MW01134066

PAST THE LAST
ISLAND
- REVISED EDITION
A MISFITS AND HEROES ADVENTURE

Kathleen Flanagan Rollins

KATHLEEN FLANAGAN ROLLINS

Revised edition, Copyright 2015, Kathleen Flanagan Rollins
All rights reserved

ISBN: 1514214806
ISBN 13: 9781514214800
Library of Congress Control Number: 2015909121
CreateSpace Independent Publishing Platform,
North Charleston, SC

For Aunt Sue

TABLE OF CONTENTS

Part I – The World Is Changing 1

Chapter 1 – The Chief's Son 3

Chapter 2 – Three Conversations 8

Chapter 3 – The Stone worker's Gift 12

Chapter 4 – The White Face of the Goddess 20

Chapter 5 – The Fall from the Cliff 22

Chapter 6 – The Reading 27

Chapter 7 – A Conversation and a Plan 30

Chapter 8 – The Boat Races 33

Chapter 9 – Nulo Alone 43

Chapter 10 – Discoveries 49

Chapter 11 – The Council Meeting 52

Chapter 12 – Yon's Visit 59

Chapter 13 – Departures 62

Chapter 14 – The View from the Cliff 65

Chapter 15 – Nulo at Sea 70

Chapter 16 – Reunion 74

Chapter 17 – The Fat Men 77

Chapter 18 – Tahn's Decision 82

Chapter 19 – Fishing Talk 87

Chapter 20 – Celebration 91

Chapter 21 – Power and Magic 99

Chapter 22 – Trembling Stones 106

Chapter 23 – The Story Spreads 109

Chapter 24 – Ryu in the Sky Circle 116

Chapter 25 – Choices 118
Chapter 26 – Cave of Treasures.................................. 120
Chapter 27 – Reading the Stones................................ 123
Chapter 28 – Attack by Sea.. 125
Chapter 29 – The Last Moments of the Old World 134

Part II – Leaving the Past Behind 143
Chapter 1 – Parting Ways 145
Chapter 2 – The Shaman's Transformation................................151
Chapter 3 – Masali...153
Chapter 4 – One Boat Leaving 165
Chapter 5 – Fever Dreams 168
Chapter 6 – Nina's Choice 178
Chapter 7 – No Shadow Day 181
Chapter 8 – The Smoking Island 189
Chapter 9 – In the Cave 192
Chapter 10 – Choosing Happiness Instead 196
Chapter 11 – Toys of the Gods 199
Chapter 12 – The Flying Man 215
Chapter 13 – Red Flowers, Dark Clouds 233
Chapter 14 – The Storm's Toll 245
Chapter 15 – Aftermath.. 248
Chapter 16 – Seal Island Talk.................................... 257
Chapter 17 – A Puppet Show 258
Chapter 18 – Yali.. 265
Chapter 19 – Preparations, Celebrations.................................. 269
Chapter 20 – Attack 279
Chapter 21 – Boat Building 282
Chapter 22 – The Flattening of Time 288
Chapter 23 – Changing Stars.................................... 298
Chapter 24 – Mountains in the Sea............................. 300
Chapter 25 – On the Islands..................................... 307
Chapter 26 – A Funeral for a Chief...............................311

Chapter 27 – On the Cliff 318

Chapter 28 – Navigating a New World 327

Chapter 29 – Nina's Journey.. 330

Chapter 30 – Treasures.. 332

Chapter 31 – Fear of the Unknown 340

Chapter 32 – The New Land 348

Chapter 33 – In the Course of Days 352

Chapter 34 – Darna's Request 360

Chapter 35 - Messages... 362

THE HEROES' JOURNEY

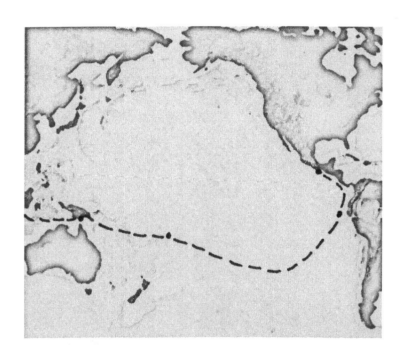

PART I - THE WORLD IS CHANGING

The South Pacific Islands, about 14,000 years ago

CHAPTER 1
THE CHIEF'S SON

Signs. I can't see any signs. I don't even know what to look for.

"It's about balance," the shaman had said. "Good and bad. You must find the signs that will determine the child's future."

That hadn't helped.

Signs. The sky deep and clear: a good sign, usually. The trees heavy with fruit: another good sign. The birth of the empty moon last night: a bad sign for mothers but perhaps not important in the daytime. Two fish hawks circling overhead: a good sign. Two crows perched on the top of the birth hut: a bad sign. Nasty tricksters the crows - thieves, travelers to the Underworld.

"I could kill you both," the chief muttered, pitching a stone toward them, "but that might bring something worse."

The birds stared back at him like two copies of a single creature, their heads tilted at exactly the same angle.

He considered calling one of his assistants to sit in his place while he went down to the shore to smell the sea and talk to the villagers. The trouble was they'd ask about his wife or they'd comment on some piece of the old village that washed up recently, and he had nothing useful to say about either subject. Hunkered down, his back wedged against a tree, he pounded a stick against a rock near his feet, wearing it down blow by blow until something crashed against the hut wall. A midwife ducked out through the opening and tied the cover back, releasing a puff of smoke.

"Chief," the woman coughed, "the baby won't come out."

"Well, give Lim something to help her."

"We have."

"Then give her something else! You must know what to do."

The woman pursed her lips and looked out toward the sea before she nodded and headed back to the hut, untying the covering and letting it fall back into place behind her.

The chief set the battered stick aside, squinted at the hawks circling near the sun, then closed his eyes. *My parents would have known what to do. They would have taught me how to be a father and sung the long song for the newly alive. But they're gone, the old village is gone; the whole world has fallen out of balance. Now the people turn to me to rekindle their hopes, and I don't know how.*

When he looked around again, everything seemed unremarkable. The sun moved along its usual course, already spreading its heat across the land. Down the hill, the sea rolled up onto the shore and pulled back again. Past the shore, though, something different caught his eye, out in the open water, beyond the drowned trees. A great silver-blue fish flipped in and out of the wave tops then leapt straight out of the water, twisting high over the sea so the sunlight flashed along its back. For a moment it paused, suspended between the sun and the sea, before it plunged back into the water, still pulsing with light.

"A lightning fish," he cried, scrambling to his feet. "A lightning fish!"

He watched the spot where it had disappeared, worried for a moment that he'd imagined the great fish. *No, I saw it, right there. Why doubt the clearest sign ever given? The other signs don't matter. The child is destined for greatness! He'll leap beyond his world. He'll be extraordinary. He'll be the one people sing about in the new songs, the ones his children's children will learn. He will make the difference.*

The midwife ducked out through the opening again, holding aside the flap. "Chief?"

"Yes? Do I have a son?"

The woman lowered her gaze. "Yes, it's a boy. And your wife will recover, I'm sure."

4

The chief didn't notice the crows still perched on the roof of the birth hut, each watching him with one dark eye. With his head held high, he started toward the hut, already imagining people congratulating him on the birth of his son. When he was halfway there, Naia, his old servant, joined him, placing her thin fingers on his arm as if to hold him back for a moment. In front of them, the hut had gone silent, leaving the air oddly empty. He slowed his pace to tell Naia about the great leaping fish he'd seen, but before he could speak, his wife shrieked.

The chief flinched.

"I'll go in with you," Naia offered.

"Yes, good." His knees went weak. *Perhaps the child didn't survive. Many didn't.* The vision of the lightning fish faded as he pushed aside the curtain, releasing a cloud of smoke. He hardly recognized his wife collapsed on the birth mat, her body battered, her face twisted in rage as she pointed to the infant in the midwife's arms.

The woman held out the baby, a bloody newborn who squirmed in her grip, crying as his legs churned. The chief fell back a step. The infant's head was too large and deformed from the birth. His skull was lopsided and lumpy, as if his features had been pushed to one side. His eyes were uneven, his cheeks too big, his chest not big enough to balance the strange head. The rest of his body was much too small, with short arms and legs, miniature hands and feet.

"Say something!" the mother yelled at the chief. "Say *something!*"

A pale cold flooded him, rushing through his chest and down his limbs. This strange dwarf child wasn't what he'd been promised. He'd seen the sign; it couldn't have been clearer. He'd been cheated. Perhaps the crows had stolen his fine son, dragging him to the Underworld before he could live his glorious life, leaving this horrible thing instead. This bloody creature the midwife held out to him - what was he? Nothing. The terrible chill ran up to his scalp, down to his fingertips.

5

"He is nothing to me. Nothing," the chief announced as he backed away. "He does not exist."

"Come back!" Lim shrieked. "Come back here. Don't leave me. Don't you dare leave!"

Pausing, still holding back the entrance flap, he looked at his wife and the baby the midwife still held, wishing they both belonged to someone else's world.

"This is a punishment for something you did while it was growing in your belly," he spat as he threw back the door flap. "I'm sure you know what it was."

"No! Wait!"

When he didn't return, Lim tried to grab the baby. "Give it to me! I'll kill it right now! I'll kill the monster!"

"I'll take the child," Naia announced, stepping between Lim and the terrified midwife. She caught the midwife's eye as she lifted the infant out of the woman's arms and tucked him into the crook of her arm. "I'll see that he's taken care of."

The midwife nodded. Deformed babies were either killed outright or simply abandoned for the forest to claim.

"It'll be good to pull this hut down tomorrow," the midwife commented, not caring whether the mother heard. "It carries bad luck."

She didn't bother to save the baby's umbilical cord. There'd be no naming ceremony for this baby when he could sit up unaided, no splashing with seawater, no placing of the cord in a cupule in the rock where all the other village births had been recorded.

As she walked away, Naia stripped off long leaves to wrap around the infant, leaving his face free, and tucked him into the sling she wore across her chest. No one commented or stopped her as she made her way out of the village into the forest where ancient trees wove their branches against the sky, blocking out the sunlight. Only a few paths penetrated the area and only one led where Naia was going: the highest spot on the island, an opening in the cover where flat rocks formed a platform under the sky, a sacred place close to the spirits.

At the top, thinking the unmoving, silent infant had died on the way, Naia took him out of the sling and was surprised to find him alive and looking right at her.

"You're a strange one," she murmured, cleaning him up with the ends of the leaves. "Ugly little thing looking at me as if you know me. A lot of trouble back there in the village because of you. A lot of people in pain. Though I don't suppose it's your fault. It's not as if you chose to be the way you are."

The child's gaze was so strong she could feel him watching her even when she looked away. "Maybe you *were* brought up from the Underworld. That's what people would say, you know. They'd say the crows stole the other baby and left you in his place." His uneven eyes never looked away, never blinked. "If your mother didn't kill you, someone else would. That's the truth."

Out where the light of the old sun still warmed the flat rocks, she set him down carefully and sat back on her heels. The reddened sky arched just over her head. She knew she shouldn't stay. She needed to get back while she could still find her way down the path. Besides, this place was dangerous. People sometimes felt the sky so close here that they slipped away into it, never to return except as shapes in the clouds.

She pushed herself up. "Don't be an old fool. You've been sitting here too long."

"You're right," Naia answered herself. "It's time to go home."

Bending down, she tucked the long leaves around the infant, reached one hand under the misshapen head and the other under his back, then settled him back into the fold of her sling. Above her, the flaming colors of the sky dome hid the world of the spirits, but she knew they could see down through holes in the clouds.

"I said I'd take care of him," she said, looking up, "so I will."

CHAPTER 2
THREE CONVERSATIONS

Lim and a Friend

"I know he's alive, Rissa. I'm not stupid. I see things and hear things. Still, I can't do anything while Naia's protecting him. She raised the chief you know, nursed him. She's a great favorite of his, if anyone is now. Anyway, that's why this stupid arrangement goes on. I know she has the boy and she knows I know, but no one can do anything because the chief declared the boy doesn't exist. So, if he doesn't exist, he can't be a problem and Naia did nothing wrong in taking him; she can't be punished and I can't confront her. It's ridiculous, the whole thing, like saying this rock doesn't exist even though everyone sees it right here." She grabbed a basket of trade shells and threw it past Rissa. "One day, though, she'll make a mistake and then I'll get rid of both of them. Then things will go back to where they were before."

"I hear the chief's new wife is already -"

"Quiet! I don't want to hear about it. Anyway, things can happen, you know, accidents, misfortune of one kind or another."

"What are you saying? You'd poison her?"

"I didn't say anything like that. I only said accidents happen sometimes. Unfortunate events. Everyone knows that."

Rissa changed the subject. "Are you going to the naming ceremony?"

"So I can watch other women splash seawater on their babies and stuff umbilical cords in holes in the rock? I don't think so.

Though now that I think about it, maybe I *should* go. If Naia brings the boy, she'll be breaking the chief's law by saying he should have a name like any other child. Then I can demand she be punished and the child returned to me." She clapped her hands in satisfaction.

"It's too late."

With a different, louder clap, she spun around to face Rissa. "It's never too late! A life can be changed, repaired, remade any day up until the very last. The problem needs a solution, that's all. He needs to be removed. 'A flame that doesn't exist can be extinguished without notice.' That's how the saying goes, isn't it?"

Rissa glanced at the woman she'd known since childhood. Lim's dark hair fell untended across half her face, hiding some of the raised dots across her cheeks she'd received when she became the chief's wife. Dark tattoos beginning at her wrist and rising up her arm marked first her family sign, then the moment she'd left childhood behind, and finally the completion of each of three initiation tests. Once, these signs decorated a friend. Now Rissa saw only a stranger who looked eerily familiar.

"It's not fair," Lim continued, looking out at the sea. "Why should people's lives change forever because of one moment? What about all of the other moments? Weren't they important too? I used to be the most beautiful girl in the village. Every man wanted me. Why isn't that moment the one I have to live in forever?" She poked absently at her decorated tunic. "Remember when this was new and he wanted me so badly? He gave me one gift after another. I wear it every day now so he'll have to remember."

For a while, Rissa tried talking about other news in the village. When nothing she said got a response, she stood up, saying something about needing to get back to her family. Lim didn't seem to notice.

* * *

9

Nina and Ryu

Nina hesitated, still holding onto the tree trunk as she leaned slightly into the clearing Naia's family claimed as theirs

"Ryu!" she whispered.

"Ryu!" she hissed again. The young man she was trying to attract was bent over a sea chart he was making out of bent twigs, holding one part while he tried to bend another into its place.

"Ryu!" She threw a pebble in his direction, aiming it right in front of him.

Jumping up as it hit the dirt, Ryu dropped the construct and held his hand up to block the sun as he scanned the area. Blue initiation tattoos ran up the length of his arm, with the navigator's star added on his shoulder.

"Ryu!"

He glanced up, seeing her half-hidden behind the tree. "Nina? What is it? What are you doing here?"

"Be quiet for a moment and I'll talk quickly. I have a message for your grandmother from my Aunt Rissa. Just tell her and then forget you saw me or heard it from my aunt."

"I don't understand -"

"The message is 'Don't take the boy to the naming ceremony. If you do, he'll be killed and then you will.' Do you understand?"

Ryu stood looking at her, waiting. He recognized her, of course. She was Laido and Darna's daughter, Tahn's sister; he'd often seen her down at the shore, helping her father, the master navigator, build and repair boats. He'd never seen her like this, though, so worried as she spoke, and he'd never seen her alone. She wore the hand tattoos of the girls who had become adults and her family sign but none of the later markings. Interested, Ryu approached, clapping the dirt off his hands. "What's all this about dying? Who's dying?"

"Listen to me. This is important. My aunt wouldn't have asked me to deliver the message if it wasn't. She's betraying an old friendship to help Naia. Please tell her." Across the clearing, a woman emerged from one of the huts with a crying child in tow. "I have to leave now. Tell her," Nina repeated, keeping her voice low.

As she slipped back into the forest, Ryu set his half-finished construction behind a stone and went to find his grandmother.

* * *

Ryu and Naia

"Then we'll name him ourselves," Naia countered when she heard the news from her grandson. "If he's nothing to the chief, we'll call him Nulo: he who is nothing."

"But once nothing has a name, isn't it something?"

"Of course, Ryu. We're only trying to find a way to let him live. If he's nothing, the chief can't complain that we disobeyed his command. If I've saved the life of nothing, I can't be punished, nor can you for warning me, or your friend for warning you."

"You can't make all that happen just by choosing a name, Grandmother."

Naia waved away his concern. "It's the chief who saved him by saying he didn't exist. The boy will grow up in the shadows, officially not alive, but every day he'll grow a little more, and finally he'll be grown. By then, people will have forgotten his poor start and he can choose a new name."

"Maybe," Ryu replied, looking at the line of tattoos on his arm, "and maybe not."

CHAPTER 3
THE STONE WORKER'S GIFT

Naia was only partly right: while people got used to seeing the odd-looking boy sitting off by himself under the trees or walking along with Naia, no one forgot what had happened. They couldn't. Lim reminded them constantly that the boy did not exist; therefore they shouldn't speak to him. They didn't hurt the boy but they didn't interact with him either, not even other children. No talking, no playing, not even any bullying. No one pushed him down or made fun of his short arms and legs, his small feet and hands. If other children stared at him, their mothers dragged them away, scolding them for staring at nothing.

Naia talked to him, but never in public, and Ryu sometimes included him in a conversation with his grandmother, but mostly Nulo grew up ignored, speaking so seldom it was hard for him to string together the right words when he needed them. The world he lived in was wordless, all one piece with no boundaries between named items, somewhere between the world of people and the world of dreams. Objects sang to him: the crescent moon, the very old sun sinking into the sea, storm clouds, chill winds, banyan trees, twisted seashells, stingrays, different rocks he collected along the shore and sorted into piles.

Watching him humming as he hunkered down, working on his piles of stones, Naia sighed.

"Nulo," she called. "You like the different stones. Why don't you watch the men working stone? You might be able to learn how they make the different tools." When he didn't reply, Naia pointed toward the stoneworkers' area.

The following day, peering out from his hiding place behind a tree, he watched as five men worked pieces of stone and shell on a flat stone, fashioning the scoop of a shovel, a grindstone and bowl, a knife blade, a fishing spear.

The men didn't mention his presence. They talked as they always did while they worked, low slow talk about the stones and the weather and the sea. The oldest and most skilled of the group took a new stone out of the cooling pit, turned it over in battered hands, then hit it with the hammerstone, shunting off the piece that fell off the bottom, flipping the core over, hitting it again, letting the remainder fall to the ground, flipping it again, all in a rhythm. When the scraper was complete, he set it aside and reached down for one of the discarded flakes. As he straightened up, he glanced over at the boy hiding in the trees, the one who crouched, ready to push off against the tree and run away. As the day went on and the sun moved across the dome of heaven, he checked several more times. The boy never moved from that spot and never looked away from the stoneworkers.

At the end of the workday, the old man left a core stone and the round hammerstone out where the boy could find them.

"Maybe he won't even notice them," he commented, tamping out the fire.

"Maybe he'll steal them," his friend replied.

As the men walked back up the hill to the village center, Nulo picked up several rocks and climbed down into the clearing, scanning the area before he laid the rocks out on the work surface. The hammerstone lay where the man had left it, waiting for him, humming against the flat rock. Nulo raised it up and brought it down with all his strength against the closest rock, but it only slid off. He tried a different rock. Nothing. He hit it harder, sending it flying into his chest. He set up the last stone wide part down, point up. As he brought the hammerstone down, it slid down the rock and smashed into his hand. Stifling a cry, he tried it again, swinging the hammerstone high and slamming it back down, missing the rock completely, then again, when it hit the stone and only bounced back up, and again, when it smashed his holding hand once more. More attempts, hitting faster and harder, left him gasping. Tears slid down his cheeks. He switched hands, with no better results. His hands trembled so the stones slipped out of his grasp. When he smashed his hand again, he dropped the stones on the work surface, tucked the battered hand under his arm, and stumbled back into the forest.

As soon as the new sun shed its light the next day, he went back, hiding in the same place. Again the men gathered, took up their work, and talked their slow talk as they went from one project to the next. Nulo moved closer, right to the edge of the shadow. Some men worked pieces of giant clam shells, chopping off the flanges to make bowls, ladles, and shovels. Others worked big lumpy stones they turned into blades, cutters, scrapers, knives – whatever was needed. The old man ran his fingers along the surface of the stone he'd selected, seeing how the reflections fanned out. Sometimes he'd tap it lightly with another stone before he wedged it against the palm mat he set over his leg. From his spot, Nulo couldn't see exactly how it happened. It seemed the man looked the stone over for a long time before he hit it with the hammerstone. Each time he hit the stone, pieces dropped off the bottom of the core into his waiting hand. Most of the time the man swept the pieces to the ground and kept going, but sometimes he put the piece in one of the piles on the work surface. The man never missed the stone or knocked it away.

When the stoneworkers left at the end of the workday, Nulo climbed down to try once again, but his hands were too swollen to hold the hammerstone or the stones he tried to hit. Sometimes he'd miss; sometimes the striker slid off its target and slammed into his bad hand, doubling him over in pain.

As he tucked his injured hand under his other arm, he felt something heavy press on his shoulder. The old stoneworker stood right behind him, holding him down. When Nulo tried to escape, the man pointed to the stones Nulo was using, shook his head, and pitched them into the grass. After a moment, he let go of Nulo and settled down next to him, waiting. Nulo didn't move. The old man picked up the core stone he'd left on the work space, turning it over in his hands several times, pointing to different spots before he tapped one particular area, took up the hammerstone, and struck the core at that very spot. As if on command, a piece dropped off the bottom of the stone into the man's hand. The old man nodded, taking up the piece in his thick fingers. After tapping one side, he turned the piece over and struck it several times along one edge. He flipped it back over, pointed to a series of uneven, sharp points and made scraping motions with it as if he was removing a layer of inner bark or the scales of a big fish.

Nulo nodded.

Setting it aside, the man took up the core once again and turned it so the last rays of sunlight caught the wave pattern on one edge. He drew his finger along the waves and back to the point where the waves began. Then, pressing the stone against his leg, he struck the place he'd chosen with the hammerstone. Immediately, a long, slim piece fell off the bottom of the stone. Setting aside the core, the old man took up the piece, pretending to run his finger along the edge before he jerked his hand back and looked at the finger. Nulo nodded. The man pointed to one edge before he started working it, holding it against his leg mat with one hand while he took up a whale bone section with the other. Pointing to the edge, he pressed the cut bone against the thin edge of the blade, taking off a curved section, like a bite out of the blade. He worked all the way up one side before he stopped to look at his work. Satisfied, he turned it around to work the other side, knocking out one small curved piece after another. To finish the piece, he checked the edges, adding another bite where needed to make it even. Then he held it up to the boy. When Nulo wanted to grab hold of it, the old man shook his head, pointing to the edge, pretending to touch it, and sucking on the finger as if in pain.

When Nulo nodded, the man handed the boy the blade, watching as the boy turned it over carefully in his hands. As the last of the day's light faded, the man put his hand on Nulo's shoulder for a moment before he walked away. Still holding the blade in his hands, Nulo watched him go until the man disappeared into the forest shadows.

The next day Nulo came back, waiting half-hidden behind the tree until the men finished their work. By the time they'd tamped out the fire and headed back up the trail to the village center, Nulo had picked up the core stone left on the work space, turning it over in his small hand, pointing to the fracture points and nodding the way the old man did. As he lifted the striker, he felt a hand press down on his shoulder. Nulo dropped the stones and twisted around. The old man stood behind him, his head tilted to one side. The tattooed lines across his cheek bones rose at the corners of his eyes. After a glance around the area, he slid down next to the boy and handed the core stone back to him, pointing to the same platform Nulo had seen. Nulo took up the round hammerstone, looked at it and the core rock, then hit the exact spot he'd wanted. A narrow blade dropped off the bottom into his hand. As he grabbed it to show it, he cut his hand on the sharp edge. The lines on the old man's cheeks rose again as he nodded, pointing to the rock slab. Nulo set the blade down. The old man flushed out the cuts with a gourd of water and waited. While his hand bled, Nulo took up the core once again, turning it over in his hand, pointing to the next spot, nodding as he looked to the old man. The old man nodded with him. So they worked until the sun disappeared into the sea.

The next day, Nulo watched from the same spot in the shadow of the great tree, watching every move the stone workers made, slipping closer as the sun grew older. As soon as the men left, he scrambled down, picked up his stones, studied them the way the stone workers did, and tried to work them the way the old man did. After a while, the old man hunkered down next to him, checking his work.

Day by day, piece by piece, the old man taught the boy, without saying a word. He showed Nulo how to lean into a piece of bone to take bites off the edge of the blade – just enough, not too big or too small. When the piece he was working was ruined, the old man showed him why, pointing to the unusual fracture line or the cut that went too deep. When this happened, the old man shrugged and swept the broken piece to the ground before he pointed to the next.

When Nulo couldn't reach around a stone to hold it, the old man set up a piece of driftwood with natural openings big enough to hold a stone. One day Nulo brought a giant sponge that had washed up on the beach. It didn't work at all, but the old man's tattooed lines curled up around the edges of his eyes.

After they'd worked the hard stone for many sessions, the old man showed Nulo how to make tools: punches, chisels, awls, and burins, pointing out how they were different, how they had to be handled. After those, they worked pieces of giant clam shells to make picks, shovels, and bowls, then bird bones and whale bones, stony corals, even urchin and ray spines. They worked with heated stone and cold stone, experimenting with slow cooling and rapid cooling. They tried different drills. When Nulo's hands bled, the old man washed out the cuts and waited to see if Nulo would keep going. Each time he did.

"What's going on here?" the old man's friend asked when they'd started work one morning.

"Where?"

"There." The man waved toward Nulo's spot in the shadows. "Here." He pointed to one of Nulo's blades.

The old man turned the point over in his hand. "Not my best work."

"I know you're teaching him."

"Who?"

"Him. I see him standing there. Every day."

"Who do you see standing there?"

The other man hesitated. "You know."

"No I don't. Who are you talking about?"

"You know what I'm talking about, right?" he asked the others, but they were bent over their work. "Never mind," he added after a moment. "Forget I said anything."

The old man shrugged and went back to his work.

"Other children would like to learn to work the stones," the friend complained to his wife that night. "Why give this one special treatment?"

"What child is that?" she asked.

He started. "I don't remember, exactly. I was just talking to myself."

"Do you mean the chief's son?"

"No, of course I don't," her husband corrected. "It's nothing. It's only that I'm hungry."

"Others have seen him, you know: some women out pounding coconut husk into sheets noticed him hiding in the bushes. Men cutting reeds for thatch saw him watching them. So now he's watching your group? Interesting. I heard that -"

"Stop talking now. It's not good to talk about this," her husband said, turning away.

His wife went back to her cooking, humming as she worked.

So the days passed. Nulo and the old man worked clam shell and whale bone, sea urchin spines, abalone, stony corals, ray spines, bird bones. When storms rolled through, they waited. When the sky cleared, they went back to work. One season led to the next and the next. While other boys joined their first initiation groups and received their wrist tattoos showing they'd left childhood behind, Nulo learned the stones. During the day he learned whatever he could from watching others or he wandered along the shore, collecting stones, shells, sponges, corals, feathers, turtle shells picked clean by the seabirds. These he brought to the old man.

Though the old stone worker was the first, others came to include him as well. When a fisherman had an unusually large catch, he waved Nulo over to help clean, fillet, salt, and wrap the fish before they went bad or the shore birds stole them.

"Why not?" the man remarked when he was sitting around his fire with some friends. "He was hunkered down right there, watching, you know the way he does. He wanted to help. Besides, I didn't say anything to him."

Nulo made gifts for the people who helped him: sharp scraper blades cut from the wings of the clamshell, fish hooks, a bone flute. For the fisherman who'd first asked him to help, he designed a woven fish cage that could be tethered to a rock on the sea bottom and allowed to float just below the surface, a place to store live catch until it was needed. Within days, most of the other fishermen had made cages just like it.

"People get used to what is," Naia remarked when Ryu told her about the fish cage. "After enough days go by, Nulo will be just another part of the world they live in."

"The fish cage is good," Ryu admitted, "but it doesn't change the facts: Nulo's skin is empty. He'll have no initiation group, no brothers in the village to stand up for him, no wife, no children. He'll never be seen as a man, no matter how many days go by."

Naia shrugged. "Many things can happen. He's talking a little now. That's how it will go - one foot in front of the other until he gets where he needs to be."

CHAPTER 4
THE WHITE FACE OF THE GODDESS

Ryu studied the stars. While everyone in the village knew the familiar patterns in the night sky and the stories they told, Ryu looked at the night sky as a living design left by the gods at the moment of creation. On a clear night, when most of the villagers slept, he often lay out on the shore, observing the world that was hidden by day. He followed the night visitors, lights that wandered slowly through the fixed pattern of the regular star figures, sometimes disappearing into the Underworld only to reappear on the other side of the world many days later. For Ryu, movement in the heavens reflected movement on the earth and life on earth reflected life in the stars. They were inseparable. Laido had told him that's why certain stars rose over their island. When he knew them, he could always find his way home at night on the sea. Those stars were tied to his island forever.

One night, he settled back on his favorite spot, his fingers intertwined under his head as he ran through the familiar star figures above. Scattered clouds obscured some of the stars. The brightest visitor pierced thin clouds in the west. Farther up, the visitor he'd been following had moved a little farther away from the spot where he'd seen it last. And across the way, he spotted something else he'd never noticed before, something fuzzy. He checked with only his better eye, looked away then back, squinted, and checked again, yet the blurry shape did not resolve itself into something more usual. Forgetting the other wonders of the sky, he watched the fuzzy light, waiting for the clouds to pass. The bright, elongated object didn't change.

"How could I have missed you?" he complained aloud. "What are you?"

Storm clouds moved in the following night, hiding whatever mystery might be unveiling itself in the sky behind them. The following night more clouds appeared. By the next night, Ryu had convinced himself that the fuzzy star was only a star behind thin clouds. To make sure, he settled into his usual spot and scanned the star patterns. He found the two visitors he'd been following, then caught his breath. It wasn't a trick of the clouds. The fuzzy spot stood out very clearly, larger than before. He looked away, focusing on nearby stars before turning back. It was still there.

"It's not a spot of light," he told his friend Chad the next day. "It's long and blurry."

"You're the one who studies the stars. I don't know anything about it. Ask Owl Man. He knows all kinds of strange things."

Ryu hesitated. "Maybe it's gone by now."

It wasn't. It grew larger and clearer each night. And others saw it, too – the bright light with the fuzzy trail behind it.

"What does it mean, Ryu?" some asked.

When he had no answer, they went to Owl Man and begged him to explain it.

"You're seeing the white face of the goddess of death," the shaman announced to the waiting crowd, "with her terrible white hair spread out behind her."

People gasped, repeating the shaman's words as they stumbled down to the beach, pointing all over the sky in their confusion. Some started screaming in the dark.

"I saw it first," Ryu muttered.

CHAPTER 5
THE FALL FROM THE CLIFF

In the morning, the new sun rose, spreading its light across the sky, washing out the dark omen of the night before. One by one, the villagers went back to their usual chores. At Owl Man's urging, the chief walked around the village, talking to people and inquiring after their families. At the shore, a woman offered the chief a woven sack full of clams she'd dug. He looked at the clams for a long moment before he nodded his thanks, wrapped the tie around his shoulder, and headed toward a group of men repairing a boat.

"Chief! Wait!" The woman ran up behind him, grabbing his arm. "There's a child on the cliff! Look – there!"

The chief spun around, stumbled, then scanned the cliff, spotting the child who stood dangerously close to the edge.

"You have to do something!" the woman cried.

"I'll – I'll climb up the cliff," he called as he forced himself to run. "Send others around the path."

"Stay there!" he shouted to the child as he jumped up onto the first of the rocks. "Don't move. I'll come and get you."

Hand over hand, he hauled himself up the rocks, looking for good toeholds, swinging himself from one solid point to the next. After he'd climbed the first section, though, he gasped for air. Pains shot through his head and neck. When he looked up to check that he was heading in the right direction, the sky looked black, the rocks shining white and shifting. He turned his head slowly, looking for a place to rest. The closest spot seemed to be the ledge he'd passed on the way up. Sliding one foot down the rockface, he felt for the last toehold. When he didn't find it, he slid farther down until he'd gone as far as he could, his right leg fully extended, his left knee bent so tight it hurt. He pushed his fingers deep into the groove in the rock, hoping he could see the ledge before the world started spinning again, but as soon as he moved his head to look at his feet, the rock seemed to move as well, dropping down, flipping the sky over as it turned. The fingers he'd wedged into the groove turned thick and dull, the rock face soft and crumbling. The bag of clams slipped off his shoulder and crashed onto the rocks below. The rock face turned again, taking him with it. Someone screamed on the beach. The sky rotated, with white seabirds wheeling against the blue sky, the rocks so close, the white birds, the rocks. Then it got dark.

* * *

Below, the people watched as the chief slipped off the rocks and fell, slowly at first, then suddenly faster, crashing onto a rock ledge and landing in a heap on a flat area.

On the cliff, rescuers pulled the child back from the edge before scrambling down the rocks to the fallen chief. One pulled on the chief's shoulder, turning him over, finding the breath of life still in him.

"The chief is alive!" the rescuer shouted down to the crowd on the beach. "Call the healers!"

Back at the chief's hut, the healers gave him saltwater baths and offered healing teas. He didn't drink any. He never sat up or spoke or opened his eyes. Though he was still alive, he lived somewhere far away.

* * *

In the chief's compound, villagers hunkered in small groups, talking, arguing, waiting for news. Some said they knew what the fall meant: the death goddess had brought this. Her curse would kill the chief first then spread through the whole community. Others thought the chief was only injured; the healers would cure him.

The healers didn't share that optimism. Standing together just outside the chief's hut, they whispered about probable causes and possible cures, but these were only words passed back and forth.

"A protective charm," one suggested. "That's what we need to make."

The others didn't reply.

Nulo, listening from his spot under the bushes, scrambled to his feet. "I know some healing herbs," he offered as he approached, touching the man's arm. "Please let me -"

Lim grabbed him by the shoulders and spun him around to face her.

"It's your fault! All of this!" she screamed. "The air here is poison. Your poison. It's not the white goddess in the sky. It's you!"

"Is that Lim?"

"What'd she say?"

"Something about the white goddess and the boy."

"What?"

Leaving Nulo behind, Lim approached a couple of women in the crowd. "That's right," she said. "The boy poisoned the chief. That's why he fell from the cliff. He was too weak to climb the rocks. I'm telling you the truth!"

"He poisoned his own father!" one of the woman shouted.

"Monster child, born evil."

"Keep your evil away from my family!"

"Look at him," Lim said to a different group. "He's the one who brought the curse down, on his own father. He blamed his father for what happened to him." The news flew through the crowd: Nulo had brought this sickness down on his father, hated his father, blamed his father, poisoned his father, hated the village, cursed everyone in it, all for revenge. He'd brought the death goddess in the night sky. He'd probably brought other illnesses and injuries as well.

Lim waited for the right moment, then pointed at Nulo and yelled, "He did this to the chief! And it's only the start! He wants you all to sicken and die! *He can cause it.*"

"Freak!"

"Monster!"

"Killer!"

"Leave us alone!"

"He brought the white goddess of death!"

"End the curse!"

One woman threw a stick at him; others threw stones. He crouched, putting his hands over his head as the first stones found their mark.

Naia pushed through the crowd and lifted Nulo to his feet, pulling him away, glaring at the accusers as she passed. "You blame this boy for bringing the death goddess? That's ridiculous. He doesn't control the sky spirits. He didn't push the chief off the rocks any more than you did. He didn't do anything except be born ugly. Some of you are far uglier right now."

* * *

Though the crowd let Naia take Nulo away, the restless fear that drove them still lived. Lim urged Raidu and other council members to ask Owl Man how to keep the boy from killing them all.

When the shaman replied that only the spirits could bring sickness, the people weren't satisfied.

"What happened to the chief?" they called out. "Will he recover?"

"Did the boy cause this?"

"Was this sickness brought by the white goddess? Will it spread?"

"What will happen to the village now?"

"Read the omens. We need to know."

Piling up their few treasures outside the shaman's hut, they pleaded with him.

"You have to help us! Tell us what you see!" one man cried, grabbing the shaman's sleeve.

Jerking his arm back, Owl Man swung around to face the crowd. "If you leave me alone until I have something to tell you, I'll do as you ask. You must give me two days to read the omens."

CHAPTER 6
THE READING

Owl Man waved his two apprentices over. "Set up the sweat lodge. Prepare the fire. I'll need a large turtle also, caught today. And keep everyone else away."

While the apprentices worked, he prepared a red mushroom extract and set the bowl on a flat rock, studying the liquid power it held. It could grant him knowledge gleaned from the spirit world, or it could kill him. Worse still, it could leave him trapped forever between the world of humans and the world of the spirits, unable to live in either. He bowed before the bowl, acknowledging the shaman's path he had chosen, the destiny that gave him mighty powers yet kept him forever separated from other people.

When the lodge was ready, he stepped inside, stripped off his robe, and stood before the fire. The assistants had built it with a strong base of dry wood then added wet seaweed and rotten bark, so thick smoke filled the hut and flowed out the smoke hole, rising up into the sky between the treetops, becoming clouds in the heavens. Falling to his knees, the shaman let the smoke take him, fill him. Only then, when he was no more than the smoke that lived between the earthbound fire and the sky clouds did he drink the potion, tilting his head back and swallowing the liquid.

At dusk, his assistants left the turtle shell they had prepared according to his directions, calling out to the shaman from outside the hut before they set the shell down, bowed and withdrew. Owl Man heard their voices on the other side of the smoke. Trembling, sweating, he pushed aside the flap and dragged the shell to him, pressing it against his chest with one hand while he stoked the fire with the other, adding dry wood until flames shot through the smoke.

Then he hurled the shell into the heart of the blaze.

Flames licked the shell bottom, moved up and over the edge, slid down across the interior, all the while spitting and crackling, dipping and rising as they fed on the scraped insides like scavengers. The fires came from both sides, bobbing through the ribs before spreading across the open sections. After they had read every part, the flames came together over the shell, rose up in the center and claimed it. In response, the shell hissed, convulsed, gave in and cracked explosively. When the sound died, the shaman dragged the shell from the fire and stared at it as the potion flooded his mind.

A wave of cracks started at one end, flowing toward a large, ragged smudge of black in the center of the shell. Thin black lines fanned away from the dark center then disappeared close to the sides. Farther down the shell, a dozen lines went off in different directions.

"No. It cannot be."

He squinted, rubbed his eyes, looked again. The pattern began to move. The shell started humming as the lines moved along slowly, like old rivers, from the neck opening of the shell. When the lines reached the center, the noise grew into a terrible pounding that only increased as the lines moved faster, sweeping everything along with them, too fast, too loud, too much, so that he knew just before the sound tore through him that it would all explode, leaving only the smudge of darkness. Shrieking, a few lines fled from the explosion, but they too disappeared. Stillness and silence followed. After a moment, a few short lines at the bottom of the shell started up slowly, wandering in different directions, crying like seabirds.

Slumping to the floor of the hut, the shaman put his hands over his ears and closed his eyes. After a while, he looked at the shell again before he dropped back to the dirt floor. Shivering in the heat, he shook his head. "How can I tell people about this – about the vision you have given me? What would they gain from this?"

As the sun rose, he looked once more at the shell before he set it aside, stood up, put on his robe, tied on his medicine bundles, took up his staff, and stepped out of the lodge. A crowd waited.

"The reading is inconclusive," he announced. "There are some good omens and some bad; a balance. There will be some sorrows and some celebrations." The people called out questions, demanded more information, but Owl Man turned back into the sweat lodge, ignoring all of them.

Council member Raidu followed him inside, pulling on the shaman's sleeve, forcing him to turn. "You should've given a good reading. The people need it. They're tired of waiting for the new age to begin."

"I can't provide an augury to order. The spirits give omens as they will." Owl Man withdrew his arm and ushered Raidu out of the stifling hut. "I'll speak about this another time. I'm tired now."

"I don't like being ordered around."

"And yet you do it so well."

"Don't forget our agreement."

Owl Man leaned heavily on his staff and sighed. "I won't forget. Now leave, please."

CHAPTER 7
A CONVERSATION AND A PLAN

Without stopping to request permission or be announced, Raidu walked into the chief's compound. He found the area deserted; most people had stopped waiting for news of his recovery. Two healers spoke quietly in front of the chief's hut. Raidu barely nodded in greeting.

"Where is Lim?" he demanded.

They pointed to a hut near the edge of the compound.

The chief's first wife was staring at the dead cookfire behind her hut when Raidu found her.

"Smells wonderful," Raidu remarked.

Spinning around, she studied her guest for a moment before turning back to the fire ring. "Then you're hungry for cold fire or burnt sticks."

"I'm hungry for many things. Food isn't one of them at the moment."

"Is that supposed to impress me? What do you want?"

"To talk to you."

"And what else? You never wanted to talk to me before. Did you forget your wife and children pining for your company?"

"You're going to need a friend to stand by you."

"Oh, thank you. I don't know how I managed before now."

Raidu moved closer and lowered his tone. "You managed because the chief was alive to protect you. Once he dies, they'll come after you. You're the boy's mother. If he's evil, it must have come from somewhere. Someone might say you were a witch. That would be an easy rumor to start. Then all that poison you've been spreading will come right back at you. I can see it now; it's not pretty."

With her head tilted slightly, Lim considered the man confronting her, his large face crisscrossed with a series of tattooed lines that accentuated the set of his jaw.

"So you think I might need a friend. That's you, is it? I'm not sure what kind of friend you'd be," she answered.

"What kind are you looking for?"

She looked him in the eye as she put her hand on his chest. "One who's not afraid of trouble."

Grabbing her hand, he laughed as he twisted her arm around behind her, pulling her close to him. "You may find more of that than you planned."

"My friendship has a price."

"I'm not sure friendship can be bought."

She pushed him away. "Of course it can. That's why you're here."

"A mutually beneficial alliance, then. I'll take care of a problem that has bothered you for a long time if you'll help me. See that the villagers are busy tomorrow at the beach. Organize boat races. Give each winner a trade cowry. Have musicians play. Make it a happy event. These poor people have spent too many days under a cloud. They need some sunshine."

"Keep them too busy to see you getting rid of potential rival?"

"Oh, no. *I'll* be at the races, talking about important matters with the fools on the council."

"And if I don't agree?"

"You will." His hand tightened on her arm. "To more than this."

Twisting out of his grip, she backed up a step. "You flatter yourself."

"And you delude yourself. Your husband is dying and I'm going to be the next chief." Slowly he ran his finger down the line of her cheek and across her lips. "Why be a discarded second when you can be first?"

"You're sure the boy will be gone – for good?"

"Such tender feelings for a mother."

"Promise me! Otherwise there's no agreement."

"Gone for good, or bad. Forever."

"You're right," she said, turning away from him. "A day of boat racing will be just what the people need to lift their spirits. I'll arrange it."

CHAPTER 8
THE BOAT RACES

If it seemed strange to have a day of racing while the chief lay so close to death and the future flooded with uncertainty, no one mentioned it. By the time the sun had reached its height on race day, most of the villagers were caught up in the festivities. Boat racing was their shared passion. Like most of the villagers, Ryu and his friends spent a good part of the time they weren't racing figuring out ways they could go faster next time. What if the boat was lighter? Thinner? Longer? Wider? What if the hull was thinner, the paddle wider? Sometimes they helped each other, sometimes they gave bad advice on purpose, and most of the time, they hid whatever advantage they'd figured out until after race day.

Race rules weren't complicated. Typically, the boats were long and thin, with just enough room for the racer to stand and work a long paddle. If another boater came too close, there was nothing barring the racer from hitting him, tipping his boat over, stealing his paddle, or pushing him overboard. Males raced males according to their initiation status; females raced females according to theirs. Winners of their races faced off in the final race.

As the racers neared the finish in the first race, the two leaders got into a fight, ramming boats. When one tried to swing his paddle into the other, he threw himself off balance. As he toppled into the water, his boat crossed the other boat, throwing that paddler backwards. As he wheeled his arms, trying to keep his balance, he dropped his paddle, and a skinny boy who'd been a distant third passed both of them to claim the first prize shell.

On the shore, other boys yelled insults at the two competitors still struggling to bring in their boats while all the other racers watched, sitting on their beached boats.

"That's almost as bad as Ryu's mat attempts," one said.

"Ryu's boat's too narrow. Of course any kind of wind on the mat would make it tip."

"You know all about it, do you?"

The boy shrugged. "I watched Laido put his models out in the water to test them. He said the wind mat would pull the boat over unless the boat was wider and deeper. He thought maybe two boats together would work better. That's the last model he tried. Didn't you see it?"

"No, but I saw Ryu make a fool out of himself, bragging about his tall mast and big mat. He hardly got out in the clear water before his boat flipped."

"I heard Laido's building another one - a raft on top of two narrow racing boats."

"How's that supposed to work? Is it finished?"

"I don't know. Since the chief fell off the cliff, nobody's talked about building boats that ride on the wind."

The next group of racers poled through the surf, flipped their paddles around, and waited for the signal to start.

"They'll be coming in right around here. We better pull the boats up farther," one boy said as he grabbed hold of the bow rope.

* * *

Up the hill from the shore, Laido, the master navigator and boat designer, watched the races with his son and daughter.

"Let's race the new boat!" Nina urged her father. "I could take it in the girls' race."

"You mean I could take it in my race," her brother, Tahn, corrected.

"No, I meant what I said," Nina pouted. "It was my idea to put the two boats together as the base."

"I'd get it to go faster. You know I would."

"But -"

"Enough," their father interrupted. "I hate to hear you two arguing. Neither one of you can take the new boat in the races. There's no boat like it to race against."

They waited.

"Well?" Nina prodded.

"We'll ask Ryu to try the new boat," Laido announced, "after the races are done."

"Ryu?" Tahn cried. "He hasn't put any work into this boat!"

"No," Laido agreed, "but he's been willing to try new ideas. He's worked with a wind mat before."

Tahn jabbed a stick in the dirt. "He's crashed every time he's tried to use a wind mat. And he lost his race today after he fought with Hadi."

Laido waved away the criticism. "You two can help me launch the boat. We'll watch and see how it works. Then we'll know what we need to fix. Go find him, Tahn. Let's see what he thinks of our new boat."

When he looked at the raft tied over two canoes, Ryu had his doubts. "It's probably stable, but how do you steer it? No matter where you are, you're too far away from the boat's center. It'll just go in circles."

"What if you paddled from the back of the boat," Nina offered, "just turning the paddle to head one way or another, like when you're paddling in the cove?"

"Possible," Ryu said, "but the mat's still a problem. You can't control it while you're steering. Maybe one person can't do both."

"Well, let's try it out after the races," Laido said. "We'll learn something, even if it's a failure. Give us a hand getting it down to the water."

As the final group headed toward the finish, Ryu, Laido, Nina, and Tahn dragged the raft toward the water. By the time the winners had celebrated their victory, the raft floated just beyond the waves, held steady by Nina and Tahn.

"You take it, Ryu," Laido said as they pushed through the waves toward the raft. "Don't be afraid to make mistakes. Every mistake will teach us about how it handles."

"Or doesn't," Tahn added.

Nina passed the paddle up to Ryu after he'd jumped onto the raft. "Good luck," she added.

"It's too high above the water," Ryu complained. When he tried to move the boat out into open water, he found the paddle barely reached the water even when he held it by the top of the shaft. "It's too short!" he called, but Nina and Laido were out of earshot, pushing their way through the surf toward the shore. Securing the paddle in a fixed position with a rope, Ryu started to tie the mat up on the pole, pulling it tight and tying the loose end. As he worked, the steering paddle slipped its rope and fell loose, leaving the boat to turn with the wind and tide. When he spun around to grab the steering paddle, the wind filled the mat and jerked the boat toward the rocky shallows inside the line of rocks that ran from the island out into the sea. Racing to beat the wind filling the mat, Ryu pulled the mat down, swung the paddle around and rowed hard to get the boat back into open water. Then he tied the steering paddle once again and reset the mat, wrapping the control rope around a peg before he grabbed the paddle again. This time, the wind caught the mat hard, jerking the boat forward under his feet. By the time he got his balance, he could feel the boat lift underneath him. It wasn't moving through the water; it was flying. The raft skimmed along before the wind far past the point Ryu wanted to turn. He tried digging in the steering paddle, but the boat was fast approaching the line of black rocks sticking out of the water, surrounded by white fringes of surf. At the speed he was going, the rocks would wreck the boat and kill him.

With a shout, Ryu ripped the mat down and hurled it onto the raft. Back-paddling hard, he managed to turn the boat before it crashed, but a wave rolling off the rocks tipped it. He'd just steadied it when a wave flipped it up. Ryu raced to the high side, throwing his weight down. For a moment, it dropped back onto both canoes. As Ryu jumped back to the steering paddle, another wave caught the same side, tipping it up in the air while the other side dug down, catching between two rocks. The raft twisted to a sudden stop, throwing Ryu into the sea before the corner broke off and left the raft free again. Ryu grabbed hold of the edge of the raft once it righted itself and pulled himself back on. The paddle floated up against the rockline, slipping onto the other side with a wave. Ryu paddled with his arm until he could use the pole to get the boat closer to the shore where Laido and Nina waited to pull it into the shallows.

Kicking aside the mat, Ryu jumped off the boat, turned and slammed his fists into the raft before walking away, leaving the others to bring it in.

Laido caught up with him on the shore. "Don't worry. It was fine. We saw what it can do. Now we have to learn more."

"What? But -"

"Keep trying. Push it until it falls over. I don't care if we ruin it. This is the closest we've ever been. There's no failure here, only learning. Do you understand?"

"It's all right to fail?"

"It's necessary to fail. We have to know, right now, what this can do. It can't wait even until tomorrow."

"Why? What's going on?"

Laido shook his head. "Better to talk later. Will you try it again?"

"Well, the paddle -"

"I brought a longer one," Nina said, joining them, "the longest I could find."

"Remember," Laido said, "risk it. Try anything you want. Take care of yourself, but don't worry about breaking the boat."

"Understood," Ryu said, climbing back onto the raft, working the long paddle to get the raft moving. When he'd reached open water away from the rock line, he set the mat to catch the wind, tied the guide rope, and waited. As the wind caught, he felt one side of the boat lift, but instead of moving to the balancing side, he moved gradually to the lower side, staying there until the boat fell over into the sea. Ryu slid into the water, grabbed the steering paddle, pushed the lower canoe down as he pushed the mast up, and jumped back on as soon as the boat righted.

He let the wind fill the mat, then turned the boat so hard it immediately fell over into the sea. With a shout, he threw his head back and closed his eyes, letting the spray cover him.

* * *

On the shore, the race-goers were packing up and heading home, leaving the grassy area empty except for a couple of men talking by the rocks. Raidu had spent the race meet talking to several council members, using a combination of threats and flattery to persuade them to agree with his proposal. The exception was Pactu, the current Council Leader.

"Everyone but you sees it has to be done," Raidu said, poking Pactu in the chest.

"And I don't." Pactu replied, backing away from the jabbing finger. "The boy did nothing wrong."

"Perhaps he made his father sick."

"You don't believe that, Raidu."

"What matters is what the people believe. They'll kill him when the chief dies."

"You mean 'if the chief dies,'" Pactu corrected.

"It doesn't matter. Everyone's tired of waiting. We're calling a council meeting to elect a new chief."

"What?"

"The members agreed."

"I didn't."

"That's why there was a vote. Majority rules, you know."

"There was a vote?"

"You seem to be dragging behind a bit here, Pactu. Yes. A vote. Today. I polled the members one by one. They agreed we need a functioning chief and that the boy has to be taken somewhere – safer."

"But –"

"Eloquent, but a little late, I'm afraid." Raidu waved Pactu aside then stopped, shielding his eyes as he looked out to sea where Ryu was leaning off the side of the raft as it skimmed across the water faster than eight strong men could paddle it. As he watched, the boat tipped too far, but Ryu let the rope slip so the mat loosened and the boat righted itself.

"Look at that, Pactu. You know what that is? It's the future."

"What?"

"Never mind. You'll understand eventually."

"Understand what?"

Without bothering with an answer, Raidu headed over to Laido and Nina.

"Is that your raft?"

Laido started. "It's just an experiment. We all worked on it."

"Well, leave it on the beach when you're done. The council wants to see it."

"It's not ready."

"I'll decide when it's ready." Raidu clapped Laido hard on the shoulder. "I'm sure the new chief will find it useful."

Laido glanced past Ryu and the raft. On the horizon, storm clouds were piling up. "I don't think anyone's going to be out in a boat for a while, unless they want to be caught in a storm."

Raidu grunted. "Then pull it up high on the beach. Once the storm passes, I'll have a real boater see what it can do."

Laido signaled Ryu to bring the boat in, expecting Raidu to leave. But he didn't. As Ryu turned for shore, Raidu planted his staff in the dirt and folded his arms across his chest, his eyes trained on the raft.

As soon as he got within shouting distance, Ryu called, "Did you see it that time? The turn?"

Laido held up his hand, moving it side to side in front of him, as if erasing the words. Silenced, Ryu brought the raft in, jumped off, and stood next to it, waiting as Laido took down the mat and rolled it up.

"Take these up to the hut," Laido said, his hands shaking as he handed the mat to Ryu and the paddle to Nina, "so the storm doesn't wreck them." As they walked away, he turned back to Raidu. "I'll let you know when the boat is ready."

"It's ready now. And it's *my* boat. As future chief, I claim it."

"When the boat is ready, I'll make you one. Now leave us alone."

"No." Raidu swung his staff up, holding it ready. "It's mine. As the new chief, I can claim anything I want. Your boat, your wife, your daughter, anything I choose."

"I don't remember anyone appointing you chief."

"Oh, they will, and you'll regret being on the wrong side of this. I can destroy you, Master Navigator, and I will. Believe me. Now, I'll take the boat. We'll discuss the rest later."

As Laido lunged forward to challenge Raidu, a cry stopped him.

Stumbling across the beach, her legs churning through the loose dirt, Naia ran toward them, gasping for air. "Where is Nulo? Where is he? What have you done with him?" She grabbed hold of Raidu's arm, forcing him to look at her. "They told me you'd know. *Where is Nulo?* You! Answer me!"

With a backhand slap to her face, he sent her twisting, crashing down in a crumpled heap against a pile of deadwood. "Control yourself, old woman. The council decreed he should be relocated."

She shook as she tried to sit up, struggling to get one elbow under her. "*Relocated?* What does that mean?"

"It means you shouldn't care about someone who never existed. If you do, you will be punished for defying the chief's decree. Besides, aren't you the one who kidnapped the boy in the first place?"

"Where is he?" she wailed.

Raidu turned his back on the figure on the sand.

As Laido knelt by Naia and helped her sit up, Ryu dropped the mat he was carrying and ran back across the beach, straight at Raidu.

"Fool," Raidu muttered as he dropped into his fighting stance. With a solid kick to Ryu's chest, he sent Ryu flying backward, crashing down on his shoulder. Holding his arm tight against his chest, he rolled to his feet. Before he got his balance, Raidu caught him across the back with his staff, throwing him face-first into the dirt.

Laido jumped to his feet, but Naia reached out to stop him. "Stay, please. If you fight, he'll call for help. If you don't, he'll leave," she whispered, "and you'll still be alive. So will Ryu. Please."

Laido knelt back down next to Naia.

Seeing no one move to attack, Raidu dusted off his tunic before heading back up the hill. "Good. I'll have someone pick up the boat," he called over his shoulder.

"Take care of Ryu, please," Naia begged Laido. "His parents are gone, and I'm not strong enough."

"You'll be fine."

"No, I won't." Her voice sounded thin and watery. "My days here are ending. But Nulo – I wish I could have helped him. He has something special."

"I'll look for him," Laido offered. "He can't be far."

"If he's still alive," Naia whispered.

Running out from the bushes where she'd hidden, Nina went first to Ryu and then to Naia and Laido.

"Papa," she cried, sliding down next to him on the sand, "what should I do?"

Putting his hand on his daughter's shoulder, he looked out to the storm clouds gathering over the sea. "Stay with Naia and Ryu while I get help. Then we have many things to do, very quickly."

* * *

That night, the goddess of death took away the chief, who'd grown tired of his strange existence stranded between the living and the dead. The next day, Naia joined him, helping him along the Travelers Path in the night sky, just as she had helped him along the island paths when he was a child.

Yet the goddess still appeared in the dark sky, night after night, her terrible white hair spread out behind her.

CHAPTER 9
NULO ALONE

Although Raidu had ordered Yon to leave Nulo with no way to survive, Yon packed several baskets of supplies at first light and stowed them in his boat. When he delivered Nulo to the island, he waited for the boy to thank him for all his trouble. Nulo, however, said nothing; he didn't even move.

"You can't go home, you know, even if you figured out a way to get there," Yon said before he left. "Raidu will kill you - or have someone else do it."

Rocking back and forth, his short arms hugging his chest, Nulo stared at the sea.

"Well, good luck," Yon called as he pushed his boat back into the water. "I hear there are others out here, somewhere. Owl Man said there's a whole community of outcasts on that long island." He pointed vaguely to a spot across the water. "Maybe you could find them." When Nulo didn't respond, Yon gave a nervous wave, jumped into his boat, and paddled away.

Nulo sank down to his knees and rocked back on his heels, watching the boat get smaller and smaller. Above it, the sky turned thick and pasty, its colors blurring into the sea. The boat shrank to a speck between the water and the sky. Eventually the old sun flattened into the sea, spreading its colors across the water and sky before it sank. As soon as it vanished, darkness rushed in around him.

He waited by the shore, but Yon didn't return. No one appeared. Overhead, clouds hid all but a few stars. In the terrible darkness, he closed his eyes and sleep claimed him.

* * *

He dreamed he was swimming back toward his home island when a giant crocodile grabbed hold of him, pulling him under the water, swallowing him whole. It was very close and dark inside the beast, yet in the strange way of dreams, he could move through its many chambers, each a separate room. He passed piles of fish bones, wooden masks and feathers, cooking pots, giant sea shells, cook stones, baskets of seaweed and coral, sweet berries and root vegetables. Beyond them, he heard the sound of voices jumbled together. He climbed up the piles to get closer to the voices, and the higher he went, the more the crocodile rose with him. Grabbing handholds on the baskets of fruits and brined bird eggs, he pulled himself up, feeling the crocodile heave itself out of the water and into the dark sky. As Nulo scrambled higher, through bundles of reeds and kindling, the monster switched its huge tail and soared into the stars.

In the silence Naia's voice spoke to him. "You must look for new worlds, Nulo, not here. This is the Otherworld, land of the ancestors." Another voice, his father's voice, seemed to agree, saying things Nulo couldn't quite make out.

The crocodile lurched sideways, throwing Nulo against the piled-up baskets and sacks, forcing him to crawl along. Dropping out of the sky, the crocodile splashed down in the water and twisted as it swam. Nulo pushed his way back through the chambers until he reached the crocodile's head. He could feel the head lift, the powerful legs push, the body twist back and forth as the beast heaved itself onto land. Then it opened its mouth wide so that between the rows of sharp teeth Nulo saw the island's forests shining silver against a dark sky. For a long moment, he stayed there, looking through the opened jaws, stuck between worlds.

On the shore, a canoe with an unfamiliar design waited for him, loaded with his belongings. On the sand, in a small bowl filled with water, a narrow stone twisted one way, then the other, then back. Finally, Nulo stepped out between the huge open jaws. Behind him, he heard the beast's jaws snap shut before it heaved itself around and slid back into the sea.

* * *

When Nulo awoke, the sun had already risen from the sea and warmed the land. The beach looked more familiar, more important now that he'd seen it in the dream. As he pulled Yon's supplies off the beach, he searched for the strange canoe he'd seen in the dream but found only thick layers of rocks and shells thrown up by the surf. Rocks and shells. Rocks. The special rock, the moving rock, that's what the dream had shown him. He waded into the shallows, studying the rocks, but none of them moved like the one in the dream. They only sat in the sand or tumbled in and out with each new wave. He tried setting them out in rows in the shallows, turning them over, arranging them in different piles. When he set a long one on top of a round one and tried to spin it, it only slid off into the sand.

A distant rumble made him abandon his search. Storm clouds filled the sky over the sea. Soon they'd bring the storm. Nulo gathered pieces of dead trees he could use as supports for a shelter, dragging one after another across the dirt, but it was slow work. As he lifted the first support and jammed it against the rock face, he felt the wind rise. Before he'd lifted the second one into place, lightning forked out across the island, splitting the air, dragging cracks of thunder behind it. Moments later the wind and rain came on hard, slapping the shore, throwing over the lone support. Abandoning his project, he grabbed the closest baskets and wedged them into a crevice in the cliff rocks. Lightning exploded in a white flash in front of him. Thunder broke behind it, crashing down in waves around him while the rain beat down. On the shore, trees bent under the torrents, their branches dragging in the dirt. Nulo flattened himself against the rock, pushing back as far as he could, finding not solid rock behind him, but a larger opening. Running back out into the storm, he snatched up the other baskets and shoved them inside the opening, then pressed himself in after them while the storm raged across the island.

Naia had told him that people who ignore lightning insult the spirits that travel along its light from one world to another. People that foolish would be killed, she'd warned. From where he stood, the lightning looked like rivers of light. After the lightning had struck the land, the path remained, like a memory of the light. With a shiver, he stepped out into the rain, letting it pound against his skin, pour down his hair and face, his arms and legs, pool up in his outstretched hands.

"Lightning spirit, touch me," he whispered into the storm. "Take me to another world." He turned his face up into the pounding rain.

With a blinding flash, the light struck the ground in front of him. Nulo staggered back, his hands pressed to his eyes. Rain lashed him, coursing down his face along with his tears. The storm raged around him and through him, reading every part of him, and when it was done, it moved on as suddenly as it had appeared, rolling off over the sea, leaving behind only the dripping trees and the smell of lightning.

When the sky reddened with the dying sun, Nulo returned to the rock crevice to retrieve the baskets. As he leaned in, high, buzzing sounds from the interior stopped him. Something was moving inside the rock, getting closer and louder. He ducked down, covering his head as the first of hundreds of bats emerged, followed immediately by the rest of the colony, a living, squeaking mass pouring out of the opening past him. Naia had warned him never to bother bats, saying they were messengers that went between this world and the Underworld, creatures of darkness that killed people who bothered them and carried the bodies away. So he waited, pressed against the rock edge, until the last ones had passed him by. When darkness fell, he slept where he was, never moving until the bats returned, rushing back in the same fluttering, squeaking mass.

The next day, he started once more to build his camp, but after he'd moved a few pieces of wood, he abandoned the effort. Instead, he walked along the shore, looking along the shore where the storm and the tides had undone all his piles of rocks. But one rock he remembered remained. The long skinny stone lay suspended by the rising tide over a round rock. As the next wave came in, spattering itself out on the shore rocks, it pushed the skinny rock around, parallel to the shore. As soon as the wave passed, the stone turned back to face into the sea. Nulo stared. The stone was turning itself. Other stones under it and around it kept it from being washed ashore or out to sea. So it turned and aligned with the beach when the wave pushed it. As the wave receded, it turned back, pointing to the sea.

Nulo hunkered down, watching, at once desperate to touch the stone and afraid it would lose its magic if he did. Finally, he lined the bottom of a large clamshell with smooth shore rocks, dipped the shell into the surf to fill it, lifted the narrow stone out of its home in the shallows, placed it on top of the rounded stones, and waited.

It didn't move.

He winced. "Why show me these things only to take them away?"

He settled the shell bowl into the dirt and studied the stone that used to dance. The long slender rock lay imprisoned between other rocks.

Starting over, he took everything out before he replaced the round stones and the water, placed the narrow stone back on the round base, and stood back, breathless. When the water stopped moving, the narrow stone slowly turned, facing seaward.

He caught his breath. "Why are you different today? Perhaps the lightning awakened you or the spirits of Naia and my father tested me." He stared at the stone as he picked up the shell and turned in a circle, slowly - one step, another, all the way around. Then he went faster, circling until he staggered. No matter how he turned, the stone always returned to the same position. When he went faster, the stone turned faster. When he slowed, the stone slowed, as if following his lead. He walked off, stopped, circled, backed up, lurched around, all the while clutching the shell to his chest.

"The dancing stone! Grandmother, I have it!"

Afraid to leave it, Nulo sat on the shore with the bowl and the stone for the rest of the day and all night. When the moon rose and the stars appeared, the stone pointed to the great serpent in the stars, the guardian of the cave at the center of the sky. *A thing of the earth linked to the stars,* he thought, *forever connected to both worlds. A great thing. A gift.*

CHAPTER 10
DISCOVERIES

At first light, Nulo awoke with a shiver, afraid he only dreamed about the dancing stone, but he found it balanced on the smooth stones in the shell, exactly where he'd left it. He set the shell down away from the shore but tucked the stone into his sash before he climbed back up the hill to retrieve the supplies he'd left in the rock opening. As he twisted around to pull out the closest basket, a glimpse of something strange stopped him. Pushing aside the baskets, he squeezed inside. Early sunlight streamed through the gap between the rock slabs, sending a broad beam all the way across the cave and illuminating the back wall. Above, the ceiling was covered with bats hanging upside down, their leathery wings wrapped tightly around them. Piles of foul-smelling guano covered the floor, bearing no tracks except his, and yet there, on the far wall now lit by the young sun, seven red handprints stood out clearly against the rock face.

Nulo held up his own hand next to the red prints. *All the right hand, with a twisted little finger. A child? A small adult? One person left all of these - Why? Why seven prints?* He searched the rest of the walls, looking for other marks, finding none. As he examined the prints, the shaft of light that brought them to life gradually narrowed, so only the middle prints were lit and the rest disappeared into shadow. As the light narrowed to only a finger's width, Nulo traced the lines of the handprint, lingering on the crooked finger, acknowledging this stranger, this companion. On his way back across the stinking piles of guano, Nulo turned to see the last of the prints disappear with the changing light. *Does each hand stand for something? Persons or days or moons? If it does, what does each hand measure? One? Five? Some use their finger joints to count, so maybe each print means more? Did you know, you who left these prints, that the light would shine exactly on this spot when the sun was first born? Did you know how the light shaft would move and narrow? Did you make your prints in exactly that place so the light would find them? Did you know that the handprints would whisper to me, saying words just a little too muffled to understand?*

At the entrance to the cave, Nulo bowed in honor of the person he'd never met, this companion who shared his space, who'd left a message he couldn't understand. But the message was less important than the artist who'd left it.

"I am more because of you," he sang over the conical pile of stones he built, remembering a song Naia used to sing to him,

> "I am better, stronger, kinder
> because of you.
You add to all things,
> even the sky.
When you leave,
> the stars will remember you,
> the sea will sing for you,
> the rocks will carry your name.
In another time, I will see you again,
> somewhere behind the sun,
> where tears turn into flowers."

All day long he could feel the presence of the one who'd left the prints, someone he knew had meant to talk to him, to relay something important. Or perhaps long ago, a lightning being had come down and left the prints before returning to the sky.

That night, he climbed to a rock basin high on the cliffs where rainwater collected until the basin overflowed and the water ran down the rock in rivulets. There he swam in the stars. The Path to the Otherworld arched high above him and reflected deep in the still water around him, receding infinitely in both directions. Familiar star figures surrounded him: the winged Creator Mother and Father whose long tails intertwined; the great bird rising in the east; the leaping whale; the lost children, and high above him, the Bridge of Birds that spanned the dark river in the Travelers Path. After a while, even these familiar outlines faded, leaving only the field of stars, immeasurably high and deep, and in the center of them all, the feeling of his breath. Then he let that go too. He swam in the darkness that was the other half of the stars, unaware of his own being and undivided from everything else.

All around him the rising sky filled with music: the bright stars airy and high-pitched, flowing into strange and beautiful harmonics; the dark stretches between the stars heavy and sonorous, resonating inside him.

He was alive at the center of the singing universe.

CHAPTER 11
THE COUNCIL MEETING

A young woman hurried into the meeting lodge bearing a bowl of painted eggs. Behind her, at the entrance, Owl Man's apprentices summoned the Council members, crying "The chief is dead. You must choose a new chief! Take your places!" Along the far wall, Owl Man pounded the point of his staff against a block of wood, pushing members to move faster. His tattooed face remained motionless while the black feathers on his staff and rows of bone fragments and shark teeth on his robe jerked in unison with each beat. Pushing through on-lookers crowded along the wall, careful to give Owl Man a wide berth, the young woman with the bowl found a clear spot near the front where she arranged the first set of vote eggs. She'd painted each one of the hollowed eggs with a different pattern using red ochre mixed with fine sand, charcoal, and egg yolk. Once they were laid out, she nodded at her work. But the newly thatched roof couldn't match the rain falling outside. A large drop splashed into the bowl, ruining the design on the top egg. She hurried toward the entrance to get a replacement egg, but the crossed staffs of the apprentices stopped her.

"No more people may enter!" the apprentices yelled. "No one may leave until after the vote!"

Watching their angry faces, the artist hardly recognized the two apprentices as men she'd known all her life. *I saw you race along the shore as the sun dropped into the sea. I loved you both, though those days and that shore are gone now. I remember when you used to wrestle fish. And you sang songs so beautiful that my heart sang with you. You were strong and smart and beautiful, nothing like the frightening men I see before me. You knew when you started that only one would be chosen to continue the shaman's training, but it hadn't mattered back then. It was an adventure. Now, too many days of competition have changed you. You find the closeness of the other unbearable yet you refuse to yield the space. You look as if you would fight to the death if the other simply raised a hand against you. My beautiful friends from other days, you poison the air with this intolerable tension. You breathe it in and you exhale it, so it moves through the entire lodge. I can feel it spreading.*

Pactu showed the council members to their seats, but they quarreled about the arrangement. When he called for nominations for the new chief, the members refused to support any candidate, arguing against the candidates and each other. To settle the question, Pactu called for the artist to distribute the voting eggs so each member could place an egg in one of the bowls designated for the candidates. As each member voted, the others watched then voted so that no candidate had enough eggs in the bowl to win. Frustrated, Pactu called for the artist to empty the bowls and asked for new nominations. When they were chosen, the artist laid out the vote bowls and distributed the eggs. Again the members watched each other vote then altered their vote if necessary to ensure no candidate had enough to win. When the artist collected the eggs once again, the beautiful designs had smeared into red blotches.

At the end of the first day, the council hadn't reached a decision. Pactu sent them home, telling them to be back the following morning at first light. "Rest well," he called after them. "We'll do better tomorrow."

But the next day was no better. At Pactu's order, the artist distributed the smeared eggs for each vote and collected them after each failure. She knew why the designs were ruined, why the elections failed: evil air mixed with the crowd's fears. Council members wouldn't speak to each other. Each time it seemed one candidate would have enough votes to win, the other members voted for someone else. If Pactu suggested a compromise arrangement with more than one candidate, they all disagreed. Once again, he sent them home at the end of the day, telling them the next day would be better.

On the third day, Raidu refused to sit with the other council members at the start of the session. As the others took their places, he paced back and forth, staring at them.

"You call yourselves council members?" he shouted, standing behind them so they had to swivel around to see him. "I don't see any counsel here. No leaders. No wise advice. Only stubborn, stupid people arguing with each other. It's no surprise the young men of the village are useless - playing about in boats instead of learning the skills of a warrior. What kind of life is this? When will you stand and fight?"

"Stand and fight? No one's attacking us," another member countered. "We have a good life here."

"It's a pathetic life. What do you have to show for your days? Real men are fighters. They know they have to kill or be killed in order to preserve their place in the world."

"Who would you fight? We have no enemies here."

"This place? This isn't the home we deserve. This is a refuge for exiles. We were pushed out of our rightful home."

"War, then - is that your plan, Raidu?" Pactu interrupted, standing up. "And for what reason? Boredom?"

"Reclaiming what's mine. Standing up instead of running away. Where will you stop running? When you reach the edge of the earth?"

"That happened many seasons ago, on the old land," an older member countered. "We were run off because they had giant war canoes and many more warriors. None of that's changed, I'm sure."

Raidu smiled. "Oh, but it has. We now have wind rafts that will be much faster than war canoes."

"You mean that disaster Laido and Ryu have been working on?"

"It works better than they want you to think. In fact, Laido should be training all the men to use them. They'll be a huge advantage in battle."

"You speak as if the war is already decided," said another member.

"The wrong has already been suffered. If you're too weak to exact punishment for it, then you should get out of the way and let someone else do it."

"The attack happened long ago, in a different place," Pactu reminded the group. "Why seek revenge now? Those people probably don't even remember."

"But I do! And now we have what we need to even the score."

"Didn't they have something like the wind raft?" a voice called out from the audience.

"Yes," an old woman replied. "They came in under cover of darkness, set fire to our huts, and killed those who tried to stop them. We fled with nothing more than we could carry."

In the silence that followed, Pactu tried again. "Why do we need their used-up land? This land supports us very well. We're happy here."

"You're wrong!" Raidu closed in. "You're whimpering in a little hole. The world belongs to those who take it for themselves, not to those who flee! Sooner or later, someone will try to take this land and you'll have no place left to hide. Then you'll wish you had taken a stand!"

"This argument has no merit," Pactu objected. "You say we should go to war because we should go to war. That's not enough. What do you lack here?"

"On the surface - nothing. Inside - everything. I have enough to eat but I'm hungry for something more than food. I have an island but I want the world. I want greatness – for all our people," he added after a pause. "I look at the sun and stars, and I want to shine like them. That's the destiny of great men."

"We should see this wind raft," one member responded. "Then we could figure out how to use it. Did you say Laido made it? Where did he get the idea?"

No one replied.

Owl Man spoke slowly as he stepped forward. "Perhaps he is the medium of one of our enemies. An idea must come from somewhere. It doesn't just float through the air to be caught by anyone passing by. However, if his spirit was somehow linked to this past warrior, he would know the design of the boat."

"It's not the same design," Grandmother corrected, but her remark was lost in the overlapping comments that filled the lodge.

"Wasn't Laido's family killed by the invaders of his island?"

"Maybe that's just the story he told. How did he learn how to read the sea?"

"Why would he lie? He was a child when he was brought here."

"We're here to elect a new chief," Pactu interrupted, "not to condemn innocent people on some rumor."

Raidu warmed to the contest. "The chief sets the direction. He chooses the strongest and bravest. He weeds out the troublesome and lazy. Look around. I see a bunch of whining children fighting with each other. You could be so much more! All you need is a leader who'll take you there, someone who's not afraid to aim higher."

"That's someone like you, I suppose?"

"Greatness is for those who would fight for it, Pactu. Those who do nothing but stare stupidly at the old village under the sea or whine about their pains get nothing in return. They don't like how things are but never bother to change them. Have you no hunger for a real fight, a battle for greatness?"

"Many honorable people here do not share your thirst for blood," Pactu complained.

"Then they're weak and will be pushed aside."

"You sound as if you're already chief, Raidu, but you haven't been elected," one council member pointed out.

Throwing his staff to the floor, Raidu glared at the seated members and at the artist waiting by the side of the lodge. "Then vote! Distribute the vote eggs! Council members, stop stepping on your own feet. Go somewhere. The world is changing, right here, today. Yesterday's world is gone. It went away with the old village when the sea moved in, so stop pining for it. There's a brand new world opening up in front of you. All you need to decide is whether you're going to be part of it or not. It's no place for cowards. Only the brave will survive."

Four men who had been waiting in the back of the chamber moved up on his signal and stood with him.

Pactu pleaded for reason, his voice strained. "There is nothing different now from three days ago when you came to this hall to elect a new chief. Your families are the same. Your neighbors are the same. The world is the same. Raidu's speech was just meant to scare you."

"Raidu's right," a council member called. "We need a strong chief. I nominate Raidu."

"I nominate Pactu," another voice called.

"Let's vote, then, and be done."

After they agreed to another vote, silence fell over the group. One by one the members rose and placed their eggs in the candidate bowls. When all the vote eggs were placed, Pactu had to announce the final count: ten eggs in Raidu's bowl, two in his.

"It's decided, then," Owl Man declared, extending his staff toward Raidu. As the artist collected the vote eggs for the final time, Raidu nodded to the council members and Owl Man, acknowledging his election. The members waited for him to address them as their new chief, but he waved them out impatiently.

"Your work is done. Go now."

As Owl Man followed the others out of the lodge, Raidu grabbed the shaman's arm, motioning for him to stay.

"It went well, don't you agree?"

"It went just as you said it would," Owl Man said, twisting out of Raidu's grip

When Owl Man reached the entryway, the two apprentices fell into step behind him.

Raidu watched them leave, his eyes narrowed.

CHAPTER 12
YON'S VISIT

Wheeling and crying, flocks of shorebirds flew up as Yon jerked first his boat and then another boat onto the shore of Nulo's island.

"Nulo," he started, even though he hadn't seen the boy, "I need to talk to you. Things have changed at home. Your father is dead, Naia too. I'm sorry to have to tell you this way, but I don't know any way that would make the news easier to hear. Raidu is the new chief." He glanced around the beach area. "Nulo?"

"Yes," Nulo said, stepping out of the bushes.

"Yes," Yon echoed, twisting his hands. "You're alive, anyway, that's something. See, Raidu told me to take you here. I brought the supplies myself because it seemed wrong to leave you here with nothing at all." He paused as if stuck.

Nulo waited.

"Now Raidu wants you killed." Yon's thin hands moved in jerks as he spoke. "He sent me here to kill you. That's it. Now it won't matter if I kill you or not. Raidu doesn't trust me or anyone else. He'll check. If you're still here, he'll have you killed and then kill me. So you need to leave this island. You can't go back home and you can't stay here, so you have to go somewhere else." He glanced up at Nulo and back down, locking his hands together again.

"I could take you somewhere. Owl Man mentioned an island out that way that has other 'left-over people.' Do you want to go there?"

Nulo stared past Yon.

"You have to tell me. You have to say one way or the other: yes, you want me to take you to this island or no, you don't. Do you understand what I'm saying?"

"Did you bring that boat for me?" Nulo said, working on the words.

"That?" Yon looked at the second boat. "Yes. Well, I stole it. I thought you might need a boat. If you want it, that is. I could take you in my boat, which would be fine, but you'd have more room in that boat. You don't seem to understand what I risked. I'm trying to save. I'm saving your life. You have to say something. Nulo!"

The boy only hunkered down, staring at the beach.

After pulling the covered baskets out of his boat and throwing them on the damp sand one by one, Yon turned back to Nulo. "Maybe your balance has gone. You were always strange, but now you're not even a person."

Slowly, Nulo turned his head to consider Yon's darting eyes, his tunic soaked with seawater, his thin legs twisting when his hands were locked together, his words falling fast and hard, plink, plink, plink, plink, like pebbles on the rocks.

"Thank you for your kindness. I'll go by myself."

"If that's what you want. Make it soon. Good luck." Yon untied the second boat and hurried his own back into the water. "There's salted fish, berry-fat cakes, root flakes, things like that in the baskets. And a better knife." Out of things to say, Yon held up his hand in a formal farewell before he vaulted into his boat.

* * *

None of Yon's words mattered to Nulo. Only one thing held his attention: the dugout canoe resting on the sand where Yon had left it, tipped slightly away from him, its tow rope lying half in the boat, half on the sand, its row of sea turtle designs running along the waterline, the middle two obscured by wet sand, exactly as they should be. The same paddle with the chipped blade. The same oiled, burned-out interior with the light spot near the bow. All the time Yon was talking, Nulo had studied the boat, going over every part of it.

It was, in every detail, the boat in his dream, the one he'd seen on the beach when he'd stepped out of the crocodile's mouth.

CHAPTER 13
DEPARTURES

Pactu slumped against a post in his hut. "I don't understand, Mara. What do they want? How did this happen?"

His wife sat on the floor, sorting through piles of dried fish wrapped in palm leaves, strings of shells, fish traps, bundled roots, mats and baskets, bark cloth, precious stones, quills filled with salt and medicinal powders, plaited leaf bowls, iridescent feathers, carved wooden figures of her ancestor spirits. "They were afraid. They *are* afraid. Raidu's men have been all over the village telling people that they must follow him or leave. People thought it was a bluff at first, but now they believe him."

"The council would have come around. They always did before." His voice trailed off. "I can't believe it happened like that."

"Well, it did. If we stay, you'll have to support Raidu, no matter what he does. He won't tolerate criticism."

"Of course we'll stay. Where would we go? My whole life is here. We just need to get it back to the old way. We'll have a new Council session and vote in a new chief. It's simple."

"Look around, Pactu! Who would dare vote against Raidu?"

"I would."

"You already did. You lost."

"Why are you so set on running away? Isn't that exactly what Raidu accused me of - always running away from a fight?"

"I'm trying to save our family," Mara said. "I know there's no promise of a good life out there, but I know what will happen here."

"How can you know? Maybe it's all just talk."

"It's not talk. He means everything he says."

"Well, I won't run away. I'll stay right here." He paused. "But you can go. Take the children and wait for me."

Mara threw down the bundles in frustration. "Where? When? What are you talking about? We don't know where we're going! How could you meet us there later? And why would you abandon us? We need you!"

"If I go, he'll be right. I have to stay. I have to fight."

"For what? Fight for what? Your community wants Raidu. They voted him the new chief. Unless you persuade the Council to stand against him, his word is law."

"There must be a way," Pactu sighed. "There must be another voice. Who was the other vote for me?"

"No one seems to remember. I asked." Mara handed him a small bowl. "Here, I made you some tea."

Pactu drank deeply. "It'll work out, you'll see. The people just need some time."

"For what?'

"To realize they don't really want Raidu. They were just tired and frightened. Once they get some rest, they'll see that. They'll see Raidu isn't the chief they really want." When Mara didn't reply, he went on, half to himself, "Why didn't the members choose me? Do they really want to go to war? Maybe they do."

For a moment, he stared at the piles of supplies on the floor of the hut. "I don't know what to do, Mara. The whole election seemed strange." He finished off the bowl of tea. "It was the rain, you know. Too much rain. And the air was heavy. It wore people down. That's it. Too much rain. Bad air," he repeated as he slumped to the floor, sound asleep.

"It'll be better later," his wife murmured as she packed up their belongings.

Mara and the children loaded their boat after dark then guided the very groggy Pactu to the shore. When he started to protest, she told him she needed his help getting the boat into the water, so he helped push it into the shallows then climbed in slowly. As the children took up their paddles, heading away, she tried to see the familiar parts of the island that had been her family's home, but darkness covered everything except the last bits of a fire still burning in the village center.

* * *

Later that night, Laido and his family also left, towing the wind raft behind their big canoe. Ryu went with them.

CHAPTER 14
THE VIEW FROM THE CLIFF

Yon lied to Raidu about Nulo, spinning a long story about how he'd killed the boy with a stone and dropped the body into the sea. He'd expected Raidu to challenge him, ask for proof, maybe accuse him of lying and punish him, maybe even kill him right in front of his supporters. But Raidu only shrugged at the news of Nulo's death.

"The important thing now is to make sure Laido doesn't leave with the wind raft – or without it. Keep watch by the shore tonight. Don't fail at this, Yon." Raidu eyed the younger man who clasped his hands together to keep them still.

When another supporter joined the group, Yon slipped away, climbing up the cliff rocks to a ledge where he'd have a perfect view of the beach. There he hunkered down, pressing his back against the stone, watching the sky darken and the stars appear out of the dark, listening to the wave sounds change as the tide came in. Later he heard other sounds – muffled voices, boats being dragged across the sand, paddles being thrown into the boats, people splashing through the shallows. Yon recognized the voices and the boats, but he didn't alert Raidu.

When the night passed, Yon looked out at a grey sea and a grey sky divided by the thin line the old men used to call the dark serpent of the sea. On the shore, he saw rows of footprints and lines where people had dragged their boats into the sea. Wrapping his thin arms around his knees, he looked from the dark line of the serpent to the dark lines in the sand and shivered.

* * *

On the shore, a man walking close to the water's edge shed his tunic and dropped it in the wet sand. From the opposite side, another man appeared, his motions the mirror image of the first. The two headed straight for each other, slowly at first, then a little faster, yelling each other's names in challenge. Stripped down to their loin wraps, they could have been any two men except for the long black feathers they'd worn tied into their hair since the first day of their apprenticeship to the shaman. As they closed the distance, they broke into a run, drawing up at the last moment as one raised his ax and the other his club. Their weapons flashed at the same moment, slamming into each other. Staggering back from the blows, they recovered, raised their weapons, attacked again. Then again, and again, each time perfectly and terribly matched.

From his perch on the cliff, Yon could hear their grunts and cries, the crack of their weapons, but the men seemed unreal, battling like grey ghosts under the grey sky. They stumbled, fell, pushed themselves up, and rushed in again. Blood ran in dark rivers. As they tired, the swings grew wilder. After both fell hard, they struggled to their feet, took up their weapons, and threw everything into one last assault. With a scream, one slammed his club against his enemy's head while the second drove his ax into his enemy's chest. In the moment they crashed to the sand, broken and dying, the hatred that had driven them spewed into the air like spores from a poisonous plant, carried on the wind across the shore, up the hill, and throughout the village.

Yon didn't move from his perch on the ledge though he felt the air change around him the way it did before a storm. As he watched,

villagers coming down to dig for clams discovered the dead apprentices. Two ran up to the village center shouting the news. When
they returned, families and friends of the apprentices came with
them, gasping at the sight of the two slain men. At once, they took
up the desperate fight because the apprentices had left it to them: a
gift and a demand from the newly dead. The families yelled about
avenging their kin and fought each other where the apprentices lay,
stepping across the bodies as they screamed and battled, drawing
the poisoned air inside them with every breath.

While they fought, the man whose boat Yon had stolen ran
up and down the beach, grabbing one man after another by the
shoulder, spinning them around, yelling, pointing to the shore. One
argued back, shoving the fisherman, shouting something at him.
Another stepped between them, raising his arms. One of the fighters grabbed him, twisting his arms around. Another spat at the first
then pushed aside the second. The men fought without allies. A
kick to the midsection. A blow to the head. A cut across the arm.
Friends moved in and took up the fight. Friends became enemies.
Every fight drew more people into the middle of it.

All the while, the troubled spirits of the two apprentices
watched, still hungry for something to destroy.

Women ran into the middle of fighting groups, yelling,
throwing rocks at the men and at each other. One threw a slop pot
at another, covering her in filth. Screaming, the woman tore the
shell necklace from her attacker's neck, throwing the shells across
the sand. The attacker swung the pot at the other's head, trampling
her precious shells as she went.

Tears ran down Yon's face as he watched the fighting, the
combatants appearing interchangeable and unreal. He watched as
someone tried to break up a fight with a long paddle but someone
else grabbed it and smashed it into the man's head, digging a bloody
track. The hurt man lunged at his attacker, throwing him down
into the sand and kicking him. Another figure knocked the winner

down as well. Someone else grabbed the paddle, swinging it in great arcs through the crowd. Red blood sprayed across the dark sand, trampled under struggling feet.

Yon moved to the cliff edge, each heartbeat amplified, each image intensified, and stood for a long moment looking at the braided layers of grey sky hovering over the dark sea. He imagined himself falling, slowly, arms outstretched like the wings of a hawk, until he crashed into the white surf below, where he'd be released from this long line of mistakes.

"No," he called to the grey sky. "I need to finish what I started." Exhaling a ragged breath, he started down the cliff rocks.

On the beach, several people ran past him to escape the fighting, but they only pulled the conflict with them up the hill and into the village center. Raidu's men couldn't stop the fighting; they had little experience controlling a mob. When they blocked the main paths to keep the crowd from entering the village center, fighters simply found other ways.

The more people destroyed, the more they wanted to destroy. Like a demon lover, chaos took them. Someone threw a burning branch onto a rooftop, setting the thatch on fire. Once flames leaped from the hut, they moved to another. Those who'd lost their huts ripped out burning stakes and used them to burn others' huts. Some tore down the lodge built for the new chief. Although Raidu stormed into the middle of the crowd, yelling and threatening, even his booming voice had no effect.

Villagers escaping the fires trampled those too slow to run. Yon pushed through and pulled a child out of the path of the mob. When he heard a cry, he handed off the child and pushed his way back to a burning hut. Inside, he found an old man yelling about a ghost holding him there, refusing to let him escape. As Yon took the man's hand to pull him to safety, the man pulled back, shaking his head. Yon's head swam. He couldn't breathe. Two warring ghosts filled the hut, battling with flames, turning sometimes to look at him. The old man screamed as the ghost flames found him. Yon grabbed the man's arm and pulled, but the figure seemed to be made of stone. Breathless, Yon collapsed on the hut floor while the thatch burned overhead and the ghosts hurled flames at each other until they became fire figures moving into the flames that consumed the hut and everything in it.

By the time the madness cooled, eight people lay dead and twice that many wounded. Half the buildings in the village had been damaged. Some had burned to the ground. In the hills, children hid in the banyan trees, afraid to go home.

* * *

Afterward, the villagers remembered their dead, treated their wounded and repaired their huts, but they found it hard to look at each other. Something still smoldered inside many of them, waiting only for the right conditions to break into killing fire. When Raidu offered them the chance to go to war, they took it without a second thought. Others were so disgusted by the darkness they'd witnessed that they fled immediately without knowing where they'd go or what the future might hold for them. They only knew they couldn't stay any more days in the place evil had claimed in a moment.

From his vantage point off to the side, Owl Man closed his eyes. It had all happened exactly as foretold in the cracks of the turtle shell.

CHAPTER 15
NULO AT SEA

By the time Nulo paddled past the tip of his island, the old sun was flattening, spreading into the sea under a bank of purple clouds. He found no sign of the island Yon mentioned, only bits of treetops sticking out of the water where islands used to be.

As the light dropped to a thin red line on the sea, a bitter wind rose, turning the canoe sideways. Since he knew he couldn't fight the wind, he let it take the boat, assuming it would push him right back to his island. Instead, the wind strengthened, driving the waves before it, pushing the little boat farther from the island. Lightning snaked across the underbelly of the storm and down toward the water, showing him no land, nothing but the dark sea rising around him. Thunder cracks broke the rain loose from the clouds. As the rain ran down his body and pooled up at his feet, he tucked his best stones deep in the fold of his sash and tried to steer the boat straight over the waves. Once he could feel the waves rising directly under the boat, he braced the steering paddle under one arm while he bailed with the other. When the steering paddle slipped, the boat skidded sideways down the troughs and seawater lapped over the edge. He went from steering to bailing and back again until his hands were raw, his arms had no strength left, and he was too tired to manage anything but steering.

Morning brought just enough light for him to see the sky swelling with the next storm. The seawater sloshing in the boat smelled foul. His supplies floated in soggy masses around him:

snake fruits, root bundles, soggy bits of fat-berry cakes, a broken basket lid, bark cloth, one of the water gourds. Thirsty, he lifted the gourd, pried out the wax and grass stopper, and took a long drink. His hands shook as he tried to push the stopper wad back in the gourd.

While the sea was quiet, he bailed out more of the water and sorted out the supplies worth keeping. Before he'd finished, a new storm rose, its dark clouds pulling the sea up and then dropping it, making the boat twist and roll with the waves. No thunder or lightning this time, no gradual build-up, only the wind rising suddenly, pushing the sea before it, making it slop over the side of the boat. Thirst rose in him again, but the gourd floated well past his reach. He tried to find his way through the water and wet bundles, but he was thrown back as the boat rode up a wave front. He pushed himself up, grabbed the paddle, and corrected the angle every time the boat twisted away from straight into the wave. When the rains came again, he opened his mouth as he steered, nearly gagging on the water. As he reached for the bailer gourd once again, the boat twisted down into a trough and an oncoming wave topped the side, splashing across the boat, lifting the bundled supplies and sweeping them out the far side in a single motion. Shoving the paddle under one arm, he grabbed at the baskets with the other and reached nothing.

The waves rising underneath the boat felt like so many sea creatures pushing him into the wrath of the storm, whose face filled the sky. "Kill me, then!" Nulo yelled, shaking his paddle at the storm. "Kill me if you will! What sort of fight is this? Look at me!" As the storm roared at him, he yelled back even as tears slipped down his face. "I'll fight you, spirit of the storm on the sea!"

As darkness fell, a series of storms rose, one after another. Blue-white lightning struck nearby, spreading across the wave tops in ghostly fingers. The thunder crack boomed across the water, bringing on more wind and rain and heaving seas. The storm's bitter strength wore Nulo raw. When the last of the storms blew past, he huddled in the storm water at the bottom of the boat because it was warmer than the air.

When he awoke, the sky to the east was brightening behind the morning star. "So bright," Nulo said, addressing the star, "so bright and clear, and the land underneath you, so dark."

Land. Land under the star. He took up his paddle again, even though his hands were raw. That dark shape with a cloud hovering over the top had to be an island. It would have a good place to land and a fine river or spring-fed pool, he promised himself.

As he neared the island, he realized it was bigger than he'd thought, with lush forests, a good landing site, and what looked like a river draining into the sea. Steering clear of the dying trees that stuck up through the water, he brought the boat to the shore and half-fell into the shallows. Stumbling, he pulled it just far enough onto the shore to keep it from floating away before he plowed through the brush to the river.

Dropping to his hands and knees, he put his head in the river and drank. For a long time, the chuckling of the water between the rocks and a silver flashing sound filled him. He drank until he couldn't drink anymore, then dunked his head under the water, letting it run down his face and chest. Slowly he rose and walked farther out, feeling the river dimple under his trailing fingers. In the deepest part, the water washed over him completely. Then, because all things must be in balance, he extracted his most beautiful red stone from his sash and buried it in the river bottom. A gift for a gift.

When he surfaced, he heard irregular knocking sounds in the forest around him, first on one side and then on the other. Hollow sounds, not rhythmic patterns. Tap tap tip tap tip. Silence. More tapping. Silence. More from the far side. Silence. Like a conversation with sounds instead of words. Standing in the river's moving light, he realized only people could make sounds like those. In case of attack, he probably couldn't get back to the boat fast enough.

More than that, he didn't want to go back to the sea. He wanted to be right where he was, with the sunlight in the river. So he stayed even though he heard the tapping start again, quite close to him. The sunlight glinted on the water as he stood, feeling the change coming nearer.

But the hand on his arm still came as a shock. Someone silhouetted by the sun pulled him out of the river and leaned in to get a look at him.

"Nulo?"

CHAPTER 16
REUNION

"Come with me. I'll help you up to our camp. It's good to see you, but you can't stay here."

"*Ryu!* The storm - boat -" Words stuck.

Ryu handed Nulo a water gourd and a handful of mashed nuts as he helped him up the bank. "Don't worry about your boat. It's been taken already, as well as anything in it." You need to get off the shore. I'll take you to our camp. Laido and his family are here too."

The camp was a collection of hastily constructed lean-tos in a clearing in the forest with a view of the shore and easy access to the river. When Ryu and Nulo arrived, Tahn slipped out without speaking to either of them while Darna, Laido, and Nina gathered around, asking him about his journey, passing him bowls of food and water, and arguing with each other over details of their own trip.

"Thank you. The food and drink are good," Nulo managed, "and you've all been very kind. I don't understand."

Before they had a chance to explain, Nulo's eyes closed and his head slumped to his chest. Darna caught him before he fell over.

When he awoke, he found the sun was already high and the camp area empty except for Darna.

"Welcome back," she said, looking up from the torn mats she was repairing. "Once you're settled, you can help me split some reeds until the others get back. Did you bring your tools?"

"Lost in the storm."

"You might want to look around the island for some replacements. Stonework could be your contribution for the Fat Men."

"Fat men?"

Darna set her work down. "I guess no one had a chance to explain it to you last night. The winds that brought us here brought others before us. The first two people here were the Fat Men. Their names are Fuhua and Liwei, but everyone calls them the Fat Men, just not to their faces. They control the water. If you contribute to the group, you have access to water. If not, you don't."

"Anyone could get water from the river."

"No, they couldn't. And it's not really about water though that's where it started. It's really about control. When newcomers arrive, they have to give the Fat Men a gift. It might be valuables - shell, jade, tools, beautiful carvings, that sort of thing. Or something new, like the wind raft. Or a skill, like fishing, cooking, building, curing, singing, storytelling, weaving, painting, carving - anything that the Fat Men want. That's how people get permission to stay here."

"What did you give?"

"Well, Laido offered the wind raft, a special boat he designed. And I'm a master weaver, so I told them that both Nina and I were fine weavers, though Nina really is only a beginner."

"Why would you say something untrue?"

"It was necessary. Girls are not welcome in the boat building group. Girls with no skill become Entertainment Girls. So she became a weaver."

"What if you have no treasure or skill they want?"

"Then you serve in an assigned work group or the Guards. The Guards are young people, mostly, who act as observers, enforcers, private servants, whatever Fuhua and Liwei need. You probably heard the scouts' signals when you arrived."

"Tapping sounds?"

"Their code. Each scout carries two wooden tubes. When struck, they make a low or high sound that can be heard over a wide area. Their code's secret, but it's built on a series of sounds for each idea, so they can tell each other many things, including when someone new has landed. While you were drinking from the river, they were already ransacking your boat. If you had any valuables, the Guards would have taken them, squabbled over them, and eventually turned some of them over to the Fat Men. If not, they'd simply take the boat for themselves."

"Is this the island of banished people Yon told me about?"

"No one here was banished, or at least no one will say so. They're all refugees from somewhere. You'll get to meet them at the celebration they call Brightness Day."

"I don't think anyone will be happy to see me."

"You'll be surprised," Darna said as she resumed her work. "It's different on this island. People don't all look the same. You might find a new life here. But first you have to see the Fat Men to get permission to stay."

CHAPTER 17
THE FAT MEN

Two Guards emerged from the forest by the camp without making a sound. Wearing dark loin wraps and pectorals of bird bones, they stood wordless in front of Nulo and Darna. Tangles of black hair fell across their expressionless tattooed faces. One of them motioned to Nulo to come with them.

Pushing himself to his feet, Nulo followed them along barely cleared paths. When he fell behind, they slowed their pace without looking back. Around them, the forest rang with cries of monkeys and birds. From an open flooding, crowds of white herons rose, beating longs wings in rhythmic strokes as they flew into the tree tops. Nulo stopped to watch the flash of white wings against the dark sky. *They carry the ghosts of the ancestors,* Naia had explained long ago. He wondered whether one was Naia still looking out for him. When he looked back to the trail, he saw the Guards disappearing in the dense brush. With a last glance at the herons, he hurried to catch up. In the deep forest, he followed exactly where they walked for the trail seemed invisible to him. Past a sapling tied down to the ground, the Guards turned abruptly onto a different path, one carefully smoothed and wide enough for three men to walk side by side. From there, they motioned Nulo toward a flattened hill at the end of the trail before they slipped back into the forest.

Nulo had never seen a hill like this one. It stood at least twice his height, very wide at the base, tapered on the sides, and perfectly flat on top. Stone steps led from the bottom of the hill to the top where two large huts with thatched roofs stood. A Guard at the top of the steps pointed to the first hut, where a fat man sat cross-legged on a low platform, watching him. His large, bald head was framed by long ears with elongated lobes set with green stones. His fleshy cheeks, marked with swirling designs, drooped down past his jaw, merging with the rolls of his neck and flowing into his enormous belly. His wide arms couldn't reach around his midsection, so he rested them on his bulging stomach. Only his eyes moved, impatiently taking in the figure before him.

"Well? You are called Nulo, are you not? What have you brought me?"

"I have only one treasure. It was given to me in a dream."

"A dream learner, then," the fat man nodded. "I am Liwei. Show me this amazing thing you gained in a dream."

Nulo pulled the stone from his sash. "It is a dancing stone. It needs a bowl of water and some rocks."

"An odd stone that needs water." Liwei clapped his hands and a Guard appeared. "Fetch us a bowl, some rocks to fit in the bowl, and a water gourd."

When the Guard returned with everything requested, Nulo put the dancing stone down on the floor and emptied the stones out of the bowl one by one. As he set the last stone down, the dancing stone turned toward it. Nulo moved the stone, but the dancing stone kept pointing to it. As Nulo moved the stone closer to the dancing stone, it slid across the space between the stones until the two were touching.

Liwei leaned over the edge of his platform, following every move of the stones. "What is this?" he demanded. "What is happening?"

"I don't know. Before, it always pointed out to sea, toward the dragon in the stars." Nulo moved the dancing stone back, but when he released it, it slid across the floor to the other stone, touching it in exactly the same place.

"A worthy gift! We must learn what it means. Tomorrow we will speak to the Circle of Learners about this. I will keep it until then. Very interesting." He sat back, clapped his hands, and ordered the Guards to escort Nulo back to the camp.

"Sir, the stone was a gift to me."

"It still is, but many will learn from it now. You will come back and show it to the Learners tomorrow."

The Guard who stood by Nulo's shoulder tapped him on the arm and motioned for him to follow. As they turned to leave, Nulo saw Liwei reach his staff down to test the stone's magic once more.

* * *

As Liwei had directed, the Learners gathered the following day: a mixed group, different from each other in every way except their curiosity and their desire to learn. Out of the five men and three women, one was very old and one had barely left childhood behind. Some wore the headdress and skins of the far northerners; some wore the fine weavings of the west; some wore almost nothing. Some had patterned scars decorating their faces and circling their arms. Some had narrow eyes and flat heads; others had round eyes and flat noses.

Without telling them what had happened the day before, Liwei had them sit in a circle and then directed Nulo to set out the extra stones. "And now the special stone," he ordered.

When Nulo set the dancing stone down, it didn't move toward the stone it had been drawn to the day before. As he moved the other stone closer, the dancing stone moved away from it, turning slightly on the floor. The Learners moved closer.

"But, yesterday, it was not that way; it moved directly toward the other," Nulo said.

"Try to do exactly what you did yesterday," one of the women advised.

Nulo put all the stones back in the bowl and the dancing stone back in his sash. One by one, he tried to recreate every action exactly as he had done it before. When he set the dancing stone down near the other, it immediately slid towards the stone it had shunned moments before.

"Surely it is possessed by spirits!" one Learner gasped.

"It is a living stone!" said another.

"No stone is alive. It doesn't breathe or grow."

"Yet it moves."

"And so strangely. Why does it go one way and then the other?"

"There must be something different this time. Something we're not seeing."

"Turn it around," an old man said.

Nulo turned the dancing stone around so that the opposite end faced the stone it sometimes liked. Immediately, it moved away, as if suddenly repulsed by the stone it had befriended.

"Turn it again!" cried several voices. When Nulo did as they asked, the dancing stone slid back until it touched the other stone.

Liwei was also entranced. "What happened when you put it in the bowl, Nulo?"

After Nulo explained about the dancing stone pointing out to sea and to the sky serpent in the stars, the group called for him to set it up that way again. When the bowl and stones were fetched, he set the dancing stone exactly the way he had it back at his island, but the stone did not move.

"The rock that bewitches it is in the bowl," one pointed out. "It's too close."

Nulo held the bowl against his chest and removed the rock. To his surprise, the dancing stone moved - to point to the rock. As Nulo moved the rock around the outside of the bowl, the dancing stone moved to point to it.

"It *is* bewitched by the other stone," a Learner named Walissu said. "Hand it to me. I'll hide it." He put the rock inside his tunic. Immediately, the stone in the bowl aligned north and south.

"Yes!" they cried. "It needed to be free of the spell!"

The Learners passed the bowl around. Some turned around, some walked back and forth. One jumped up and down, splashing water out of the bowl. Always the stone returned to its starting position. Until it found the rock hidden in the tunic. As Walissu steadied the bowl against his torso, the dancing stone turned from its regular position to face the rock that had been tucked away.

"It knows you've hidden the rock, Walissu!"

The Fat Man's tiny eyes shone. "This is powerful magic. Very useful." He turned to Jin, the head of the Guards. "You know where to find other rocks like the one Walissu has?"

"Yes," Jin answered.

"Bring them. Some bigger than this one and some small. We need to find out more about the magic stone."

With a clap of his hands, Liwei ordered sweet treats and drink brought in for the group. As they celebrated, he added, "We have much to learn about the stone before the festival. Its magic will be very impressive."

"The dancing stone was a gift," Nulo repeated. "A gift connected to the stars."

"Of course," Liwei said, nodding to Jin.

Jin tapped Nulo on the shoulder and motioned for Nulo to follow him back to Laido's camp.

CHAPTER 18
TAHN'S DECISION

High in the island's interior, Tahn wove his way through an ancient banyan tree's maze of trunks. On both sides, heavy branches dropped aerial roots that thickened into new trees, so a whole community grew from a single parent. Clusters of orchids drooped from notches in the trunks above his head. Tahn watched a family of monkeys swinging through the canopy, set his bundle on the ground, leaned back against the great trunk and closed his eyes.

Why would he choose Ryu instead of me? Giving him the wind raft to try, asking how it handled, looking for ways to improve it. We built it, not Ryu. Inviting him to join the family when we left the old island – as if he was the son. And Nina so taken with him, staring at him when he was working the boat. Why did we leave the old island anyway? I hate it here. Father leading the boat group now, the master navigator teaching the other men. And Ryu, the magic day counter, gathering numbers he thinks no one else can understand. Both so proud of themselves. Nina weaving with her group even though she'd rather be taking the boats out on the water. Mother weaving fine mats and bowls with the others, talking away as if everything was fine. Nulo showing up, another misfit to adopt into the family. Even crazy Nulo working for the Fat Men. Everyone working for the good of the community. That's what they tell me. Well, I won't. I don't care about the jobs they give me.

It's better here, under the tree. Cool and dark. No people to bother me.

In the canopy, green and yellow parrots screeched and flew off. Opening his eyes, Tahn searched the area and found nothing except the maze of banyan trunks and roots. Except that one of the shapes nearby wasn't a drooping root bundle. It was a man, watching him.

Tahn tensed.

A dark brown centipede as long as his forearm moved up his ankle and headed up his leg, its yellow legs working in ripples as it moved. More than anything, he wanted to knock the creature off him and smash it with a stone.

"That's not a good idea," the other man said.

As Tahn bent down to grab the stick, the centipede stopped, sensing the arm close above it.

"Stop, fool! Do you want to get bitten?"

Pushing himself back up, Tahn felt it move again. Another one followed, twining up his foot and around his leg.

"Move sideways against the trunk. I'll try to get them off," the man said as he approached. "You probably woke them up. Now they're unhappy." He kept talking, ignoring Tahn as he pressed a flat stick against Tahn's leg in front of the top centipede. "Yes, very unhappy," he went on easily as the animal bit the stick. "You were having a nap when this man walked right over your home. So you weren't pleased." Pushing another stick under the centipede, he moved both sticks away from Tahn and down to the leaf litter, leaving it still curled around the stick while he removed the other and set it down next to the first.

"Kill them."

"Why?"

"Because they were going to bite me."

The man shook his head. "Wrong reason. You don't know what they were going to do since they didn't have the opportunity to prove you right or wrong. In any case, you're more likely to die at sea. Will you throw a rock into the sea?"

"That's stupid."

"So is your idea."

While Tahn glared at him, the man killed both centipedes with a stone and wrapped them in long leaves. "The right reason to kill them is that they're delicious."

"Go away."

"I just saved you from a very painful bite."

"I could have killed them."

"No, you couldn't."

Tahn considered his options. He could run. The problem was he didn't know where to go and the man looked as if he could run very fast. For that matter, he looked as if he could beat Tahn in any kind of fight. Tall, lean, strong – a warrior, with his hair shaved back and tattoos across his forehead. The same designs appeared on his shoulders. Across his chest he wore a necklace of trade shells and a rope sling. The hilt of a long knife stuck out of his wrap.

"Who are you?" Tahn said. "What are you doing here?"

"Jin, Captain of the Guards." When Tahn didn't reply, Jin went on in the same tone he'd used to quiet the centipede. "I was sent here to find you because you apparently weren't happy on the forest work crew, and they weren't happy with you. So the situation needs to be sorted out, one way or the other. Would you like to tell me your side of the story?"

"No."

"Why did you leave?"

"It doesn't matter."

Tahn waited, body tensed. Moments slid by, but the man didn't move.

"Well, go ahead, then!" Tahn yelled.

"And do what?"

"Attack. That's what you're here for. So do it."

Jin shrugged. "All right." With a single fluid motion, he drew out his knife, sighted along it, and let it fly. It landed right next to Tahn's head, digging into the tree behind him. "You could reach for it," Jin said easily, "pry it out and use it against me."

Sweat rolled down Tahn's face. The blade had hit so close to his head it caught part of his hair. He couldn't move his head without wrenching the hair out of his scalp.

"I'll let you think about your answer," Jin said, turning to go.

"Wait!"

"Why?"

"I -"

Hunkering down, Jin poked at the leaf litter with a stick, waiting.

"I don't know where to be," Tahn said finally.

"Where do you want to be?"

The question took Tahn by surprise. "I don't get to decide. No one does. The Fat Men decide where people have to be."

"That's an excuse. The Fat Men try to put people where they want to be. You didn't want to be anywhere. I'm asking where you want to be. It's a simple question."

"I don't know."

"Well, then," Jin said. Another giant centipede emerged from the leaf litter, curling aggressively around the stick. Without hurry, Jin dispatched it, wrapped it up, and added it to the collection.

"My family -" Tahn started.

"The question wasn't directed at your family. Only you can pick your path."

The knife was embedded so deeply that Tahn needed both hands to work it out of the tree. Once it was free, he thought about throwing it straight at the other man, right at his heart. He could picture the man jerking forward, clutching the knife buried in his chest as he fell forward with a scream of pain.

"And what would you do then?" the man asked as he packed up the wrapped centipedes. "That's always the question to ask."

Tahn's head hurt. The knife lay heavy in his hand.

"You can keep the knife," Jin said. "If you'd like to join the Guards, bring it back to me. If you choose to stay here, it might help you survive, for a day or two."

Tahn flipped the knife over in his open hand: a long blade of white stone with a red vein running through it, carefully worked on both sides, perfectly balanced between blade and bone handle - a warrior's knife.

"I'll think about it," he said, looking up, but the other man was gone.

CHAPTER 19
FISHING TALK

Almost everyone worked on some part of the Brightness Day festival preparation. While Darna cooked and Nina wove simple palm leaf bowls, Ryu and Nulo were sent off to catch fish, which they interpreted as a chance to experiment with the wind raft.

"I see why Raidu wanted this," Nulo said as the boat skimmed the water, powered by the wind and yielding to Ryu's command.

"He's probably gotten someone to make him one just like it by now."

Ryu watched the shifting patterns of the wave tops for a while before he turned back to Nulo. "Things weren't good at home after your father and my grandmother died. Everything started to fall apart. Raidu wanted to go to war, to get the old lands back. This raft was going to be his secret weapon."

"Many people fled?"

"I don't know. Some talked about it. I left everything behind. Except for Laido and his family," he trailed off.

Nulo nodded. "Did Raidu start his war?"

"Who knows?" Ryu pulled the mat toward him so the wind rushed past it and the boat slowed. "We should probably catch some fish."

"This boat flies over the water."

"When it's not tipping over."

They settled into the rhythm of fishing, pulling in their catch and resetting the funnels, dispatching the fish and wrapping them in seaweed.

"Is the wind raft your contribution to the Fat Men?"

"No. Laido and the other boat builders are working on new designs, but the Fat Men were more concerned with day keeping, so that's what I do for them. I had started doing it back home. Owl Man taught me some of the cycles, and from there, I kept adding more."

"You keep days? What does that mean?"

Ryu reset his funnel. "I track the visitors and the resident stars in the night sky. I count the days the Morning and Evening Star spends in the Underworld. I mark sun swings, moon cycles."

"Does the sun swing?"

"Periods between no-shadow days."

Nulo shivered. "I remember Naia's warnings about the dangers of No-Shadow days, when the ancestors cannot see the living. Why were you given this work?"

"Because the sky rules the earth. The moon cycle makes the tide cycle; the heavens order what happens on earth. If the sun and the stars and the visitors are all in cycles, we can know what will happen in the future because the pattern of the past will repeat itself. We'll know exactly when the rainy season will start, when the fish will spawn."

"You could look."

Ryu pulled up his trap, removed the fish, and lowered it again. "You wouldn't understand. It's more than just seeing. It's *knowing* everything about the sky and the earth and the sea, the entire world. It's all connected. I understand them and they belong to me."

Nulo wrapped a fish, adding it to the growing pile. "You can watch those lights, but they don't belong to you. They belong to the sky."

"Of course they belong to me! No one can live outside the rule of the sun and the stars. Their spirits establish our world, our seasons, everything that happens. We'd die without the sun. Everyone is under its control. It gives us light and power, from the first day of our lives to the last."

They went back to fishing, their backs turned to each other.

"The sun is the measure of our lives," Ryu continued without turning around. "The stars mark our destiny."

"How do the stars make a destiny? What do the stars know of us?"

"The stars create their own patterns based on their combinations and positions. The person born under their light shares their energy, left over from the time the gods made the world."

"Did the stars make me ugly?"

"It's too much for you to understand," Ryu replied. "It's a system. I can tell what will happen in the sky before it happens. The sun today will be born at a certain point in the sea and die at a certain point in the sea. The path tomorrow will be slightly different, a new day made and measured by the sun. You'll wake up because the sun has risen. You'll go to sleep because it's gone down into the sea. You look at the sun and measure how long you've been working or traveling."

"Naia said a day of sorrow lasts half a lifetime. That's true no matter what the sun does."

Ryu jerked his fish funnel up by its ropes, hauled out two large fish, dispatched them with two jabs of his knife, and wrapped them up.

Nulo changed the subject. "The Learners are trying to understand my stone."

"What stone?"

Nulo explained the dream, the stone, and the peculiar ways it acted when he showed it to the Learners. "Liwei said the stone would be useful."

89

"Of course it's useful," Ryu said. "It's magic. Magic is power."

They went back to fishing. As Nulo listened to the sky singing, breaking into multiple layers of sound as the clouds bumped into each other, Ryu thought about the sun on its perfect course across the sky, the path shared by the star figures he knew so well.

CHAPTER 20
CELEBRATION

The Brightness Day Festival began with a dance for the dead. Four drummers pounded on a hollow log with lengths of whale bone, and four singers started the songs of the dead. The dancers formed their circle and set it in motion, facing the center, moving in the direction of the sun through the sky, right foot first, left foot crossing over, four beats forward, one still.

As they circled, a masked dancer leapt into the center of the circle. One side of the mask represented a human face, the other a skull. As he leapt and twirled with his arms stretched wide, he turned back and forth in front of the dancers, alternately appearing as life and death, forever connected and opposite.

After the masked dancer jumped out of the center, the circling dancers began the naming of the dead. One by one they called out the names of the people they'd lost and their relation to that person: father, mother, sister, brother, son, daughter, aunt, uncle, niece, nephew, grandparent, grandson, granddaughter, friend.

In the quiet after the last name, the chanters took up the final song for the dead, first on their own, then joined by the circle of dancers, and finally by everyone watching.

Come then, you who are alive
Dance the memory of those who are dead
Their sunshine and laughter,
Their darkness and pain.

Live well and carry them with you.
Their memory sings in your blood.
It dances with you.
It dances with you.

Dance for the dead,
Dance for the living,
Dance for each other.
We who share the breath of life
are all connected.

Come then, you who are alive
Dance the memory of those who are dead
Their sunshine and laughter,
Their darkness and pain.
Live well and carry them with you.
Their memory sings in your blood.
It dances with you.
It dances with you.

Dance the circle of life and death!
Dance the circle of death and life!

Nulo didn't intend to be seen at the festival, let alone sing
with the others, but he was drawn into the song. Ryu and Nina
too. The dead sang and danced and were loved. At the last word,
the circle of dancers stopped, knelt, and placed their heads on the
ground, then rose and waved their hands high, shouting and crying
out as the drummers pounded hard and fast until it was done and
the drums went silent. For a moment, the people held the silence
like a vigil. Then the drummers started a different beat, a skipping rhythm. A guard called out, "The dead are sung. Now you are
invited to the feast!"

The dancers said their goodbyes, exchanging smiles with those who'd shared the song. Children ran up to greet their relatives and pull them back to the present. As the dancers filed out, one passed quite close to the rocks where Nulo perched. She was not a child, as he'd assumed, but a very short, slight young woman, bearing tattooed lines and dots across her wrist like those worn by girls who've left childhood behind, but no initiation or marriage marks. A necklace of dark and white shells graced her neck; a length of twine held her dark hair in a thick braid. Her belted tunic, decorated with bird designs around the bottom, fell almost to her knees. Below it, her tiny legs and feet were bare.

"Nulo," Nina gave him a nudge, "it's probably better not to stare."

He started. "She's so beautiful," he said, trying to find the words. "She reminds me of these handprints I found."

Nina and Ryu didn't hear his comment. The celebration was moving, and they were already finding their way down the rocks. By the time Nulo caught up to them, he'd lost track of the girl in the crowd.

* * *

The cooks arranged salted fish wrapped in seaweed next to rows of skewered grubs, scorpions, centipedes, and caterpillars, giant water bugs in coconut oil, hearts of palm, bitter greens, bee larvae and mango, fermented breadfruit. On the beach, men dug up steamed shellfish and heaped them on huge clam shells to carry up to the village center.

As the drums thumped, people gathered, waiting. After ten rapid beats, Fuhua and Liwei gestured expansively, inviting everyone to enjoy the food.

Nulo, Ryu, and Nina wandered along the displays of food, trying everything, greeting people they knew from their work groups, introducing Nulo, meeting others for the first time. Nulo hesitated, but no one attacked him. No one fled in terror. When people introduced their friends and family to him or asked him how he liked life on the Fat Men's Island, he nodded, searching for words. All the talking left him confused. Only one thing remained clear – the girl he'd seen. He went back over her image in his memory, searching the crowd for her, wondering if she'd noticed him when she passed by the rock. Even though he knew it wasn't possible, he kept thinking the handprints he'd seen in the cave were hers, that she'd left him a signal.

"Nulo?" Ryu called. "Everybody's moving to the arena. Let's go."

A Guard directed people to the edges of the open hillside where they could watch. Once they'd settled in, he called the two flute players who were then backed up by drummers on hollow wooden tubes. They picked up a skipping rhythm as the first group filed into the center of the arena.

They were children, each one led in by a parent or adult friend. As each child stepped forward, the adult gave the child's name and the names of family members. No one mentioned how or why these children happened to be so far from their homeland or what kind of life they'd left behind. As each introduction ended, the boy or girl stepped away from the adult and joined hands with the other children who'd been introduced. One by one, more joined the line, clinging to each other's hands. With the last introduction complete, they faced the crowd and bowed while onlookers called out welcomes. At a signal from the Guard, they ran across the arena, many jumping and shouting as they rejoined their families.

In the quiet that followed, the same Guard ran the circumference of the arena lighting torches against the fading sunlight. He finished with two large torches next to the benches where Fuhua and Liwei sat cross-legged, ready to preside over the competition.

As the drums sounded three times, Fuhua held up his staff, calling for silence. Behind him, the Guard waved the torch back and forth until the crowd quieted.

"Winners will be judged by acclamation at the end of the dances!" he announced. "You will decide who gets the prize: ten large polished beads of green jade, the Stone of Wonder."

In reply, people started shouting and stomping, slapping their legs and arms in rhythm.

As the drums started once again, Fuhua announced, "The Red Winds!"

One dancer stepped quietly into the stillness of the arena. A single flute joined the drums as he stood with his head bowed, his body wrapped in a dark cloak.

"It's Tahn!" Nina whispered to Ryu.

As two more drums joined in and the pace quickened, Tahn leaned down to loose the lines of rattles at his ankles then rose and threw off his cloak, revealing a face painted with red ochre and a necklace of blue trade shells. Rows of cone shells flashed along the hem of his wrap. In each hand he held a reed hoop.

At a signal from the Guard, the big drum thumped. Tahn jumped up, landing as the drum called, swinging the hoops over his head and down along his body, switching both hoops to one arm then the other. The hoops seemed to have their own life, spinning as Tahn moved under and over them. They pulsed with the drums, with the flicker of the torches. They flew around his head and neck, down his body like living things. When they reached his legs, he kicked out, sending them flying up in the air, one after the other. They'd hardly fallen before they were airborne once again. They moved down the arm that caught them then launched themselves away once again. The rattles on Tahn's legs caught the light, calling to the people, to the flying reeds. His body moved in flashes of light and sound, like the reeds. The crowd shouted along with the drumbeat, slapping their legs.

At the Guard's whistle, Tahn leaped to the side and dropped to one knee. Another dancer ran into the circle across from him, also carrying two hoops. Like Tahn, he remained expressionless behind his red clay mask as he sent the hoops spinning before he stepped through them, working them up his body until they flew along his arms, up in the air and across to the opposite side. At the second whistle, Tahn jumped to his feet and the two dancers faced each other, sending their hoops in wild arcs, first over their heads and then across to their partner, then down the arm that caught them, then aloft once again. All the while, the beat grew faster, the drums more intense. The crowd shouted with the drums, calling to the dancers and their strange companions.

As the Guard whistled again, the dancers jumped up in the air twice, throwing the hoops above them each time and dropping to one knee to catch them. When they stayed down, two more dancers ran up. A young man and a young woman who wore the same red masks and tunics dropped to their knees and rolled over before they sprang up to catch the circles that lived in the air. They tossed the hoops, switched places, and caught the new ones. The hoops never lost their flight. While the handlers remained expressionless, the hoops exalted in the drumbeat and torchlight.

At the next whistle, the dancers lined up, two in front and two behind. As the closer two threw their hoops to their partner, the back two threw theirs higher, so twin beams crossed with the drumbeats. As the front dancers lunged side to side, the back dancers did the opposite, leaving the hoops crossing in two tiers. As the drums grew faster, the throws got higher, the angles more extreme, yet the hoops never fell, never lost their flight. They went so fast they turned into a blur of light and sound. The onlookers stomped and shouted. At the final whistle, the dancers threw the spinning hoops into the crowd and bowed.

"Perfect!" Nina yelled.

"The Red Winds!" Fuhua called to the crowd, pointing to the dancers. Immediately, the crowd picked up the cry, shouting their name as the four ran out of the arena.

"The Red Winds! Tahn, you're wonderful!" Nina cried.

"Yes," Ryu added after a moment.

As soon as the area was clear and the crowd settled, the Guard announced the second group: "The White Fire Lizards!"

"They probably won't be as good," Nina commented.

With the old sun sinking and the night sky rising in layers of purple and red behind them, four dancer dressed in simple dark wraps stepped into the arena. Fire pulsed from both ends of the long sticks they held out in front of them.

At the Guard's whistle, the drummers took up a rapid beat. Two of the dancers stepped forward, swinging the fire sticks in unison, first to one side and then to the other, turning and twisting so twin fire circles rose and fell together, in front and behind. Leaning back, the fire dancers worked the sticks directly over them, their upturned faces lit by the fiery glow while the rest of them became lost in shadow. As they brought the fire sticks down, only their legs were visible in the turning light.

At a whistle, they turned and threw the flaming, twirling sticks toward each other as the crowd gasped. With practiced hands, the dancers caught the center of the batons, spun them overhead then threw them back. As the last of the flame circles sputtered, two more dancers jumped in, spinning their bright fire sticks, throwing them up in the air and catching them as the first two dancers took new burning sticks from the Guard. Two faced two as they danced with their fiery partners, swinging the sticks in large and small arcs to create circles within circles in front of them, behind them, back and forth between them. Then they turned and threw their fire to their partners. The crowd screamed.

With the last of their flames, they moved closer together and swung the sticks so carefully that they never touched, so the audience saw moving circles of fire hovering over the earth, lighting their handlers with a ghostly glow, showing now a face, now an arm, now a set of feet, disjointed pieces lit by the flash of the turning fire.

The Guard whistled, the drums stopped and the four dancers killed the last of the fire in the dirt and bowed to the shouting crowd.

"White Fire Lizards!"

"White Fire Lizards!"

"Well, they were very good," Nina said, as she began slapping her arms in rhythm with the others. "Not as good as Tahn, you know, but quite good."

Nulo found the noise overwhelming, pounding through him so hard he couldn't breathe. As he looked around, wondering how he could slip away, he saw her, the girl from the dance for the dead, across the arena, looking straight at him.

CHAPTER 21
POWER AND MAGIC

Helpers lit more torches around the arena as night fell. A Guard whistled for silence before announcing the third group: "The Black Hawks!"

"I have to leave for a little while," Nulo muttered to Nina.

At the Guard's signal, four young men entered the arena, each wearing a line of black and white feathers tied into his hair. Long black lines down their faces and chests echoed the lines on their loinwraps. Each one held a long cord with whale vertebrae tied at both ends.

"Take the children home," the leader shouted.

Curiosity kept everyone rooted to the spot. Eventually, Fuhua waved at a Guard, sending him off to complete the order.

Grumbling, the parents dragged their reluctant children away, just as Nulo was trying to get through.

"Out of the way!" one irate mother yelled at Nulo.

"I want to stay!" her child wailed, grabbing hold of Nulo's arm as an anchor.

"Come along!" the mother cried, wrenching the child away and throwing Nulo off balance.

When he got to his feet, Nulo found himself in the middle of a group of parents and children. As he ducked back, pushing toward the entrance, a Guard grabbed him by the arm and spun him around.

"Are you lost?"

"I'm looking for someone," Nulo replied.

"The children have all gone home."

"I need to find her."

"Her? Your sister? Maybe your girlfriend?" the Guard laughed. "She left with somebody else. She decided she'd rather have a whole man than half of one."

Nulo looked past the Guard, searching the area.

"Hey!" The Guard jerked Nulo's arm. "Pay attention."

"I have to find her -" he started.

"Listen to me, slow one. Your girlfriend isn't here. She never was. Move." He pointed, pushing Nulo along with the others. "That way."

Nulo took one step and another, but he'd lost his nerve. Abandoning his search, he joined the crowd at the edge of the arena. Once the parents had taken their reluctant children away, four dancers lined up, spaced evenly across the arena as the drums and the Guards' signal woods started, picking up a syncopated sound that came and went out of the regular beat like a conversation. At a particular tapping sequence, the first dancer began to swing the cord he held, first slowly then faster around and across his body until the bone made an eerie moaning sound. Shortly after, the second man joined in, swinging different, smaller bones that made a higher-pitched wailing noise. The third joined in with a thunderous roar, the fourth with a piercing shriek. The arena filled with screeching, wailing sounds, as if the newly dead had come back to relive their last suffering. Nulo winced, covering his ears. Next to him, people screamed and cowered. They would have fled except that more Guards in Black Hawks costumes ran in, circling the arena. Each one carried a long spear tipped with a white point that flashed in the torchlight. As the dancers stopped, they shouted together, brandishing the spears high over their heads.

The big drum sounded again. The first four dancers set aside their roaring bones, picked up their spears, and joined the other

Black Hawks as they formed four lines of four young men each. Spears held high, they stopped, waiting. The big drum stopped. The crowd held its breath.

At the tapping of the signal woods code, the second and fourth rows took one step to the side, and all the men lowered their spears so the bottoms touched the ground next to them. As soon as the signal changed, all of them lunged forward, thrusting their spears straight ahead. With so little room between them, they barely missed each other as they swung their weapons. Again, the signal changed. The entire group made a quarter turn and lunged forward so their spear tips ended up only an arm's length from the reclining figures of Liwei and Fuhua. The crowd gasped. The two rulers never moved.

When the signal woods spoke again, the dancers formed two circles, one inside the other. The inside circle moved slowly, the men bowing their heads and bending their knees while the dancers in the outside circle leaped in the air, yelling and waving their spears. At a subtly different signal, both circles stopped completely. The dancers on the inside dropped to one knee then leapt up, raising their spears straight up. At the moment they jumped up, the dancers in the outside circle dropped to one knee, jumping from that pose straight into the air as the others dropped down. The two circles rose and fell, the spears flashing above the leaping dancers with each jump. The warriors formed a beautiful and deadly beast, part earth and part sky.

At the next signal, both circles began to move in opposite directions, all dancers still dropping down and leaping up opposite each other. Sweat poured down their faces from the exertion, but no one faltered. No spear touched another man.

A string of staccato beats on the signal woods told the warriors to re-form the original four lines. Each man took the spear in his right hand, drew it across his chest, then grabbed a lower hold and swung it in a double-loop pattern over his head. Gradually each one moved his grip down the spear so the arcs grew bigger, so big that they intersected the arc of the spear next to him. But the precision was so great that no spears touched. Instead, each dancer stood still, left arm by his side as his right arm increased the deadly circle of the spearhead. As the crowd watched in silence, each dancer let the arc grow again, just enough so the tip of the spear touched the upper arm of the next dancer. As the blades swung around, one dancer after another nicked the left arm of the dancer nearby, so lines of blood trickled down his left arm even as his deadly right arm marked the next man. When the signals told them to switch directions, they repeated the sequence, once again extending the arc of the blade until it just pierced the skin of the next dancer.

At the final code from the signal drums, the big drums took over, pounding toward their finish as the dancers ran toward the edge of the arena, spears up. When they neared the benches where Fuhua and Liwei reclined, the front line of dancers dropped to one knee and held their spears straight out. The second line, staggered behind the first, thrust their spears at an angle slightly higher than the first group. The third line pointed their spears halfway between horizontal and vertical. The fourth row joined them, their spears vertical. As one, they yelled out as the drums stopped. For a long moment, no one moved. The dancers held their position in the sudden quiet, chests heaving, arms bleeding. The crowd made no sound.

After a moment, Liwei laughed and began a hearty clapping. The crowd responded, screaming, shouting, slapping their arms and legs, jumping, stomping. The dancers returned to their lines, standing motionless until the crowd quieted.

"I suppose you win the prize," Liwei said, holding out the jade beads, "though how you'll divide ten gemstones among all of you, I do not know."

Jin, the leader, stepped forward and took the stones, giving the smallest of bows, never meeting Liwei's eyes. Instead, he turned to the crowd and held up the string of beads like a trophy.

"They *were* really good," Nina admitted. "Though the others were too."

Ryu didn't answer.

Nulo flinched as the crowd roared. On a hill rise, he searched for the best way to get back to Nina and Ryu. Instead, he found her, right there, in the crowd, looking straight at him. While her body seemed small and delicate, her gaze was so strong he found he couldn't look anywhere else as he moved toward her. When he stood so close that he could see the wisps of hair escaping her braid, the line of her cheek bones, the curve of her lips, he could find no words at all.

As the people around them slapped and stomped, she said, "I am Aeta."

"Nulo," he managed. He knew he should say something else, something about her or how he'd noticed her after the dance for the dead or how he'd looked for her earlier or how beautiful she was but all the words stuck in his throat like sticks in the river, piled up on one another so that none could escape.

"Quiet!" a Guard called after the dancers departed with their prize. "Liwei wishes to speak to you! Move closer! Move into the arena!" the Guard repeated, drawing people, including Nulo and Aeta, into the competition circle.

As the Guards opened a path for him, Liwei strode through the crowd. People standing closest to him pointed out the large jade serpent suspended from a cord around his neck and the many lines of trade shells that decorated his wrap. When he reached a thin wooden slab with fine bark cloth draped over the edge, he stopped and waved the people closer yet. In response, they pressed in together, pushing others aside to get a better view. Behind Liwei, Nulo and Aeta found an open spot.

On the table in front of Liwei sat dozens of stones, each carved in the likeness of a person. He held up some large pieces and some smaller ones no bigger than a man's finger, then pointed to the two in the center, which were twice as big and bore an obvious resemblance to Fuhua and Liwei. Around the edges were pieces that looked like the dancer Guards, complete with spears.

"Look at this," Liwei said, holding a hollow gourd near his mouth to amplify the sound as he spoke. People pushed in closer as he waved his free arm toward the stone figures in front of him. "You know that the power of the spirit, which is all around us, lives in both people and objects. It cannot be seen, you know that. Yet I will show it to you."

Nulo cared more about the young woman who stood next to him as if she'd always stood next to him. She smelled of spice leaves.

Liwei pointed at a group of statues near one side of the table. "See, this group here - these are some representatives of our community. Good people. Kind people. Hard-working people. If you could see the power of the spirit among these people, it might look like this," he continued, throwing something onto the table.

"They move!" the people in the front called out, pointing.

Others pressed in for a better view.

"They do! It's magic!"

Indeed, the slivers of stone moved, danced, slid across the surface until they formed a circle around the statues he had pointed out. A gasp went up from the crowd as the word spread.

"And people need leaders who share this spirit and who take care of their people," Liwei continued, throwing more slivers of rock to the table. They too skipped and jittered across the surface until they formed a circle around the Liwei and Fuhua stones.

Next to Nulo, Aeta said, "They say he can make stones move."

"Stones – move?"

"Yes, with magic."

"We must see this," he said, taking her hand as he pushed his way through, looking for a better spot.

"But sometimes," Liwei was saying, "there is a voice of discontent, a ghost song that rings in your ears, telling you to destroy that which you have worked so hard to sustain. Then," he paused, "you need to know the truth." He threw slivers of stone at the periphery of the circle, where the stone guard dancers were placed, but the slivers immediately jumped away from the dancers and slid back toward the Fat Men stones at the center of the table.

At Liwei's signal, his assistant dropped a whole bowlful of stone slivers onto the table, and every single one jigged its way across the board into a thickening circle around the Fat Men figures. As the people shouted out, astonished, Liwei held both his arms up to the sky in triumph. The crowd roared its approval, stomping and slapping their arms, calling out Liwei's name. Several people were so moved they wept.

Nulo and Aeta finally reached the table only to find the show was over.

"I wish you a good night, my friends!" Liwei called over the wave of noise. With a final wave to the drummers, he called for the end music.

On their way out, many stopped to admire the stones before they bowed to Liwei and Fuhua, thanking them for the celebration.

"What a wonderful day!"

"Truly. Amazing."

"A festival to remember! And the last part – so moving."

"Good food, good company, good entertainment."

"We're so lucky to be here."

"Thank you!"

"You've made a great community here. It's our home now."

Only the Black Hawks dispersed without saying a word to the Fat Men.

"Magic is the key," Liwei remarked to Fuhua as they too headed out.

"Magic and a good spy network," his brother added.

CHAPTER 22
TREMBLING STONES

Waiting behind, Nulo studied the stones on the table while Liwei's assistant cleared them off. As Nulo expected, two people crawled out from under the table.

"Hey! You have to leave!" one of them yelled, waving Nulo away.

"I know about the stones. The first dancing stone was a gift from my dream."

"Well, you can't be here."

"And yet we are here."

"I'll call for the Guards."

Nulo ignored him, studying the remaining stones, mostly slivers of stone the assistants hadn't picked up yet. "Look!"

Curious, the assistant joined Aeta and Nulo to watch the pieces of stone on the table. They weren't sliding across the surface as they had when they were telling Liwei's story. They were shaking, moving back and forth like a person with a chill. A few with round edges rolled slightly, bumping into others.

"What?" the assistant cried. "There's no one under there to move them!"

In the silence that followed his statement, the stones quieted, losing their bizarre shiver.

"You must have shaken the table," the assistant declared, whisking the stones off the table. "Excuse me; I need to finish my work." Turning his back to them, he tossed the little stones into a basket and hurried away.

"What does it mean?" Aeta asked.

"Something moved the stones. It wasn't us; it wasn't the assistants. The dancing stone I gave the Fat Men doesn't shake all by itself." Picking up a few fragments that had fallen on the ground, he set them down on the table, spaced far apart.

They waited and watched. The stones remained motionless. A Guard walked the edge of the arena, extinguishing the torches.

"I must go. Good night," Aeta said, taking his arm in a formal gesture.

Putting his hand over hers, he held her there for an instant. "This night," he paused, "- filled the sky."

Briefly she touched his hand before turning away.

He watched her fade into the darkness beyond the arena, joining the others heading out. Overhead, the young moon sailed through the sea of stars.

"Nulo?"

Spinning around, he found Nina calling his name.

"We've been looking all over for you," she said. "Are you all right?"

"Yes."

"What are you doing here?" Nina pressed.

"Watching rocks," Nulo said, pointing to the bits of stone on the table, expecting them to be motionless.

"What's happening?" Nina cried. Even in the thin light, she saw the stones were moving, wobbling back and forth.

"Here you are, Nulo," Ryu said, joining them. "What's going on? We need to get back to camp."

"Ryu, look over here!" Nina pointed.

"The table?"

"What do you see?"

"Nothing."

"The rocks!"

"What about them?"

When Nina looked back at them, they lay completely still.

"I saw them move," she said, "and so did Nulo."

"You must have pushed the table," Ryu said. "Come on, we have to get back. We spent quite a while looking for you, Nulo."

Nina was still staring at the surface. "What does it mean, Nulo?"

"It means we've wasted enough time here," Ryu broke in. "I'm going to the Sky Circle."

"The earth is breaking," Nulo said as Ryu walked away.

"The earth can't break, Nulo," Nina said. "It's made of rock."

He could find no explanation for what had happened, so he said nothing while Nina talked about the night's entertainment.

"I still think Tahn was best, though the Fire Lizards were amazing."

"Yes."

"And of course, the spear dancers."

"Yes."

"And Liwei's stones were magic."

"Yes."

Nina stopped suddenly, studying him. "You talked to that girl tonight, didn't you?"

"I did."

"I'm glad," she said, leaving the rest for him to say if he wished.

"I met her on the night the earth started breaking."

CHAPTER 23
THE STORY SPREADS

"I told you it's not possible," Ryu repeated to the group as they sat around the fire the next night. "It was from a tree falling, someone stomping on the ground, puffs of wind."

Laido asked Nulo to go through it all again, from the dancing stone and the Learners group to Liwei's magical set-up to the shaking stones. "If they can be manipulated from below, couldn't something still be there - maybe a stone the assistants left behind?"

Nulo shook his head. "I searched under the table."

"And what of Ryu's idea of strange winds that come through and then dissipate?"

"It was calm."

"What if walking near it was enough to rock the stone?" Darna suggested.

"It would have moved when Liwei was standing there, waving his arms around," Nina pointed out.

Ryu turned on her. "So *you* believe his story? It's ridiculous. The earth doesn't break. You said so yourself. It's just Nulo. He's always imagining something. Singing trees. The smell of colors. That sort of thing. It means nothing. If something terrible was going to happen, I'd know about it. I'd see it in the night sky."

"It's true that you saw the white face of the goddess before she struck the old village," Darna admitted.

"That's right," Ryu continued, "and I've seen nothing unusual. If Nulo's right about the stones Liwei used, there was probably some

109

energy between the stones on the table left over from the show. When people walked by, they nudged one of the stone bits close enough to get it to move. Once it moved, the next one did and so on, until they were all moving."

They were about to settle on that when Nulo spoke up again, slowly. "The earth is breaking underneath us. Cracking and heaving up."

After Nulo spoke, Tahn slipped away into the forest.

"Let him go," Laido said as Ryu jumped up. "He needs to be somewhere else."

"But he'll tell the Guards about Nulo's crazy idea."

"Perhaps," Laido said. "Then they can argue about it too."

"There's nothing to argue about. It makes no sense. Motion comes from the movement of the stars in the heavens, not the ground."

"Maybe the stones looked as if they were moving because the torches threw moving shadows," Darna offered.

"We saw the stones lie still in the torchlight," Nina said quietly.

"You don't understand anything about it!" Ryu cried.

"I'm only saying what I saw."

"You mean what you think you saw."

In the fire pit, the flames clicked and hummed at Nulo.

"Nulo," Ryu challenged, "you started all of this. Say something."

He had to pull his gaze away from the fire and search for the words. "Something imprisoned inside the earth is trying to break out."

Ryu laughed. "There! What more do you need to know?"

Nina shook her head. "All we saw were some wobbling pebbles, Nulo. Not a monster."

"I'm sorry. I wish it was something else. Truly. The force inside will break the earth."

"Ridiculous," Ryu snapped. "Earth monsters breaking out of the rock. What do they look like, Nulo?"

"Fire," Nulo said slowly.

"What do you mean?" Laido asked. "Describe it."

"You're looking at the fire," Ryu broke in. "That's why you're seeing fire."

"Strings of fire," Nulo went on. "Rivers of fire. Red and black."

Ryu started pacing behind Nulo. "Rivers of fire. And where do these rivers come from?"

"From the ground. Under the rock."

"And how does fire, even in a red and black river, travel through the rock?"

Nulo only listened to the flames' jittery snapping.

"I told you - it's just another Nulo dream. He hears sea sponges singing. It's no surprise that he sees stones moving."

"You need to leave here," Nulo said, still watching the fire. "All of you. Soon."

"That's crazy!" Ryu snapped. "A pebble moving on a table doesn't mean some fire monster is breaking out of the earth."

"It might mean exactly that." The voice came from Liwei, standing at the edge of the fire-lit area, flanked by Jin and Tahn. "I need to hear from the dream learner first." He motioned for Nulo to follow. "Send for the Learners, Jin. We need their counsel. Tell them it's very important."

* * *

When the Circle of Learners gathered, Nulo described the stones and the vision.

"Some pebbles moving? A dream vision from looking into a fire? Everyone sees strange images sometimes. Dreams, nightmares, fever views," the Learner named Garah said. "They're not necessarily visions of the future."

"You're right" another agreed. "Maybe it was a daydream. I sometimes see figures dancing in the flames. Beautiful girls, usually."

"Sick people can have strange dreams, you know."

"I once dreamed the sky was raining fire. The next day the sky was clear and the sun was shining."

"Exactly," Garah agreed. "We could sit here all night exchanging stories of strange dreams."

A woman named Kiah, however, disagreed. "Didn't you dream about the dancing stone? Isn't that why you experimented with it until it turned the way it did in your dream?"

"Yes," Nulo answered.

Garah waved away the idea. "A curious person works on a problem during sleep. I ask you: Has anyone else here seen this monster inside the earth? Does anyone know of someone who has?"

The man sitting next to Kiah said. "Nulo has." His comment set the arguments in motion once again so the circle filled with overlapping conversations.

"Quiet." Liwei waved his arm. "I have other news, which you can now understand more easily. I just wanted to see how you would respond to Nulo's vision." He waved forward a man named Bondel. "Explain the pots."

Holding up a shallow white clay pot, Bondel made sure everyone could see the inside and the outside. "I placed sun-dried pots like this at different locations around the island and on the little island offshore and put one measure of red-clay slurry in each one." As the Learners watched, he poured a measure of a red liquid into the bowl. "I marked the highest point of the slurry," he added.

"What does all this mean?" Garah interrupted.

Bondel explained how the porous white clay would record any movement of the red ochre water. To demonstrate, he held up another pot so everyone could see it, pointing to the places where the red liquid had moved above the line.

"So, something moved the pot," Garah called. "It's not a mystery. Wind, rain, falling tree branches, animals, curious children, careless adults – there could be many reasons the water moved."

Bondel explained again how the sensors were placed in areas away from the settlement. In order to prevent anything from disturbing the pots, he had placed them inside rock depressions or caves where wind, waves, rain, and animals wouldn't disturb them.

"Why did you do this?" Garah asked. "And why weren't we informed?"

"Liwei told me to place the pots."

For a long moment, Liwei seemed lost in thought; then he leaned forward to address the group. "I have seen this thing that Nulo saw. I asked Ryu to keep track of the days because I thought I would know the day it would happen again. Instead, the dreamer has seen it. It is just as he said – a river of fire exploding out of the land. Before it breaks free, the earth shakes and heaves. Then the god of fire escapes, screaming, from underground. It covers the land, killing everything in its path, until its river of fire plunges into the sea, hissing as it makes white clouds."

"This is the stuff of old tales, as fantastic as the boy's dream," Garah scoffed.

"Yet it is true."

"How are the clay pots connected with this fire?" Walissu asked.

"Before the fire god appears, the land shakes. The pots mark the shaking of the land." Liwei turned to the group, looking for a response, getting none.

"There's more," Bondel continued. "The dark rocks at the top of the island were warm last night, long after the sun had gone."

Garah shook his head. "None of this is proof of some great disaster looming. Why stir up everyone's fears? Maybe the rocks felt warm. Maybe your feet were hot. Sometimes mine are too. The land is full of surprises. I say we need to learn more about these things before we run off in a panic to – where?"

A chorus of assent followed.

"And, in the future," Garah continued, "I don't want to be called on to render a decision based on nothing more than a strange dream. We all take pride in our knowledge, real knowledge, not intuition or premonition. Frankly, Liwei, I am surprised that you would bother considering this – what did you call it - dream learning? If I dream about a beautiful girl tonight, should I report to the group about her? What about if I dream of a delicious meal? Would you like to hear about that?"

The group laughed.

"At least it would be entertaining!" one called.

"So would the beautiful girl!" another laughed.

Liwei looked around. "So, you have decided?"

Garah took the lead. "Yes, we've decided that this is all just fog on the sea. It will clear by itself."

Many agreed with him.

Liwei called for refreshments to be served, marking the end of the discussion. "Thank you for your thoughts. As always, I appreciate your views."

After most of the Learners dispersed, two stayed behind: the woman named Kiah and her partner, Colbee, the stocky, flat-faced creator of the boat known as the Flying Fish.

"We're sure the vision is true," Kiah said to Liwei.

Liwei studied his hands. "Then you must act on it." They waited. He looked up at them, nodded. "Prepare to leave, but do it in stages: first, set aside the things you would need if you had to leave tonight. Next, set aside the things that would make a journey easier but would take more room. Finally, set aside everything else you would want to take with you. I'll send a messenger to you if it becomes clear we must leave right away. On the other hand, if we have the luxury of more time, we can bring everything useful, even plants and seeds, with us. If your neighbors criticize you, hide your efforts from them. Each person must decide the right course here, but some will try to decide for everyone."

Colbee turned to leave and then stopped. "Where will we go?"

"That will depend – on many things," Liwei said vaguely. "Good night. It's been a long day."

Nulo dragged himself back to Laido's camp, feeling empty, as if all his insides had been pulled out and set out on the sand for others to poke at with sticks. As soon as Nulo joined the group around the fire, Ryu left.

CHAPTER 24
RYU IN THE SKY CIRCLE

By the light of the young moon, Ryu wandered down the trail to his Sky Circle. His feet knew every rock, every bend; even in the grey light, he knew where the poles were set, where the neat lines of stones were laid out. Before he looked up, he knew exactly how the stars would be aligned over the posts, where the visitors would be, all as familiar as friends. Night after night, they explained their mysteries to him. All the information was recorded here, even the course of the Morning and Evening Star, now at its incredible brightest, and the sun, its partner, with its own secrets and variations. He'd begun counting days and learned that each day had its own character, drawn from the mix of influences on it. The days of the dark moon belonged to the death spirits, yet the reappearance of the Morning and Evening Star could change them. When the Great Serpent of the night sky rose out of the ocean and spilled water through the sky or left its breath in the clouds, heavy rains flooded the land. Red Moon days were filled with danger. It was his work, measuring the day shadow, following the moon, marking the progression of the stars. All his records were here, embedded in this place where the sky was linked to the earth and some great mystery awaited his discovery. He couldn't leave this behind, no matter what the red clay marked on the white pots.

Lying down next to the sun anchor pole in the middle of his Sky Circle, he closed his eyes, picturing where every star group lay, then opened his eyes to find all of them exactly where they should be, taking their regular places over the marker stones in the circle. They resonated perfectly, exactly as the gods had left them. The stars belonged to him here as surely as they belonged to the night sky.

CHAPTER 25
CHOICES

In the morning, Nina found Ryu still curled up in the center of the circle. Though she called his name, he didn't open his eyes.

Nina hunkered down behind his back. "Father's group is building a very large wind raft as well as two other large boats. They started the work right after we got here. Why would the Fat Men have ordered the boats if they meant to stay here forever? Liwei ordered Bondel to start placing the sensors before we even arrived. He must have known this fire river was a possibility. Nulo's vision simply confirmed what the sensors were showing."

Ryu didn't move.

"It's true I don't understand what you're doing here with these posts and stones. I only know that all of this matters to you." She set something down on the flat earth by his feet. "Perhaps you could find a way to record what you've learned so you could take it with you." When he didn't reply, she put her hand on his shoulder for a moment before she rose and walked away.

Long after she'd gone, he could still feel her hand on his shoulder and hear the sound of her footfalls. When he pulled himself up, he found a green sea turtle shell she'd left for him. The carapace had been oiled, showing off the line of six-sided center scutes and the large lateral scutes flanking them. The interior, cleaned and rubbed smooth, was divided into sections by eight ribs that went down each side.

"It's a fine gift," he said to the absent donor, "but a wasted effort. How could I put my circle, anchored to the earth by the birth and death places of the sun on No Shadow days, into something as limited as a shell? Anytime it was moved, it would change everything. It isn't even circular. It's too long, too uneven, too broken up by the lines of the ribs."

He ran his finger along the inside of the shell from the dark center line out to the edge. Directly behind his hand was one of the posts in his circle.

"It only works because my circle is here," he muttered, setting it aside, only to come back to it again, turning it different ways. With the shell in the center of the circle, he lined up his most northerly post with the second rib down from the neck opening. Moving carefully to the other side, he hunkered down, imagining the line continuing across the shell to the opposite post, crossing the edge of the shell at the second to last rib on the far side.

"It might be possible," he conceded, as if she still stood near, "to poke a stick through the center and make marks to count the days between No Shadow days." He lingered, studying the shell. When he stood up, he brushed the shell and sent it spinning unevenly across the packed dirt.

"It will never work! It moves with a touch or a brush of wind. It cannot tie the heavens to the earth, not ever!"

He stomped away, then turned back, considering the sections of the shell, bending down to sight along the ribs as he held it motionless. With a charred stick, he made a single mark: a dot on the smooth inner surface.

When he stood up, he considered the mark, the shell and all its divisions, then dragged it away from the circle and tossed it behind a rock. "I'm not going anywhere!"

CHAPTER 26

CAVE OF TREASURES

After hearing the news of Nulo's vision and the red dye pots, Fuhua hurried away from his fine hut on the hill to a cave that lay at the end of a trail purposely obscured with stones and piles of brush. It was one of two caves on the island. The one most people knew of was considered a portal to the Underworld, a place of the dead, frequently festooned with flowers and offerings. This one was a private treasure trove.

As Fuhua pushed aside the brush and picked his way through the stones, he didn't notice the person following him, the one slipping past the thrown aside branches, and waiting, pressed up against the rocks at the mouth of the cave. That person watched as Fuhua made his way up and down the path in the center of the cave, gesturing extravagantly to the piles of baskets and boxes and muttering as if he was talking to them.

In front of a dark wooden box carved all over with vines and flowers, he stopped and bowed deeply before lifting the box and setting it down closer to the cave opening. Heading back in, he waved his arm over the piles of treasures as he passed by, pointing to some and shaking his head. He walked the length of the middle aisle, turning side to side as he went, stopping, pointing, commenting. He emptied a hide pouch full of pearls into his hand, considering each one before putting it back in the sack. After a moment, he tucked the sack in his sash. He tried to add a collection of knives, hand axes, and spear points, but they proved too much to carry at once, so he took one load to the front of the cave, retreated to the back of the cave, and returned with another bundle. He added dark wood carvings, footed bowls, a matching stool and headrest. When he came back with a cinnabar figure of the of the wind god so deep red and deadly, he lingered over it, running his fingers over it before adding it to the growing pile of objects near the cave entrance.

On the next trip, he carried only Nulo's dancing stone and its bowl of stones, setting it with the wind god figurine.

As the watcher kept track, Fuhua kept adding items:

A pile of fine weavings so heavy he struggled under the weight

A necklace of shark teeth

A leaf bag of polished blackstone pieces

Carved bone rattles

A paddle marked with the sign of the light on the sea

Coils of three-strand rope

Three decorated staffs

A cape of long blue-black feathers

A basket of iridescent trade shells.

After he set the basket down, he turned unsteadily, leaning on one of the decorated staffs as he headed back into the cave. Along the way, he unwrapped two long spear points made of white stone with red veins, nodded, and wrapped them back up before adding them to the pile at the entrance. From the very back, he took a black rock marked with many holes and added it as well, setting it down next to the bone box he'd brought out first.

As the other man watched, Fuhua moved two whale bone carvings from the pile by the entrance back into the cave only to bring them back out again. Twice he stumbled as he turned. When he lost his balance, he fell into the pile of treasures, sending baskets, trade shells, and carvings tumbling across the floor. As he bent over to pick them up, he stopped and held the sides of his head. Slowly, he picked through the pile, searching.

From his hiding place, the watcher tried to guess at the value of all the treasures piled at the cave entrance. When Fuhua headed back into the cave, the watcher edged closer, leaving the safety of his cover and stepping out into the open, finding the pile of treasures so close he could reach out and touch it. He could hear Fuhua mutter something as he moved a number of bone flutes across the aisle then back to their original spot before he set them down and bent over, staring at them. When he straightened up, he stepped back, tried to steady himself against the cave wall, lost his balance, and lurched forward, knocking over piles of baskets and woven sacks as he fell into the cave wall.

Jin looked at Fuhua's body lying motionless on the floor of the cave and at the treasure lying heaped up all around him, like a funeral offering for a chief. "It was easy to follow you, big powerful man, to watch you sort through your treasures, all those fine things lying at my feet, so many wonders in one place that each loses some of its value because it's thrown in with so many others. I used to serve you, bowing to you and doing as you ordered. Now you're nothing more than a lump on the cave floor." Stepping over the man's outstretched legs, Jin pushed farther into the cave, hardly able to take in all the riches that lay before him. But the air smelled acrid. His head hurt. "You would have noticed the air was bad except greed made you stupid."

From the pile of gems Fuhua had left near the entrance, Jin chose a single fine greenstone and tucked it carefully into his sash before he picked his way around the fat man and out into the fresh air.

Then, with a sigh, he turned back and dragged Fuhua out of the cave.

CHAPTER 27
READING THE STONES

In the lead boat of Raidu's war party, Owl Man took out his omen stones and laid them in different sections of the wooden tray in his lap. He had been counting days lately, days since the death of the chief, days since the burning of the village, days Raidu's warriors had been at sea, days since they'd discovered the settlement they planned to attack was flooded and abandoned, days since regret and loss had cloaked the boats in fog, days since Raidu had split open the head of the warrior who dared to call the trip a waste. To each of these numbers he assigned a stone, and these stones he placed in the tray, studying them in different formations.

The shaman thought about his father, a famous reader of the omen stones, the wise man of the old island who had taught him about herbs, stars, signs, and visions. His father had such perfect balance in the world of men and beyond it that he could pass between realms at will. Once, he'd confided in his son that he could fly when he was in a trance state, or at least he could become one with a spirit bird. He shouldn't have said that because gifts from the gods are easily taken away, but he did, so his son would know. Later, Owl Man wondered what it was like. He never had the gift, and he resented his father for it until his father died. Then it seemed an irreconcilable loss.

He added a stone for his father to the collection in the tray.

Next he chose two stones, one milky white and one red, breathing on each one before he set them in the tray. They were for his mother, who had died when he was very young, and his wife, who had died shortly after giving birth to their stillborn son. After all these days, he still couldn't think of them without seeing the great dark space in the stars where powerful spirits managed the universe. Alongside these stones, he placed others for Raidu, for himself, and for the spirits of the sky, earth, and water. Finally, he placed the stones of war. To his surprise, when he read the assembled stones sitting on the tray, the message wasn't about war or ancestors, or Raidu, or spirits. It was about fire. Removing them all from the tray, he began again, placing them purposefully, looking for omens of war. Instead he saw murder.

Raidu came over and looked at the tray. "What do the omens say?"

Owl Man didn't look up. "It's difficult to say."

"Perhaps a better shaman could read them."

"Perhaps," Owl Man replied as he put the stones away and covered the tray.

CHAPTER 28
ATTACK BY SEA

"Sir," the lookout said, waking Raidu, "I think we've found it."

"What?"

"A large island with boats pulled up on the shore."

Jerking to his feet, Raidu confirmed the sighting and shouted, "Gather your weapons, men! Prepare for battle immediately." When a few didn't respond, he kicked them. "Wake up! The battle is upon us."

Half-asleep, the men stumbled around, assembling their weapons.

"Yes!" Raidu sucked in the air. "Finally."

* * *

On the island, lookout scouts sighted the boats heading for the island and signaled the others, tapping out information that was transferred to the rest of the Guards and the Fat Men. Racing to the closest lookout, Tahn gasped when he saw the lead boat and the boats behind it, including a wind raft, just like the one his father had built before they'd left the old island. Since Tahn couldn't leave his post to warn his father, he tapped out a message for others to relay: "Warn my family! The warriors *will* attack. Four boats. Be ready on the beach."

* * *

In Laido's hut, Darna had almost finished packing their belongings. Laido and Nina were hauling the bundles down the slippery trail to the boats when a Guard relayed Tahn's message.

"Raidu's war boats!" Laido yelled as he ran back to camp.

Panic spread with the news. People shouted the same things over and over, running to the village center, to the Fat Men's huts, looking for direction and finding none.

"Nina!" Laido called as he hurried down the trail. "I'm going to help organize the people in the village center. Tell your mother to leave whatever she hasn't packed and get to the boat. We need to get everyone out before Raidu's men land. Get Ryu. Take the wind raft. We'll try to split Raidu's force. I'll meet up with you as soon as I can." He hesitated. "I wish Tahn was coming with us."

In their camp, Darna was tying up bundles of seed pods and separating them into piles.

"You'll have to leave them, Mother. We need to go now." Nina tried to keep the panic out of her voice.

"Where's your father? I think he went to check on something."

The signal tapping started again, close to them.

"Come with me, Mother. We need to leave. I'll take you to the boat."

"Oh, no, I haven't finished packing yet. Besides, I need to check that we're not forgetting anything."

Nina took her mother by the arm. "Father told me to bring you to the boat."

"On the beach? No, I think something is going on down there. The Guards have been signaling like crazy."

"We'll stay out of their way," Nina said, walking her mother out the door.

"I have to bring my seeds!"

"I'll get them," Nina said, scooping up the bundles and hurrying her mother down the path.

At the shore, Laido stood knee-deep in the water next to one of the boats, helping others get aboard. As soon as Darna was settled in, he pushed their boat into deeper water and jumped in. Other families were doing the same, shoving yet more people and belongings into the already weighed-down boats, shouting at remaining family members to hurry, pushing off into the choppy water.

"Separate!" Laido called to the other boats. "Make it harder for them to catch us."

* * *

When Nina reached the observation circle, breathless from running, Ryu was bent over a line of small stones that ran from the sun pole at the center toward one of the stones in the circumference.

"It's the shadow count," he said, glancing up at her and back at the stones.

"My father needs you to take out the wind raft. Raidu's attacking the island!"

"I thought he'd show up here eventually. It's where the currents lead."

"What's the matter with you?" Nina yelled. "Look at me!"

"Go on, Nina. Take the raft. You can work it. Get Tahn to help you. Or Nulo."

"How stupid you are!" Nina spit, kicking the rows of little stones in every direction. "You care more about your little stones than you do about the people who love you. Fine. Raidu wants someone to kill. I'm sure he'll be happy to make you the first victim. You can die here with your circle. That's what you seem to want. Maybe he'll add an extra stone for you."

"It doesn't count people," Ryu muttered.

"You won't listen to Nulo because your pride is hurt. You wanted to be the first to know everything. What does it matter now? We're under attack! People need your help to survive. How can you be so selfish you'd refuse your friends?"

When Ryu didn't reply, Nina ran around the circle, kicking every line and pile of stones she could see. If she had had the strength, she would have pulled down the pole and standing stones as well. "I'm leaving now. My father and others are fighting while you count little stones. You -" Unable to finish, she turned back toward the trail, but he grabbed her arm, pulling her back to him.

"Why didn't you say anything to me before?"

She wrenched her arm away from him. "I've said many things in my own way. You're the one who won't hear. It might be nice to talk but we have other things to do. I have to leave now. Are you coming with us or not?"

He drew in a long breath as he looked around his circle. "Yes, I'll come with you. Just wait a moment. I have to bring something with me."

"Raidu will be on the island soon. I have to leave *now*, with or without you."

"It's not far away," he said, lifting the turtle shell from behind a stone. The inside was covered with rows of lines and dots separated by the ribs.

Together, they raced down to the rocky trail to the cove, pushed the wind raft into the water and poled their way into deep water.

"Where's Tahn?" Ryu called as they attached the mat.

"He's staying with the Guards on shore. Nulo too."

* * *

"Who are these people in boats?" Raidu shouted to Hadi, the commander of Boat Two. "Are they attacking? Fleeing right into our path? Stop them. Take Boat Three also. As I thought," he added as he pointed to the wind raft. "Overtake that raft and kill everyone on board. Go!" As they paddled away, he called to his son, Bokai, commander of the Boat Four. "Stay close. Head for the beach."

The men pulled hard but the tide ran against them, so they made little progress toward the shore. It helped those escaping by pulling them toward the open water, but it left those fleeing too close to the attackers.

"We have to split up!" Laido yelled. "Head back toward shore a little," he called to one, "then go farther south." To each, he gave specific directions:

"Follow your uncle."

"Follow Kiah."

"Stay close to the shore. Turn past the cove."

As the boats headed off, he called out to Ryu and Nina on the wind raft. "They're sending out boats to attack us. They'll want the wind raft."

"Then we'll make sure they don't get it," Ryu yelled back

As Ryu and Nina raced to intercept the attack boats, Ryu dropped the mat lines and stumbled over them. His hands shook as he re-coiled them.

As the attackers' boats approached, a man in Boat Two called out, "It's Ryu! And that's Laido's boat!"

His commander hesitated, then shouted, "We have our orders. Load the slings! Get your spears and knives ready."

Ryu pushed the wind raft so it flew ahead of Laido's boat.

"Steer straight for them!" he called to Nina. "Aim for the closer boat."

The enemy boats grew larger as the raft's hulls flew through the chop.

"Now, go left!"

As Nina threw the steering paddle to the side, Ryu held the mat just tight enough to make one hull lift out of the water.

"Hold it there!" Ryu yelled.

In the attack boats, the men stared at the raft racing toward them half in the water and half out of it like a seabird banking into a turn.

"Hang on!" Ryu yelled.

"Grab hold of something!" the commander shouted, just before the wind raft smashed into his boat so hard it pushed the boat over onto its side. The lower half quickly filled with water, dragging it down. As the men scrambled out of its way, it rolled upside down.

The crash broke a piece off one of the wind raft's hulls and splintered part of the deck. Momentum carried it over the attackers' boat and dug it into the water on the far side. Nina managed to keep hold of the steering paddle as the boat lurched forward. Ryu staggered to his feet.

In the water near them, the attackers scrambled to get back to the boat and attempt to right it. But it had been hewn from a single great tree, left long and heavy across the bottom to make it more stable in the sea. Also difficult to right, once it had rolled.

"You should get your men out of the water, Hadi," Ryu called to the commander, a man he recognized as a friend from long ago, even with the strange dark slash across his cheek. "The sharks know you're here now."

"I knew it was you," Hadi said without looking up.

"Why are you waiting? Call your other boat."

"They'll kill you. Raidu ordered it."

"The sharks will kill all of us, once they find blood in the water. Is that what you want?"

"It doesn't matter what I want. Not anymore."

When Laido and Darna arrived, the other boat's commander called for an attack.

"Are you crazy?" Laido called, putting his boat between the men in the water and the boat filled with men who should have been his enemies. Except they couldn't be enemies. He knew them all. "Is that you, Silat?" he called to the commander.

"Yes," he said. The men stopped paddling in mid-stroke, staring at Laido and Darna.

"What are you doing, Silat?"

In the silence that followed Laido's question, Darna spoke up. "Is your uncle well?"

As the boat grew closer, Laido and Darna called out each name as they recognized the man. "Bando, Raden, Sani, Daku, Van, Awan, Waiem, Assai -" For each, they called out a relative or a friend's name. Darna added questions about the families, all of which went unanswered. The men sat motionless; the boats drifted.

"Hadi," Ryu tried again. "Get your men out of the water. If you want to kill me, you and I will fight, right here if you want, but there's no point in killing all of these other people. They're friends of mine."

"You don't know us anymore, Ryu. You don't know me."

"If I knew you once, how can that be undone?"

"That person is dead. I killed him."

Two dark fins broke the surface of the water. From where he stood, Ryu could see one of the sharks passing.

A man in the water yelled, "Something bumped into my leg!"

"Get in the boat!" Laido called as he paddled over and extended his hand. "Hurry. Before it comes back."

"No. You can't," Hadi growled.

"It's here again!" another man called. Something bumped the overturned boat hard, lifting it up to show the open mouth and enormous head underneath.

"Help the others!" Laido called to the rescued man. "Move them to the far side or we'll all be in the water."

Darna extended her paddle to draw another man closer to the boat. "Don't thrash around. Get in quickly."

In the water, the second shark moved in closer, switching its tail as it dove down, circling below the men. The closer one surfaced just after a man heaved himself onto Laido's pitching boat. As it broke the surface, Darna and one of the rescued men smacked it with paddles.

Reaching down from the broken side of the raft, Ryu extended his hand to Hadi. "Grab hold. Get out of the water."

"No, Ryu." Hadi slapped the water and jerked his legs. "Take the others. I'm already marked. That place where we raced boats and thought it was important – I can never go back there." Drawn by the commotion, the shark left the men by the boat and headed toward Hadi, the sea swirling around its fin and across its exposed back. Far below, the other followed.

"Hadi," Nina pleaded. "Please get in the boat."

"Nina." He looked surprised, as if he'd just noticed her. "Beautiful Nina." His expression softened slightly. She edged toward him, extending her hand, but Ryu jerked her back as Hadi was thrown upward by the force of the attack. The lower shark dragged him down, but the surface shark also attacked, throwing him up sideways once again. He screamed as the two giants fought over him, ripping him apart, churning up the bloody red water.

Nina staggered back.

"Get out now!" Ryu yelled at the men still in the water.

As they struggled out of the water onto the wind raft, Boat Three and Laido's boat, more sharks swam in, excited by the blood, bumping the boats. When they rose up, mouth agape, the men smashed the sharks' snouts with paddles, but it did little to discourage the predators.

"Silat, follow me," Laido yelled to the Boat Three commander. He threw a rope to Nina on the wind raft. "Tie it around the mast, Nina. We'll try to get all the boats to shore."

With the extra men aboard, Laido's boat rode low in the water. When the sharks came around, the men could see the animals clearly; they were as long as the boat, swimming past, turning and swimming directly at the boat before bumping it, diving underneath, and surfacing on the other side. Terrified, the men paddled hard, pushing the boats toward the island, dragging the wind raft behind them. On the raft, Ryu, Nina, and two of the rescued men clung to the mast as the damaged hull dragged deeper into the water.

CHAPTER 29
THE LAST MOMENTS OF THE OLD WORLD

As Raidu's force neared the shore, Jin and Tahn pulled tangles of bamboo spikes across the sand and set them down over piles of dry razor grass. As they finished, Jin threw flaming sticks into the dry grass, setting it ablaze just before he and Tahn retreated into the bushes.

The men in Bokai's boat stopped rowing when they saw the fires.

"Forward!" Raidu yelled to them. "Get to shore!"

Jumping into the water before his boat reached the shore, Raidu waded through the surf and strode up to the flaming barrier, scattering the burning pieces before him with a swing of his war club.

"This way!" he called to the men still pulling the boats onto the shore.

As they hurried to catch up, they heard tapping sounds echoing off the rocks on the far side of the beach. Raidu plunged up the trail to the village and set the first huts he found on fire He was surprised no one ran from the burning huts or challenged the attackers. The village looked deserted.

"Cowards. They've run away."

When the tapping started again, higher up the mountain, Raidu followed the sound. Behind him, his men struggled up the trail, stumbling over the rocky terrain. The tapping was always just a little farther ahead, a little higher up the mountain, until they reached a clearing near the summit, where the tapping sounds stopped. Fanning out, the men searched for some sign of the villagers.

"Look at this!" one called, darting forward. Near the edge of the clearing, unbelievable treasures lay heaped up: trade shells, green feathers, pearls, bowls, wooden boxes, stonework, weavings, sashes decorated with rows of tiny trade shell beads, polished staffs, drums, flutes, hooks, whale bone carvings. Shouting, the rest of the men fell on the pile, grabbing at pieces they wanted, fighting with each other. When Raidu yelled at them to stop, no one listened until he swung his club against the closest man's shoulder, throwing him across the pile.

"I told you to stop!"

The men backed off but they didn't stop looking at the treasures.

Hidden in the bushes, Nulo watched and waited, still holding the Guard's signal woods. While the tapping on the shore had been real, the tapping on the trail was a random string of sounds Nulo thought sounded like the Guards' signals. Once the raiders stopped, he hurried ahead along the forest trails, looking for the villagers who'd fled inland, finding them hiding in the banyan trees, high above ground in the maze of branches.

"You need to leave," he urged them. "The attackers are nearby. They'll track you here. If you can get down to the shore, the Guards will protect you."

No one moved until Aeta left the safety of her hiding place and stood with him.

"All of you! Climb down from the trees," Nulo called. "Join us!"

A few more climbed down slowly: some old people, a few parents with children.

"Take the hand of the person nearest you," Aeta urged.

One by one, more joined the group, many of them taking the hand of another as soon as they left the trees, but they couldn't move, so Aeta took the hand of the old woman next to her, who took her grandson's hand. Her daughter took the child's other hand while she held out her free hand to another child, and so on, until they formed a long line that snaked its way down the forest trail.

* * *

"It's a trap!" Raidu shouted.

"If it was a trap, wouldn't someone have attacked us by now?" one man asked. "There's no one here. They left it all behind."

"He's right," another added, leading the group back to the pile of treasures. He pawed through those closest to him and tucked a whalebone carving under his arm. "When they ran off, they couldn't take all this with them."

Raidu strode into the middle of the treasure hunters, swinging his club in wide arcs as he went. The man with the whalebone carving fell heavily, screaming when the club hit him in the back. Scrambling, the others jumped out of range of the lethal club. One man still held a fistful of pearls.

"Drop them!"

Uncurling his fingers, the man let the pearls scatter at his feet.

"Now find out where the drums went."

When he hesitated, Raidu lunged toward him, sending the man running across the clearing where he man glimpsed something moving through the forest. "There, Chief! Look!"

Raidu swung around, his club ready. "What is it?"

"Not warriors, Chief. They look like children. A line of children."

"Attack them!"

In the instant the warriors hesitated, Nulo pressed Aeta's hand with both of his, nodded down the trail, and left the group,

136

threading his way through the trees back toward the opening where the warriors waited.

"Must you kill a group of elders and children to prove you're a great warrior, Raidu?" Nulo challenged as he stepped out.

"You! I see you weren't dumped in the sea as Yon told me. It makes no difference. You're a reject, Nulo. No one wanted you, especially not your mother. And now you're trying to be a hero. How stupid you are. Yon's dead and you'll die now."

"Why did you have me kidnapped? Did you think I might be the new chief?"

"You? Chief?" Raidu laughed. "Who'd follow you into battle?"

"Who follows you?"

Raidu swept his war club in a big arc. "All of them. Because they know the penalty for disobeying. Warriors must follow the chief's orders."

"Then why have me kidnapped?"

"Your mother wanted you gone. She hated you."

In the forest, Aeta's group worked its way down the trail.

"And what about you, Raidu – did you want me gone? Were you afraid of me?"

"Listen, you ugly half-grown man. I don't care who your father was. He's dead, I'm chief, and you're no threat at all. You're nothing, Nulo. What a perfect name Naia gave you."

Nulo thought about Naia, seeing her as a white heron rising off the flooding back on the Fat Men's Island. It was her blessing. He nodded and glanced down the trail, checking on the line of people Aeta led.

Seeing the shadows moving through the trees, Raidu yelled, "Stop them!" But when he stomped his foot, it bounced back up, throwing him off balance. The earth rippled up under his feet, like a wave moving through the ground. In the forest, the convulsing earth lifted stones and great trees, ripping out the connected trees by the roots, hurling them sideways. Through the confusion, Aeta hurried the group along, clutching the hand of the child behind her, heading away from the worst of the tree falls, finding a way around others.

In the clearing, the warriors stood unmoving, terrified. Even Raidu stopped.

"You need to leave, Raidu," Nulo called. "The mountain is moving."

Raidu laughed. "The chief's son, indeed. A freak, talking to trees and rocks. Look where it got you. What are you now, Chief of Old People and Weaklings?"

"You and your men need to leave," Nulo repeated.

"You're wrong. I've been waiting for this moment, and now it's here. I promised your mother you'd be dead and I hate to disappoint her." He waved off the men who gathered behind him. "I'll handle this myself."

"Raidu, listen to me -"

"Too late, half-man." Raidu ran straight at Nulo, his arm jerking back as he swung his war club. As he closed on his victim, the earth heaved up beneath him. Catching himself, he lurched sideways and struggled back up with a roar, only to find his opponent wasn't where he used to be. As Raidu searched the area, the earth shuddered so violently his knees buckled. Above, near the summit, the mountain screamed. The rock cracked open. The mountain began to rip itself apart. In the clearing, Raidu's men screamed and ran.

"You'll die if you stay here," Nulo said slowly, emerging from behind a rock. "The mountain will kill you."

"*You're* the one who'll die!"

Nulo, unmoving and unarmed, watched Raidu's approach. His face was pulled taut, his mouth open, his eyes fixed on Nulo. As his arm swung up, wielding the heavy club, the muscles across his chest and shoulder strained. The flushed face seemed to swell, the body grow larger, the legs draw up as he prepared his stance to balance the swing.

At that same moment, a stone ax with two black feathers attached to the handle caught Raidu in the back of the neck with such force that it jerked the top of his head back then pushed it toward his chest as the whole body pitched forward, convulsing as it sprawled on the ground, the ax still buried deep in his neck.

Owl Man ran across the clearing and stopped by the chief's body, muttering words Nulo couldn't understand. Crouching, he rolled the body over and placed two stones on the man's chest and one on his forehead, speaking all the while. Then he pulled out the bloody ax, tucked it in his sash, and stood up. Behind him the mountain exploded. Ash clouds shot out a side vent. Thick streams of fire burst out of the top of the mountain. Where they fell back to earth, burning rivers grew, incinerating everything in their path.

Nulo couldn't move. In front of him, Raidu sprawled; above, the fire beast inside the mountain forced its way to freedom. Death surrounded him. Owl Man reached over, wound an extra sash around Nulo's face, leaving only his eyes free, and pulled on his arm, forcing him to move.

* * *

Near the pile of treasures, the Guards rounded up most of Raidu's fleeing force without a fight. Some refused to believe that Raidu was dead. A few begged Tahn to remember that they used to be friends.

"Yet that wouldn't have stopped you from killing me," Tahn noted.

Jin called out to the captives, "I'll speak quickly. You can surrender your weapons and take your boats back to your home island, or you can join us, with the understanding that you will be answering to me. Anyone not obeying Guard orders will be executed or abandoned. Is that understood?"

The men mumbled to each other.

"You need to decide now. The mountain will kill anyone who stays."

After more hurried talk, five decided to go their own way, led by Raidu's son, Bokai. The rest bowed to Jin, accepting the conditions.

"Get our people into the boats. We have to hurry," Jin called to the Guards, barely acknowledging the men's allegiance. Before they left, he glanced at the five who had chosen not to stay.

"Watch them, Tahn. Once we're all off the island, they may turn against us."

When the mountain screamed again, shooting thin streams of fire into the sky, he pointed to the cove. "Check on Aeta's group and the new boat. I'll check the far beach. We're missing a lot of people."

In the cove, Jin helped Liwei get Fuhua onto a boat, along with some of his favorite treasures. Liwei bowed formally. Thank you. Now you must leave too. The mountain is poisonous."

"I'll stay to help the rest."

"The mountain will kill everyone foolish enough to stay," Liwei warned, "no matter which side they're on."

"If we move quickly, it can still be done," Jin said, returning the bow. "Good luck."

Colbee had made the new boat larger and deeper than usual. In the back, he'd put a heavy, extra-long steering paddle that could be set straight down against the stern or angled away from the boat. Because he'd found some leaks during the boat's trial runs, he'd added filler and left the boat pulled up on the shore until the pitch could dry. That's where Aeta's group found it. With no other boats available, panicked people climbed aboard the beached boat, forcing it deep into the sand and dirt. Aeta climbed back out, but no one followed. When Tahn rounded the point of the cove, some passengers had tried to push the boat off the shore with the steering paddle, managing only to wedge the paddle between two rocks.

"Everyone has to get off!" Tahn yelled as he reached the boat.

No one moved. Jumping aboard, Tahn tossed the first two people he saw into the shallow water.

"Get off the boat!" he repeated. When the people still hesitated, he pushed two more into the water.

After that, some began to climb off.

"Faster!" Tahn yelled. "We need everyone to help move the boat!" Throwing ropes out into the water in front of the boat, he ordered two people to swim out and grab the lines. He threw two more lines off the stern and had people on the beach hold them.

"Grab long poles or tree trunks!" he yelled to others. "We need everyone up front. Get the poles under the boat. We have to push the boat up and out to deeper water. Grab hold. Ready? PUSH UP!" he yelled. "Again! PUSH UP!" Slowly, the boat began to move, fighting the heavy sand.

Behind them, the mountain thundered and shook while a river of fire flowed down its slopes, burning the ancient trees before drowning them in firerock.

"Start pushing forward!" Tahn yelled. Turning to the people in the water, he yelled, "Pull on the lines!"

When the boat was floating free in the water, he ordered the climbing ropes dropped over the sides. As the last people hurried up the knotted ropes, two figures stumbled out of the forest and onto the beach: one short and one tall, both choking, their skin smoke-blackened.

"It's Nulo!" Tahn cried. "And Owl Man. Get them onto the boat!" he called to the men on the lines. "Then push off and get in. Let's hope we can make it past the rocks."

Farther up the shore, Laido sorted out Raidu's men and the remaining boats, pushing the last into the sea before he climbed aboard. Behind him, the first burning rivers reached the shore rocks.

* * *

While the sun sank into the sea, friends and former foes huddled in their boats, shapes thrown into silhouette by the fires burning from the mountaintop down to the sea. Stunned, they watched the great trees ripped out and burned, rock slabs picked up and carried along in the thick fire coursing down the hillsides. At the water's edge, the red river fell spitting and hissing into the sea, throwing up clouds of steam.

That night they saw the mountain crack open yet again, releasing a new fire beast, so it too could leap into the sky, then plunge down and spread across the land, destroying everything in its path in an ecstasy of fire and death until it was conquered by the endless sea. The terror rose, subsided, and rose again. In the boats, people shuddered as they watched the old world burn.

End of Part I

PART II – LEAVING THE PAST BEHIND

In the areas known today as Melanesia,
Polynesia, and the great Pacific Ocean

CHAPTER 1
PARTING WAYS

Those who dragged their boats onto the shore of a small island days later found a place to rest and plan, not a place to live. The long flat section by the shore flooded completely at high tide, forcing them to make camp against the cliffs. Still, the rock depressions collected rainwater, palms crowded one section, and the rocky shallows teemed with fish and crabs. They had food and shelter, for the moment. They made offerings to the spirits for their survival, tended their families, and gathered food, but uncertainty filled every moment. The Fat Men's Island, their old community, had been destroyed, its leaders deposed by nature's fury. Off by themselves, the Fat Men said almost nothing and asked nothing of others. Like everyone else, they tried to determine where their future lay.

Some missed the old island so much they considered going back, even if it *was* burning. "Maybe," one woman argued, "it's like a lightning fire. It'll burn itself out and then everything will be fine again after the rainy season. We just have to wait here until then."

Several turned to Garah for guidance. He explained, as if to children, "It's not possible to live there now."

"But I liked it there," the woman complained. Others nodded agreement.

"I did too," Garah continued, "but we can't live there now."

When the tide was out, people dug for shellfish and talked. Some wanted to return to the original homes they'd left long ago despite not knowing how to get back there. Some wanted to head farther out to sea, past the fire mountain. Others began preparing for departure even though they hadn't decided where to go, collecting coconuts and palm branches, tapping the sap to make wine, gathering seaweed, shellfish, trade shells, sponges, urchin spines, medicinal herbs, animal bones, and whatever else they found that might be useful. Darna plugged the ends of hollow branches to make water containers. Kiah set out saltwater to dry in shallow rock hollows so they could take the salt with them.

Jin called Raidu's warriors together. Hunkered down in a semi-circle around him, they were a sad lot: twenty-five men, thin and worn.

"You're neither my enemies nor my prisoners," Jin announced. "As of this moment, you're free to return to your own lands. We escaped the fire mountain together. The spirits gave us a future." Picking up a long stick, he pointed back the way they'd come. "To go back to your homes, you will need to head past the fire mountain and the black rock islands. Your home island, from what I understand, is many days travel in that direction. Laido can give you the rising star sequence you'll need to follow. If you're going, you should try to go together. But know this: even if you find your old island and the people you left behind, that place is not the home you left. It's different. Changed. Damaged. You'll need to cleanse it of bad spirits and bad memories to make a real home of it once again."

"*If* we go? What else can we do? We left our families there!" a man shouted.

Jin looked at the men and the vast expanse of the sea behind them. "I understand. That's a good choice. However," he paused, searching the faces in the circle, "some may wish to make a different choice. If so, I offer a place with us."

"What place?"

"Going where?"

146

"I don't know," Jin answered. "I don't know, except to say it will be out there." He pointed out across the water. "Farther and farther. Past the last island. Until the sea spirits take us, I suppose."

The men waited, unsure.

"Back in my homeland," Jin explained, "my whole family died of swamp fever. I was the only one spared. For what reason? I think it's because I have to find something extraordinary, something I can show them when I meet them again. It's not enough for me to walk the old paths and fish the same waters. I must live enough in one life to give something back to those whose lives were cut off so early. Most of you probably don't understand, but if you do, I invite you to join me."

No one replied.

"You can tell me your answer any time until sunset tomorrow." He threw the stick down to the sand. "Think carefully."

As soon as Jin walked away, the warriors started shouting, debating the possibilities, bringing up problems with each suggestion. Most had already made up their minds. It was exhilarating to consider an adventure on the great open sea, but after a while, life on their home island looked like a better choice. Later that day, only Goh approached Jin, saying he accepted the offer. The rest wanted to go home.

Once word of Raidu's men's choice spread through the camp, many others decided to join them. They would have a large group to travel with, the island could easily support more people, and they'd probably be welcome there.

When Laido asked Darna if she wanted to join them, she considered her reply. "In a way, it would be easy to return. I know the place and I love some parts of it. Yet even in my best memories, it's as if another person lived her life there."

"You don't want to go back?"

Darna took his hand. "Why don't you tell me your plan instead of trying to figure out mine?"

"I need to know how you feel."

"I think when the sea flooded the old village, it was telling us the old world had ended. That worried people, so they made Raidu chief because he seemed strong enough to face the change. Instead, he used it against them. But it wasn't Raidu who made us leave. And it wasn't the raft. Those things simply made us do something we'd already planned to do."

"I know." He put his arm around her waist. "So if not back, where?"

"You already have an idea. Why won't you tell me?"

"Because it's too dangerous. I have to know that you'd choose the same path if you had every choice available."

She locked her hand over his. "If one trail is blocked, we must pick another. I would choose to see what's beyond here, but only if you were with me."

"Then it's decided," Laido exhaled. "We'll take two boats and head out to sea."

"Including Ryu and Nulo," Darna added, stopping herself before she added more names to the list.

"Of course. I consider them part of our family. There may be others who'd like to join us: Colbee and Kiah, for instance."

"Good. Yes. Very good."

When they told Nina, she thought it was a fine plan.

Ryu agreed.

Tahn didn't.

Nor did Nulo.

"I'm staying with the Guards," Tahn announced as he stood up, ready to leave. "You can go wherever you want."

His mother put her hand on his arm, keeping him there. "Wait, Tahn. Please. You're my family. I don't want to lose you."

"You found a better son, one more to your liking."

"Listen to me," Darna commanded. "*You* are my son. You will always be my son. I value you more than the breath that marks my life. There is nothing you could do, ever, that would make me stop loving you."

"Then let me go, Mother." Tahn said. "Let me go."

"Go where?"

"Jin, some of the Guards, and four of Raidu's warriors want to head out to the edge of the world. That's where I'll go."

"It looks as if that's where we're going too."

"What? You're not going back?"

"No," Laido said. "We see no future in the past."

"I'd travel with the Guards," Tahn insisted. "If we were to change course or get separated, I'd go with them."

"Agreed," Laido said, putting his hand on his son's shoulder. Surprised, Tahn returned the gesture.

"Now we need to hear from Nulo," Darna said. "He can't go back to the old island. He'd be killed if he returned."

"He left when we first started talking," Tahn said. "Didn't you notice?"

While the others debated, Nulo searched for Aeta, finding her in the farthest camp, with a frail old man. "My grandfather," she said when she saw Nulo. "He's all I have left. My brother died at sea before we got to Fuhua's island. I sang for him on Brightness Day."

"Bring your grandfather with us," Nulo said. "We're going on, not back."

Aeta shook her head slowly. "He wouldn't survive. His only chance is for me to join the group returning to Raidu's island."

"No. Come with us."

"You have no say in what I do," she snapped. "Nor do you understand why. I don't want you to change your plans for me, and I won't change mine for you."

Words twisted together in his throat, choking him.

"You have to leave now, Nulo. Goodbye."

"I'll come with you, then."

"No. I don't want you to."

"If -"

"If things were some other way," she sighed, "then we might be some other way as well."

Behind them, her grandfather called for her.

"I have to take care of him."

"Take this," Nulo held out a flute he'd carved from a seabird bone, marked with dotted lines that formed two serpents twining around the holes.

Glancing at him for a moment, she nodded, tucked the flute into her sash, and turned away without a word. In another time and another place, her acceptance of his gift would have meant something important. Now it seemed to mean nothing at all. She tended to her grandfather, her back turned to him on purpose.

He waited. Finally, he turned away.

CHAPTER 2
THE SHAMAN'S TRANSFORMATION

In the end, only Owl Man still struggled with his choice. While no one blamed him, he'd killed a man he knew, attacked him from the rear without warning. The act might be excused but never erased. When the others were ready to leave, he refused to join any of the groups.

"How can we persuade him to join us? Laido asked.

"You can't," Nulo replied. "But you can leave him a boat so he can leave when he's ready."

When Laido and his the group left Owl Man behind, they called his name as they paddled away, wishing him well, pointing to the little boat with yellow eyes painted on both sides of the bow. He didn't return their farewells. Instead, he stared at the edge of the sea where it melted into the sky.

When he looked into his past, he saw nothing except regrets. While he knew he could go with the explorers, he was nothing there either. So he stayed where he was.

In the days and nights that followed, the shaman never moved. The yellow-eyed boat blew over in a storm. Rains fell on him, and sunlight and moonlight and spray from the waves. His hair grew so long it reached down his back to the ground. His toenails twisted down into the sand. A swift perched on his shoulder.

Inside he discovered a great space filled with sky that he rose up into, pushing through it with his uplifted arms, stretching out his fingers until he reached the very heart of the sky. Just before he had it under his fingers the swift stopped him, saying, "It's not given to you to know the heart of the sky."

So he returned and reached down into the earth, solidifying into a guardian tree near the shore, its wide trunk greater around than the reach of six men, its branches reaching higher into the sky than any other tree. Red macaws claimed it and tiny wax bees, grey monkeys, a python, a wide-eyed tarsier. Most of all it belonged to the swift, who, as the shaman's other, gave him the gift of flight, just as his father had known so long ago.

CHAPTER 3
MASALI

Nina drew the salt air into her lungs, threw her head back toward the sun and closed her eyes as the wind raft skimmed the sea like a bird. Around it swam schools of fish as dense as forests, dolphins threading through the wave tops, dark whales far larger than the boats, sea turtles and giant rays. Above, seabirds sailed just beyond her reach. As the days went by, she forgot the world she'd left behind: the busy groups on the Fat Men's Island and before that, the old island where she was born. The world became the sea and sky, its only people those in the boats.

So it came as a shock one day to see strange boats pulled up on the beach of a little island and four men digging with clam sticks in the shallow water.

"People!" she called, pointing.

As soon as Laido called out a greeting, the men dropped their sticks and ran into the forest, leaving their baskets of clams behind on the beach.

In the second boat, Fuhua brightened up immediately. "Go ashore!" he waved. "Maybe we can trade."

On shore, he and Liwei set out a pile of interesting but not very valuable items: a plain bark cloth wrap, several baskets, a couple of bone knives, some small pearls. Once he was satisfied with the presentation, Fuhua sat cross-legged on a mat across from the baskets of clams. The rest of the group brought their boats near shore and waited.

After a while, one man stepped out onto the beach, grabbed two clam baskets and ran back into the forest, catching a glimpse of Fuhua and his trade goods.

"Patience," Fuhua said, patting his belly. "A fish needs to be worked carefully before it can be caught."

When the others were ready to give up, they heard a rustling in the trees. Brushing aside the branches, four men walked out and stopped at the edge of the forest, watching Fuhua, looking over his offerings. Long curved bones pierced their noses. Their skin was empty, their dark hair oiled and pulled back, with shells woven into the front strands. They stood lightly, ready to flee.

Fuhua waved expansively, as if they were the very people he had been looking for. "Come, see if you like anything. Perhaps we could trade," he said pointing from his pile to their baskets.

The men took out the clams and set them in three piles. One pile had only one clam, but it was huge, with a shining gold edge. The second pile looked unimpressive, until a man cut a clam open and dug out a small pearl with a rosy glow. The third pile held dozens of small clams. The man pointed at it and made eating signs.

Fuhua took out the bone knives and the baskets and set them apart, pointing at the large clam. The men pointed to the pile of small clams and pushed them forward. And so the bargaining began. Fuhua clapped his hands and laughed. The head fisherman copied the gesture.

One of the others went off into the forest and returned later with a snake as long as a man wrapped around his shoulders. He held out the snake's head and tail while one of the other men laughed.

"Lazy. Lazy snake," one said. "Too lazy to bite."

"It doesn't need to bite," Liwei replied. "It can kill by squeezing its prey."

Interrupting the bargaining, Laido said, "I don't think we need it on the boat."

"Probably not," Jin agreed, "though it might be good eating."

Eventually, the men agreed on a trade. Fuhua took the giant clam, three pearls, and a basket of small clams, in return for most of his selection of goods. The basket of clams he gave to the group; the other pieces he added to his new collection of treasures.

"You come to my land," the head bargainer said, pointing out to sea. "Land of the Dangerous Bird. Three easy days in boat. Many treasures there. And friends too."

His companions laughed as they packed up Fuhua's trade goods. "Maybe," one of them said.

After the strangers left with their new treasures, the group set up camp on the island while Laido, Jin, and Tahn stood on the shore, considering the strangers' invitation.

"Fuhua and Liwei are set on going there," Laido said. "But I don't know."

"We'll make sure we're armed when we go," Jin added, "and send the Guards out first. We'll have to leave someone with the boats and agree on an alarm signal."

Ryu dragged the wind raft up onto the beach and joined them. "If it's a trap, what good will the alarm be?"

"We can split into two groups," Tahn suggested, "so one group will land at the main beach and the other will land farther down the coast, or even stay in the water offshore, in case there's trouble."

"We're blind here," Laido objected. "We have no idea what we're heading into."

"Then we'll have to guess based on what we know," Jin answered. "We know the strangers will tell them we're coming. They know Fuhua has treasures and wants to trade. We didn't lead them to believe we are hostile. On the other hand, they know we have warriors and weapons. I think we're in a fairly good position."

Nina and her mother joined the group, along with Kiah and Colbee.

"I could stay offshore with the boats," Nina offered, "in case of trouble."

"I wonder what the name 'Island of Dangerous Birds' means," Darna said. "Are birds dangerous?"

"Only when flying overhead!" Colbee laughed.

* * *

As the fisherman had said, it took three days to reach the island, but they saw it long before they reached it. The closer they got, the larger it grew before them, bigger than any island they'd ever seen, with mountains rising in the center. At the shore, thick tangles of mangroves laced their roots into the sea. Beyond them, endless forests rose in waves of dark green straight into the sky.

"There's no place to land here," Laido said. "Let's look for something better."

Farther down shore, giant trees grew to the land's edge, throwing long branches out over the water. Flowering bushes crowded the bits of light that remained on the shore, blocking the travelers' view of the interior.

Laido waved them on. "Keep looking."

"There!" Ryu called, pointing to a stretch of sandy beach.

"Well, let's go!" Fuhua yelled.

As agreed, they pulled the wind raft and the Flying Fish up onto the beach, and left the two war canoes tethered to rocks in the water. When they finished, only one person waited for them on the beach. She sat cross-legged on a flat stone in the middle of the sand, facing them but looking up at the sky. Thick twists of dark hair dressed with oil and decorated with shells, monkey fur, extravagantly curved green feathers, and lizard tails fell past her shoulders and down her back. A long bone pierced her flat nose. Around her neck, she wore a curved shell necklace under strings of trade shells and cinnabar beads. Between her breasts hung a lizard skull that examined the visitors with greenstone eyes. In one hand, she held a double-ended spear decorated with crossed designs. In the other was a large white flower. A monkey with a huge nose sat on her knee, half-buried in the grasses of her skirt. On her shoulder rested a bright green bird sporting very long tail feathers like the ones in her hair, which made it hard to tell where the bird ended and the headdress began.

As the group stood on the beach, staring, more people emerged from the forest. Their faces and hair were covered in red or yellow clay marked with different lines and dots so that each was different, yet together they formed a band of ghost warriors. Each held a spear and a shield of dark wood covered with white designs. Around their arms, tightly wrapped bands held dried grasses, shark teeth, snake skins. Some of the men had rows of raised dots running along their arms and backs; almost all had painted bones through their noses. Some wore only a simple loinwrap; others had elaborate belts and wraps with gourds, shells, bamboo rattles, and skulls. On their chests, they wore necklaces of bones. They stood behind the woman, taking their place one by one, their gaze locked on the newcomers.

"Thirty men," Jin whispered, "probably all capable of killing us."

Laido bowed to the woman. "Madam, we are visitors here and ask your hospitality."

She ignored him.

As both groups stood locked in silence, considering each other like animals waiting for the fight to start, Darna stepped forward. "I want to know why this place is called The Land of Dangerous Birds."

The woman looked at her. "Who are you?"

"I am the Queen," Darna answered. "Who are you?"

"You do not look like a queen."

"And you do not act like one. We lost our home to fire, and we ask for your hospitality. It doesn't seem much to ask of someone such as yourself."

The woman jumped to her feet, upsetting the monkey and bird, plus a number of large moths, so the air seemed to whirl around her. "Much to ask? We ask nothing of you, except to leave us alone, yet you feel free to ask much of us. How is that? Do you have more of a right to ask than I do?"

"Are we free to leave?"

"It's too late for that."

"Why?"

"You have already shown yourselves to be thieves. You have stolen the fishermen's precious shells."

"We traded for them. If you feel the trade was unfair, we will give back what we received when you give back what you have received."

"We received nothing! You stole the shells."

"Not true. I watched the trade."

"Then you are one of the thieves."

"You argue in circles: You say I must be a thief because I must be a thief. Neither part is true. Perhaps others have wronged you, but not us. We have done nothing except to pull our boats up on the beach."

"Your words are like snakes, moving fast so no one can follow."

"In my land, when a stranger is in distress, she is welcome to ask for help. Perhaps it is different here."

"I know what you want. It's more than help. You'd leave a few trinkets and then take everything you want from our land. You'd steal our long-tailed birds, take our precious gold-lipped shells. Sometimes, voyagers think our young women are beautiful, and they want them too. They leave behind only suffering."

She stared at Darna. "You want to know about this land? I'll tell you. This is Masali, the place of bad spirits, and I am Alu, the queen of those who eat the dead."

She pointed to one side with her spear. "On this side are the birds that will kill you when you touch them; they send their poison through your skin." She swung the spear to the other side. "On this side are poisonous beetles and frogs. If you touch them, you will die within moments. We use their poison on our spears." She swung the spear out towards the sea. "There, the great sharks will kill you. And in the jungle, big snakes will crush you, the crocodile will drag you into the brown river to drown, the red tiger will hunt you in the dark, the lizards that stand like man will bite you, the thorn tree will rip the skin from your hands. And when you run from the forest in fear, we will kill you. Right here. We do not want your cheap gifts."

Darna looked straight at her. "We were invited."

"You were entrapped. Do you understand the difference?"

Nulo walked up to Darna and stood next to her.

"What is this?" Alu demanded.

"This is Nulo, my advisor," Darna answered.

Nulo motioned to the line of warriors flanking Alu. "Many more used to stand there. Where are the others?"

Alu sucked in her breath. "Where are the others? Dead! They're all dead, or dying! Dancing with death, lying with death, birthing death, walking with death leaning on them, shaking like a rattle in death's hand. That's when people are real, when they embrace death. Everything else is a lie. That's why we eat them, because they have the purest energy, the clearest spirit. The rest," she pointed to the group, "are imperfect." At this, she turned around and showed the human skull that hung from a rope on her back. Strings of beads and feathers had been laced through the eye sockets.

"If you really were the Queen of Death," Darna said, "you wouldn't need all of this costume. You would be all-powerful on your own."

Alu spun and hurled her spear. Darna never moved. The spear flew past, barely missing her, sticking in the sand. With a scream, Alu ran at Darna, curved dagger in hand, and Alu's warriors ran at the group, spears leveled.

Jin released the Guards in a full attack. The two forces rushed at each other, weapons flashing. The islanders hurled their spears. One of the Guards took a spear through his calf. As the toxin spread through his system, he screamed in pain and collapsed onto the sand, convulsing.

As the killer cheered, four warriors threw their spears, striking four islanders and silencing the celebration. From that point on, it was man to man, dagger, knife, club, staff, spear, battling on the sand. Nulo was knocked down and trampled in the surge. Ryu was fighting with one man when another hit him in the back with a club studded with shark teeth. He stumbled forward, blood running down his back. As his opponent swung the club again, Liwei and Fuhua waded into the fray with their staffs, landing a powerful blow on the man's head then helping Ryu to his feet. They proved to be formidable fighters, fending off several opponents, splintering arms and legs with terrible blows. Kiah and Colbee fought with canoe paddles, the only weapons they could find. Jin and the Guards slipped under the swing of the poison spears to throw their long knives.

While the others were fighting, three islanders tried to sneak around and steal the boats. Nina, hiding in the canoe, heard someone splashing through the water toward her and felt the canoe float free as he untied it. When he threw himself up and over the edge of the boat, she rose and hit him hard with a paddle, pushing him back into the water. At her cry, two of the Guards ran back toward the boats. The other two islanders, alarmed that a new force waited in the boats, rescued their comrade in the sea and abandoned their quest, running back into the forest.

Seeing her mother being attacked, Nina jumped out of the boat and ran ashore but forgot to drop the second anchor stone.

While the warriors clashed, Darna and Alu fought their own battle. With a knife in one hand and a poison-tipped spear in the other, Alu drove Darna backward. Stumbling over driftwood piles,

Darna struggled to her feet as Alu closed on her. As Alu raised her knife, Darna caught the wild woman's arm and twisted it around. Screeching, Alu swung the spear around like a club and caught Darna in the face, whipping her head back, throwing her to the sand.

As soon as Darna fell, Alu dropped her spear and grabbed Darna's hair, preparing to cut Darna's head off. Instead, a powerful kick to her side sent her sprawling in the sand. When she sat up, she found herself looking at a younger version of Darna. Nina stood between the wild woman and her mother. In her hand was Alu's spear.

"What is this?" Alu yelled. "Witchcraft? Are you the ghost of one not yet dead?"

"I am the Daughter of the Queen," Nina said. "And *you* are the witch. Look around! Look at what you have done here! This is evil work. Your work."

"More lies!" Alu yelled as she lunged at Nina. Nina planted her left foot behind her, pointed the spear at Alu, and wedged the end of the shaft against the arch of her left foot. As Alu lunged at her, Nina threw all of her strength into holding the spear and steadying it against her right thigh, even as Alu's weight hit it. Alu's contorted face grew so close it filled the space between them, overwhelming Nina. The flapping shells, the wild tangles of her hair filled with green feathers, the lizard tails, the green eyes of the lizard skull staring. Alu's body falling onto the spear, crashing down, carried by the momentum of rage, falling into Nina, pushing her backward, knocking her down, crushing her. Alu's fury flooded Nina's body, carrying with it ghost warriors, lifeless lizards and birds, skulls with golden shell eyes, the enormous weight of the dead queen. They piled on top of her so she couldn't move, couldn't breathe. The stink of death surrounded her.

Laido ran to Darna, reaching her side just as two islanders tried to attack her. "Leave her!" he yelled, lunging at them. "Or I will cut off your arms!"

"We're not afraid."

Jumping to his feet, Laido swung his bone knife, jabbing the closer attacker in the leg, leaping up, jabbing again and again. He flew at both, yelling "I will see your blood flowing like rivers in the sand!"

Through they tried to stab him with their poison knives, he moved just ahead of each blow, forcing them back as he attacked. He struck one in the face, tearing the flesh from the eye socket down to the jaw. The other he raked across the shoulder before stabbing him deep through the chest, burying his knife in the man's flesh.

Only when the two attackers had slumped to the red sand did his fever cool. He shivered as he kneeled by Darna, who was now protected by two Guards. She was weeping as she took his hand in hers.

Ryu pushed Alu's heavy form off Nina and lifted her head. It dropped to one side as he moved his hand. "Nina!"

Kiah hurried over, rolled Nina onto her side to get her to breathe and checked for the river of life inside her. "She's alive and yet not with us."

"Like the chief?" Ryu worried.

One of the two fishermen they'd met before came up behind them and held out his hand. "Here, take this." Across the palm of his hand, liquid silver beads jumped oddly as his hand shook. "Cure. For her. Forever life."

Pushing him back, Liwei stepped between the man and Nina. "No. It's poison. It's driven all of you mad."

The man jerked his head back and forth. "No! Forever life! Forever clear!"

"It's deadly," Liwei said, shaking his head. "It kills your mind, your eyes, your legs. Don't you see what's happening here?"

"Forever life! Forever clear! Watch!" he yelled, as he popped the rolling silver drops into his mouth.

162

"No!" Liwei yelled. "It's poison. It's killing you."

"See?" the man mumbled as he backed away, jerking his arm as he motioned to his friend. "See? Forever clear!" he called back as they headed into the forest.

"Those red beads," Liwei said, pointing to one of Alu's necklaces. "When you heat them over a fire, the silver drops ooze out. I've seen them before." After a moment, he added, "Fuhua had some red cinnabar carvings."

"He did?" Ryu said. "Like those? Why?"

"They're beautiful. She must have gotten them in a trade," Liwei remarked, contemplating Alu's inert body.

Not far away, Nulo crouched next to Ryu as he held Nina.

"There's too much pain here," Nulo said, "in the people and the air, ghosts who haunt the forest, in her. You must remind Nina of who she is. Tell her about her mother's courage and her father's fury. Call her back."

The limp form in Ryu's arms grew suddenly light, as if filled with air. "I have no great words to call her back. I don't know those words."

"Just say your words."

So Ryu spoke to Nina while others buried the fallen Guard at the edge of the forest and sang a death chant so his spirit could go to the Otherworld peacefully even after his violent end. The islanders dragged away their dead and wounded, including Alu, and disappeared into the forest. Guards watched for a second attack, but none materialized.

"I need a fire to clean me," Laido said. "Evil grew inside me."

Liwei and Fuhua threw the debris of the fight onto a great pile of wood. Jin knelt in front of it, striking sparks off his fire rock onto heaps of dry tinder. As soon as embers flared in one spot, the fire rose, spreading its arms through the pile, dark red shoots reaching through black smoke. Laido stood in the thick of it, striking himself with a switch until he bled, letting the smoke rise to the gods, carrying his blood offering. When he fell onto the sand, Darna washed his wounds, laid her jade amulet in the middle of his back, unrolled her mat and slept next to him.

Through all of this, Ryu stayed with Nina, speaking to her, his voice rising and falling like a river over rockfalls. When night fell and the others set up camp on the beach, Ryu remained by her side. As the stars appeared, one after another, he told her their stories, explaining how the stars' stories and the people's stories were all intertwined, as if a web of ropes climbed from the earth to the top of the sky. All the people and all the animals were tied into it, and the sun and moon and all of the star figures also, so that if one event made the rope tremble, it could be felt all across the universe. He was tied to the stars. So was she. Her life was tied to his.

He called her back that night, yet in the morning, when she moved against his arm, he was startled at her nearness, embarrassed by his own emotion. Instead of speaking to her, he called to Laido and Darna. They filled the space with their shouts and embraces so it was easy for him to slip away.

CHAPTER 4
ONE BOAT LEAVING

The shadows of Masali clung to them long after the battle ended.

"This is stupid," one of the men from the Fat Men's Island remarked. "We'll die here. We should have gone back when we could."

"Gone back where? To the Fat Men's Island? It's gone. And your old home? How would you find it?"

"I bet none of the others made it back," another answered.

"You can't leave," a third added. "You don't have a boat. Don't you understand? We're stuck on this journey into madness. We'll all end up like *her*. We won't even remember the old life."

"We could make our own boat."

"And spend a moon here with the crazy people?"

"I could take one of Laido's boats," one suggested. "I could leave one night when everyone's asleep."

"And do what with it? You couldn't paddle it home by yourself. Besides, you couldn't find your way. You get lost paddling around the cove."

Jumping to his feet, the man kicked out and knocked the speaker to the ground. As he went to kick again, Jin dragged him away from the fight.

"Settle down!" Jin hissed as he flung the man to the ground.

"It's his fault."

"It's always someone else's fault, isn't it?"

Laido took Jin aside. "We've got to get them to work or they'll turn on each other."

"The problem is they're afraid of the forest."

"Then we'll work out here. We'll find supplies along the beach. The boats need some repairs."

When Jin told the men about the plan, they agreed immediately. One even offered to gather some of the gold-lipped clams before they left the area. "They're very valuable."

"They're certainly valued here," Jin admitted.

"The greatest treasure they have."

"You found them nearby, offshore?"

"No, we looked," the warrior said. "We'd have to go back to the other island."

"That's more than two days each way!"

"Yes," the man admitted. "Is that too long?"

Jin hesitated.

"If the four of us went," another added, fingering the beads on his necklace, "we could go faster and be back sooner. Of course, it's up to you. If you think we'd be more useful here, we'll stay."

Across the beach, Jin saw Colbee directing the group repairing the damaged canoe. Everyone helped, hauling materials, building a fire to heat the pitch. The man standing in front of him hadn't offered to help. None of them had. He and the others had piled their possessions near the boat, as if they already planned to leave.

"If you're sure you can be back in five days, go ahead. I'm sure we have that much work to do on that boat alone. More than five days though would be too much. Everyone's anxious to be away from here."

The man gave a quick nod. "We'll leave as soon as we can. The tide's with us right now."

Laido and Jin watched the warriors load the heavy canoe and push it into the sea. Once they were out of the rocky shallows, the men vaulted in and started paddling through the surf without a backward glance.

"Where are they going?" Laido asked

"They said they were going to collect gold-lipped clams. But they won't bother looking for them. It would only slow them down on their way home."

"You let them take the boat?"

Jin shrugged. "They would have taken it anyway. It's easier this way. No one got hurt. None of us, at least."

"And if they come back with the giant clams?"

"I'll be *very* surprised."

Laido sighed. "There are more dangers than the poisonous frogs and birds here. I'll be glad to get off this island."

"We all will," Jin agreed. "Let's get the work done and go."

"Did all of the new men leave?"

"Goh stayed. He's helping Colbee with the repairs."

Laido nodded. "One good man added, four problems solved. Good choice."

CHAPTER 5
FEVER DREAMS

The warriors didn't return after five days, or seven. Past ready to get off the island, the group hurried through the last of the preparations, dragging in extra palm branches, packing salt and cloves, medicinal herbs, bundles of bamboo. With a shout, they pushed the three boats into the sea and left Masali behind. Its heritage of pain, however, went with them. Nulo was the first to fall ill. Three days out, the boats were making good time with a favorable wind when the sickness overtook him. After he vomited, his terrible headache got worse. Then he couldn't stop shivering, couldn't move. By the time Nina noticed something was wrong, he was shaking cold, his face wet with sweat. She covered him with wraps, but they didn't still the shaking.

Darna gasped when she saw him. "It could be swamp fever. Maybe we brought it on with the branches. Keep him very warm so he can sweat it out of his body." She moved over to Laido and crouched down next to him. "Nulo's sick. We need to go ashore so I can get some herbs to help him." In a voice only he could hear, she added, "We may all face this. If we get medicine now, it may save us later."

* * *

Nulo heard none of the conversations going on around him. The boat and the people in it faded, replaced by the sound of the water slapping against the boat, the drumming of the stars hiding behind the daytime sky. At the place where the sky met the sea he saw a flooded shoreline dominated by a giant tree. Its branches, filled with arcs of blue lightning, punched through the sky to the Otherworld. Aeta knelt by the tree, weeping, her head thrown back, eyes closed. As her body collapsed inward and her head touched the ground, lightning in the tree top exploded in fireballs. Wild flames shot upward then coursed back down through the heart of the tree. The halves screeched as they broke apart and crashed to the ground. When the smoke cleared, Aeta was gone, the tree destroyed. Only the yellow-eyed boat still rested on the flooded shore. A single swift perched on its higher edge. In the water beyond, darkness rolled toward the island like a cloud. At its edge was a war canoe with five men aboard.

"Aeta!" Nulo tried to run toward the spot where she'd been, calling over and over, trying to get his feet unstuck. "Where are you?"

"Nulo, it's all right. You're safe here, with us."

He opened his eyes, more confused than before. Images of Nina and the sky above her crashed into those of Aeta and the smoking tree. "The guardian tree is destroyed! I have to help her!"

* * *

Several days later, Tahn spotted a promising island, and the men pulled the boats up on a short beachfront. Nina offered to help her mother, but Darna waved away her concern.

"The ferns I need should grow close by. You'll be able to see me."

But immediately past the beach, Darna found nothing useful, so she struggled up the hillside into the forest, pushing thick branches out of her way while insects buzzed, diving into her hair, settling on her bare arms and legs. A family of grey monkeys watched. Parrots squawked at her approach. Farther up the hill, giant ebony and teak trees stole the sunshine, leaving her in green darkness. She leaned against one of the great trunks, watching thin streams of light pouring through the canopy openings to the forest floor. *I should have brought something useful*, she thought, *like an alarm conch or dye powder. I didn't even bring any water. It seemed simple: find and bring back the wormwood fern. But it isn't simple.*

"I wonder if I could persuade you to move away from the tree," a voice said.

She jumped, suddenly alert.

"It's just the caterpillars behind your neck," the voice continued. "They don't look like much, but their spines are poisonous."

Darna sprang away from the tree bearing the bright green caterpillars with blue dots, jumping again when she realized the source of the voice was close behind her. A hunchback bent his head sideways to look up at her. Faded tattoos marked his forehead and cheeks.

"You're sick," he said. "Fever."

She squinted, trying to see what was real and what wasn't. "Yes," she said finally. "One of our group is already sick. I was trying to find some wormwood fern, but I got lost."

"The fern you want grows closer to the shore, where it has more light."

"Forgive me," Darna stammered, "but who are you? How are you here, in the middle of the rainforest, on an island far from – anywhere?"

One side of his mouth turned up in a wry smile. "How am I, indeed. I am because I chose to be." He looked past her into deep woods. "I was abandoned," he continued after a moment. "Most defectives are abandoned. Then people can assume that they went away. I didn't, though I considered it for a while."

Darna studied this bent figure with the bald head, wondering what lay behind that bland expression. It was hard to tell how old he was; he had the bearing of an old man and the face of a youth. "I am Darna," she said.

Again the small smile. "You can call me Hao. My real name is too long to bother with."

"I'm tired," Darna said. "And I didn't find the ferns."

"Yes, but you must walk out. I'll get your ferns." He handed her a short staff. "Follow me."

She watched his bent form recede into the bush and trudged after him with no idea where he was headed or whether he was friend or foe. The trip back to the shore took so long that she wondered if the island was bewitched by this man, so that there was no way out. Ahead, he moved on in his rocking gait and said nothing as they pushed through spreading palms, tree ferns, twining creepers, drooping bell flowers.

She remembered a story her mother told about an old man who lived alone in the forest. One day, he came upon a toad being eaten by a big snake. The toad's hind legs were in the snake's mouth, but his head and front legs were free. When the old man walked by, the toad pleaded with him to save his life.

"But the snake must eat too," the old man said.

"Then find something else for it to eat," the toad answered.

"But what if that something else begs me to save it?"

"Give the snake something with no voice," the toad answered.

The old man went looking for something to give the snake.

"Hurry!" cried the toad.

The old man came upon a rat, which tried to bite him; a mouse, which squeaked loudly; and a turtle, which had just laid her eggs in the sand.

"You have so many eggs," the old man said to the turtle. "May I have two?"

"What will you give me in return?" the turtle asked.

"This gemstone," he said, removing a shiny dark stone from his sash. "You can carry it on your head; it will glow when you are in the presence of poison, and it will help you find your way back home, no matter where you go. It's very valuable."

The turtle considered this offer, then nodded. The old man put the gemstone on the turtle's head, and it immediately sank inside, disappearing completely before she lumbered back to the sea. He gathered up two eggs, covered the rest, and patted down the dirt.

When the old man returned to the desperate toad, he placed the eggs in front of the snake's nose. In the instant it opened its mouth to grab them, he snatched the toad out. After that, the old man and the toad became friends, of a sort, and the toad taught the old man about the plants in the forest, especially the ones that were useful medicines.

Darna looked at the figure brushing through the broad leaves in front of her. "Do you have a toad friend?" she asked, aware even as she asked the question that it sounded slightly odd. "I mean, do you have a friend that is a toad?" That didn't sound much better.

He turned and gave her that odd half-smile. "We'll take care of that fever. You'll feel better soon."

* * *

Laido built a smoky fire to help Darna find her way back and blew the alarm conch repeatedly. He hadn't watched where she'd gone and found tracking difficult in the heavy growth near the shore. Tahn and Ryu said they'd help, but all three men were sick, moving heavily. As he backtracked to start over, Laido looked up the beach and saw Darna stumbling on the rocks. A stranger grabbed her arm when she fell. With a shout, he ran down the beach to her, pulled her toward him and drew his knife on the stranger.

Hao set down a bundle of cut ferns and backed away. "I'll just leave these for you."

"No!" Darna shook her head. "He's good. He's the toad's friend."

Too tired to take another step, she sat down where she was.

Laido looked to the hunchback for an explanation. "I don't understand."

"She got lost while looking for medicine ferns."

"Hao," Darna began, "found me and the ferns – and you."

"Thank you. I appreciate your help," Laido said after a moment.

Hao nodded. "I'm happy to give it."

The sickness swept through the group, striking one after another with shaking chills and nausea, leaving them limp and weak when they emerged from the fever spike, then striking them again. By the time Darna recovered, four days had gone by. As she stood up on wobbly legs, she saw Hao, Fuhua, Laido, and Colbee on a flat section of beach talking, waving their arms, and pointing to something in the sand. Though she wanted to join them, it was too far, so she sat down and watched the sea.

After a while, Laido joined her. "Welcome back. We were worried about you."

"My legs don't -"

"They'll recover. It takes a little while," he said. "And you were right about the ferns."

"I didn't find them. Hao did."

"He calls you the toad lady. What does that mean?"

Darna only smiled.

On the sand, Hao built a map. He put down palm branches for the big islands and shells for the smaller ones, sticks for currents, twigs for harbors, thorny seed casings for dangerous places, red flowers for each person in his network of discarded people.

"It can be done, what you want to do," he said to Laido, Colbee, Ryu and the others, "but there are only some places the sea will let you pass through. Here," he said, jabbing a stick into the sand, "is our island. We'll call it Steep Beach. You want to go out here."

He drew a long line to one side. "But you can't. Not from here. The currents would carry you right back. You would need to go up and back," he said, marking a dotted line around a circle of islands. "The currents there are very strong and changeable. You need to watch the waves, read their direction. First, the waves will go in two directions, arguing with each other. Then, beyond that, you will see your current."

Drawing a curved line around the edge of the map, he went on, "At night, you'll need to follow four rising star points, starting with the tail of the Great Bird." He made seven marks in the sand.

"We call it the Seven Warriors," Laido commented.

"And for us, The Snake Bird," Colbee added.

"In any case, once it's risen, you'll need to turn to keep the Great Bird's wings directly in front of you." He drew the three-star line that marked the bird's ribs and the two bright stars that marked the tips of its wings.

"The Hand," Laido said, pointing to the line of three stars and the bright stars below it.

"The names don't matter," Ryu broke in. "If I can see any section of the night sky, I can fill in all the rest. In the daylight, I can see clouds over islands, birds returning to roost, changing colors of the shallow water over the reef – all the standard markers. I can smell land, even before I see the faint gleam on the horizon. I can find my way."

Hao smiled. "And what will you do when you cannot see the sun or stars? How will you know where to steer?"

Ryu hesitated. "How do *you* know? Can you see in the dark?"

"No. But there are other tools that are useful."

"I can return to any island I've seen," Ryu snapped, "and find this island you're talking about – Seal Island."

When no one replied, Ryu turned and left.

"He's a good navigator, but he's young," Laido remarked, turning back to Hao's map. "What tools do you recommend?"

Do you have a direction marker and a speed rope?"

"What are those?"

"They're easy to make. You probably don't even need the direction marker, but when it's hard to read the waves, it's useful. Hollow a gourd, fill it halfway with water, and tie it to a length of twine. You want it to ride in the water, not be blown about by the wind on the surface. The gourd will be pulled in the direction of the current. Simple.

"The speed marker is also useful. Weave a long length of twine and lay it out on the sand. Then walk its length. Every twenty paces, stop and tie a big knot. It's a good idea if it's dyed a different color from the rest of the rope, so you can see it easily in the water. When you are going well, let out the rope. The current will take it out of your hand quickly if you are going fast and slowly if you're not. You can measure it by counting the number of knots that play out in ten heartbeats. It's also useful for taking depth measurements. Just tie a stone to the end and count the knots as you drop it."

The group stared at the map until Jin broke the silence. "It seems impossible now."

Fuhua disagreed. "Perhaps Nulo's dancing stone could also help us. I'll get it."

The stone fascinated Hao as it turned in its bowl of water. "I've seen something like this only once before. It was suspended in the middle by a string. The navigator simply held the string out from himself to read it. This would be useful, I think, when clouds block your view of the sky."

Laido studied the map and its maker. "Would you come with us?"

"I'm pleased you asked, but it would be a decision for the group to make." Hao retraced some of the lines on the map. "There's more you need to know, things you would need to consider about the whole trip. Perhaps it's best that I tell everyone about them."

"We'll eat first," Darna announced.

After the meal, the whole group, including Ryu, gathered around Hao's map.

"It's too much," Ryu complained. "The rainy season will arrive soon, catching us when we're beyond any sheltering island. The storms will push us out into the void."

Goh worried, "Maybe no one is allowed to go out there. Where's the honor in dying at the edge of the sea?"

Hao didn't try to persuade. He waited. Finally, he said, quietly, "Sea turtles swim great distances in the sea every year. So do whales. People have done it before you. It is difficult, and yes, many died. You'll die someday, too. Perhaps it will be here. Perhaps on the sea. Perhaps in a new land. The question is what you do with the life that you have. You are exceptional. Why would you settle for an ordinary life?"

The murmurs stopped.

"There's more you need to know," Hao went on. "You'll need to bring everything with you, including living plants, water, tools. The greatest challenge is a long stretch of nothing you'll need to cross. Those who have crossed it describe it as the flattening of time. The sun stays motionless in the sky. You see nothing except the ocean; at night, nothing but the stars, which reach all the way down into the sea. People can go mad out there. They're used to things that are scaled to man, where man is important. A person on the great ocean is a speck, a nothing. You must be able to deal with that. If you cannot, you will perish, and the sea and stars will not notice."

After a long silence, Jin said, "How do you know these things? Do you know anyone who has crossed the void on this route?".

"Yes," Hao said. "And he returned."

"Why did he return?"

His people were here, and he missed them, so he returned, but only to the edge. He stays there, between worlds, forever drawn in both directions. He understands how others are drawn to it. He'll help us on our last stop before the void."

"And you?" Nina asked, "Are you also one of those?"

Hao studied her. "Being one of the discarded, I do whatever I want. Nothing I do is recognized or rewarded."

"That's not exactly an answer."

"What do you know of the other side of the void?" Nulo asked.

"It is a land of choices. When you've passed the flattening of time, the currents will divide again. You must choose to go north or south. After that, you must choose where to land and what to do with every day you are given."

"Every day is a choice, no matter where you are," Ryu noted. "Why is the choice more important somewhere else?"

"Perhaps because you risk so much to get to the edge of the world," Kiah commented. "The life must merit the place."

"I'm going," Jin announced. "Can you teach me these things you mentioned?"

"Of course."

"I'm going!" Fuhua shouted. "Who knows what treasures we'll find along the way?"

"I am too," Liwei added. "How could I refuse?"

"I'm going if Kiah will go with me," Colbee said.

She gave a little smile as she nodded. "Yes, to both."

Jin, Tahn, and the other Guards all agreed.

Laido and Darna agreed, as did Nina.

"If everyone else is going, I am too," Ryu added after a moment.

"I'm very sorry, my friends. I can't go with you," Nulo announced. "I have to go back for Aeta."

CHAPTER 6
NINA'S CHOICE

"She's on the island where we left Owl Man," Nulo explained. "You don't have to go back. I have to. She's in danger."

"I'll go with you," Nina said.

"What?" her mother gasped.

"I will too," Ryu answered.

"But, you – Nina, you - Maybe we should all go," Darna stammered, looking to Laido for support.

"You'll have many decisions to make," Hao said. "I'll leave you to consider your choices." With a suggestion of a bow, he headed off toward the forest.

The quiet that followed Hao's departure suddenly filled with overlapping conversations.

"How do we know he's not crazy? He's been wandering around the woods by himself. Look what isolation did to Alu and her people."

"He seems to know a lot about navigation. Why would he make that up?"

"Maybe he plans to get us out in the middle of the ocean and then kill us."

"What good would that do him?"

"It's a way out of here for him."

"And into where?"

"He didn't kill Darna. He helped her."

"How would it be different if he didn't help? Would we be better off?"

"Nobody does something for nothing. He's got to have a reason. Maybe he just wants to get back to another island."

Eventually, the speakers broke into smaller groups, but the discussions continued long past nightfall.

Darna took Nina aside. "We can't keep splitting up the family, Nina. Tahn's going with the Guards and the Fat Men. And now you want to go off on your own? You've never undergone the traditional training. You, a young woman, travelling with two young men? Who would protect you? The world isn't always kind to young women. Almost never, in fact. And how would we know where you were or what had happened to you? What if you couldn't find the rendezvous point on Seal Island? What if you got lost? What if you were sick or injured?"

Nina listened to her mother's concerns without interrupting. When Darna had talked herself into silence, Nina sat on her heels in front of her. "Nulo needs to do this, and he can't do it alone. I can help. We need another person to work the wind raft, and I know how. I'm good at it. Papa and Hao can give us a course. Besides, Nulo and Ryu are my friends. I can't think of anyone I'd feel safer travelling with. If we get into trouble, they'll protect me."

When her mother didn't respond, Nina went on, "If Aeta *is* there and she's in trouble, we need to try to save her." Nina reached up and took Darna's hand. "We have restless spirits, Mother. If we were bound by the old ways, we wouldn't be trying to leave the only world we've ever known. I know my choice is dangerous. So is yours. I know you care for me and want to keep me safe from all harm, but you can't, and I wouldn't want it even if you could. I need to do this on my own."

"But there are so many things you don't know -" Darna began.

"I'll learn," Nina said.

"You seem to have grown up in a moment," Darna sighed, holding onto her daughter's hand. "Are you sure about this?"

"Yes. We'll meet you on the Island of Seals."

Darna looked at her daughter as if she didn't quite know the person before her. "Is this just something of the moment? Will you change your mind tomorrow?"

"No."

Darna rubbed away her tears. "If Hao is correct about the Island of Seals, we'll stay there while we gather everything we'll need for the voyage. Colbee wants to build a new boat, I think, and Hao says we need to make a food boat, so we should be there for a good while. You'll join us there?"

"Yes, Mother, just as we said," Nina said, embracing her mother. "I love you very much."

CHAPTER 7
NO SHADOW DAY

Leaning out over the front of his boat, Bokai squinted to get a better view. The shape he saw might be a boat on the shore of the island. "There!" he pointed. "Laido's boats! Just like I said."

The four men behind him stopped paddling while they strained to see.

"I see one. Where are the rest of the boats?" one man called. "If it's Laido's group, they should have at least four."

"Probably around the other side of the island," Bokai answered.

"That boat's half-full of water."

"It's very small," another added.

"They're here, on this island," Bokai shouted. "I know they are."

"The same way you knew how to get us back home?"

Bokai swung around. "You wanted to find Laido's group and I found them for you."

"You've been lost since we left the fire mountain," the man replied, daring Bokai to attack. "Your father would have known how to get home."

"Raidu didn't know much more. Look where he got us."

"Let's get to shore," one of the others said as Bokai twisted around to challenge the speaker. "Killing each other here won't help."

"What happened to the tree on the shore?"

The closer they got, the larger the downed tree became; its split trunk spread across most of the beach.

One man hesitated, his paddle still dripping in mid-stroke. "I don't like that."

"Don't be a fool," Bokai said. "It's a tree. Lightning struck it. That's all. Get the boat to shore."

As they dragged the boat up and stepped over the branches of the fallen giant, the nervous man noticed something else. "No shadow," he said, pointing to the ground next to him. "It's a No Shadow Day."

"Forget that nonsense," Bokai called, striding ahead.

"You can't connect to the ground," the man continued, "so you float in the air. There's nothing behind you. No past. You can't remember how you're related to everything else."

"Fan out," Bokai called. "Look for tracks. Maybe they have a village near here."

One looked at the tipped boat, half-filled with old storm water and seaweed. "No one's used that boat lately."

"Here!" another called, pointing at a set of footprints in the dirt. "They're recent. Small. A child, maybe."

"Usually, children's prints are shorter and rounder. These are more like a girl's footprints."

"I don't see any other tracks. Just those."

Bokai studied the prints in front of him, putting his own foot next to them. "When the mountain exploded, the tiny woman – in the woods, remember? She was leading the line of people down the mountain. Then Owl Man attacked my father, threw his ax when my father's back was turned."

"How do you know this print is hers?"

"I just know. We were led here so I could avenge my father. His ghost brought me here. The woman was there, and Nulo. Then the mountain blew apart and I ran away."

"We all did, Bokai. We would have died if we'd stayed."

"The river of fire reaching my father's body. Owl Man, the traitor. The ax protected by magic buried in his neck. If it hadn't been for Nulo and the girl, my father would have seen Owl Man, would have killed him."

"That was a long way from here," one noted.

"He sent me here," Bokai continued, stepping on top of the small footprint. "He haunts my dreams, crying for revenge. We have to right a terrible wrong. We have to find all of them. Here on this island."

"We don't know who's here."

"They're all here!" Bokai yelled. "All of them!"

"Bokai! I saw someone moving up on the rocks. Over there."

"Show me," Bokai commanded, pushing the doubters out of the way.

* * *

Aeta was watching from the rocks when the boat came into view. She thought maybe a boat had gotten separated from the main group or needed repairs so they had to return. It wasn't until the men pulled the boat on shore and looked at the tracks that she began to worry. By then, she couldn't think of anywhere to hide.

A swift fluttered in front of her, chittering in alarm, pecking at her hair. When she waved it away, it came back, louder and more insistent. It flew off, back to her, off again in the same direction. When she paid no attention, it darted at her bare feet, pecking at them until she followed. She had to run to follow it across the flat rocks and down through the forest, past a tangle of vines to a small opening in the rock. After the swift flew through, she pushed through the entrance, trying to calm her own fears as the light faded into darkness and the opening narrowed. She scraped her shoulders along the walls and hit her head on the ceiling. In the narrowest parts, she had to crawl, extending her hand in front so she could find the opening. When she felt the opening widen, she got to her feet and took a tentative step forward, but the floor dropped down so precipitously she pitched forward, bouncing off the wall and banging her knee on a rock ridge. As she pulled the hurt knee to her, she heard the swift fluttering and chirping. When she tried to see it, she thought she could make out the outline of one side of the tunnel farther down. She started moving again, following the light edge. When it disappeared, she kept on, trailing her fingers along one side so she could feel the twists and turns. She hit her head on a low ridge, ducked underneath. When she lifted her head, she saw light along one rock edge, showing a bend in the passage.

Beyond the bend, the tunnel opened into a large, high-vaulted chamber pierced by a series of shafts that ran up to the surface. Through them sunlight flowed in distinct streams through the chamber, pooling on the floor.

* * *

From the shore, Bokai saw her flee.

"Follow her!" he yelled, running into the forest. "Find her tracks!"

"It looks like a child. Why follow?"

"It's her. If she's here, Nulo's here, and Owl Man," Bokai spit. "She'll lead us right to them."

"I've found tracks. Recent. It looks as if she ran through here."

Bokai pushed the man aside. "Unless she can fly, we have her now."

"Except her trail seems to end right here," the tracker remarked at the cave entrance.

"It can't. She can't go through rock." Bokai slashed at the rock, breaking the shaft of his spear against the stone. Though they all tried, none of them could fit through the narrow opening.

"Maybe she turned into a bat. No Shadow day."

Bokai knocked the speaker to the ground. "Start a fire!" he yelled at the others.

As Bokai cut away the vines around the cave entrance, the men gathered downed wood full of powdery black rot and stinging insects that crawled up their arms.

"I can get the traitors out of there," Bokai said as he tried to get a spark going in the wood. When it wouldn't light, he whirled around to face the watching men. "Bring dry wood from the shore!"

The men scattered.

"This is your last chance!" he yelled into the cave. "Owl Man, Nulo! I might have expected you to hide instead of fight. After all, look what you two did to my father. One pretended to be concerned about him while the other snuck up from behind! The great shaman never warned his victim! Never fought a fair fight. You killed your chief! I could have been chief after him. Now even the air I breathe is bitter. Everywhere I see his ghost. He calls to me in the night, in the storms."

Hearing no reply, Bokai piled the wood against the cave entrance, added a pile of tree fern spines, and struck his spark stone to them. The pile smoldered, sending out thin trails of black smoke, but no flame.

"Where's the dry wood?" he thundered.

A man hurried up with an armful, and threw it on the fire.

"Get more!" Bokai yelled. "All of you! Bring dry wood!"

The men hurried back with more dry wood from the beach and hurled it on the smoking pile.

"Owl Man! Coward! Traitor! Nulo, accomplice, this is for you. Your burned bones will appease my father."

Tongues of fire licked around the bleached wood and burst into flame, swelling up through the pile, popping and cracking, spilling sparks out into the dry peat that ran along the edge of the rocks. One of the men started stamping out rogue fires in the peat, but Bokai pushed him aside.

"Let it burn!" he yelled. "Let it all burn! Hiding in their cave won't save them when the whole area is burning! Smoke will drive them out."

"It's just a girl in there. Only her tracks, remember?"

"They're all there!"

"How could they get in there if we can't?"

"The shaman arranged it somehow. They're hiding in there."

"I told you," one man whispered to his friend, pointing at Bokai's feet. "It's like moon madness."

Bokai stepped toward the man, drawing his knife. "What did you say?"

The man turned and ran. The moment he took off, the others did too, as if they'd been waiting for a signal. Bokai ran after them but they split up, plunging into the thick growth. Dashing after one, then another, he looked for signs of their path, but the forest hid them.

"Run faster! Traitors! If I catch you, I'll kill you with my bare hands, choking the life air out of you. Cowards!"

He heard no reply to his taunts, only the sound of people crashing through the forest.

"Run away, then! Your failure will pursue you forever!" he yelled.

Hands shaking, he built more wood piles and lit them, working his way back from the cave along the dry peat swamps. Black smoke billowed from the burning peat. On the beach, he piled driftwood up in lines, setting them alight and adding dry palm branches that sparked and spit.

With the fires spreading, he worked his way back to the cave, where he found the brush he'd piled up against the entrance undisturbed. No one had emerged.

He threw his head back as he dropped to his knees. "They're dead! Father, I give you their bones as payment. Give me a sign, Father. Accept my gift." Thick smoke turned the trees into dark figures hulking toward him. "Father? Is that you? I can't see!" he choked. "I can't breathe. Father. The fire, it's inside me."

* * *

In the cave, Aeta heard Bokai yelling, setting the fires. As the smoke drifted in, she searched for the few shafts where fresh air came in. The swift was gone.

Trying to avoid putting her weight on the injured knee, she searched for a pointed stick or a rock to make a mark, but the floor was smooth, covered with a fine layer of silt. The walls were also smooth, except for a bumpy bulge at one end of the room. When she looked closer, she realized the bulge was stalactites, not rock.

And they were decorated.

Carefully drawn across their bulges were marks in red and black: concentric circles, wavy lines, circles and dots, wavy lines and dots, wavy lines and circles. Two bones about the length of her arm lay on the floor parallel to the formation. Along the wall next to the stalactites were seven handprints in an uneven row, some in red, some in black, some a negative image with red all around a blank hand. They were all the size of her hands, or smaller, and they were painted just where her hands would be if she touched the wall.

Just beyond the handprints were the other inhabitants of the cave.

In a dark recess three human skeletons lay on a rock slab. The two adults were her size. The child was an infant, with a clay figurine by its feet: a strange humanoid creature sitting on its heels, except the arms were feline front legs, and the hands were paws. The face had large feline ears and eyes, but a human mouth. The two adults had shell necklaces and pectorals. One had a carved greenstone circlet on the arm. Only knots remained of their wraps.

Aeta sank to her knees before the family. "You are my family too. That's why I was brought here, so I could be with you, so you could take me to the Otherworld. I know you should be sung, but I can't remember the songs from my village. Many days ago the sickness killed everyone there."

When she tried singing the song from Brightness Day, her voice came out tiny and broken. Instead, she picked up one of the bones to make a mark on the walls to go with the others but found it wasn't burned at one end to make the black marks; it was purposely cut and finished. At the end of the bone was the same design as the one on the stalactites. She touched the bone to the stalactite, dragged it along its length, then tapped the spot with the mark. It made a surprisingly loud sound. She backed up, considering the marks on both bones. When she tapped another stalactite, a different note filled the cave. She tried it farther up, where the other marks were, getting a clear, resonant tone. Moving to the other marks, she tried tapping each one in the order of the marks on the bones, getting a different sound from each that echoed in the chamber and filled her mind. "The sounds will be your chant," she said to the family as tendrils of smoke dropped into the cave. "I'll play your death song until it becomes mine."

CHAPTER 8
THE SMOKING ISLAND

When Ryu and Nina brought the raft up to the island, black smoke filled the forest beyond the beach. Red flames pierced the fog.

"It's not the same boat as in the vision," Nulo cried, pointing to the boat hauled up on the shore. "It's all wrong. We're too late."

"Look, there!" Nina called, breaking into a run.

Past the broken tree, a figure lay slumped on the burned palm litter. Under the soot, his skin and eyes were red, his hair scorched. His blackened mouth hung open.

Nina took his arm to help and jumped back at the feel of his flesh.

"He's – I think he's -"

"It's Bokai," Ryu said slowly, "Raidu's son."

Nina couldn't look away. "It used to hold a life. Now it's lost its air, like a terrible imitation of him. What happened here?"

"We have to find Aeta," Nulo said. "Please. We'll take care of him later."

"Where should we start?" Ryu called.

"We'll have to wrap our feet and face in soaked cloth," Nina said. "And stick together. If any of us is overcome with smoke, the other two must agree to leave, even if we haven't found Aeta."

Nulo nodded. "I understand."

"Someone came out of the forest up there," Ryu pointed. "They look like Bokai's prints."

The path Bokai had taken out was easy to follow, but it wandered through the fire centers without any clear direction. They followed every twist and loop until they were back where they started.

"Try that way," Ryu pointed. "It looks as if three or four people went through there earlier."

"Are they here now?" Nina worried. "How many?"

"Bokai left with four other warriors when Jin offered -"

"Quiet!" Nulo shouted. "Listen!"

"What do you hear?"

"It's only the sea."

"No, it's not." As Nulo pushed farther into the smoking forest, he heard it again, not the pulse of the sea or the cry of an animal, but a pattern of sounds, sometimes so faint he lost it completely.

"I hear it too!" Nina called.

"It's a messenger made of music," Nulo said.

It pulled them deeper, encouraging them when they fell, when it hurt to breathe. When they reached a flattened hilltop, the distinct melodies resonated clearly, even though they seemed to have no clear source.

"Where?" Nulo cried. They searched the area but found no prints, no broken branches or crushed undergrowth. All around them, charred tree trunks stood mute as stones. Above them a cloud of smoke obscured shadowy branches. Even the birds had gone silent. Yet they could feel the sounds rising around them as the old sun sank lower toward the sea.

"Aeta! Where are you?" Nulo pounded a stone on the ground in rhythm with the music.

The sounds stopped.

Nulo started again, beating the same rhythm on the ground. This time the reply came from underneath them, slow but definite. The tones decorated each beat of the stone, answering, explaining, improving the single sound given.

While Nulo pounded the stone, Nina and Ryu searched, pulling aside the underbrush, signaling their finds to each other, narrowing the range until they found an opening.

"It's much too small to get through," Ryu whispered when he saw the size of the shaft.

"Aeta?" Nina called down the opening.

CHAPTER 9
IN THE CAVE

"It could be a long cave," Ryu said, "with an entrance a long way from here."

"How can we find it?"

"Since the vents are here on top of the hill, let's split up and look for lower entrances while we listen for the sounds."

We should make torches," Nina added. "Soon the sun will be gone."

Nulo didn't wait.

"I'll make several," Ryu agreed.

As he worked his way down the hill, Nulo banged another stone on the earth. In response, Aeta tapped out a reply. Nina passed out torches. They worked in ever-widening circles and found other openings, some almost large enough for a person to squeeze through, but none of them led to Aeta. In the torchlight, every shadow looked like a hole. Rocks hid under thick vines, tripping them as they slid down the hillside.

"Nina, stay by the vent," Ryu called. "At least you'll know where we are. If one of us finds the opening -"

"I'll tell you," Nina finished.

Nina could hear the music from below, but not words. She called down, asking questions, hearing no replies.

In the cave, Aeta tried to remember the path she'd taken through the forest. Mostly she recalled the swift in front of her, its wings swept back in a dark crescent as it slipped between giant trees until it perched on the vertical rock surface at the cave opening. The searchers would never find it, especially in the dark.

Music kept her alive. Lying on the floor as the cave grew darker, she hit the stalactites, building melodies she'd never heard before, assuming they were gifts from the family who lay not far from her and kept her company. She wondered how they died, how they came to be laid out in this musical cave, who had figured out the sounds and labeled the places. Their spirits seemed near, strong, reassuring. She gave them names and talked to them as she made the stalactites ring.

Nulo pulled away thorn vines that covered the rocks. Beyond a jumbled mass of moonflowers, he noticed a rock outcrop that could be an entrance, but as he pushed toward it, something hit him on the top of his head. Stopping short, he held up the torch and looked around. Nothing moved in the circle of light. As soon as he started back toward the outcrop, something hit him again. He spun around, looking for it, and fell over a rock. When he got to his feet and held up his torch, he saw nothing.

"Are you all right?" Nina called

"Something hit me. Maybe an owl," he said.

"Then go a different way," Nina offered. "Maybe it has a nest nearby."

As Nulo held up the torch and struggled to his feet, he realized the thorn vines around him weren't just burned, they'd been cut. Clearly, someone had swung a long blade through the brush, slashing at it.

"Ryu! Come look at this!"

Before Ryu reached Nulo, he saw it too. Someone had been cutting back the undergrowth in a hurry, moving it, dropping pieces. Even by torchlight, he found prints that were far too big for Aeta.

"They're not all from the same person," Ryu said, pointing to one print. "See? This one's shorter and wider, and this one has a roll to the outside."

"What have you found?" Nina called.

"Brush piles," Ryu called. "Stay with Aeta. If we get close enough for her to hear us, ask her to signal."

"I don't know if she can hear me. I can't hear her voice – only the sounds."

Whoever had cut the vines and branches had dragged them to a big pile that hadn't burned easily. Ryu found more prints near the pile. This time they all seemed similar.

"Someone spent a long time here," Ryu noted, pointing to the prints in front of the pile and noting their depth.

Nulo was already trying to pull aside thorn vines that bit him and stuck to his tunic. "Hold up your torch, Ryu!"

Ryu couldn't believe a person could fit through the opening. "Maybe it's just another vent. We should look farther down."

"No, I think this is it. That's why Bokai piled the brush here. To trap her."

"No one can fit through there."

"I might," Nulo said, as he pushed his way into the cave. "You stay here."

"Mark your trail," Ryu advised.

Past the opening, Nulo found the cave widened. His torch provided a thin circle of light that showed Aeta's track in the fine silt. But farther down, the cave shrank to a tube. Nulo had to push the torch along the floor ahead of him as he crawled. At a junction where other tubes opened up on both sides, he stopped, finding no track in the smooth floor, no sign of any kind to guide him.

The rock closed in around him like a cage. He struggled with a fading torch against an enemy made of darkness. Fear tainted the air he breathed. He forgot Aeta and his friends and the world outside where the sun lit the sky. No one could live inside this rock;

it was only waiting for the right moment to crush him. Burning through its last fuel, the torch flared up, offering him a clear view of his prison before it died, leaving him in total darkness. He couldn't move at all.

So faint he thought he willed them to exist, he heard sounds coming from the channel running to his left. High and low tones, pieces of melodies, calling him, speaking to him as the old songs spoke to the children who sang them: teaching them, guiding them. He felt his way along the passage, dragging the spent torch, hanging onto the tones like an invisible rope. Wedging his way through the narrowest part on his belly, he pushed on until the passage started to open up and the melodies became nearer, clearer, more beautiful as they sang to him in the dark. They became his sight, resonating through his bones, filling in images made of sound instead of light. He closed his eyes and breathed in the music, swallowing it, tasting it on his tongue. She was there, in the dark, twisting threads of song, weaving a world, waiting for him.

She reached out for him. "I was supposed to die here, Nulo. But the Others left me the music and you came back for me."

CHAPTER 10
CHOOSING HAPPINESS INSTEAD

All night Nina waited by the shaft, eventually falling asleep right next to it. When the sun rose high enough to give them a little light, Nina dropped torch branches and a firestone down the shaft.

To keep busy, Nina gathered mangos, scorpions, spice berries, crickets and grubs, wrapped them tightly and set them in the fire. Ryu filled the water containers and added fresh fish to the fire. They said little while the wait dragged on. When the food was cooked, Nina pulled it out of the coals and left it on a rock, unable to eat.

"Maybe I should go help," she suggested.

"You can't fit through the opening. Neither can I."

"I could try."

"If you got stuck, you'd block their only way out."

She glared at him. "We have to do something."

"We could help Aeta up the hill."

"What?" Nina spun around as Ryu jumped to his feet.

Aeta and Nulo stood at the mouth of the cave, squinting at the sun.

* * *

That night, Nina, Ryu, Nulo, and Aeta sat on the beach and talked while stars rose high above their fire. The stories they told came out in pieces, mixed in with pieces of other stories, on top of each other and out of order. Aeta said she and her grandfather had been left behind once the others in the boat knew he was dying. After he died, she was alone on the island. Ryu and Nina told about Darna's meeting with Hao, about the plans to meet on Seal Island, about finding Bokai's body.

"Why did Bokai's men take Owl Man's boat, Aeta?" Ryu asked. "Wouldn't their war canoe have been better?"

"Maybe they were afraid of being recognized as his men after they left him," Nina suggested.

"Who would know?" Ryu pressed, but no one had an answer.

When Aeta told them of the breaking of the great tree on the shore and the swift that had led her to the cave, Nulo nodded. "Owl Man. He took you to a safe place, a place you needed to see because of the family buried there."

During a lull in the conversation, as they looked at the stars over the sea, Nulo asked Aeta to be his wife.

"What?" Ryu interrupted. "You're not -" Nina gave him a sharp push. "Not well-acquainted," he amended.

"He means I never underwent initiation," Nulo explained. "An uninitiated male with empty skin is never considered a man."

"Who makes this judgment?" Aeta asked.

"The ones who have become men," Ryu answered.

"Are they here now?"

"Only one," Nina said.

"Actually," Ryu admitted, "I never completed the final phase before we left."

In the quiet that followed, Aeta said, "Am I allowed to answer now?"

"Of course," Ryu said. "I only thought -"

"What did you think?"

"Well, Nulo's father -"

Aeta waited.

"His father said Nulo didn't exist, so he could never be initiated, never take a wife. Isn't that right?"

"Yes," Nulo answered.

Aeta let the silence flood the spaces between them. "The old ways belong to the old villages," she said finally. "It's up to us to make the new ways. I'll understand if you withdraw your offer, Nulo, for I was never properly initiated either. Therefore, perhaps, I don't exist."

"I didn't mean -" Ryu started.

"I don't." Nulo said.

"I wasn't fully initiated either," Nina added.

"Don't what?" Aeta asked.

"I don't withdraw my offer."

"Then my answer is yes. The problem is," Aeta added, "I no longer have the flute you made for me. I gave it to my grandfather so he could have something beautiful in the Otherworld."

"I will make you another."

"May you have a wonderful life together!" Nina cried, clapping her hands.

"On the wings of birds," Ryu added the traditional wish, after a moment.

Later on, Aeta thought she should have shared her secret right then, before anything else happened, should have told them about all the people who'd died in her village — at first the children and old people, then whole families. She should have told them how the villagers thought she was a witch because she never took sick at all, how her grandfather had to sneak her and her brother out by night.

She should have told them, but the moments passed and she didn't.

CHAPTER 11

TOYS OF THE GODS

The Flying Fish, Colbee's boat, moved easily through blue waters. With several days to go before they reached the Island of Crested Iguanas, the travelers had plenty of time to sit and talk.

"You say these kites are made out of bamboo and big leaves, or bark cloth, and they're used for fishing?" Fuhua asked.

"Yes, fishing and many other things."

"And they fly like birds? How can that be?"

Hao pointed up to the Flying Fish mast. "See how the wind blows along the mats?"

"Yes. It pushes the boat, just as it pushes the branches of the palms."

"But does it push the birds?"

"Yes – sometimes," Fuhua hesitated. "They turn their wings just as we turn the mats, so it's more than just being pushed. They use the wind."

Hao held his left hand up flat and pushed against it with his other hand. "With a kite, the wind is trying to push it, but the handler with the string is preventing it from being pushed forward. That push has to go somewhere, so it goes up. The kite rises into the air."

"How would that help to catch fish, other than flying fish?" Fuhua laughed.

"Imagine you're standing here," Hao put a stone on the boat deck. "And I'm standing here," another stone, "and before us is a fast-moving river full of fish." He laid a stick beside the two stones. "If you walk out into the river, the current will sweep you off your feet. If you take a boat, you'll find it hard to stop long enough to catch the fish. So you use a kite. You have a kite shaped like a bird with a long tail - the bird is the ancestor of all kites - and you have two strings, one from the middle of each wing. Or, perhaps, you have one string coming from the heart of the bird. In a nice wind, you can make the bird rise, turn, and swoop down, just as a real bird does. Since you want the bird to fish for you, you fasten bait and a hook on the end of its tail. Then you fly the kite over the river, working the lines so that the bait moves in and out of the water, attracting the fish."

"But what will the fish do, jump onto the kite?"

"In a way. If you're lucky, the fish swallows the bait and hook."

Fuhua pointed to the two stones. "But now you have a kite in the middle of the river, with a fish stuck to it. How does it get back to us on the shore?"

"That part is a little harder. You can't let the motion of the kite stop. It has to be going in a circle, so the hook touches the water when the kite is coming back up. The weight of the fish, especially if it's thrashing, can make it a real challenge to land the fish. Yet I've seen it done."

"I'll believe your fishing kites when I see them."

"Oh, you'll see many kinds of kites on the Island of Crested Iguanas and on Seal Island. Kites were born out here. They're considered the toys of the gods. According to the stories, twin wind gods had a contest flying kites, but the tail of one kite came off, causing it to falter. The older brother was considered the winner."

Colbee came up to join them.

Fuhua said, "You should talk to Colbee about your fishing kites. He can build anything."

"Really," Hao said. "That's good to know."

Colbee ignored the exchange. "So, what's it like on this island we're going to?"

Hao looked up with his sideways smile. "I think you'll find it - memorable. The village has a big festival this time of year, with boat races, kite-flying competitions, music, dancing, intoxicating drinks, and delicious food. Oh, and gambling. They love to gamble."

"Gamble? With what?"

"With whatever you have that someone else wants," Hao answered. "Be careful. It's easy to get tricked into betting. As soon as they see a stranger, they look to see what valuables he has. Then they figure out a way to win them. Not always fairly," he added after a pause.

Fuhua sat back. "You're right. This should be interesting."

* * *

By the middle of the day, when they pulled the boats onto the shore, the beach was already filled with boats of different shapes and sizes, including two with masts and mats similar to theirs, though nothing that looked quite like the Flying Fish. Darna had little interest in the festival and Laido avoided crowds, so they stayed with the boats while the others went to look around. Fuhua brought along some of his treasures. As soon as they stepped onto the beach they met the island's namesakes: giant crested iguanas that hurried up, their bodies swinging side to side, their long tails leaving deep curves in the dirt.

A man standing nearby threw food down on the beach to distract the long-tailed scavengers. "They can stand up on their hind legs," he called, "and their bite hurts. Everybody pays them sooner or later. It's their island. Hurry up. I'll take care of them for you."

"Thank you," Fuhua called as he hurried past.

At the village entrance, food vendors called out, inviting people to trade for their wares. "You!" one called to Fuhua. "Fat man! You must be hungry. I have just what you would like. Come, see," he cried, pointing at his crayfish and crab bites wrapped in seaweed, "Very beautiful and delicious!"

Fuhua looked at the tiny creations, with their lumps of crab meat carefully surrounded by pieces of sweet and sour fruit, all folded into a seaweed cup, so they looked like flowers. "Perhaps later," he said. "I want to see the flying kites first."

"But these are delicious right now."

"You are probably right," Fuhua said, nodding before he moved along

In an open area, musicians played drums, bamboo flutes, and gourd shakers while a singer entertained the crowd with a song about strong warriors, beautiful women, and foolish enemies. A stilt-walker and two jugglers worked the crowd, asking for gifts when they finished their act. By the time Jin saw them, they had quite a collection of large and small shells, two live crayfish, a purple orchid, and a small woven bowl.

At the edge of the music area, a group of men sat half-listening to the music and half-talking to each other, but mostly enjoying a local drink made from trench-fermented breadfruit and palm hearts. They waved to Jin, inviting him to join the group.

"It probably won't kill you," one laughed as he passed a bowl.

After brief introductions, they asked where he was from and where the group was headed. "Few people make Crested Iguana Island their final destination" one remarked.

"From here we'll head to Seal Island," Jin answered. "After that, as far as we can get in the open sea. This hunchback, Hao, said he can help us. He knows people who have gone there."

Several men broke out laughing. One said, "Is that what he's calling himself these days? As good a name as any, I guess, and better than some he's been called."

"What do you mean?" Jin cried. "Are we trusting a liar?"

The man laughed again. "Oh no, he's no liar. He's a very good navigator."

"Then why are you laughing? Tell me!"

"Well," a flat-faced man began, "he's crazy."

"And he can't drink without doing something stupid," added another.

"And he gambles compulsively," put in a third.

"And once he gets out to sea, beyond sight of land, he becomes possessed by demons. The last time he went out there, he tore up his own boat because he thought it was trying to kill him. He had to be dragged out of the water before the sharks got him."

"But don't worry. I hear he's much better now, since they sent him off to live on his own on that island."

"Thanks for the warning," Jin said, looking out into the village center. "I hear a lot of gambling goes on here. Where do the biggest gamblers go?"

"To the kites, of course. That's why most people come here – for the kites and the gambling."

"Yes. The rest is just little stuff, a little fun, a little music, and a lot of chances to relieve the visitors of their valuables."

"Nicely, of course," the flat-face man added. "We want them to have a good time before they leave."

"And to leave their goods when they do!"

Laughter rippled through the group again.

"Don't worry, friend," one said to Jin. "I'm sure he's much better now."

"Why, he'd bet on it."

"You'll probably find him over there, through the trees out by the long beach."

"Good luck!" another called as Jin marched off.

In the market place, Kiah stopped to admire a large, shallow reed bowl with a pattern of alternating light and dark blocks.

"It's beautiful," Kiah remarked to the maker, "but I have nothing of value to trade."

"Try your luck at the kites," the vendor recommended. "Perhaps you could win enough for the bowl."

"I'd like to see them."

"They're on the other side of the trees. The kite-flyers need the wind coming from behind them, so the kites fly out over the water and not into the trees!" The woman laughed. "Come back and see me afterwards. Perhaps we can work out something else. It's nice to talk to someone who appreciates my work."

Kiah nodded.

"Oh, and the contests are impossible to win," the woman added. "Only the locals know the secrets."

"How can I win the price of your bowl if only the locals know the secrets?"

"You bet on the people, not the contest. Bet that someone will beat someone else. That way, even if neither one wins the whole contest, you can still win your bet." The woman smiled. "Or make up your own bet. People here will bet on anything, including which ant will cross a line in the sand before another."

Kiah waved to the weaver. "I'll see what I can do."

At the shell games, Tahn, Goh, and Colbee were quickly separated from their treasures. Though they were sure they knew which shell covered the pearl, they were proved wrong time after time. The game master would turn over the chosen shell to show it was empty; the pearl lay under another. The drink the shell master offered them didn't help their concentration.

"I know you do that somehow," Colbee said thickly. "I just can't sort it out."

"Well, friends," the shell master said, "I'm sorry you lost your valuables, but I'll tell you, you can get back everything you lost and add many more treasures if you win at the kite contests. You should give it a try. Just be careful of the side bets. You'll never win on those – too many arguments. Just stick to bets on the big contests. Then it's clear who won and who lost."

"Thanks," Goh said. "We'd give it a try if we had anything left to bet."

"Oh, you can bet anything, not just treasure," the shell master said. "Your fine knife, for instance," he said to Goh. "A ride in your boat perhaps," he added, winking at Tahn. "Anything of value to someone else."

"We need to get going," Tahn snapped.

"Wait! We have to see the kites!" Colbee objected.

"The kites! Yes, we have to see the kites," Goh added. "I wonder what kind of bet I could make with my knife."

Liwei and Fuhua joined the group watching the kite-flying contest at the far end of the beach. The contestants, mostly young men, played out lines wrapped around sticks that tethered kites rising into the brisk breeze: bird shapes made from bark cloth dyed red or yellow, very light kites made of single huge leaves, mat kites with woven designs of star figures, birds, or fish, kites with long streaming tails of coconut fiber, kites with short fluttering tails made of feathers, kites with no tails at all. Most had protective charms attached. A few dangled cut bamboo pieces that whistled and shrieked in the wind.

Hao appeared at their side. "A beautiful sight, isn't it?" he said, slurring slightly. "This is the highest flight contest."

Liwei studied the soaring kites. "How would they know which kite is the highest? Some kites may be smaller and only look higher."

"Yes, indeed. That's why the contestants mark their line. Every twenty paces, they put a mark, light or dark, so the judge can measure how many marks high the kite is." Hao laughed. "Of course, the theory has many flaws. A child's stride is shorter than an adult's, so twenty paces would be a shorter space. Everyone uses the smallest child they know to mark the line, even babies."

"How would they measure it once the kite is in the air?" Fuhua asked.

"Well, they're supposed to measure when the contestant brings the kite down, but, you see, that allows other things to happen in the meantime. If a kite never comes down, it doesn't count."

"I don't understand," Liwei began. "You mean -"

"Oh, you'll see," Hao said, waving as he backed away. "Now, you'll have to excuse me. I need to talk to someone."

In the sky above the beach, kites started bobbing and shifting like attacking birds. Many of the flyers had coated their lines with fish glue and attached splinters of sharpened stone. When they moved their lines, they sent their kites veering sideways, slicing across their opponent's lines. When two fighting kites were disabled, the handlers traded insults, then moved on to kicking and pushing. Bets on the fight flew back and forth through the cheering crowd. Friends of the combatants handed off their kites so they could join the fight. Once the melee grew, more flyers tethered their kites so they could join the fray. One boy then ran along the line and cut the lines to all the tethered kites, which then flew off, accompanied by the cries of the flyers, as the boy disappeared into the woods.

Only four of the original twelve flyers still had kites aloft.

The gambling intensified. People yelled bets up and down the beach. Fuhua wondered if anyone was keeping track of all of these bets and how someone knew if a bet had been accepted. When the four flyers kept their kites aloft for a while, the betters began running up behind the flyers, yelling insults at the ones they wanted to lose. A few gamblers poked the flyers, trying to distract them or make them fall. In response, other gamblers ran in to protect their flyers, and more fights broke out. People bet on the secondary fights as well, yelling their offers of beautiful gems, or their family's lodge pole carvings, or fish nets, or sexual favors, or shark teeth strings, or stingray spines, whatever someone else might find valuable.

Then one kite string broke, severed by another. Freed from its tether, the kite floated away, followed immediately by a gasp from the crowd as many saw their winnings disappear. Some denied they had ever made those bets, which brought on more fighting and more betting on the fights.

The last three flew their kites in a fight to the finish. No one cared about which was the highest. Knowing the winner would be the one that vanquished the others, the flyers maneuvered to slash at other lines. When they couldn't cut the lines, they tripped, jabbed, kicked, or ran into their opponents. All the while, the brawlers continued their fights, right into the paths of the flyers, who flew their kites against their opponents and darted around the fighters. When the feather tail of a large leaf kite got tangled in a mat kite's line, the mat flyer wrenched his line sideways, pulling his kite away, tearing the tail section from the leaf kite. The wounded kite floundered, making great awkward spirals downward until it plunged into the sea. While the crowd screamed, a betting frenzy erupted as the gamblers realized the contest was down to two kites.

Not for long. The extra weight of the defeated leaf kite pulled the mat kite dangerously close to the sea. In a last attempt to win, the mat kite flyer slashed at the remaining kite, a bird with a long serpent tail. Despite the attack, it flew ever higher and farther, until it hovered way out over the sea, watching the chaos on the shore with a red eye.

The betters pushed forward and yelled louder, both for and against the great bird kite in the distance. Its supporters formed a protective circle around its flyer, pressing closer and closer to him, making it hard for him to manage his kite. The mat kite flyer tried to cut the line again before his kite crashed into the sea, but as his kite ditched, the judge of the event, who had been nowhere in sight for most of it, stepped forward and proclaimed the bird-serpent kite the winner.

Self-proclaimed winners mobbed the boy as he hurried to bring in his kite, cutting his hands on the sharp line as he looped it around the stick. The crowd rushed to see the kite, grabbing at it, fighting over it, lifting up the boy and carrying him along awkwardly. Powerless, he dragged his kite behind him.

By the time Colbee and Tahn found Jin, the next contest, The Egg Roll, was already underway. Each contestant was given a fresh bird egg, a handful of flexible bamboo shoots, and a coconut in the husk. They could use whatever tools they could find or borrow, including awls, hatchets, knives, picks, hooks, and drills. While others competed in the Highest Flight contest, they built protective cages for the eggs that would allow them to survive, intact, while the cages were rolled. According to the rules, which no one followed, the first roll was down a gentle slope that ended at a rock cliff. Each contestant rolled another contestant's egg, so the roll was not a gentle push. If the cage didn't roll at all, the contestant was eliminated. Past that, anything was worth a try.

Unlike the Highest Flight contest, this one included several girls and women as well as men and boys. Many of the women were good weavers who could build a sturdy cage quickly.

Colbee wandered down the line of contestants, fascinated by the designs. One woman had built a circular cage of bamboo, opened the coconut, extracted the meat, inserted the egg, tied the coconut back together with coconut fiber, and put the coconut in the circular cage.

A girl wove a coconut fiber web around the egg and then tied the ends of the web to an oval bamboo cage, so the egg's web was attached to the cage at six different points.

A boy hollowed out the coconut husk, removed the coconut, chopped it in half, filled it with coconut fiber, inserted the egg, and tied up the coconut inside its husk. The bamboo shoots he wove into a nice sitting mat for himself.

A woman put the egg inside a small cage, then built a larger cage that she stuffed with coconut fiber before inserting the smaller cage.

A man wove the bamboo into a long tube, put the egg in the hollowed coconut, then wrapped the long tube around the coconut several times and secured it with coconut fiber.

Another chopped the coconut in half, inserted the egg in the liquid, tied the halves back together and then drilled small holes at an angle all over the surface of the coconut. Through these he threaded the slender bamboo reeds in loops, so that the finished product looked like a flower with bamboo petals sprouting in all directions.

Others filled the coconuts with various items not allowed, like feathers or bark cloth, to cushion the eggs.

Gamblers wandered up and down the line of contestants, asking about the designs, so it was easy for Colbee to talk to the people building the cages.

"The hard part," one boy said, "is the fall down the cliff. That kills most of them."

"So what do you have to do to protect the egg?"

"Assuming it gets to the cliff," the boy laughed, "I'm hoping I can keep the egg from breaking on the coconut shell or the cage. Of course, if both of those break, I'm in trouble."

Colbee looked at the boy's sturdy cage. "What do you mean 'assuming it gets to the cliff'? Won't it roll that far?"

The boy looked up at him. "You must be new here. Of course it will roll, but usually, someone hits it, or throws it off the cliff."

"I didn't know about the complications," Colbee said. "It sounds more like an Egg Roll with Random Dangers to me."

"That's what makes the contests fun," the boy said. "Want to bet on my kite?"

"Sorry, I have nothing left to bet with. Good luck!" Colbee called as he left.

He wished he had something to bet, just because he wanted to be part of the celebration. He wondered whether anyone ever collected on any of these bets, or if by the end of the day, everyone owed everything to everyone else anyway, so it didn't really matter. Maybe it just allowed them to ask favors later, simply by reminding someone of the kite festival wagers that were never paid. Probably no one had a very clear memory of anything they'd done at the festival.

The contestants were lining up for the Egg Roll when Jin finally found Tahn and told him what the men had said about Hao.

"It's hard to tell what's real here," Tahn said. "Everyone is crazy. I wouldn't worry about it. They were probably just trying to scare you."

"They did a good job," Jin remarked, studying the contestants and their egg cages. "Where is he, anyway?"

"Hao? I don't know. I haven't seen him in quite a while."

The first contestant handed over her egg cage to a man who rolled it down the gentle hill. Before it had gotten far, two boys ran out, one kicking the cage, and the other kicking the kicker. Forgetting the egg cage, they fought until they were pulled off by onlookers. The egg cage bounced down the rocks and sailed over the edge of the cliff, falling from ledge to ledge, breaking into pieces. At the bottom, a girl collected the pieces of coconut and bamboo, all smeared with broken egg.

The next contestant offered to roll his own egg, but the official took it from him and set it rolling down the hill. It was barely an arm's length down the hill when a man ran out to kick it, but he was knocked over by another. A third came out while they were fighting, pushed them out of the way, and booted the cage over the cliff. It too suffered from the fall from the cliff, leaving a trail of feathers and coconut fiber behind as it hurtled down the rocks, splitting open near the bottom, leaving a trail of yellow splatter on the rocks.

One cage never made it to the cliff edge. One of the fighters fell so hard on it that it split open along its seam, spilling its contents across the hill as the gamblers fought over it.

One survived intact all the way over the cliff and down to the rocky shore, but when the coconut was opened, the woman found the egg inside was broken.

The betting began to pick up as the field of contestants narrowed. Even Colbee got into it, betting his fine knife that the boy he had spoken to would win. The one accepting his bet was none other than Hao, who leaned against a rock to steady himself.

"Wonderful, Colbee. Good bet. And there are so many other opportunities!" he said before he pushed himself up and moved away.

Colbee wasn't sure what Hao had bet in return, if anything, but he watched with new interest as one egg after another came to grief on the cliff rocks. Only the double-cage design worked, although the outside cage was broken in the fall. Then the egg in the coconut in the husk made it to the bottom successfully, despite a hard bounce on a rock ledge. The cage with the loops of bamboo also arrived at the bottom with the egg intact, though the loops were badly damaged in the fall. That was the egg cage Colbee had bet on, so he walked up to congratulate the boy.

"Oh, it's not done yet," the boy said, with a grin. "But it was a good first round."

Colbee looked at the hacked apart egg cage. "What else is there?"

"Now we have to make it float," the boy said.

"On the water?"

"No, in the air," the boy said, picking up his egg and the remains of the cage. "We drop them off the cliff."

"Can't you just do what you did before?"

"No, it would just fall then."

The three winners set to designing something that would float down the cliff. The double-cage winner reworked the bamboo into two curved mats with the egg braced between them. The coconut fiber she stuffed into the lower sides of the mats.

The whole coconut winner reassembled the coconut and husk as he had before and then took the mat he had made to sit on and attached it to the coconut husk with long twined coconut fibers that ran from the four corners of the mat to holes he drilled through the long ends of the husk.

The loop cage winner made the bamboo loops into wings; the whole thing looked like a bird with a small, fat body and long wings.

As the gamblers shouted at their favorites, the winners lined up on the edge of the cliff. Spectators were not allowed near the cliff edge, so some stood on the shore below and some cheered from behind the competitors. The betting was fierce. Colbee, with nothing left to bet, just yelled with the others.

First to go was the girl with the curved mats. She held the egg cage aloft while people screamed all around her. When she released it, the wind caught it and it floated nicely, but then the edge of one of the mats caught on a rock ledge. With a crunching sound, the mat tore off the coconut and the cage careened down the rocks, smashing its precious cargo before it was even halfway down. A sympathetic groan went up from the crowd at the bottom.

With the field down to two, the gamblers became frantic, yelling bets multiple times. Again, a protective line formed around the competitors, but the din was terrible as the crowd pressed ever closer.

When the loop cage winner released his winged creation, it soared out away from the cliffs until the weight of the coconut made the front dip down and it crashed into the shore rocks. Both the coconut and the egg were shattered in the fall. Colbee found himself hoping the third one would break also. Then they would have to try again. He joined the throng yelling at the one remaining contestant, until there was an indecipherable wall of noise around the single boy on the edge of the cliff.

The boy held out the coconut husk with its attached mat while the crowd screamed behind him. Then he launched it. The crowd strained to see. No one was saying what had happened. There was no sound from below either. Some ran to the cliff edge.

"What's happening?"

"It's floating, I guess," someone yelled.

Some called to the people below. "Can you see?"

A man on shore yelled, "It worked! It didn't break!"

"It's in one piece! He won!"

More yelling on the cliff top. People forgot their bets and ran down to the beach to see for themselves. The judge took the husk apart, pried out the coconut, and removed the intact egg. The crowd roared and swept the boy up, hauling him by his arms and legs in an attempt to carry him back up the hill in glory. They threw flowers and coconut husk pieces, congratulating him, yelling at him, yelling at each other, stumbling up the hill, tripping over each other's feet. By the time they had made their way back up to the top, the fishing contest had started, so they set the boy down and headed off to the lagoon.

Colbee went looking for something to eat at the vendors' market, where he met up with Goh. They were trading betting stories when Jin and Tahn joined them, and the talk turned to Hao's strange reputation.

"Where is he, anyway?" Jin asked.

"Hao? Colbee asked. "I haven't seen him since he took my bet on a losing Egg Roll."

"What?"

"One of the contests. I lost."

"I'm suspicious," Jin said. "I heard he's crazy."

"Probably. I think everyone here is!"

"No, I mean it. I don't think we can trust him, especially out at sea."

"Perhaps not," Colbee answered, "though I don't know what he could do against all of us. He may be crazy, but I don't think he's vicious."

"No," Jin hesitated, "I don't either. Still, we're putting a lot of trust in someone we don't know."

Goh finished his meal with a satisfied sigh. "We have lots of time to find out about him. Let's give him a chance before we decide he's dangerous. Maybe the rumors are just gossip from drunks."

"Maybe," Jin said.

CHAPTER 12
THE FLYING MAN

On the boat, Laido and Darna were surprised to find a group of people gathering nearby, asking if they could come aboard to look around.

"No one is allowed on board," he told the strangers.

Laido's refusal didn't stop people from milling around the boats, peering into them and asking each other questions about the value of the boats and their contents. When the crowd pressed closer, Laido took up his knife and spear, ready to strike the first one to set foot on the ship. Darna wielded her double-edged knife. The crowd backed away but settled on the beach to continue their debate on the combined value of the boats. When the sun was getting old and the others started returning to the boats, their presence pushed the onlookers a little farther away. Fuhua and Liwei helped Hao to the shore, but since he was too drunk and sick to manage getting on board, they left him on the beach.

In the morning, Hao was gone.

"I knew this would happen!" Jin cried.

"What? We don't know what happened," Laido replied. "Let's get the whole story first. Then we can decide who's to blame."

"If there's trouble, Hao's at the bottom of it," Jin retorted. "I knew it yesterday."

"And what would you have done, Jin? If you know a storm is coming, you still can't stop it."

"Well, I could have stopped this storm if I had tied up that hunchback." Jin swung around, glaring at the group on the shore. "What are all of these people doing looking at our boats?"

"So far, just looking," Laido said.

"Let's get off this island," Jin said. "Just leave him here. He's happy. He can get drunk and gamble and act stupid. People here love that. They'd laugh at him and he'd never even know."

Darna stepped in. "That's very harsh. Hao saved my life. Probably he saved all of us. Give the man a chance, Jin."

"Fine," he snapped, "but I'll kill any of these fools who try to get on the boats."

"They know that," Tahn said. "That's why they're way over there."

The next day, when the sun had warmed the land, the festival organizer asked for a conference with Fuhua and Liwei on shore. At one point, the organizer had both men stand side by side, then pointed to Liwei and nodded. He then moved off and motioned for the crowd to leave the vicinity of the boats, which they did, slowly.

Liwei called Laido to join them, and Darna jumped into the shallows after him.

"I've been on that boat too long," she said by way of explanation. Most of the others joined her.

"They've taken Hao hostage," Liwei explained to the group. "He's not hurt. They just wanted to be sure he didn't leave before he had made good on his bet."

"Why? What did he bet?" Jin called.

"It's a little complicated. Apparently, he kept losing bets at the kite contest, so the next bet had to include everything he owed the last person, plus more. Of course, he lost all of them except the bet he made with you, Colbee, and he didn't want to take your beautiful knife, so he made one big bet that would pay off all of the others." Liwei paused.

"And?" Darna pressed.

"And he bet that Colbee could make a man fly," Liwei said.

Colbee was the first to find his voice. "What? He bet what?"

"No one would believe him, at first, so Hao described the Flying Fish, saying it was a boat, but it moved like a fish in the water and a bird in the air. He probably got to bragging a little. A lot, maybe."

Laido said, "So that's why they were looking at the boats?"

"Not exactly," Liwei sighed. "When no one would believe him, Hao bet the boats."

"He what?"

"In return for what?"

"What are we supposed to do if he loses?"

"I told you we should have left when we had the chance. He's a compulsive gambler. He'll take everything we have."

"Only if he loses," Colbee said, half to himself.

"There's one more bit of bad news," Liwei said.

Laido looked pained. "You might as well tell us all of it."

"It's me. The man. The man who has to fly."

The group looked at the great bulk of Liwei and groaned.

"Could we just cover him up – make him disappear?" Goh offered.

"No," Colbee said. "We have to make him fly. How long do we have?"

"Today. And part of tomorrow. It has to happen before sundown tomorrow."

"That's ridiculous! I say let them keep Hao."

"But -" Darna started.

"Then we need to get going," Colbee interrupted. "Darna, Kiah, I'll need your help with weaving. Goh, I need you to contact as many of the flyers from yesterday as you can find. See if they can bring their kites from the contest or any others they may have at home. We'll need a lot of help making and flying this thing."

"What thing?" Laido asked.

"I'll explain as we go along," Colbee said. "I have an idea."

Fuhua nodded. "That's what Hao was betting on."

"Jin, you and Tahn protect the boats. The people are afraid of you."

"With good reason," Jin grumbled.

"Fuhua, Liwei, scout the area for anything useful: treasure, trade goods, materials for the new ship. If you find anything interesting, talk to the organizer and negotiate a better deal. I want to set the stakes high, a lot higher than just rescuing Hao. If they don't agree to your terms, although I'm sure they will, then we don't have a bet. You have to make them understand that."

"That will make it much more interesting, for everyone," Fuhua said. "We'll see what we can find."

When they had gone, Colbee poked at the sand with a long stick. "Laido, will you help? I have an idea, but I'm not sure how to make it real." He drew a series of lines in the sand. "I've thought of two possible solutions: one huge kite or a series of smaller kites all connected, like this."

The two men hunkered down, drawing configurations in the sand, considering them, talking about what Colbee had seen the day before, what they knew from the mats on the Flying Fish and the wind raft. While they considered possibilities, Goh returned with several of the contestants from the day before, all carrying their kites. Happy to have adults who wanted to listen to them, the boys explained how they made the kites and how the kites flew best. Each had its strengths and its weaknesses. The very light kites were easy to fly in even a slight breeze, but the heavier kites could do more tricks and attack better. Tails helped stabilize the kite, but they added weight. When they were done, Colbee asked the boys to show him how they flew their kites. One by one, they flew their kites, talking as they did.

"Could you tie it to the ground and walk away?" Laido asked.

"Sure," one boy said. "The only problem is the wind. If you've got a really strong wind, it will pull your kite stake right out of the ground."

Another broke in, "And out of your hand, sometimes."

"A big kite in a strong wind is hard to hold onto." A boy held up his hand, showing a long scar. "This is what happens when you try to hold on anyway."

Laido looked at the two designs on the sand. "A giant kite would be hard to hold, even if we tied it down. We'd need a strong rope, stronger than anything we have on the boat, and we'd need to anchor it to something unmovable."

"Like what?" Colbee asked. "A big rock? A boat? How would we get the rope around it? More than that, how would we launch the kite in the first place?"

"Have you ever flown more than one kite on one line?" Laido asked the boys.

"Sure," one said, "but it gets really hard to hold onto more than one."

Colbee looked at the drawings in the sand and started drawing new lines on it. "What if we had several ropes coming down to flyers on the beach, not just one? Wouldn't that spread out the stress?"

"How would the flyers get the ropes?" Laido said. "We can't have people standing out in the ocean."

"We could," Colbee said, "if we had to."

The whole group hunkered down around the drawings, considering different possibilities. One boy said, "What about the cliffs? You could launch from up there and have people down on the shore."

Laido stopped him. "Too dangerous for Liwei. It's better if we have him off the ground but not way off the ground. He just has to fly, not become a fish eagle."

"Pick the spot with the best updraft," Colbee said, "and put the helpers on the extra lines in a big circle at the base. Then they can share the pull, but we don't have to worry about ropes tangling in the kites."

"How will Liwei hang onto the line?"

One of the boys drew a new diagram in the sand. "We had to move people over the river when the bridge was out, so we made something like this. The person sat on this wooden base. Ropes went through holes in the ends, underneath the seat and up the other side. To keep it from being too tippy, we put a shorter wood piece higher up. We got everyone across on it."

Colbee studied the diagram and turned to Darna and Kiah. "We're going to need the strongest rope you can find. Try using regular ropes and braiding them together. It has to hold the weight of Liwei and the pull of many kites. If it breaks, Liwei -"

"Liwei breaks," Darna finished as she looked at the diagram. "How will his sling be attached?"

"Good question," Colbee said. "Can you weave a handle right into the rope? And a big strong wooden ring into the handle?"

Kiah drew a design. "Like this?"

"I think it has to be a smaller handle and a bigger ring," Laido said. "If the handle is too big, only the bottom section will take the weight."

"Where can we find the ring?"

"Maybe one of the boys can help us," Colbee said, turning to the collection of keen faces behind him.

One bowed. "I will get it for you, Uncle."

"You can call me Colbee. And you are -"

"Fen. But I would rather be called Colbee."

"Then how would anyone know which Colbee was being called?"

"I would say I was Colbee second."

Colbee sent the boy off with a smile to find the important wooden ring.

Laido smiled. "You may have gotten yourself into something there, friend."

"I'll worry about it later. First, we have to make a fat man fly. Laido, will you and the boys familiar with the river transport make the sling for Liwei? And give Darna some idea of how long the rope needs to be? The rest of you boys, can you bring all the good kites that people are willing to lend us? I don't know what we can offer them in return except the chance to try something brand new. Maybe it will even work!" Colbee laughed. "And if it doesn't, people will still talk about it!"

As the boys started for their homes, Colbee called after them, "If you can find some men who would be willing to help hold the lines, tell them to meet us at the launch site. Then we might actually be able to bring Liwei back down again!"

When they had gone, a single girl walked up to Colbee but did not look directly at him. "I also flew a kite in the competition. I know about kites and would like to help."

Colbee stopped and studied the slight figure before him. Her dark curly hair, dark eyes, and broad flat nose reminded him of the children from his homeland. "Do you know how to add things that would make this series of kites look dramatic? Wings, shells, maybe, or long tails?"

"Yes, Uncle. All of those."

"And could we add them without adding too much weight to the kites?"

"You are already making a fat man fly. A few decorations will not make a difference, except to those watching," she said.

Colbee nodded. "Very true. And you are - ?"

"My name is Light of Wind. And there are many things we could do. If it is getting dark, we could ask the man to shoot flaming arrows or throw flaming wood pieces. Or, if it is still light, we could attach things that twirl in the wind or make noise in the wind. Some make a frightening noise," she added. "Of course, we could also add tails on the kites, so they look wonderful streaming out into the sky. My people, in my homeland, believe this is the way to talk to the gods – in the sky."

She looked at the sand while Colbee considered her ideas. "How many of these could you make happen, today?"

"Do you want an impressive show?"

"Yes. It has to be so impressive that people won't notice that Liwei doesn't actually fly, he just hovers."

"I understand," she said. "I will meet you where you are launching the kites."

"We're thinking of the cliffs - not all the way up, but far enough to get a good updraft to help us," he called to her.

"Yes, I know. And at least one flyer should be in a boat," she added as she turned to leave.

Darna and Kiah found several women happy to help with the critical task of weaving the rope. One had worked on the rope across the flooded river, so she knew what would hold the weight. Because the lowest part of the rope would take the most strain, they made that first: big, heavy, and strong, with handles sewn in every twenty paces, so the flyers could attach control ropes. For the highest parts of the rope, they used sections of rope they already had and attached them to the lower parts. Darna was concerned the sections would split apart with the strain of the kites, so the women sewed in wooden rings that went through the rope both below and above the joints. If the rope did fray at the joint, the rings would help hold it together, at least long enough for the flight. The strongest ring was the one Fen brought for Liwei's sling, which Kiah carefully sewed into place.

It took everyone to move the heavy finished rope to the cliffs where Laido and Colbee were constructing the sling and assembling the kites. When he saw the rope, an enormous heavy serpent coiled on the sand, Laido sighed.

"We'll never lift that," he said to Colbee. "We might as well fly a boat."

"Let's try it," Colbee said, waving the boys over with their kites. "We'll attach the ropes and the kites and see what happens."

"It won't matter how many kites you attach."

The boys suggested a couple of ways. They could launch the kites first, then attach the line to the rope. Or they could take the end of the rope up the cliff, where the updraft was strongest, attach the kites and launch only the end of the rope until the kites were aloft, then play out the rope.

Colbee liked the second idea, so the boys went up the cliff with a dozen kites and attached them to the line. Then, all together, they lifted the rope into the wind. The kites caught the wind but floundered against the weight of the rope. As the boys looked to Colbee for another idea, the breeze picked up, rising up the cliff face and picking up each kite in turn, launching them all skyward. Colbee yelled and grabbed onto the bottom of the rope, just as the wind took over the kites, pulling them up in a long line straight into the sky. The boys yelled, first in delight and then in alarm. Only a few had remembered to attach their control line as Colbee had advised, so the line of kites dragged farther and faster into the sky.

"Pull!" Colbee yelled to the boys. "Pull on your lines!"

Laido reached up to the wooden ring and grabbed it with both hands, using his weight to drag it down. Darna and Kiah grabbed hold of the handles and pulled, throwing their weight backward, cutting their hands on the rough wood. Other women grabbed hold and pulled too, seven people on the beach and a dozen boys on the cliff all pulling on the rope, trying to bring back to earth the creation they had sent into the sky.

Fuhua and Liwei each grabbed a handle too. And the line of kites stood still, in a momentary balance of forces.

"Perhaps," Liwei said, breathlessly, "my brother should accompany me on my flight."

"There are a few problems to work out," Colbee laughed, "but at least we don't have to worry about lift!"

"No," Laido said, hauling on the line, "some other big problems, but not lift."

With the help of everyone in the area, they pulled in the rope and untied the kites. A few vendors were already setting up food booths near the launch site. Laido asked them to move farther back so they wouldn't get trampled if the support flyers had to move quickly.

"Too far away and no one will see us," one complained.

"Too close and you will be run down, along with your wares," Laido answered.

When the kites were detached and the rope coiled up, Laido said, "We need to try out the sling."

"Of course," Colbee said. "Were you able to put something together?"

Laido nodded as he looked at his crew of sling builders. "Oh, we built a fine sling, but we'll need some help getting it here. We wanted to make sure it would be enough to support Liwei, so it's big and strong, and heavy."

"Let's get it."

* * *

From a distance, Fen's father watched Colbee and Laido, followed by a line of children, heading toward the village center.

"Who are these people?" he complained to his neighbor. "Strangers, that's who they are. They don't belong here. Who gave them a right to order people to do things for them? What made them so powerful?"

His friend agreed. "It's our land. Strangers only stir up trouble, give the children bad ideas."

"We need to stop them."

"I'm ready. And I know some others who'd join us."

Fen's father and his friends watched until Colbee's group left the rope to get the sling. When the area was clear, they dragged the great rope away from the cliff, across the sand and rocks, and shoved it off into the cove on the other side of the spit. Satisfied, they watched it tangle in the seaweed beds and sink. To make sure it wasn't found right away, they swept away the marks the rope made in the sandy ground. Then they left the scene, going back to their homes, making sure their neighbors saw them working outside their huts.

Light of Wind knew. She came to the cliffs to deliver the whirling decorations and found the heavy rope gone. Only some kites remained, anchored with rocks. She followed the footprints and scrape marks in the sand until she lost them on the flat rocks. As she was searching the spot where she'd lost track, Colbee's group arrived, lugging the sling.

"The rope's gone!" one boy yelled.

"Search the area," Colbee called.

But the only tracks they could find were the girl's.

"She must have taken it!"

A boy grabbed her arm and spun her around to face him. "Where is it?"

She wrenched her arm away. "I didn't take it! I was trying to figure out where they took it, but you just walked all over the tracks!"

"Who? Who took it?" another called. "How do you know?"

"Because she took it," the first boy said sullenly.

Colbee stepped in. "What we need is some information." He turned to Light of Wind. "Did you see anyone here?"

"No," she said, pointing. "But I saw tracks leading from over there to the flat rocks. I couldn't see anything past that."

"We'll start here," Colbee said, walking away from the cliffs and pointing to footprints in the dirt. "These are the tracks we want. Spread out. See what you can find."

Only Fen refused to join the group. He went home, sick at heart.

Light of Wind went to find Darna. There were new plans to make, and the day was fading quickly.

* * *

Fen found his father leaning against the wall of the hut, drunk. When he saw Fen, he laughed.

"So, how's the great flying thing going? Oh, not so good? Too bad."

"I saw your tracks, Father, with the twisted big toe. How could you do it? How could you destroy this? It was wonderful! It was the most -"

Before Fen could finish the sentence, his father's hand crashed into his face, sending him reeling backwards. Once his son was down, the father reached for whatever he could find, hitting the boy over and over.

"I didn't destroy something wonderful - You did!" he yelled. "You made me do this! Following this stranger, embarrassing me, forgetting your own people, insulting your own people, insulting me!"

Fen fell against the hut wall as his father raged on.

"Stupid boy, I'm your father, not this stranger, and I *will* teach you to respect me!" He turned to grab his war club as Fen scrambled to the opening. The club crashed into the brace behind him. Fen pushed himself to his feet, made his back straighten, made his legs move, gulped air into his chest, and ran. He could hear his father stumbling outside the hut, yelling, and he could think of only one place to go.

On the boat, Jin was restless. As the sun sank, he heard someone wading into the water next to the boat. Silently, he grabbed his spear in one hand and his knife in the other, but no one jumped into the boat. When he heard a voice, he darted to the edge of the boat but found only a boy standing knee-deep in the water, one hand on the side of the boat, talking to himself.

"Who are you? What do you want?" Jin called.

Fen turned his head, looking at Jin with one eye.

"I need to talk to Colbee," the boy said, working on the words. "The rope. My father – he threw the rope in the sea."

"Stay here for a while," Jin said, noting the boy's battered face. "Tahn will look after you. I'll relay your message."

Soon, they all knew. Colbee's group traced the tracks to the cove, but when they swam out to retrieve the rope, they found it completely soaked and tangled in seaweed, much too heavy to lift with the kites.

Back at the boats, Fen didn't move or speak as the group debated their plan for the next day.

"Maybe Jin was right," Tahn said. "We could still just leave."

Goh said, "It seemed like fun until it turned ugly. Maybe we should leave before it gets worse."

"No. Too many things unfinished," Laido said, without naming Hao or Fen.

"What can we do by tomorrow sundown?" Fuhua asked. "We've used up our store of good will and cooperation here."

Colbee scanned the group. "Where's Kiah? And Darna?"

"Meeting with the girl who flew the kite - I'm not sure where," Laido said. "They should be back soon."

"We are back, and your conversation can be heard all along the beach," Darna said as she and Kiah climbed into the boat. "It's a good thing you weren't planning something secret. Everyone knows we could leave tonight. That's why they're watching. We had a setback. They want to see if we'll run away or see it through."

"See what through?" Laido said. "We lost the rope. We used all the ropes we could find to make it. How are we going to change that?"

"What if you don't do exactly the same thing?" Kiah asked. "What if you have a different flying fat man?"

"They said it had to be Liwei," Colbee pointed out. "Remember?"

"Well, it seems to us," Darna said, looking at Kiah, "that this island is full of gamblers. They don't always stick to the rules, but they want to see something happen. So, we showed everyone there today that we could have made Liwei fly. In fact, we almost sent him off to the clouds! So the question is not whether it can be done; the question now is whether we can keep going even after we've been robbed."

"A fine thought," Laido said, "but we can't make even a sea turtle fly tomorrow."

"Now that would be a sight to see," Goh commented.

"That's what they're counting on," Kiah said, "that we'll put on something really special, a sight to see. We talked to some weavers, and we think we have an idea for tomorrow. It'll be a little different, but still impressive. Enough to rescue Hao, at least. Part of it is Light of Wind's idea."

"Who?"

"She is a very good flyer," Fen murmured.

"And inventive," Darna added. "If half of her ideas work, it'll be quite a show."

"You've given us no idea what you're talking about," Fuhua said, "but I'm intrigued."

"I'm confused," Liwei broke in. "Am I to fly without a rope? Certainly a more challenging proposition and a good deal more frightening."

Darna smiled. "Something that looks like you will fly, Liwei. Does that help?"

"Only a little."

"What do you need?" Laido asked.

"All of your flyers, including their kites and lines," Darna said. "That means you too, Fen, if you would like to be part of this."

"Yes, I would."

"And," Kiah added, "we need long sticks, as long as you can find, six armfuls of dried palm branches, two handfuls of dried seaweed, some spare bark cloth of any size, clam shells, bamboo pieces about the size of your hand, cut sideways, long twisting seed pods, four torches all ready to light, tapa cloth, a whole coconut with the husk, bamboo branches, palm oil, colored clay -"

"We'll never remember all of this!" Tahn cried. "Let's split up the tasks, so each person has only a few things to recall."

"Good idea," Kiah said, "I was losing track of the list myself, and I made it!"

"How do you always talk us into doing these things?"

"I'm a little bit of a gambler, Jin, and I think we can win this one," she said, with the hint of a smile. "Fuhua, you need to re-establish the high stakes. We want to go away with some fine things, especially boat materials, if we make this happen."

"It will be my pleasure," Fuhua said.

* * *

At first light, the groups scattered to their tasks. Perhaps because the curiosity had waned or because the festival was over, the villagers went about their regular work rather than following the flyers. Only a few people watched when the weavers pieced together the tapa cloth or sewed on the coconut husk or patted the seaweed on the top of the husk. With no crowding or shouting or betting, locals came and went as usual and ignored the group working on the cliff.

The rope the women found was too fine to hold much weight, so Darna wove some of the strands together to form the base of the kite line. The line farther up could be finer, but this had to hold all of the extras. Kiah attached the "fat man" they had created from tapa cloth, seaweed, old wraps, and bamboo poles. With some padding and clay paint, he would look convincing, especially if he was flying high above the viewers. To hide his feet, they added sandals from Liwei's own collection.

"I'm bald. I don't like his hair," Liwei complained.

"It's seaweed," Kiah explained. "It adds to the effect."

Above the fat man were the kites, and between the kites were Light of Wind's creations. She attached a string of long, curving seed pods soaked in oil to the main kite rope, and she ran oil-soaked palm leaf ribs between the seed pods, so that once one was burning, it would pass the fire to the next. Between the fat man and the kites, she put baskets of dried palm leaf litter.

"If it works," she told Kiah, "it will be something no one has seen before."

As the day wore on, Laido became concerned that the boys weren't showing up with their kites. It seemed too quiet. Perhaps the villagers thought there was another way to win this bet: for no one to show up to make it happen or to watch it happen. Indeed, no one appeared all afternoon. As the old sun neared the sea, Laido wondered whether he could just rescue Hao and leave, when a single boy appeared with a kite. He struggled up the slope, dragging his kite, but he kept coming, as if he was fighting an invisible wind that dragged him backward. He seemed to be pulling an entire village behind him, one step at a time. It was Fen, leading the flyers to the cliff, though the sun was so old the sky flared red behind it.

Colbee and Light of Wind helped connect all the kites and extras. Kiah and Darna made sure the fat man figure was connected and secure. Laido secured the base of the line around a heavy rock. The flyers fanned out at the base. On Colbee's signal, they launched their kites, and the line soared into the reddening sky, taking the fat man with it.

Few people turned out to watch.

"Fine," Darna said. "We'll give them something to see."

She signaled Jin and Fen, who took up the long bamboo poles and lit the ends that had been soaked in oil. With the ends blazing, they lit the first of Light of Wind's hanging pods. The flame spread up the whirling pods to the connecting palm ribs and on to the next set of pods, until the whole string was alight.

"Light the baskets!" the girl cried.

Jin ran to the first basket of dried palm debris and held the light to it. It flamed up so quickly it almost lit the kite line, and Jin yelled for the handler to pull the line. As he did, the basket tipped, dropping a shower of burning pieces that flew on the wind and lit up the growing darkness.

A shout arose from the people who had been lurking out of sight.

"Light the others!" Light of Wind called.

As Jin lit the other baskets, the flames jumped from one to the next, showering pieces of fire into the sky.

Finally, Light of Wind took Darna's arm. "We have to do something amazing."

"Isn't this it?"

"No. We need to light the man."

"We can't," Darna said, "He won't burn."

"Yes, he will. I made him to burn. I made him as an offering to the gods of the sky."

Darna looked at the girl, so intense and so sure. "Then you will need to do it yourself."

The girl nodded. When Jin gave her the long pole, she lit the figure. When it caught fire, the entire figure of the man blazed in the night, the final offering. The sparks and smoke rolled up into the sky, into the hands of the gods. Truly, the man flew. The crowd burst into the launching area, running, crying, cheering, shouting.

Fen dropped to his knees and stared at the spectacle in the sky, its glorious fire reflected in the tears rolling down his cheeks.

* * *

The next morning, six men accompanied Fuhua back to the encampment, each carrying a basket on his head and bundles under his arms.

"We've done very well for ourselves," Fuhua said, patting his belly contentedly. "It wasn't so much the main bet as the side bets that won us all this. We gained trade goods, tools, boat building supplies, food stuffs, and -" he gestured toward a cage the last porter set down in front of him, "a special gift for Colbee."

"Sea turtles?" Colbee asked. "They'll be dead soon in that cage."

"No. They're land turtles. A seafarer brought several of them here many seasons ago and traded them for supplies. The villagers have raised their offspring. These are apparently quite young. I thought we could take them along as an emergency food supply."

"We'll spend all day finding food for them," Kiah complained.

"When they eat too much," Colbee said, "we'll eat them."

"I prefer the other treasures," she said, reviewing the assortment of goods set down in front of her: a large honeycomb, several fine weavings, bright green feathers, bamboo tubes stuffed with salt, two carved flutes, a small drum, needles and awls made of bone, three large dark pearls, two of the enormous gold-lipped clam shells, dye stuffs, an ebony spear decorated with designs of fish and water lilies, sheaves of bamboo, various mushrooms and herbs, nuts, a necklace of bird claws and one of shark teeth.

As they were examining their prizes, Hao walked up, looking old and dirty, missing his usual placid smile. "I suppose you won't be looking for my help on your voyage."

No one seemed anxious to answer him until Darna spoke. "You're wrong, Hao. We would like to have your help."

"We would?" Laido blurted.

But when Laido looked at his wife, he nodded. "Yes, we would."

A hint of the old smile returned to Hao's face. "Well, then, we've a lot to do. I should probably start with a bath."

Fen watched this exchange from the cover of the trees.

CHAPTER 13
RED FLOWERS, DARK CLOUDS

Nina had planned to weave a fish trap, but the reeds fell loose and tangled as she watched the silver river flowing past, whirling into pools, gurgling and gushing, full of rapid water talk as it found its way around dark rocks. Above it, on the far shore, hibiscus flowers nodded at her from tall stalks. Abandoning her work, she found her way across the river and picked one of the extravagant blossoms. Bright red, it demanded attention, its wide red petals lying open, revealing a long column from which sprang dozens of anthers, each with its dusting of pollen. At the end of the column, it split into five parts. A single drop of nectar hung from the center. She studied the flower it as if she'd never seen one before. Her mother used the dried flowers and stems as cures for coughs and digestive problems and Nina had helped her prepare them. This was somehow very different.

"I wish I had gone through the traditional training," she said to the flower in her hand, its petals fluttering in the breeze like wings. "I wonder if I would understand if I carried the initiation tattoos on my body. Silver river, red flowers. A whole world turned red and silver." She ran her finger along the petals before she tucked the flower behind her ear, crossed partway back over the river, and stopped, balanced on a stony point. "If I could make up my own tattoo, I'd put the red flower in it. And the river. You would be my marks."

When she reached the other side, she knelt down, rocked back on her heels, and drew designs in the dirt. "On my shoulder and down my arm, I'd have swirling lines of light on water. And on my back a bird -"

"Nina?"

She saw Ryu right in front of her and jumped up, throwing down the stick and knocking the flower out of her hair as she rose. "What is it?"

Ryu picked up the flower and held it out to her. "You dropped this."

Nina didn't move.

Ryu still held the flower in his outstretched hand as he turned and looked at her designs. "What are these?"

Nina hesitated then took the flower from him, looked at it, and put it back in her hair.

"My tattoos," she said, feeling the words fill her mouth. "It's just a design. I have no way of getting them now."

"Show me," he said, leaning over the patterns.

The wind blew through her, taking her old breath away with it. "Since I never went through the training, I never received my tattoos. I wanted to design my own, just as -"

"You already said that. I meant explain these."

She knelt down across from him and went through the designs, one by one, explaining each, adding a row of dots around a curling edge. The large design of the bird, with the wind swirling up underneath its wings, she saved until last, worried it was too grand.

"And this?" Ryu asked, pointing to it.

"It's a dream I had." She couldn't say more. Suddenly it all seemed a mistake. She stood, erasing the bird design with her foot.

"No!" Ryu cried, taking her arm. "I will give you these, if you'll let me."

She couldn't look at him. "Yes. That would be good."

Once he had collected the materials he needed, he marked out the design on her left arm with a charred stick: a spiral that started on her shoulder and continued in five wavy lines down her arm, honoring the spirits of light and sound on the water. To make the lines permanent, he held a sharp blade above the lines, tapping it against her skin as he moved, concentrating on the tattoo. Above that design he put the undulating lines of shining heaven reflected on the water. When the marks began to ooze drops of blood, he dusted burned caterpillar powder on them and pressed healing leaves over the marks. Neither one spoke as he worked. Under the sun, there were only the two of them and the river and the red flowers watching, nodding.

On her right arm, he drew the South Star design, then dusted the finished image and blotted it. As the marks became part of her skin, he pressed crushed leaves over them, exhausted from concentration and desire, overwhelmed by the closeness of her.

When he finished the designs, he couldn't leave her, couldn't separate himself from her.

"This is what I want," he said, pointing to the hibiscus flower. "Put this design on me."

Slowly, she turned to study the flower and the young man so close to her, then took the blade from his hand. On his left arm, under the traditional sea marks of a young navigator, she tapped out the hibiscus flower outline and rows of dots along the inside of each petal.

Close above them, the sky flared red as the sun dropped near the sea. As the drops of blood rose from the flower lines, she put her hand over the design and pressed down, then put her hand, marked with his blood, on her own chest.

He laid his hand over hers.

"I want to be part of the red flower under the red sky," she said.

* * *

When they lay side by side, looking up at the patterns of stars in the black sky, Nina pointed to the figure of the enormous bird rising in the north. "That's what I want for my sign: the Great Bird rising, beating its wings as it lifts into the sky. Is it wrong to want something so grand?"

"It would be shameful to pretend to be less than you are," he said.

They sank into each other with a luxurious indolence, forgetting to do anything ordinary or useful. Ryu drew the Great Bird on her back, exquisite in its detail: the great bird with its head lifted up and facing left, its left wing lifted slightly higher than the right, pushing off into the top of the sky. For the dark lines, he used charcoal and burned caterpillar dust. For the red-purple sections, crushed hibiscus flowers. As he worked, he described the image to her.

When they tired of exploring the land, they took to the wind raft, making it fly across the water, pushing it ever faster, hanging out over the side to balance it. Above them, the sky opened into the high blue vault that housed the sun.

As they brought the boat back to shore late one day, Nina noticed the sea covered rocks that were usually bare at low tide.

"Storm swell," Ryu said as he jumped off the boat and found seawater up to his waist instead of his knees.

On the beach, Nulo and Aeta were waiting for them.

"We have to prepare for a bad storm," Nulo announced.

"We felt the swell," Ryu said. "It's not unusual this time of year. The heavy rains are coming, finally."

Nulo shook his head. "This is different. The storm carries death with it."

"What are you talking about?"

"Can you take apart the boat?"

"Take it apart? No. Not without destroying it. If you think it's not safe here, we'll move it farther up the shore."

"We can't move it far enough," Nulo argued. "If the sea rushes across the shore, it will throw the boat against the cliff rock."

"It's rain, Nulo. It won't hurt a boat."

"Maybe Nulo's right," Nina said, watching the waves hurrying into the shore. "My father says, 'Waves run from trouble. When they run fast, they bring trouble with them.' They're running very fast right now. And we felt something was different when we brought the boat in."

"So you think I should tear apart my boat?"

"We know something's coming," Nina started, choosing not to comment on the fact that it was actually her father's boat, "and Nulo can sense things. He's been right before. Why not trust him on this?"

"If you think it's not safe on the shore, I suppose we could break it down into pieces that we might be able to put together again. Or we could be stuck on this island without a working boat because you made me take it apart."

"Tell me what to do to help," Nulo continued. "Also, we'll need extra food and fresh water."

Ryu and Nina glanced at each other. They had almost none.

"Nina and I will see to the food and water while you two manage the boat," Aeta announced as she set off inland, waving Nina along.

"These marks on your skin," Aeta said, without turning around, "you wanted them?"

"Yes, I did."

"They're not traditional. What do they mean?"

"That I am on a journey."

"I hope you find happiness along the way."

"Thank you."

"We have much to do. Did you count the waves on the shore?"

"Yes. I counted a wave every twelve beats. Not very high, especially with a storm coming."

"Good. That gives us time to prepare. I'll show you the cave we found between the mountains. We'll need to secure everything there: as much water as we can manage, since the river may become contaminated with sea water -"

"You think seawater will reach that high? Not possible."

"Nulo thinks it will happen," Aeta explained.

They used every container they could find for water, picked fruits, dug root vegetables, gathered firewood and stacked it, roasted waterbugs, caterpillars, and beetles, brought in piles of palm fronds and bamboo, dried seaweed, and smoked strings of tiny fish. While they worked, Ryu and Nulo took the wind raft apart and tied the pieces together.

"Tomorrow, we'll build a shelter for the boat," Nulo said.

"Then, when the rainstorm passes, I'll have to figure out how to rebuild my boat," Ryu complained.

"It would be destroyed if left on the beach. This way it might survive the storm."

"This whole thing is another one of your stupid ideas. I'm going fishing," he announced, walking away.

When Nulo caught up with him later, Ryu was cleaning his catch as seabirds wheeled overhead. "Mackerel and crabs, good work."

"Look, Nulo, I know you think this is important -"

"I know it is."

"I've seen storms before. We drag the boat off the shore and let the storm pass. It's not the end of the world."

"Not the end of the whole world. Just ours, here." Nulo looked out to sea. "I felt it, Ryu. I felt my hair being pulled up. The air bitter like lightning. A witch as big as the sky with white hair swirling around her. She was screeching, drawing up the sea and spitting it out in floods across the island. Dead sea creatures lay piled up at my feet so deep I had nowhere to step. This storm means to kill us, Ryu."

Ryu didn't look up from his work. "No one made you chief, Nulo. Don't give me orders. If I'm meant to die, I'll die."

"I would never give you orders," Nulo said, with a slight bow. "You will always be my oldest friend. Do what you think best."

As Nulo walked away, Ryu tossed the fish to the hungry seabirds and walked down to the shore. The sky was clear. If anything, it looked even brighter blue than it had the day before, though the swell, he noticed, was now very high. Still, storm swells were common. They brought high water and stirred up the bottom; they didn't kill people. And now his boat lay in pieces because Nulo saw a white-haired witch.

Nina came up and put her hand on his shoulder. He drew her down next to him, glad for her company, but she stared past him.

"What are you looking at?"

"The waves," she said. "I've been counting. They're more frequent now."

He let her hand drop.

"Have you seen the swell today?" she asked.

"Yes."

"And?"

"And, yes, somewhere around here, they're going to get a storm. That's what happens at the beginning of the rainy season."

Nina stood up. "Are the fish ready?"

"No, I threw them to the birds. They were hungry and had seen visions of someone cleaning fish for them."

"I'll get others."

Ryu did not join the group for dinner.

Nina slept by the river.

The next day, Ryu was up at first light, padding through the water's edge and watching waves scudding into shore. White clouds massed on the horizon and low clouds streaked by overhead. Farther along the beach, toward the windward side, white caps and streaks of foam decorated the waves. While he watched them, the wind picked up. One moment it was only the usual offshore breeze; the next the wind was pushing against him, whistling in his ears. Then the first fat drops fell, splatting on his face and arms. A warm rain - not a good sign.

When he turned around, the wind pressed him forward, catching loose sand that stung the backs of his legs as he tripped over rocks. Clouds raced by just over his head. The air felt charged.

As he headed inland, the rain changed, falling in sharp pings on the rocks, then changed again, with so many drops crowding into each other they became a mass of falling water shifting with the winds. Huddled behind a large stone, he searched for a route he could take up to the shelter, but sheets of rain threw everything on the hillside into a confusion of grey. The wind rose to an incessant roar, tearing branches off trees, throwing them into the storm. Rain flew past him in bands. Under his feet, muddy water carved new channels, dug away at roots, wrenched bushes out of the earth and carried them away. As he struggled toward the mountain, grabbing handholds on standing rocks, fighting the pull of the mud, he couldn't remember which way to go. When he looked up the slope where he thought the cave was, he saw only newborn rivers tearing through the forest, cutting through the land, racing downhill.

Just behind him, a tree trunk snapped off in the wind and whipped across the back of his head and shoulders, throwing him down onto the rocks. When he managed to pull himself up, his head throbbed. Blood ran down the side of his face, dripped down onto his chest only to be spattered away in the rain. With every step he took, sharp pains shot up his right leg. A white shard of bone stuck out of a gash below his knee. Shivering, he grabbed a rock for support.

Something crashed behind him. Half a tree flew past. A parrot scrambled in the wind as it was blown over his head, its green feathers spread and twisted. New winds rose, ripping whole trees out of the ground and flinging them down against the rocks. On the shore where he'd been walking, the sea hurled gigantic waves against the beach, dragging sand, stones, shrubs and trees into the sea only to churn them up again with the next assault. Ryu struggled for higher ground while the mud river moved the earth under his feet, pulling him backwards. When he caught the bad foot sideways between rocks, he fell again. Pain shot up his leg. Unable to stand, he dragged himself through the mud. Behind a boulder, he curled up, his arms wrapped around his chest to still the endless shaking while the brown river surged underneath him, pulling at him.

I can't reach the shelter.

What did I say to Nulo about dying?

It was stupid.

Naia used to say that anger was a poor friend.

I'm a poor friend.

He thought he saw shapes coming toward him but dismissed them as stones half-hidden by sheets of rain.

I'm cold.

He pushed himself back against the rock though even there he felt the mud river pulling on him, dragging him down under the weight of dead things.

Something grabbed his shoulder. Thinking it was the storm spirit, he jerked away, falling sideways against the rock. Then a different form resolved itself out of the downpour, blurred and stretched by the storm. It wrapped itself around his arm and pulled on him. Though he struggled to stand, to escape, his right leg wouldn't support any weight. The wind and pain pushed him down hard before it lifted him up again and pulled him along. Then there were other winds, all pulling on him while his foot twisted and pain shot through him again.

Nulo, Aeta, and Nina reached the shelter, dragging Ryu with them. Speech was impossible; the wind's scream filled everything.

Nina made Ryu a bed of dried grasses and tended to his leg as best she could with no medicines. While he opened his eyes sometimes, he didn't speak at all.

Muddy water seeped into the cave from above. From the entrance, a stream of mud moved down the center of the cave, tiny at first, snaking its way through the cave bottom, then growing larger, forcing them to move farther up against the walls, dragging their supplies with them.

When Aeta drew out some food for them, Nina couldn't eat. Outside the cave, she could hear the storm dragging, scraping across the island, digging into the rock and soil, clawing at anything that had survived. She sat by Ryu and put her hand to her arm, where she had asked him to draw the symbols of the wind and the sea.

"I thought I knew them," she muttered, "when we were at sea. Yet this screeching witch is also the wind. Nothing has only one side. Even you. Even me."

She ran her fingers back over the lines of dots. As the storm raged outside, she lay down next to Ryu, thinking he smelled different.

When the storm's anger was spent, it dissipated, its clouds breaking from walls into sections and then into fragments. When the heat came up the next day, the island stank of rotting vegetation and foul muck. Trees lay felled and smashed, their roots filled with debris carried by the flood. Dead sea creatures lay where the raging waves had thrown them, far from shore. Seabirds scavenged in a frenzy. The beach was gone; only a rocky ledge marked where it used to be. The river, now filled with muddy, brackish water, ran between ragged banks.

In the split trunk of a downed tree, Aeta found a soaked honeycomb.

"The water won't affect its curing power, Nina" she said, prying it out and tucking the sticky bundle under her arm. "At least I hope it won't."

In the cave, she pressed the raw honey onto Ryu's leg, patting it onto the cuts. "We'll hope it cures him before it attracts stinging ants," she said, rising. "We can feed him the rest."

"If the bone is broken, how can we wrap it? Won't the wound fester?"

"We'll wrap the leg but leave the wound open. There may be some dead flesh. Don't be surprised if he gets maggots. They'll clean out the wound."

"I can't do this," Nina objected.

Aeta wrapped up the rest of the dripping comb. "Of course you can. We'll help."

"Did the boat – Is the boat -"

"I'm sorry," Aeta said, "I saw no sign of it."

Aeta didn't know the pink and white blossoms from which the bees had gathered pollen were toxic to humans. When Ryu ate the honey, it took him to a bizarre world. At one point, he found himself in a long underground passage, a tunnel that snaked deep into the earth. Nearby he could see other tunnels, and every so often he'd find a passageway from one tunnel to another. At these junctions, he could see that the network of tunnels went on forever, to the very core of the earth. Sometimes, he could hear Nina's voice, or other voices, but they were always in another tunnel. When he tried to find them, they disappeared.

The sides of the tunnels felt bulbous as he ran his hand along them, reminding him of the story Naia told of the tree that grew from the navel of the world all the way up into the sky when the gods created the world. At the top were all of the fruits and vegetables and seeds and flowers, too high for the people to reach. A wise man changed into an eagle and tried to break off the branches, but the tree was too big, so the birdman asked the help of all of the other birds. Together, they worked, pecking at the giant tree until the top crashed to the ground and all of the seeds and fruits fell to the earth. Then the great tree split apart, and the rest of the people emerged to populate the new land.

He thought he'd find the surface of the earth if he climbed. Somewhere up higher, he heard muffled voices. Occasionally he thought he could make out words mixed in with sounds echoing in the tunnels. In some places, the air had very distinct smells. One was Nina. One was a pungent cooking smell, like steamed seaweed. One was a sharp, putrid smell like rotten meat.

CHAPTER 14
THE STORM'S TOLL

Though Hao warned Laido and the others that a storm was coming, no one paid much attention. By the time Laido agreed that a major storm was brewing, he knew they needed to find a safe haven quickly.

Hao shook his head as he pointed to the rocky outcrops they were passing. "There's no place to beach a boat on these little islands. They won't give us any real shelter. The sea would wash right over the top of the island. We need to get to something bigger and higher."

"Maybe we could ride it out," Colbee said, studying the rising white caps.

"Perhaps," Hao said, "but you would have no control. Even if you weren't swamped by the water, you would still be blown with the wind. If the boats were thrown against rocks like those," he added, pointing to a sharp outcrop that marked a flooded island, "they would be destroyed instantly."

"Then we need to get to land, or farther out to sea," Laido said.

Every time they saw the outline of an island, their hopes rose; each time, it proved unworkable. The island they thought the most promising had no beach, only jagged black rocks at the water's edge.

"We're going to have to risk it," Colbee said. "Maybe we can get close enough to tie up to the rocks and unload."

Goh studied the rocks. "How will we get the boats on shore over the rocks? We'll never be able to lift them."

"We don't have long to make a choice," Laido said. "If the water keeps rising like this, any shore entry will be dangerous. Some will be impossible."

As they rounded the spit at the end of the island, Kiah cried, "There! Look there! Just what we need!" A pebble beach easily wide enough to land the boats formed a crescent behind a sheltered cove.

"That's it. Head in," Laido called.

"Drag the paddles!" Colbee yelled. "Try to steer for the middle of the beach! Keep the boats straight. Brace yourselves!"

The words were hardly out of his mouth before the sea took the boats. Jin, Tahn, Fuhua, and Liwei worked the paddles in the Flying Fish while Colbee tried to keep it lined up with the beach. The big canoes were lifted like sticks, thrown toward the shore.

"Drag your paddles!" Colbee called again as they got into shallower water.

They dragged the beautifully carved paddles against the rocky bottom. The boats caught, lurched, hesitated, then surged forward again. When the boats reached the shore, the wave carried them across the beach until the water became so shallow that the boats dropped onto the land.

"Well done!" Laido called, jumping out. "We did it!"

Hao looked at the clouds massing and at the boats laden with goods. "We need to find shelter quickly. You'll need to decide what to bring and what to leave."

Faced with a storm that might destroy all his treasures, Fuhua struggled with his choices. In the end he took only a few precious pieces and his sky rock. Liwei and the others made similar painful decisions.

Though Kiah opened the land turtle cages, the animals refused to leave. "Then take your chances with us," she said, taking the cages with her.

Once they'd hauled the Flying Fish as far onto the shore as they could, they wedged it between two large rocks. Near the top of the hill, they built a palm roof over a circular rock outcrop and then dragged in bunches of extra palms. Though they worked quickly, they were hardly done with the preliminaries before the storm hit. After the wind ripped off the roof, rainwater soaked everything and filled the depression in the middle of the rocky circle. When the storm rose to its full force, they wedged themselves against the rocks and lived inside the storm, battered by its attack, emptied by its fury. Darna tried not to think about Nina and the others except to hope they would survive.

When the storm had spent itself, they found the island's trees flattened, the land covered with stinking sludge, and the Flying Fish battered to pieces between the big rocks.

Goh, Jin, and Tahn worked all day clearing debris and building a new shelter, work area, and fire pit. On what remained of the shore, Fuhua looked in vain for his treasures. Liwei sat staring at the sea, saying nothing. Laido put his arm around Darna. Unable to find anything encouraging to say, she wrapped her arm around her husband's waist.

CHAPTER 15
AFTERMATH

Despite the saltwater baths, Ryu's leg became infected. As Aeta predicted, maggots settled in the wound, eating out the bad flesh. Ryu lost so much weight, his bones stuck out at his shoulder and chest. Although he had moments when he seemed to recognize people, the light in his eyes faded quickly. To get him some fresh air, they moved him outside when the weather was clear. Sometimes Nina sat with him, talking about what she saw or what she was thinking. She wondered if her parents and Tahn had lived through the storm, if she'd made the wrong choice in leaving them, if she'd ever see them again.

Aeta kept looking for other treatments. One day she came back to camp with six ripe Noni fruits she'd found floating in the sea. After splitting open four of the smelly yellow fruits, she set them out to age. Two days later, well-fermented, the mass smelled even worse, yet Aeta hummed while she poured the juice into a bowl and mixed it with coconut milk and the contaminated honey to help dull the bitter taste. Then she held it up to Ryu, telling him to drink the whole thing. After a couple of swallows, he turned away.

"You can drink it or lie in it," she said as she spread some of the mashed fruits on the floor and motioned to Nina and Nulo to lay him down on top of them. When he was settled, she poured the rest of the juice over him and added more mashed fruits, concentrating on his chest.

"You'll kill him with the smell!" Nina gasped.

Aeta patted the pulpy fruits against Ryu's skin. "The smell shows it's working."

That night, Ryu dreamed his flesh was rotting, falling off in a sludgy mash while he was pulled down into a pit of muck. Terrified, he thrashed and yelled, trying to reach the surface, breathe, escape the putrefied flesh all around him. *I have to get out. Get out. Get out. Get out now.* He clawed at the air as he hauled himself upright, shaking so hard the world appeared to jerk spasmodically as he looked around.

Nearby, he could see Nulo hunkered next to a cook fire, busily stirring something that smelled very bad. Outside the shelter, Aeta was pounding something and Nina was splitting open what looked like rotten fruit, scooping out the pulp with her hands, and piling it up next to her. He wondered if he was still dreaming or if he had brought the nightmare stench with him into the world of the living.

Nulo looked up from his pot and noticed Ryu struggling to sit up.

"You're awake," he said. "Welcome back, friend." After he studied Ryu for a moment, he added, "I've learned to cook."

Ryu tried to look at only one thing at a time, hoping the world would stop moving around him. Only a moment later, everyone was at his side, all talking to him at once, their faces close, their voices blurred.

"What is that terrible smell?" Ryu asked when there was a quiet moment.

"Noni," Aeta answered. "Isn't it wonderful?"

* * *

It took many days for Ryu to get his strength back. Below his knee he had lost a lot of flesh. The bone mended, but not exactly as before, leaving him with a hitch in his walk. He often felt dizzy and weak, so there was little he could do to help. He made himself walk up and down the island with a staff to steady himself. Some days he hauled deadwood and gathered crabs and snails from the shore. At dinner, he ate whatever Nulo had cooked, though he had his own opinions about Nulo's culinary talent. Designing, building, and working a boat, however, lay beyond his ability.

* * *

One afternoon the four of them sat by what used to be the beach, watching seabirds piercing the water like spears, their wings folded back as they dove for fish. When they rose with their prize, other birds dove at the flapping fish, trying to steal them.

Suddenly Nina jumped up, pointing. "Look! Two boats!"

They stared at the boats heading right for their island. Another time, they might have hidden, or at least figured out what defenses they could put together, but they had no real defenses. Besides, they were curious.

As Aeta watched the boats come closer, she also jumped to her feet.

"It's the yellow-eyed boat!"

Nulo stood and Ryu pushed himself to his feet. All four stared at the familiar boat and the larger boat, both of which were headed straight toward their island.

"They have to be Bokai's men," Ryu said, "unless they traded the boat already."

* * *

Keoni, the man steering the yellow-eyed boat, considered the group on shore. "Looks like a family. I don't see anyone else. Let's take the boats to shore," he called to his friend, Enoka, who was steering the other boat.

"Are you certain?"

"Yes. No. Wait. Those two aren't children," Keoni corrected.

"I think it's Nulo," his brother Kap said slowly. "At least it looks like him. Nulo and Ryu."

"And Nina. I've seen the other one too, somewhere."

Kap squinted. "Is she the one from the island, the No Shadow Day?"

"No. I don't think so."

"Should we still go ashore?"

Enoka hesitated. "Yes."

"Watch out for these," his brother called, pointing out ragged rocks sticking out of the water.

As Enoka tried to avoid the biggest rock, the current twisted the boat sideways. When Kap stood up to push away from the boulder, the sea slammed the boat into a different rock, knocking him off balance and pitching him headfirst into the water.

"Kap!" Enoka yelled, trying to paddle back as the current swept the boat past the rock and farther down the shore.

After a moment, Kap surfaced. "I'm all right," he called, "but I can't get to you. I'll head for shore." He bobbed for a moment, watching his brother's vain attempt to turn the boat against the sea, then swam for the line of rocky outcrops that ran from the shore into the sea. He made it partway up the closest rock before a wave washed him off the slippery surface. The next time, though he tried a slightly different spot, he still couldn't keep hold of the deep seaweed piles. The next wave washed him back into the sea. When he struggled back toward the rock, he saw two people standing on it; one was holding out a long pole to him.

"Grab hold of this," Ryu yelled over the sound of the sea crashing on the rocks. "We'll put down a mat for you so you can get some traction on the rocks."

Nina was already picking her way along the rocks with the rope mat they'd been sitting on. When she was as close to Kap as she could get, she spread it out on the rock and mashed it down until it was thoroughly soaked and conformed to the rock surface. As the next wave coursed over the mat, it stayed put on the bumpy rock. Kap, swept away by the water, swam back. When he reached the rocks, he grabbed at the pole, missed, and went under as the wave caught him.

"You'll have to swim up past us," Nina called when he surfaced. "Catch the pole as the wave comes."

Nodding, he tried again. When he got close, he grabbed hold of the pole, but the next wave caught him before he reached the rocks, so he had to let go. His breathing was ragged as he turned back once again.

"You can do it this time," Nina called. "The mat will help you. Get on your hands and knees on the mat. Don't try to stand. We'll help you."

Kap swam past the rock, caught the pole with one hand, and grabbed a wet rock edge with the other. Scrambling up the rock's sharp angles, he crawled forward until he hit the mat. As the wave hit, he braced himself, let it roll past, then continued crawling, across the mat and onto more rocks collecting seawater and pebbles in their depressions. As the next wave caught him, Nina reached out her hand.

"Thank you," he said, rising unsteadily, sucking in ragged breaths. He stared at them while trickles of blood ran down his arms and legs.

"The sea water will help clean out those cuts," Aeta said.

In the boats, Keoni and Enoka watched the rescue, unable to get close enough to help.

"Where can we land?" Keoni called to the group on the shore.

"Try going that way," Ryu yelled, pointing down the shore, "past the rock spit. We'll meet you. It's rocky, but the currents aren't as bad."

On the other side of the rock line, where the water was calmer, Keoni steered between the big rocks. The new shore, however, was littered with half-submerged trees carried downhill by the floods. The men would have to lift the boats up onto the shore. It took all of them, levering the boats over jumbled tree trunks and root fans, to get the two boats ashore. When they were done, they stood next to the boats, touching their right hand to their left shoulder in greeting, finding no words.

"It's the storm," Nulo said, inviting the visitors to join them. "It changed everything."

With a loud sigh, Keoni hunkered down across from Nulo. "It changed me, I know that." He picked up a handful of the beach pebbles around him and rolled them around in his hand as Enoka joined the circle. "We saw what it left behind. Forests ripped out, mudslides, whole villages lost. After the storm, it was bad. Bodies, even children – I'll tell you, it took the heart out of me, seeing it."

Enoka nodded. "We used to go somewhere new expecting a fight. Most of the time, we were right. It's not the same anymore. We go places and people are glad to see us, most of the time. Some places only have a few people left and they're looking for some company. They want to hear that other places weren't hit so hard."

"I'll get something for those cuts," Aeta offered. "And some food."

"I need to explain what happened with Raidu," Keoni said, though no one had asked.

"Aeta is right," Nulo said. "We'll take care of Kap's injuries first. After we eat, we can all hear your story."

"You know we were all good friends with Bokai back home," Keoni began when they'd finished eating, "my brother Kap, Liem, and me. When Raidu became chief, we didn't ask what happened to Nulo or why families fled in the middle of the night. Bokai supported his father, so we did too. We didn't know what he had in mind. We'd never been to war. It sounded exciting. But when Pactu left and Laido left with the wind raft, Raidu started ranting about killing them because they'd betrayed their chief.

"After the storms went through, we left to find the old land that Raidu wanted to reclaim. We called ourselves brave warriors. But when we got there, we found nothing. Floodwater covered old huts and lodges. A few drowned boats broken up on the shore. No sign of people, even inland. They'd all left, or died. The discovery made Raidu crazy angry. Instead of taking us home, he told us we'd search the endless sea until we found a land with people to conquer. When someone complained, Raidu smashed his head in with a war club. He told us to leave the man lying there." Enoka hesitated. "We were scared. Since we couldn't survive on the flooded island, especially with the dead man's ghost so angry, we went with Raidu. He had us then." Keoni stopped, digging his toes deeper into the dirt.

When no one replied, he went on, "Back on the island - you know, where the mountain broke open - when Owl Man murdered Raidu, we were secretly relieved. Bokai, though, he really suffered. He ran with the rest of us when the mountain exploded, leaving his father to die in the burning river, but his father's ghost haunted him. When Jin offered the chance to leave, Bokai took it. He couldn't stay with the people who'd killed his father. He needed us, so we went with him. But nothing went right after that. We couldn't find our way back home. Bokai would wake up at night, screaming, begging his father to leave him alone then promising to avenge him. We didn't know where we were or how to get home. So day after day we wandered on the sea. Sometimes we'd spot an island and go ashore but it was never the right island, so we'd get supplies and go back to sea and search for the next island. Or an answer of some kind, even if it was death.

"When we found the island with the yellow-eyed boat and saw the tracks of the woman -"

"My tracks," Aeta interrupted.

Keoni stared. "I didn't know – I thought maybe -"

"Go on," she urged. "I only wanted you to understand."

"Bokai thought Owl Man and Nulo were hiding on the island with you. He wanted to avenge his father by killing you, all of you. When you ran to the cave, he followed, tried to force his way in, but he couldn't. The fire - it started as a way to smoke you out of the cave." He looked away then down at his feet.

Enoka took up the story. "Bokai ordered us to build more fires, not just the one by the cave. When sparks lit other fires in the peat swamps, we tried to put them out, but Bokai turned on us. He became his father, swinging his club against anyone who stood against him. We didn't even look at each other; we all knew at the same moment. We turned and ran, leaving him behind." His voice trailed off.

"Were you all in the cave?" Kap asked.

"No," Aeta answered.

"And Bokai? Did you find him?"

"Killed by the smoke," Ryu said.

"He lit his own death fire," Keoni sighed. "Maybe that's what we realized."

For a moment, no one said anything; no one moved.

"The sea healed us," Keoni began again. "Bit by bit, day by day."

"It became our home. We learned the right spots for fresh water, good supplies, easy fishing," Kap added.

Enoka continued, "And we found villages. At first, we had trouble and we'd leave in a hurry. Then people got used to seeing us. They wanted to trade. A new item is worth something extra just because it's different. Once we had a regular route, we delivered messages between chiefs, or we were asked to learn how to do something and bring the information back."

"Or steal something," Kap interrupted.

"Moons went by. We delivered whatever people wanted," his brother continued. "We live at sea now. We know dozens of islands and how to reach them, how the currents run. We found Pactu's island. He wanted us to settle there and marry the girls, but we needed to get back out on the sea. Maybe we've become sea creatures. My legs don't work right on land anymore."

"We've gotten good at estimating the value of things," his brother went on. "If someone gives us a pink pearl, we know what kind of dagger it can be traded for – that sort of thing. We say, 'Well, that kind of carving was worth a gold-lipped clam shell last time.' It makes trades easier."

"So," Aeta said, "what is the yellow-eyed boat that you stole worth to you?"

"I've been thinking about that," Keoni admitted. "I thought it might be worth a trade: some treasure, perhaps, or a trip somewhere. I don't see a boat here, and we have two, more or less. In return for taking your boat, we could take you wherever you want to go."

"Seal Island," they all said at once.

Kap jerked his head up. "Seal Island? Really?"

Nulo answered, "Yes."

"Seal Island it is, then," Keoni said. "We have a little work to do on the second boat. The repairs should only take a day or so. After that, we'll leave whenever you're ready."

"That's assuming we manage to launch the boats when they're loaded with passengers and supplies," Enoka added.

"That's a small problem," Nina cried. "We'll figure out a way. We're going to Seal Island!"

CHAPTER 16
SEAL ISLAND TALK

"So you've been to Seal Island?" Ryu asked. "What's it like?"

Keoni smiled. "It's like nothing you've seen before. It's land right at the edge of the wide ocean, so it has two hearts: one belongs to the islands behind it and one to the open sea before it. Actually, it isn't even one island, except at low tide, when you can walk from one part to the other over the rocks. At high tide, it's a string of five islands. The middle island has a perfect harbor ringed by a thin circle of rock. Since it's too narrow for a village, people leave their boat, wait for low tide, and walk to the main village on the next island."

"You can find anything you want on Seal Island, for a price," Kap added.

"Except a chief," Keoni said.

"That's not quite true," his brother corrected. "Every Seal Islander is a chief, according to their law. None of them agree on anything, but they work it out somehow."

"All kinds of people live on Seal Island," Kap said, "discarded people, outlaws, runaways -"

"How do they manage to live together?"

"Oh, it's actually quite peaceful. If someone is a threat, he can't stay. If he doesn't take the warning, he's removed, permanently. On an island full of outlaws and outcasts, it's not hard to find someone to get rid of a problem."

"Interesting," Ryu said.

"Oh, it's that," Keoni agreed.

CHAPTER 17
A PUPPET SHOW

Hao assured Laido and Darna that they'd know as soon as Nina and the others arrived. "Leave it to the children's network," he explained. "They know everything about everyone on Seal Island."

Darna waited, but days slid into moon-turns without any news. Other newcomers arrived and talked of the terrible damage the storm had caused and how it had wiped out whole villages. But no one had seen the missing members of the group.

"Maybe we should go back and look for them," Darna suggested.

"Give them ten more days," Laido said. "Then we'll decide what to do."

The wait drained Tahn. While the others worked on the new food boat or bargained for supplies, he walked around the lagoon, explored the other islands, idly considered the wares available for trade at the market. During the three-day festival at the full moon, he spent his days listening to the musicians. In the moments the music filled him, it pushed out his restless sadness. By the third full moon festival, he recognized the best musicians and the pieces they played on a large skin drum, a log drum, different flutes, and a row of hanging bamboo tubes suspended from a tree branch. He even learned some of their long songs about heroes and spirits at the beginning of time.

As he sat on the hillside one day, listening to a loud, fast piece with pounding drums, a crowd gathered. A new figure joined the musicians, a woman completely covered in black. The leader of the musicians introduced her, but she never looked at the audience. Instead, she slid her arms inside a puppet which was about half the size of a person. Layers of dyed bark cloth, grasses, leaves and shells flopped about as it moved its arms. When it shook its head, a wild mop of seaweed jerked side to side.

A woman in the crowd yelled, "Agata! Tell us a fortune today, Agata!"

The puppet turned and scanned the crowd, moving in jerky motions that set its clothes and hair flying. It stopped when it seemed to be looking right at Tahn, holding up its hand up as if to see him better against the late sun. Then it held its palm to its forehead and started to moan and shake.

"Tell us!" someone yelled.

The puppet laughed, flopping up and down. "Well, okay, but it's really easy." It looked at the crowd. "Maybe too easy. Maybe I should pick somebody else."

"No, no!" the crowd replied.

"Embarrass him!" one man called.

"Okay," the puppet said, "but I need some help. Will you ask the musicians to help?"

The crowd roared, and the drummer started in with a pounding beat. Agata threw back its head, as if to think for a minute, then looked at Tahn again and pulled a small figure out of the black bag. The figure was the image of Tahn – the same long face, the same dark hair drawn up on the top of his head and tied with blue feathers stuck into the knot, the same tan wrap with rows of dark dots around the bottom, the same sash, even the same dagger tucked into it. The crowd looked from the puppet to Tahn and roared their approval.

Agata set the little figure down in front and studied it. "Yes, okay. I see - a little disappointment. A little drama. A little envy.

So common, right? The restless spirit," Agata said, as the crowd pressed closer. "Okay, so you wanted to have the fastest boat," it said, as the flute started in with a lilting melody. "Right. But there was some competition." The bamboo poles started up in a different melody that gradually drowned out the flute. "Right. There was another boat, and everyone was talking about it. Someone else's boat. Different boat.

"Don't worry," the puppet laughed, its crazy hair shaking, as it pointed to Tahn. "So, we have lots of questions and no answers, lots of wrong plans but no right plan; that's how it goes, isn't it?" Seaweed hair whipping back and forth, arms spread wide, the figure twisted as if looking at everyone. "It's difficult, isn't it? You saw other people happy but not you. That's tough, isn't it? What you think, people? It's tough, right? Tough for all of us, right?"

"Yes!"

Agata looked back toward Tahn. "And then – then – restlessness. Boredom. Waiting and searching for something you can't find -" Agata paused and looked around the crowd. "Well! At least you got a lot of company here!" The crowd laughed. "You got good friends, strong friends, and family too, but you don't remember them when you're angry, right? Just bad things. And bad things make your mind poison you."

Tahn jumped up, ready to run away, but Agata shouted, "No worry! All fun! Just for fun!" Its clothes jiggled and spun, its seaweed lumps jumped. "Wait! Yes!" One arm pointed off into the distance then dropped back down. "Or maybe not." Agata looked at the crowd. "But -"

"But what?" someone yelled from the crowd.

"But something new coming." The puppet lurched and swayed. "Exciting. So different, you see! Very happy. Maybe," Agata added wistfully. "Everything always maybe." Putting the figure back in the bag, Agata stood up, waving to the crowd, shaking its arms and hair and clothes. "Hope you liked the show! Please show your appreciation so we can eat something. Wait, I don't eat anything! Show your appreciation anyway – and to the musicians too. They're very good, right?" Agata asked, sweeping a floppy arm toward the musicians. People slapped their legs and yelled as Agata bowed, falling forward so that its head brushed the floor before rising again to more cheers.

As the musicians started up again, the woman in black slid off the stage as mysteriously as she had appeared. Tahn didn't move. Around him, people joined the group, listened for a while, then left. Tahn stayed. He couldn't shake the feeling that someone had turned him inside out, that his insides were lying there in a heap for everyone to see, and they weren't pretty. A while later, a very tall, thin woman in a hooded cape sat down next to him. He thought at first she was the puppeteer, but then remembered he'd seen a tall, hooded woman helping the puppeteer get ready before the show. Though she said nothing, he could feel her voice, as if she was asking him questions without making any sound. Annoyed, he turned to tell her to leave him alone, but the words stuck in his throat. The dark hood had protected her face from casual view, but the right half of it was distorted, as if the bones under the skin had been rearranged, or crushed, and the eye was glassy grey.

"I was punished for being a witch," she said. "They broke my face with a tree trunk."

Then she turned to face him. The other side of her face wasn't just normal, it was beautiful.

"I'm sorry," he said.

The woman looked away. "Did you enjoy the puppet show?"

"Enjoy?" Tahn said. "No. I felt myself being sliced open for the entertainment of a crowd of strangers."

"The crowd is irrelevant. The show was for you. We, Rana and I, put it together for you."

Tahn tried to read her expression, but as he looked at her, he was more curious about her life since this terrible thing had happened. "Are you happier now that you're here?" he asked.

She gave him an odd smile that lived on only half her face. "An interesting reply. And a difficult question."

They listened to a ballad singer tell the epic story of the hero and the crocodile. The hero's village had been attacked, and the people had fled into the sea, but a large crocodile swam up to eat them. Reading its thoughts, the hero jumped onto the croc's back, and convinced it to carry the people to safety. As more people climbed onto the croc's back, it grew bigger. Then it moved out to sea and became its own island. All of the bumps on its back became mountains. The people made a new home there. Nowadays, it doesn't move much, although it could if it wanted to. It was a very old story, but it was a favorite of the crowd.

When the ballad was finished and the crowd had shown its approval, the tall woman stood up. "Come by, if you'd like. We can have something to eat and you can meet her."

"Meet her?"

The woman pulled the edges of the hood forward to hide her face as she turned to leave. "The puppeteer, of course; her name is Rana."

For some reason, Tahn didn't want her to leave. "Where are you staying?"

"In the camp behind the marketplace. If you can't find us, just ask someone." With a slight bow, she slipped away into the crowd.

He had forgotten to ask her name, or give his. It was all very strange, part of a strange day. On the stage, three masked dancers had joined the musicians. New people had arrived, part of the ever-changing audience. A mother tried to keep track of three children, all going in separate directions. Four men seemed to be celebrating their arrival with any stranger who'd listen to their story. A vendor worked the crowd, selling root cakes wrapped in palm leaves. Another had breadfruit. A couple stole a few moments together. One of the ubiquitous child messengers ran past. And then, standing behind the musicians' platform, he saw two unmistakable figures:

a dwarf and a tiny woman. They were talking to a couple he didn't recognize: a thin man leaning on a staff, and a woman -

With a shout, he leaped to his feet and ran down the hill, yelling their names, knocking over several people in his path, dodging others, bumping into a fruit vendor's basket, and running, running, not caring about the spectators or the musicians or the dancers or much of anything except seeing his sister and his friends again. When he reached them, he fell on them with a shout, feeling as if fresh air had just swept through him, blowing away the black smoke and leaving behind only gratitude that they were all there, after all, just as they had planned, though they had all doubted that it would ever happen. They were, all of them, shining with amazement.

"I've been looking for you," a messenger boy said, addressing the talking, crying, hugging people in front of him, "Actually, we all have been, all the messengers all over the island. The message is -"

"I think we already know what the message is," Nina said, with her arm around Tahn's shoulder. But the messenger child looked so disappointed that she added, "We would like to hear it anyway."

The boy cleared his throat. "Master Hao gave me the message to deliver. It is to say that he and his nine companions are well and waiting for you to join them." He paused for greater drama. "And they miss you terribly."

That set them all off again, and it took the messenger a while to lead them to the camp. Laido was arguing with Goh about how to store the new supplies when Goh tapped Laido on the shoulder and pointed to something behind him. When Laido turned and found his daughter smiling at him, he was so suddenly happy he found it hard to breathe. With a shout, he wrapped his long arms around her and lifted her into the air. Darna was there too, and Fuhua and Liwei, Jin, Kiah, and Colbee, and behind them, Hao, looking up sideways at them with his sweet smile, so Nina, Ryu, Nulo, and Aeta were all swept up into the celebration, a chaos of people so joyful that they seemed to float.

Behind them, fireflies glowed in the bushes and the sky stretched in reds and purples away from the sinking sun. Silhouetted against the sunset, standing, sitting, bringing food and drink, listening to each other's stories, they were there, all of them, plus a woman in a hood and a puppeteer, and Fen, who had found his own way to the island. Later, the men from the boat with yellow eyes joined them. And then, since the celebration had obviously moved with the group, the musicians and dancers followed, as did a crowd of people happy to share someone else's good fortune – and food and drink, of course.

* * *

Darna watched the familiar figures move like shadow puppets against the red sky. She knew that Nina and Ryu were lovers as soon as she saw them. It wasn't the way things used to be done, but she couldn't think of any part of the picture she would change. They were busy talking about boats with Laido and Colbee, drawing pictures in the sand, straining to see what someone else was pointing to as the light dimmed. They seemed so much older than when they left, not so long ago. *Life lived in a hurry*, she thought. And over there, at the edge of the celebration, Nulo and Tahn were speaking to the puppeteer, while Aeta and Sula, the hooded woman, built a fire. *What a strange pair they make, one so tall and one so short, yet their movements seem so smooth, as if they've worked together for years. Our family is growing.*

CHAPTER 18
YALI

Since the first light of dawn found most of the islanders still sleeping off the party of the night before, only a few people rose early enough to see a burly man pull his boat onto the beach. As soon as he'd beached the boat, he shouted at the onlookers, demanding to see the chief of the settlement. Since that meant everyone on Seal Island, a fisherman who'd been working on his boat walked up to him.

The man grabbed the fisherman by the shoulders. "My son has been kidnapped! Help me find him! I'll kill those people, I will!"

When the fisherman tried to get more specific information, the man only shouted the same accusations. The noise drew a small crowd from down the beach.

The fisherman tried again. "What is your son's name? What does he look like? Who do you think kidnapped him?"

"Fen!" the man yelled. "He looks like a boy! What else would he look like, a fish? Don't you people listen? I knew he'd sneak out again, especially after the kite. It's them, I know; he thought the dark one was something special. Oh, so smart, so talented. So he snuck off somehow. I know he's here. All the rejects end up here."

The listeners looked at each other and shrugged.

"The man makes no sense at all."

"Wasn't there a boy named Fen at the party last night?"

"Get the alarm stick. We'll head over to Laido's camp."

Hearing the pounding of the hollowed-out piece of wood, Laido stepped out of his hut, rubbing his eyes.

"What -" he started.

Fen's father ran into him, butting him with his lowered head, throwing him backwards into the hut.

"Kidnapper! Thief!" he screamed, moving in to kick Laido.

Jin, Tahn, and Goh were on him instantly, holding him back.

"It figures! Too scared to fight for yourself, right? Need your bodyguards to fight for you?" His face was flushed red, the veins throbbing on the sides of his forehead.

Struggling to get his breath, Laido walked up to the man. "Who are you, other than a raving madman?"

"Yali," he spit. "Father of Fen, the boy you kidnapped."

Colbee stepped forward. "We didn't kidnap Fen. He came here on his own."

"You lie! No boy could find this place on his own. Especially him. Sniveling coward, always hiding in the dark. He had to have help. Who else would have helped him?"

"Tell me what the problem is," Colbee said, moving between Laido and Yali. "Are you worried about Fen? Would you like to talk to him? If he told you he was all right -"

With a yell, Yali squirmed out of Jin's grip and lunged at Colbee, wrenching a bamboo knife from his sash. His hand never reached its target. Colbee deflected the blow with his left arm and grabbed his opponent's arm with his right, twisting Yali around as his own momentum drove him past. Screaming, Yali fell to his knees, his arm twisted up behind his back.

"We'll ask the Islanders to decide," Laido said. "It's the law here." He made no attempt to help Yali, nor did anyone else. The man stayed there, on his knees, spitting and seething with his arm twisted over his back, until a group of locals gathered to hear his story.

"That one there kidnapped my son," Yali yelled, pointing at Colbee. "And the other helped."

One the locals motioned Yali to stand up and asked, "Where is the boy now?"

"I'm here," Fen said, from the back of the crowd. "And I came here on my own. No one kidnapped me. I ran away. I heard some people saying they were on their way here, so I hid in a pile of yagal mats until we were too far away for them to turn around and take me back. Actually, they were nice to me. They gave me food and water. I wouldn't have made it without their help."

"And why did you want to come to Seal Island?" another man asked.

"Because," he said, then paused. "*They* would be here."

"I'm his father!" Yali interrupted. "I don't care what these people said. They probably lied to him. What does he know, only a boy, they might sell him or leave him to die on the sea. He needs to be at home. I need him to help me catch fish, mend nets, that sort of thing."

"Of course," said a woman hidden in the crowd. "You want him back in your happy home. And where is your wife, sir?"

"My wife died," Yali said, searching for the woman who had asked the question.

"How did she die?"

He jerked his head up. "Who needs to know? She fell."

Fen stepped forward. "He killed her," he said quietly. The crowd buzzed with people asking what he had said, so it was repeated down the line, like an echo.

"She fell! Fell on the rocks and hit her head," Yali said. His teeth clenched, he repeated the words one at a time: "Fell. On. The. Rocks."

After the islanders conferred for a moment, their spokesman turned to Fen. "The choice is yours, son. You're welcome to stay or go."

"I want to stay."

"Then you must go," he said to Yali. "By island law, you are officially not welcome here."

"Who cares about your law? Who's going to stop me? I could kill any one of you, or all of you." He pointed to Colbee. "That one first."

Six islanders specially picked for their talents approached Yali to enforce the decree. Each one looked as if he could crush the bully with his bare hands.

Backing away from the men coming toward him, Yali yelled, "Fine! Stay here. It should suit you here, living on an island full of killers and witches. But you'll be sorry later. You'll be sorry you didn't come home. Really sorry." He spit at Colbee and Laido. "Really sorry."

That night Fen crouched by the communal fire, sliding burning sticks out of the flames, holding them up so he could see everything around him, then pushing them back into the fire.

Rana knelt down next to him and felt him shaking. "It will never go away – completely," she said, putting her arm around his shoulders, "but having friends who understand can take away some of its power."

"It's not just me," Fen answered. "He could kill any of you now because you stood up for me. You're in danger. It's my fault. I didn't think he'd bother to find me."

"No. It's not your fault at all. We all chose to do what we did. And we want you to be here with us."

Fen started shaking again as he tried to form the words. "I want to be here," he managed, "but I'm scared."

CHAPTER 19
PREPARATIONS, CELEBRATIONS

Laido called the whole group together, explaining first that no one was obligated to continue on the next part of the journey.

"I won't try to minimize the difficulty or the danger," he said. "You know the stories. It's hard to explain why anyone would even attempt the journey. You will probably never come back to this place. You may die on the way. We do not know what lies on the other side. The effort makes no sense at all, except to the few dreamers who can't pass up the chance to find out what lies beyond the edge of the known world." He paused. "Take your time before you commit to this trip. Go with us only if you really want to. Don't let anyone else persuade you." He looked from face to face, feeling their gazes locked on him. "We're an odd bunch," he laughed.

"And proud of it!" they shouted back to him.

"We have two boats to build: a new passenger boat and a garden boat. To plan accurately, we need to know how many we are! Tell me clearly whether you plan to go or to stay. Either answer is fine, but don't assume I know how you feel."

Nulo and Aeta stood together. "We wish to cross the sea with you."

Fuhua and Liwei were on their feet to add themselves to the list before the sentence was finished. And Kiah and Colbee. And Darna, Nina, Ryu, Tahn, Jin and Goh.

"And I, if you will have me," Hao offered.

"And we would like to come, if you would have us," Rana said.

"I need to hear from each," Laido said. "It's important."

Fen spoke first. "I want to go with you."

"I want to see what is beyond the edge," Sula said as she looked at the group standing on the hill. "And I cannot imagine finer companions on such a journey."

A shout went up from the group, confirming their identity and their will.

"Then we have a lot of work to do!" Laido yelled. He gave some special assignments: to establish a stock of trade goods, to design the new boat and oversee building it, to oversee the setup of the new garden boat, to see to the navigational aids, to gather the tools and weapons needed, and to organize the process of making new cloth and baskets. Anyone without a specific task was expected to help with others. Rana asked if she could bring her puppets, and after some discussion, the group decided that they would find room for them.

Laido didn't deal with the questions that had been bothering him: what to do if someone, or everyone, panicked once they were far at sea; what to do if they got separated; what to do when they reached, or didn't reach, the other side. Some questions would just have to resolve themselves.

* * *

Ryu approached Laido after dinner. "Sir, may I speak to you for a moment?"

"Ryu, there's only one thing I can think of that would make you address me as 'Sir.' If her answer is 'Yes,' and I know it is, then mine is also. I couldn't be happier. But you will have to tell the rest of the family."

When Ryu spoke to Darna, she listened without interrupting though she'd already heard the news. When he finished, she asked her own questions, listened to his answers, and then gave her consent.

"This is the journey of a lifetime, Ryu – filled with dangers as well as delights. Nina is your partner in that journey. You must take care of each other. Otherwise the journey will end in distant cries of pain. Do you understand?"

After he nodded, she looked past him. "Are Nulo and Aeta married?"

"I suppose they are. They married themselves. He asked, she agreed, and that was it."

"That's not it," Darna replied. "We'll add them to the celebration."

"But, they don't want -" Ryu started.

"What?"

"I don't think they want a big celebration."

"Of course they do," Darna said. "I'll talk to them."

"No," Aeta said. "I don't want it."

Darna put her hand on Aeta's arm. "I'm not trying to do something you don't want, but it's an occasion that should be marked."

Aeta's fierce eyes looked back at her without yielding.

"A nice dinner, then." Darna dropped her gaze. "Perhaps a song. Tomorrow, after the day's work is done."

The hard line of Aeta's jaw relaxed. "All right. Thank you. That's kind of you. I suppose this was bound to happen," she added, looking away.

* * *

The next day, Jin and Tahn made several trips to local merchants and stashed their bundles out of sight. Fuhua did his own bargaining, keeping his deals secret. Sula and Rana worked on something they hid from almost everyone. Kiah sent Fen off to find rose apples, water lilies, yagal fruits, and red and yellow flowers of any kind that wasn't poisonous.

When Ryu asked Colbee about raising the sides of the boat at the stern and moving the second mast farther back, Colbee seemed distracted.

"Good idea. You should try it," Colbee said as he dusted off his hands.

"Are you leaving?"

"Well, I've - I'm - hungry," Colbee said as he backed away. "I have to fix some things."

All the workers seemed to have disappeared.

"Where's Nulo?" Ryu asked Darna.

"He went to look for Aeta. She left when the sun was new."

"Going where?"

"I don't know. Up the mountain, I think."

* * *

It wasn't hard for Nulo to find Aeta's tracks and follow them up to the high rocks. As the sun rose, it threw her shape into silhouette, her long shadow reaching over the edge of the rock and continuing on the ledge below. As he approached, she stopped but did not turn around.

"You have to leave, Nulo."

"No. I have to stay."

"Don't make this worse for both of us."

"Having you leave is worse."

With a cry, she turned to him. "I wish I could be someone else, Nulo. I do. I wish I could live my life with you and be part of the family. I want to go with you but I can't. Believe me, this is the best thing I can do for you and all of the others."

"What are you saying?"

"I carry death, Nulo. It's a terrible burden I can never put aside. Everywhere I go, people die. We didn't leave our village; we escaped before we were killed. After my parents died, my grandfather took my brother and me away from our island during the night. My brother died on the boat before we reached the Fat Men's island. When I left with the others to go back to Raidu's island, some people on my boat grew suspicious when they knew my grandfather was dying. They turned around and left us back where you found me. He died within days."

"I'm sorry -" Nulo began.

"That's not the end. I knew I had to die to stop the spread of death. Every day I stood on the cliff, thinking I would jump off, yet day after day, I didn't. When the swift took me into the cave and I saw the dead family there, I thought I was meant to go with them, so I would have some company on my journey to the Otherworld. Then, somehow you found me."

"In a dream I saw you, weeping, by the great split tree, with your head bowed to the ground," Nulo said. "Why would I be given that vision if not to guide me?"

Aeta shook her head. "You say that, but you don't understand. When I make everyone out on the boats sicken, and they float, dying, at the edge of the world, you will hate me."

"Why am I not sick? Why are Ryu and Nina not sick?"

Aeta paused. "I don't know. Perhaps it will come later."

"Everyone on the boats had swamp fever. If you were spreading that sickness, all of us would be dead, yet we're not. No one is. You think you caused the illness in your village, but you didn't. Before the sun rises from the sea, the birds sing, yet they do not cause the sun to be born, even though it might look that way to someone watching."

"It's kind of you," Aeta said.

"It's selfish of you to want to leave," Nulo replied.

"Is it?" Her voice wavered.

"If you take your life, you take mine as well."

"Why would you save me?"

"Why don't we deserve to be happy?"

They were standing side by side, looking out over the sea, when Ryu found them. "What's wrong?" he called.

"It might be better if the celebration is only for you and Nina today," Nulo said.

"Why? Don't you want to be part of it?"

"It's not as if -"

"As if what? As if people cared enough to want to celebrate your wedding?"

"I was never initiated; my skin is empty," Nulo said. "Aeta and I were all right before. Why go through all this as if we were regular people?"

"You are regular people! Both of you! When are you going to understand that? Your friends want to have a party, that's all. They're worried about a long trip across the ocean that they may not survive, and they want to have a great feast and celebrate something before they go. You just happen to be the excuse. When they give you gifts, they're giving to themselves as well. We'll certainly face our share of tragedy. Let's enjoy our day of celebration and not deny it to others."

Nulo stared at the stone fragments by his feet. "If Aeta will be part of the celebration, I will be too."

"Aeta?" Ryu asked. "Is something wrong? You and Nulo seem so happy together."

"We are."

"Is there something else?"

Without glancing at Nulo, she shook her head. "No, there's nothing else. Of course we'll be part of the celebration."

"Then we don't have to spend any more time up here, do we?" Ryu said. "Let's start back. Everyone's worried about you."

* * *

Late that afternoon, Darna and Kiah set out honeyed water lily blooms and nut meats cut into flower shapes, piled in the center with roasted beetles, watery rose apples, and root cakes. The lobsters, crabs, and oysters arrived already steamed and wrapped in palm leaves, courtesy of Fuhua and Liwei. Since those two had engaged half the island's population in the preparation of the feast, they also invited everyone, so the party grew to a string of celebrations that went all the way from the town to the harbor. Many people contributed their personal favorites: roasted seahorses, grasshoppers, and cicadas on sticks, snails, tiny salty dried fish, mini-shrimp, areca nuts, roasted iguana eggs, kava leaves, snakes cooked on spits, sea grapes coated with honey. For those seeking a little more adventure, there was fermented breadfruit and palm wine, as well as sea chubs and goatfish that had been fed on lukay-lukay that made the mouth numb and gave the mind visions.

The musicians started early, providing the background to the preparations and welcoming the first guests, though it was hard to distinguish the guests from the hosts. Everyone seemed to be involved in decorating the site and bringing in food. To get things started, Fuhua called for the drummers to pound a three-beat alert. When the friends assembled on the hillside, the drums switched to the loud-soft two-beat announcement. More people crowded onto the hillside. It was filled by the time the flutes announced the arrival of the principals.

The four friends walked out together. Nina and Ryu wore light bark cloth tunics with black waterbird designs drawn on them. Around Ryu's neck and waist were garlands of red flowers. Nina wore hers around her neck and woven into her plaited hair. Long curved Bird of Paradise feathers decorated Ryu's topknot.

Nulo wore a dark orange tunic decorated with black saberfish designs and a woven black headdress topped with black feathers and yellow flowers. Aeta wore strings of yellow flowers over her orange tunic and a yellow orchid behind her ear. Her hair was pulled back as usual, but instead of being tied in a thick braid, it was plaited into braids decorated with beads and golden shells.

Ryu spoke first. "This is not a traditional wedding, but then we are not traditional people," he began. "Nina and I stand before you to make public the promises we have already made to each other. This moment binds us to everyone here. Our joy becomes your joy and your joy adds to ours. A man I once knew said people are just blown about like dead leaves in a wind. I disagree. I have friends who are stronger than the wind. They are the only reason I am standing here today."

Ryu turned to Nina and held out his hand. "I ask you, Nina, to be my wife."

She took his hand in hers as she looked at him. "I will. I ask you to be my husband. I ask also that we dare to put our lives in each other's care and to dream huge dreams."

Ryu put his free hand on top of the others. "Yes."

The crowd cheered, slapped their legs, stomped in rhythm, and banged on signal woods until Fuhua signaled for quiet once again.

Nulo stepped forward, scanning the sea of faces in the crowd. "Words have never been easy for me," he said at last, "and now they are threatening to abandon me completely. I used to try to be invisible. I'm sure some of you know what I mean: that you're better when no one sees you. But now that's changed. Aeta can see into the center of people. She saw me and found me – valuable.

"I, we, need to leave our hiding places. Others have given us a light. We need to stand in it, let it fill us, and then give it to others.

"Aeta, blue-white brightness," he said, bowing to her, "my wife." Once again, the crowd cheered.

When the crowd quieted, Aeta stepped forward. "Like Nulo, I do not have a treasure of words. I have to dig each one up, as you would clams with a stick, but I will try.

"I didn't know the kindness of strangers until I got to Fuhua and Liwei's Island. At their Brightness Day celebration, I was able to sing my brother into the Otherworld, and I met Nulo. Through him, I learned the love that others give us allows us to live all the way, not just to survive.

"Finest light, Nulo, my husband," she said, as she took his hand. Then she looked around at the group of friends. "Thank you. You are my family."

The group of friends started a syncopated slapping and stomping that was picked up by the entire crowd, growing ever louder and faster until it blended into a sea of noise.

"I think it's time to celebrate!" Fuhua called to the crowd.

And they did.

For a long time, there was a happy confusion of music and dance and food and people. When the day's light grew softer and the musicians had eaten well, Rana slipped onto the stage in her black covering, carrying a new puppet, a detailed, almost full-size version of Ryu, exact down to his tunic designs and the feathers in his topknot. Next to her, also in black, Sula carried a Nina puppet, with an exact copy of her hair and clothes. Instead of sitting down to work the puppets, they stood behind them, like shadows. When the flutes began a melody and countermelody, the puppets stood and faced each other, then bowed. As they moved toward each other, the drums joined in, adding a bass beat that was taken up by the crowd. Then the woods came in on top, as the puppets linked arms, facing the audience. The puppets' legs were strapped to the puppet masters' legs, so that, while their arms could move independently, their legs moved in concert with their shadow double behind them.

As they danced, Tahn sang, with a clear, deep voice, the old ballad of the sea spirit who wanted to dance with the sun. She tried everything the sea creatures told her, but they knew nothing of the sky, and every suggestion failed. Finally, though she knew she would not survive there, she threw herself into the sky just as the sun was sinking into the watery underworld. As the sun's light touched her, she turned from blue-green to red-orange, and in that moment he saw her and loved her. And so she became the water spirit that dances with the sun, living only for a moment, at that last flash of daylight. Sometimes you can still see them dancing together on the water, at sunset.

As the song went on and the Ryu and Nina puppets danced, they were joined by Nulo and Aeta puppets, worked by two other figures in black. The four went through a familiar dance, facing their partners, bowing, dancing side by side with their arms linked, then twirling about, arms held high. As the song neared its end, the puppets did some fancy footwork, cross-stepping, stomping, and kicking out, until the crowd yelled their approval. The puppets waved the family and friends over to join the dance, and then waved to everyone else who wanted to join them. Eventually, so many spectators swelled the ranks of dancers that they spilled out of the arena and up onto the hillside, taking with them the real Nina, Ryu, Nulo, and Aeta. Kiah and Colbee were not in the group of guests; they were swathed in black, doing a respectable job as first-time puppeteers.

CHAPTER 20
ATTACK

At the new sun rose from the sea the next day, the harbor area was deserted except for Fen. He sang as he sat on a rock by the river's edge, his feet just touching the water. He sang to the eels, calling them ever so softly, singing them up into the shallows. When he saw the first eel slither up onto the bank, he stepped off his rock and hunkered down next to it. Again he called to the eels, and more slid up onto the bank. One by one he picked them up, still singing to them while they curled lazily around his arm or hung limply from his hand as he ran his finger along them. Then he set them down gently, stopped singing, and stood up. One by one the eels woke from their trance and slid back into the water.

As he turned back toward the village, his face suddenly flushed hot; a familiar sick feeling rose in his mouth. He spun around, scanning the beach and the harbor until he spotted a flash of movement out in the harbor. Someone was on Colbee's boat.

Running faster than he ever had before, leaping from rock to rock and pounding up the path to the camp, he reached Colbee's hut so out of breath and shaken that he couldn't speak.

"Breathe," Colbee said, holding him by the shoulders. "Just breathe. Then you can tell me."

"Your boat," Fen wheezed. "He's on your boat!"

"Who's on my boat?"

"My father."

On the Sailfish, Yali swung a heavy two-headed ax in great arcs, smashing into whatever was in his way: the masts, the supports, the mats, the sides, the cover over the stern section, even the floor. He moved through the growing pile of rubble, the showers of splinters, his rage like a drug racing through his veins, pushing him to more, slashing at pieces he had already hit, ignoring his own pain. When the large mat came crashing down on him, he slashed away at it, nicking his own leg as the ax swept through the mat.

Two figures jumped onto the boat and Yali took aim, swinging the great ax and charging at the closer man. Jin twirled a short rope with monkey-fist knots at each end, then threw it horizontally so it wrapped around Yali's knees. Thrown down by his own momentum, Yali landed with a crash, hitting his face on the smashed pieces littering the bottom of the boat and burying his ax in the planks. With a bellow, he ripped the rope off and pushed himself back up, blood streaming from his face and leg. Rushing at Colbee, he swung the rope hammer into Colbee's face.

"Ha!" Yali screamed, but Jin, holding Yali's ax in one hand and his own knife in the other, stepped in front of Colbee.

Pulling up short, Yali spit at Jin. "You'll have to kill me," he said. "I'll never give up. I'll never slink away. Just when you think I've gone, I'll come back. You won't have any pretty ending. So let's see if you're man enough to finish off an injured opponent. Not even a fair fight. That's how you like it, isn't it?"

"You've never fought fair in your life," Jin answered. "Mostly you beat up women and children. You're a coward."

With a lunge, Yali was at Jin's throat, clamping his hands tight, crushing Jin's windpipe as Jin jabbed his knife into Yali's chest. As Yali staggered back and then closed once again, Jin tucked the knife back in his sash, planted his feet and swung the ax. Yali grabbed at the handle, deflecting the blow and wrenching it out of Jin's hands. Swinging it high, Yali moved in for the kill. Sidestepping, Jin avoided the ax blow by a hand's width. As it passed, Jin grabbed his knife, lunged forward, and jabbed it upward between the man's ribs. The ax had started back on its deadly arc before Yali's grip failed. The ax whirled past, crashing into the side of the boat. Yali collapsed, slumping into the wreckage as blood pooled around him

Colbee's hands shook as he knelt in the rubble to check the body. "Everything is broken," Colbee cried, "even the breaker."

"I'm sorry for your loss, friend, but there's someone over there who needs to know that there's still hope," Jin said, pointing to the shore.

Fen sat with his back to them, his head pressed against the trunk of a palm. With an effort, Colbee climbed out of the boat and sat next to the boy until his ragged sobs quieted.

Fen glanced at Colbee and pressed his forehead back against the tree. "I'm so sorry! All of this is my fault."

"No," Colbee answered. "It's not, but it's a terrible thing to see your father killed. I'm sorry."

After a moment, Fen looked at him. "I wish I had a nice memory of him to keep. He destroyed everything - people, things, even the boat."

"It'll take a while, maybe a long while. In the meantime, you can help me build a new boat."

"You mean – I can still come with you?"

Colbee put his arm around the boy's shoulders. "Yes. We need your help."

Before they got to work on the boat, the group buried Yali in a hill cave. They sent him to the Otherworld with hopes that he would find peace there, even though it had eluded him in this world. After examining the boat, Colbee felt there was little worth saving on it. Everything that wasn't ruined was tainted with death, so they towed the Sailfish out of the harbor and burned it.

There was hardly any conversation that night. Rana tried to talk to Fen, but it was too early. The wound was too new to heal.

CHAPTER 21
BOAT BUILDING

The incident on the Sailfish weakened them. Though they seldom spoke of it, many saw it as an omen.

"They need to work," Laido confided to his wife. "They need good work, hard work. They only need a spark, like tinder waiting for a fire."

"Draw them in," Darna suggested. "Close to you. Make them part of the work."

"All right. I will."

He asked all those who were not usually involved in boat design to meet him on the beach. After he dampened and cleared the sand, he gave each one a stick and asked that they draw their idea of the perfect boat. The design didn't even have to be possible, just a concept. Sula drew a boat with a high bow, topped with a carved dragon head. Fen's had a special mat at the top that flew by itself, with a boy holding on. Jin's had raised sections along the top edge where archers could take cover. Liwei's had a storage area built into the bow of the boat. Kiah added a tarp hung over a line strung between the masts. Hao wanted a table as a work surface. Rana wanted a boat that could fly. When Darna looked at Rana's drawing of a boat in the air, she drew two extremely large mats on her own boat – one in each direction, like a seabird's wings, and an arrow pointing from one to the other.

When the drawings were done, Laido called Colbee, Ryu, and Nina to look at the designs.

"It's foolishness," Colbee complained. Then he stopped and looked at each design, going back to check on some he'd already passed. "No," he added, "it's not."

A day-long discussion followed, with the participants altering, erasing, or replacing some parts, accompanied by lots of gesturing as imaginary boats hit heavy seas or high winds or shallow waters.

Darna wrapped her arm around Laido's waist. "Well done," she said.

Once they had worked out the designs they wanted, they moved quickly. With the help of the most experienced of the island's boat builders, the new boats started to take shape. Colbee wanted something similar to the Sailfish, except with a second mat and an even larger lower fin. Ryu wanted to go back to the original wind raft design of the platform over the base of two canoes, except he wanted to make them narrower, so they would slice through the water at the bow. The canoes would be the same on both ends, so the boat could be reversed easily. The canoes also could hold supplies. The boat could be beached easily, and the wide area in the center could be covered with a tarp, as Kiah had suggested. It wouldn't have a bottom fin, but the narrow canoe bottoms would help stabilize it. As the island builders suggested, they added two wide paddles that could be worked from the middle of the boat. And they agreed with Colbee's design for the mats and the large rear steering board that could be lifted if necessary.

When they were talking about the new mats, Darna asked why they couldn't have different size mats for different wind conditions. "You could have some large mats for days with little wind, one on each side like giant bat wings. Then, when the wind's stronger, you could put up the regular mats. Or add the other ones to the regular mats – somehow."

"Interesting," Colbee said. "How long would it take to make these huge wing extensions?"

"It depends," she said. "Do you want them made of strung bamboo shoots, woven yagal leaves, or bark cloth? Can we hire some of the local weavers to help with them? Otherwise, it's going to take a long time, longer than I think you want."

"I'm sorry," Colbee sighed. "I have nothing left to trade."

Later that day, Sula handed Darna a woven pouch about the size of a man's hand. "It's for the work on the boats," she said.

Darna opened the pouch and peered inside before empty- ing the contents into her hand. Pearls. Creamy white and pale blue pearls, some golden yellow, others warm pink, dark green, even some blue-black pearls, the rarest of all. Some were tiny, about the size of a ki seed, some were the size of sea grapes, and some as big as a man's thumbnail. Momentarily silenced by the wealth she held in her hand, Darna looked up, then began sputtering her thanks, but Sula had already left.

"You know how to wring the most from a bargain," she said, showing the pearls to Fuhua. "Could you see how many weavers and boat builders we could hire with these?"

Even Fuhua was impressed. "Many. Plus supplies."

"Good. In addition to the wood and mats for Colbee's boat, we need mats for Ryu's. And for my giant wings."

"Are you going to fly?"

"No, but the boat might." Darna smiled. "I have to talk to Ryu and Colbee about the wings."

Hao told them to bring food with them, so Kiah oversaw the creation of the food boat. If they were at sea for a very long time, at least they could eat something besides fish. Colbee noted that if they added some ki and breadfruit plants, they could also have something interesting to drink. Kiah planned raised beds in tiers to maximize the space, putting down a layer of river stones, crushed whitestone, humus, and topsoil. Each bed was slanted so the water could run into channels, down through the bed, and then, after it had been slowed down by water lilies, to the lower level. Over the plant beds she added a large tarp made from woven yagal leaves, which could also be used as a fresh water collector.

In addition, the garden boat housed the land turtles, trogon birds, bees, earthworms, frogs and toads. Liwei had wanted to bring some trees, but they demanded too much space. In the end, she agreed to a couple of young yagal trees. They could use every part, from leaves to roots. And, of course, they would bring a store of coconuts, as well as other hardy seeds.

With lots of help, she got all of the beds established, the seeds planted, the animals settled in. "It looks good while it's on dry land under sunny skies," she said to Darna. "The real test will come later."

As the boats took shape, islanders started offering suggestions, mostly about charms that might keep the sea monsters at bay. One old man said he'd been lost at sea without fresh water and he would have died except that a crazy man on an island had told him how to get fresh water from sea water.

"How did you do it?"

"It's not that complicated," the old man explained to Laido. "You put a raised tarp over a bowl of sea water and tie the tarp so that the ends funnel down into clean bowls or clam shells. Then you let the sun turn the sea water into cloud. The cloud rises to the tarp and then comes back down into the bowls, but it leaves the salt behind in the center bowl. You get water you can drink." He paused. "The water doesn't taste very good, but it's better than having none. And if you put the bowl of salty sludge in the sun, you'll get salt, so you can preserve your fish."

Laido clapped the man on the back. "Good idea! Thank you – What is your name?"

The man flashed a toothless smile. "I don't remember."

At the camp, Laido found a dozen women working on the new mats: stripping the outside bark from the mulberry trunks, scraping out the pulpy inner bark, sifting through it, removing impurities, pounding it, soaking it, pressing it out on the forms, letting it dry in the sun. Behind them, four men worked on the twin hulls of the wind raft, two polished the masts, and Sula carved the dragon head that would go on the Sailfish bow. The body of the boat was ready for its first coat of coconut oil, red clay, and warm sap.

"The boat needs a name," Laido said. "What do you think, Nina?"

"What about Wind Raft?"

Laido laughed. "A fine name."

Fen asked Kiah once again if he could bring some snakes. The two large constrictors that were casually wrapped around his neck as he spoke did not help his case. Hao got the table he wanted, which Ryu arranged so that it could be folded up against the sides to provide the protection that Jin wanted.

Darna worried about the size of the group - seventeen people. "Even if two people can ride on the garden boat, that's still a lot of people, two of them very large people, on two boats. If something should happen to one of them -"

Laido looked up from his work. "You think we need to build another boat?"

"Just something to tow behind, even smaller than the garden boat. It would be our way into shore if we wanted to get in and out fast."

"I don't think we'll find a lot of places to land," Laido said, "but a small boat might be useful. We could take a canoe and tie it to the back of the Wind Raft, I suppose, though it would mean more drag on the boat -"

Darna waited.

"We'll see if we can get one from the islanders," Laido agreed. "I won't mention it to the group until we're leaving. I don't want it filled with possessions people should have left behind."

Ryu and Colbee invited everyone to paint designs on the boats and the mats. In addition to large round fish eyes painted on the sides near the bow, lines of turtles, sharks, rays, and sea hawks appeared along the water line of the boats. On the mats, they added a large bat, a sailfish, cloud figures, sky spirits, the Morning and Evening Star, the dancing stone, the sky rock falling from the heavens, the rising sun, twin snakes, a crested iguana, a warrior with a spear, a flutist, a tuber vine, a red hibiscus flower. Painted with dyes made from soot, local clays, and tree sap, the figures channeled the energy of ancestors and spirits. They brought the boats to life.

Finally the boats were in the water, with the breeze catching the banners flying from the high masts and the designs along the waterline flashing among the waves. Even the Seal Island boat makers, who had seen all kinds of boats come and go, stopped and stared.

Once the Wind Raft was clear of the harbor, Ryu, Tahn, and Nina put up the batwing extensions, one on each mast. While Tahn was still struggling to pull up the second wing, the wind caught both wings and pitched the boat forward. The wind lifted the boat and it flew over the water. Nina threw up her arms and shouted as the wind tore tears from her eyes.

"I wonder what it looks like from shore," Tahn mused, "with these wings stretched out like a seabird."

"They're very effective," Laido said, "but hard to maneuver."

"We've got some learning to do," Ryu yelled as he tried to lower one of the wings. "If they touch the water, they'll pull the boat over."

Laido grabbed the section Ryu was trying to reach. "Maybe we can raise the bottom edge, or cut part of it off."

"The wings are amazing!" Nina cried. "Rana was right: it does fly."

CHAPTER 22
THE FLATTENING OF TIME

Gradually they lost the land. At first, as they pulled away, they couldn't tell who was still on shore. Then they couldn't tell how many. Later the village faded, then the curve of the lagoon, the forests and hills behind it, and finally the island itself. After the island disappeared, they felt themselves shrink to mere specks on the sea. Day after day, the sea took over all the space under the sun, with no floating mats of vegetation, no seabirds returning to roost, not even a cloud or a patch of light on the water indicating an island in the distance. When night came, brilliant stars swept all the way down into the sea, where they found their doubles in the waves. The boats became invisible. It was, Darna thought, just as Hao had said: people become completely insignificant on the wide ocean. If they cannot accept that, they will die, and the sea will not notice.

"Keep track of the days," Liwei reminded Ryu. "If we don't have any land to measure distance, we'll know by day count how far we've gone."

Ryu agreed, though after many days went by, no one asked him for the count, not even Liwei.

Laido set the star sequence for Ryu to follow on clear nights. After the sun sank into the sea on the west, the Diving Bird would rise in the east. After it was two fists high off the horizon as he sighted along his arm, the Long Eel would begin setting in the west. When that was half-way down, the Basket would rise in the east. When it was three fists high, the Maiden Star would set in the west.

At the same time the Whale would be rising on the eastern horizon, followed by the Young Whale. The Scorpion would set two fists short of west. Before dawn, the Hunter would rise in the east. Since he knew where all the figures were, he could use the two sighting points on the Wind Raft to keep on course.

Some nights, though, he had trouble concentrating. The stars didn't behave the way they had when he'd watched them from his Sky Circle. The rising full moon flooded out the stars he needed to see. With the pitch and roll of the boat, stars lurched from one spot to another, rearranging themselves at will. At times, it seemed new stars appeared. When clouds blocked the stars, Laido took over navigation, depending on the long waves as guides. Ryu tried to learn how to read the messages the water sent through the boat, but he couldn't always see the invisible rivers Laido described flowing through the sea. Ryu sometimes forgot whether he'd marked a day once, twice, or not at all. All the little dots on the turtle shell began to overlap, dancing in rows, changing places.

Some days they saw wonders: enormous whale sharks basking near the surface, their mouths agape, pods of whales resting like islands, dolphins forming a ring of bubbles to drive fish to the surface, schools of tuna and wahoo so large they surrounded the boats for days. One night, Nina found the sea around the boat filled with moving lines of light, every wave crested with a quivering line of green-gold light that rippled and danced, slipping under and resurfacing, reforming itself with the water's every move. Where the boat's hulls sliced through the water, the light fell away in a never-ending shower of stars. Everywhere she looked, the magic lines of light coalesced and dissipated, then formed again.

Ryu came up and stood next to her. "Navigators use it to read the long waves at night. I saw it from the stern: the boat's wake is all tumbling lights."

"The sea is dancing with light," Nina said.

When she tried to explain the lights to Tahn the next day, he stopped her in mid-sentence. "What we need is water. We've been rationing water for days. We're trying to supply too many people."

"Well, it should rain soon," Nina offered.

"Not a cloud to be seen," Tahn noted.

The next day the sun crawled across a cloudless sky. The day after that was the same, and the next, and the next, until they lost count. As the sun beat down on the endless sea, Laido fell sick. Others only stared at the sea. When Ryu set up the seawater converter Laido wanted, he got a little bit of brackish water no one liked. While they all drank their rations, it did nothing to slake their thirst. They caught fish and ate them raw though the salty taste made the thirst worse. Kiah offered the withered garden produce to anyone interested, but few could manage to chew the greens.

"I'm thirsty," Fen complained. "When will it rain?"

No one answered.

Their world ceased its normal time. Instead of the rising of the new sun from the sea, the growing height of it, and then the falling toward the sea, the sun slowed to an impossibly slow pace.

After a while, they stopped looking for rain, so they were caught unprepared when a storm came up suddenly. After the sun had slipped into the sea, the winds rose. Ryu, Nina, and Tahn struggled to lower the Wind Raft's extended wings. On the Sailfish, Colbee and Goh climbed up the masts to lower the mats, hoping that the flashes of lightning that helped them see wouldn't also kill them. Below, Liwei and Fuhua tried to reach the tarps that had been folded away out of sight in the bow. On the garden boat, the wind caught the cover, pulling at its ties. To keep it from blowing away, Kiah and Fen held down the ends all through the storm. Everyone moved slowly, as if they'd grown stupid from thirst and had to think about each motion. They ran into each other in the dark when they were trying to move the mats. "Take this!" someone would yell in the dark, only to hear someone else yell, "What is it? Where should I put it?"

"Set out the water collectors!" Kiah called, hoping someone would.

Hao didn't help the others. As they worked, he stood out on the open deck, arms extended, until the wind and rain were at their peak and Fuhua led him back under the tarp.

"I need to give myself to the lightning, to the storm," Hao cried, stepping back into the storm.

"That's enough of that," Jin said, giving him a sharp blow to the head.

"Something's wrong," Ryu complained after the storm had passed. "The Wind Raft is sitting different."

"A leak?" Goh suggested.

"I don't think so. If one of the hulls was leaking, the whole boat would be listing. It's something else, like it's standing still in the moving sea."

"Something's pulling on it?"

"Yes. Something we forgot." Leaning over the stern, Ryu hauled on the soaked line, pulling the dugout canoe closer. "It must be completely submerged, and we can't empty it in the dark."

"What about trying to lift one end?"

"It's too heavy to lift from here."

Even with a torch held high, Nina could see nothing beyond the line disappearing into the water. "Will it pull the boat down?"

"It depends on how deep it is," Goh said. "Right now, it's just slowing us down."

"If we had a long stick -" Ryu started.

"We could tell how deep it is," Goh finished.

"What about the speed rope?" Nina said.

"I'll get the rope," Goh said as he disappeared out of the circle of torchlight.

"It's not designed to drop straight down. It's too light," Ryu complained.

Nina tried to see beneath the scatter of reflected light. "What do we do if it sinks?"

"Cut the line. Better to lose the canoe than our boat."

Goh pushed past Nina with the speed rope, but as he leaned out and threw it, the rope tightened around his ankles, pitching him forward. Nina heard the smack of his head on one of the hulls and the splash as he fell into the water, dragging the rope with him. Nina shoved the torch at Ryu and jumped in, ignoring Ryu's call to stop. She tried to remember exactly how Goh fell so she could figure out where he'd gone under water. She swam past the end of the hull and along the downward-pitching canoe, feeling her way with sweeping arm motions. When something brushed against her leg, she sucked in a deep breath and dove lower until she found it – a loop of rope. Holding it tight in her fist, she followed it to Goh, finding it tangled around his body. She pulled hard, trying to free him, but the effort only tightened the loops around him. Frustrated, she gripped his arm and swam toward what she hoped was the surface. Somewhere above, lights danced: a torch over the water. She kicked up, one arm pointing to the lights, the other wrapped around Goh.

At the surface, she gasped for air. From the boat, people shouted words she couldn't understand. Darna extended a paddle. Relieved, Nina grabbed hold of it. Many hands reached down to help lift Goh onto the boat. By the time Nina was on board, Sula was already working on Goh, rolling him onto his side and onto his back, the palms of her hands on his stomach, thrusting up and forward, pushing the water out of his chest as she sang softly. No one spoke, afraid that any sound would break the spell she was weaving, calling the water out. The fourth time she rolled him on his side, he vomited seawater and sucked air in shaky gasps interspersed with fits of coughing and gagging. With Sula's help, he sat up.

"Thank you," he wheezed when he had the breath to talk.

"Nina found you, and many others helped bring you back," she said.

All around him, people shouted his name. Ryu wrapped his arm around Nina's waist.

"Did you get the canoe?" Goh managed after a while.

"No," Tahn said. "I suspect we won't be able to lift it until it's light enough to see what we're doing. We're just happy we have everyone back. A little while ago, I thought we had too many people on board. I was wrong. We need everyone we have."

When the new sun rose from the sea, Colbee realized the Wind Raft was far behind. With no way to communicate with the other group, he decided to float with the current and hope the others could catch up. "If that doesn't work," he admitted, "maybe we could paddle back."

"We don't know where they are," Jin pointed out.

"Then think of a better idea."

"I have one," Liwei added after a moment. "At the Brightness Day celebration, I used a piece of mica and a torch to shine a beam of light."

"That would be a good idea if we had a piece of mica."

"I know someone who does."

"Interesting that you ask," his brother said, searching for the stone. "It's one of my favorites."

On deck, Liwei held up a torch. Behind him, Fuhua held the stone, turning it back and forth, back and forth, sweeping the reflection across the water from side to side while the stars moved slowly around the center of the sky.

Goh was sitting at the bow of the boat, feeling terrible, when he spotted a light skipping on the sea. When Aeta brought him something to drink, he said, "Look out there. Do you see anything unusual?"

"Nothing other than the flashing light."

"Isn't that unusual?"

"They've been signaling to us since the sun rose from the sea. Tahn has been tapping out a reply signal for them, but we don't think they heard it."

At the stern, four people tried to raise the canoe. While they could pull the canoe close to the boat, they couldn't lift it.

"Maybe we should let it go," Ryu commented.

"It's extra space and an emergency boat," Nina said.

"I could get in the water and push the other end up. Then we could tip it."

Nina pointed to a fin breaking the water, heading for the lurching canoe. "Not a good idea."

"Brace yourselves!" Ryu called as the shape moved toward the canoe. "Hands away from the edge!"

A shark bumped the canoe and turned. Water swirled around its fin as it swam the length of the boat and back.

"Give the line three quick jerks, then cut it!"

The canoe bounced under the surface. Tahn cut the rope. As it moved away from the Wind Raft, the shark grabbed the canoe and dragged it away.

"It will tire of the canoe," Nulo said. "From its scars, it looks as if it enjoys a fight."

"If it destroys one of our hulls -"

"Do we have something that we could use to hit it?" Nulo asked.

"Tahn?"

"I'll see what I can find."

Tahn handed out clubs, long knives, and spears.

"Hit it hard," he said. "Make it terrible for it to stay. Those of you with knives, be very careful the shark doesn't pull you with it. Slash at it as it goes past. Don't touch it with your hand or arm." He paused. "We need to keep our boat – and our people."

Moments later they felt the shark bump the boat.

"Spread out!" Tahn called. "It could strike anywhere."

"Should we put up the wings?" Nina called.

"Wait a while. It's watching us right now," Tahn said.

They stood at their posts, watching the wide sea. While it looked calm, almost empty on the surface, underneath lay a different realm with its own chiefs and outlaws, its own rules of life and death, and a predator watching its prey. They waited.

"I wonder -" Nina started.

Something bumped the boat again, this time right in the middle. It took Rana by surprise, but Sula reached over and swung her club as the shark went past, hitting it behind its head.

"Be ready!" Ryu yelled.

The fin sliced through the waves, marking its path as the shark headed for the middle of the boat again. Tahn slipped into a spot on the edge of the raft, between Rana and Sula. The beast came at them, rising out of the sea, mouth open. Sula swung first, hitting it on the side of the head. As it swung its head away, Rana hit it on the snout. Falling back into the water, it swam a distance before it circled back. Tahn waited, spear lifted, watching the shark swimming close to the surface. As it rose again, Tahn hurled his spear deep into the shark's gills. Thrashing backward, the shark swung its head, trying to dislodge the spear, crashing up against the side of the boat, pushing the spearhead even deeper before the beast headed away, carrying Tahn's spear with it.

When it didn't return, shouts went up from the group.

"I will make you a new spear," Nulo said to Tahn, "one fit for a fine warrior."

"I'm only one of several warriors on board," he said, nodding to Rana and Sula.

"Let's raise the wings," Ryu said, "but keep an eye out. It's not dead; we could see it again."

Goh went to help raise the wings. "We should probably set extra watches after the sun sinks."

"Good idea." Ryu looked around. "Aeta, are we still getting a signal light from the other boat?"

"No, it stopped a while ago."

"Well, we know where they are, and this boat's faster than Colbee's." He sucked in the sea air. "Especially with the wings up."

* * *

"I was getting a signal back from them, but it stopped," Jin said. "Something happened. We need to go back. I'll try signaling again."

"Something slowed them down," Colbee agreed, "but their mats are up now, and they're heading toward us. All we have to do is wait."

Jin signaled, tapping on the side of the boat for a bigger sound.

* * *

The next morning, as soon as it was light, Nulo woke Ryu, saying he'd spotted the Sailfish. As Ryu squinted into the rising sun, trying to see the other boat clearly, he thought it looked different somehow. As they got closer, they were relieved to see familiar figures on board waving to them.

"Look at the garden boat!" Ryu called.

A piece had broken off the stern, making the whole boat twist down. The tarp lay smashed down on the vegetable beds. One of the poles had snapped off.

* * *

When they'd tied the two boats together and surveyed the damage, Jin found Tahn.

"I got your spear back," Jin said, clapping Tahn on the shoulder. "The shark attacked the Sailfish first, but then it ripped a piece off the garden boat stern. After a while it came back at the main boat."

"What did you do?"

"We hit it several times. The last time I managed to get your spear out. Once the beast started bleeding, two other sharks killed it."

"We lost the canoe," Ryu said. "Any damage to the Sailfish?"

"It's not taking on water, so that's good. We're alive, you showed up, we have fresh water, and the wind's picking up."

"Then let's get going," Ryu said.

"They did well, Darna" Laido complained, "while I did nothing."

"You're sick," his wife reminded him. "It takes your strength away. Don't worry. You'll be fine soon."

He took her hand in his but he turned away.

CHAPTER 23
CHANGING STARS

The days went by, but Laido's strength did not return. Every movement took a great effort. Most of the time he slept.

"Wake me, Ryu, if you need my help," he'd said.

Ryu nodded and mumbled something in reply. It wasn't the right moment to tell Laido that the unchanging stars seemed to be changing. Lately, the Northern Bird barely cleared the horizon before it sank again. At first, Ryu blamed the anomaly on the choppy sea. Later, when the sea was calm, it was no different.

The stars do not change, he told himself. *Only the visitor stars change. The Evening Star disappeared in the Underworld, a bad sign, yet even that cannot change the stars.*

Many days later, when there should have been a No Shadow day, there wasn't. Ryu gave up counting days. The changing stars above twisted everything around so nothing went right below. That's why his leg hurt again, Laido slept all the time, Rana fell ill with fever, Aeta slipped and crashed onto the side of the boat. People saw things in the sea. Sometimes they were real, sometimes only phantasms. After a while, the distinction didn't matter. When he was awake, Laido often saw a grey whirling, like weightless raindrops in sunshine. Darna saw faces in the sea foam, forming and dissolving, forming and dissolving, each time a different face, as if all the dead had only a single moment to reappear in the waves before being replaced by another. One evening, just before the sun sank completely into the sea, they saw a flash of green light spread out across the water. When it was gone, and the sun had died, no one spoke of it, each certain it was only a vision.

Ryu knew Laido depended on him to set the course, so he did. When the fixed points he needed to steer by seemed to move, he guessed.

CHAPTER 24
MOUNTAINS IN THE SEA

When the wind picked up suddenly one morning, it caught one of the wings and swung it back, wrenching the top clasp loose and leaving the mat flopping, and Nina volunteered to see if she could fix it. She started up the knotted rope but stopped when she saw the boat's long shadow play across the water: the raft, the mast, the drooping wing, and the figure of the woman on the top who copied her every move. She played with her shadow, moving with the light. When she looked back to the boat's shadow, she found the mast pointed toward something odd.

Unwilling to name something that might not really be there, she tried to keep her voice steady. "Goh, can you come help me fix this?" Once he was high on the mast, she pointed out to sea. "You have excellent eyes. Do you see anything out there?" she whispered.

"Yes, of course!" he shouted.

"What?"

"A giant whale and a bird with a long curved tail!"

Nina shook her head slowly. "No, I meant the mat of plants. Right there."

"I know!" he said. "The bird is right past it, sitting in the water. White body, red bill, long curved white tail. See it?"

She squinted, trying to clear her vision, but she could see only a spot that might be a bird, or the color of the sea or a trick of the eye. "It's hard to tell -"

She spun around, holding on to the mast. "Ryu! Look out there! Tell me what you see!"

That alerted everyone within earshot. One by one they strained to find something.

Goh pointed. "It's a bird! There! See? It's just sitting in the water. It's got a big curved tail. In front of that island – or whale."

"It's not a whale," Tahn said. "It's not the right shape. It's an island."

"Tahn's right. It's an island. It's a mountain," Nina added.

"Then it's more than one island."

Ryu pulled himself up the mast, ignoring the pains shooting through his leg. Near the top, he steadied himself and glanced around, at first seeing nothing but the sea in all directions.

"It's only the sea," he said. "It plays tricks sometimes, especially if you want to see something out there. Let's wait and see if it moves off."

The others didn't answer, but they kept looking, waiting for someone to say definitely. The sun sank into the sea in a blaze of purple and orange but they kept looking even as the light failed and darkness raced in.

"I'm afraid to hope," Nina whispered. "If that's land out there and we can get there, and if there's water on the island, and we can get supplies and repair the boats -"

"I know," Ryu answered. "But it could be nothing at all, just like before. We'll know when the new sun rises."

Nina couldn't sleep. She awoke so often she followed the track of the stars as they whirled in their endless circle overhead, playing out their nightly story.

"Let's go see," Ryu whispered.

The waning moon had just risen, spreading its dull white light, clearly marking the dark shapes to the east. They clasped hands, not wanting to move or talk because that view had to be kept exactly there. As the sun rose from the sea, its golden light fanned out behind shapes that most certainly were not whales. They were islands, just as Tahn had said.

Everyone on the other boat already knew. On Ryu's signal, they brought the boats close together so they could decide where to go.

"We can see some smoke on top of the closest mountain – maybe a lightning fire – or maybe set by people. Another island would be a better choice."

"Which one?" Colbee asked.

"To cover more territory, we need to split up and explore the islands. If you find water, send up a signal kite for the other boat. If you find a good harbor and water, send up an extra banner on the kite. We'll do the same."

"I'll send up a test kite first," Colbee said as they were splitting up. "Ignore it."

Fen took over the kite plans. "Why can't we attach a kite to the boat's mast? Why can't we attach someone, like me, to the kite? We lifted Liwei. How hard can it be to lift me?"

Hao said, "Perhaps the better question would be 'How can we get you back down again?'"

Fen ignored him.

Colbee attached a seat bar for Fen below the kite, attached the line to the mast, and started letting the kite line out. As the sea breeze caught it, Jin helped Fen into his seat while Colbee held the line. Once Fen settled in with a firm grip on the side pieces, Colbee played out the line and the big kite soared up. With a gasp, Fen watched the world fall away under him. He felt he would turn inside out and his insides would blow away out to sea. When he closed his eyes, the world rolled, so he opened them again.

"Are you all right?" Colbee called.

Fen had to struggle to find his voice. "Yes."

"Do you want me to bring you back down?"

"No."

"Can you see anything?"

Fen scanned the sea in front of him until the confusion of the moving surface resolved into specific shapes. "Yes."

"Like what?"

"The mountain in the sea with a cook fire on top. Big schools of yellow fins."

"Maybe you should come back down, now -" Colbee started.

"And lots more," Fen continued. "I can see an upside down whale. Just ahead."

"I'll bring you back down now."

"No! Please, no! Just look. You'll see I'm not making it up. Just look."

At the bow, Hao pointed. "It's there, the whale the boy saw."

Once it spouted, everyone found it. Instead of swimming away, it swam toward the boat, leaping out of the water, landing and rolling onto its back, its light underbelly showing clearly under the water. It rolled over again, surfaced, and dove out of sight. When they thought it had gone, it resurfaced on the other side of the boat and gave one last roll before going on its way.

While they were watching the whale, they forgot about Fen and the kite. When Colbee checked, he realized the point where they had connected Fen's seat was coming untied, dropping the bar farther down on one side. Calling for Jin's help, he tried to lower the kite, but the wind held it.

"We could just keep wrapping the line around the mast," Jin offered.

"I'm afraid we'll break the line," Colbee said so only Jin could hear.

"We'll have to try. Maybe if Fen moved off the seat bar, it would lessen the friction."

"And where would he go?"

"Higher. He could hang on to the crossbars of the kite and just keep his feet on the seat bar. That would move some of the weight off the bar."

Colbee shook his head. "What if we attached other lines to the main one, the way we did on the island?"

"The fray is too high. We could increase the pull on the line, but we'd only increase the strain."

"What if we have Fen dismantle the kite? Once the wind was out -" He stopped himself. "No, the kite would crash."

As they grew more frustrated, their voices rose. It wasn't hard for Fen to figure out what they were talking about. He'd seen the kites lift Liwei so that he almost flew off into the sky.

"Where's the direction marker?" Colbee called to Hao. "What about the speed line?"

"I'll get them."

"Jin, do we have any other rope?"

Jin shook his head. "Only what's attached to the mooring stone."

"We might need to borrow it."

When Hao ran up with the marker, Colbee climbed up the mast with it.

"Fen, we have to change the way we're bringing the kite down," he said. "The rope is fraying. I need you to try something, all right?"

Fen's reply came out as a squeak.

"We can take some of the weight off the seat bar if you stand up and hold onto the cross-brace on the kite. Just keep your feet on the seat bar."

Fen struggled to unlock his gaze from the ocean, to look up, to unclench his hands around the bars. His stomach lurched. He slid one knee up, so his foot rested on the bar, but he couldn't reach up to the kite. It would have to be all at once. *Just stand and reach up.* With nothing to hold onto except the unsteady edge of the kite, he blew out a deep breath, looked up and stood. With a lunge, Fen grabbed hold of the kite bars and felt around for the seat bar with his feet. With his face up close to the surface of the kite, he hung there, blind. The kite faltered under the additional weight. The change of pressure on the seat bar when Fen stood and pushed off against it proved too much for the rope. It began to unravel, giving way one strand at a time.

Colbee swung the marker rope. "Fen! Can you catch this?" he cried.

The boy willed one hand loose from the cross-bar and held it out. Colbee tried an impossible throw. The knotted end flew up and hit Fen's hand. In trying to catch it, he leaned over, pulling the kite down on one side and snapping the last of the frayed seat line. He missed the marker line. The kite swerved in wild loops.

Colbee grabbed the falling ropes. "Stand up, Fen!"

With the kite swinging around, it was hard for Fen to tell which way was up. He tried to align his body with the kite, moving one way or another to make the kite correct its crazy loops. He tried tucking in his chin and looking down. Past his feet there was no Colbee, no boat. Just ocean.

Ryu brought the Wind Raft closer, leaned out over the side and yelled up at the boy. "Fen, you need to bring your feet up and push the front of the kite down, so you are heading toward the water. I'll tell you when to jump off and we'll come and get you, okay?"

Fear and wind pulled his reply out with no sound. He tried to bring his feet up by throwing his legs forward. Suddenly, he felt the front of the kite drop and his head fall. He was hanging upside down, falling backward.

"That's fine," Ryu called. "Can you do that again?"

Shaking, Fen kicked his legs up and sent the kite rushing down.

"When I tell you, drop your feet off the seat bar and let them hang for a moment before you let go. Then you can drop down feet first."

Fen sucked in a deep breath and swung his feet away from the bar so he was hanging straight down. The weight pulled the kite down farther.

"The longer you can hang on, the shorter fall you'll have," Ryu yelled. "When you're ready, just let go and try to enter the water feet first. We'll be waiting for you."

Fen's arms and shoulders burned. His fingers, clamped tight on the kite braces at first, suddenly lost their hold and slid off. The water rushed up to his feet, slammed into him, bubbled up all around. Then there were hands reaching for him, guiding him back up to the surface, friends waiting for him, just as they'd promised. He could hear the cheers from the boats, calling his name.

Tears running down his face mixed with seawater.

On their way to the islands, they managed to rescue the floating kite. Much later, after everyone had stopped shaking, both Fen and Colbee dreamed about building a new manned kite.

"And the next time," Fen told Colbee, "I want to be able to see where I'm going."

* * *

The islands became a beacon for the voyagers, drawing the boats toward them. As they'd agreed, they passed the first island and headed for the large island past it, which was actually a chain of mountains with lowland links between them. Along one edge they found a passable harbor and a good beach with formidable cliffs rising beyond it. In the rocks, a few twisted trees and cactus plants clung to life. Higher up the mountainside, scrub trees hugged the rock, while the mountaintop was covered in lush forest.

"A strange place," Darna commented.

CHAPTER 25
ON THE ISLANDS

As soon as they landed, almost everyone found a reason to get away. Some headed off alone: Liwei to check the beach, Goh to check for fresh water sources, Fuhua mumbling something about gathering plants. Sula offered to stay with the boats, a job no one else seemed to want. Nina and Ryu went up the mountain. Rana headed off to see birds, or maybe iguanas. Aeta and Nulo sat on the edge of the beach under the shade of a lone tree. Though Nulo said he'd look for useful stones for tools, he didn't leave the patch of shade he'd found.

By ones and twos they wobbled away in different directions, still feeling the boat rolling under their feet. Goh wandered down the coast, stopping at the tidal shallows, watching sea stars and sand dollars, sea cucumbers, spiny sea urchins. So many scarlet crabs scuttled sideways over the rocks just above the waterline that the rocks themselves seemed to move. Life pulsed all around him. A long-tailed lizard grabbed a small scorpion. In mid-air, a large black bird stole a fish from the diving bird that had caught it. Butterflies swarmed around red and yellow flowers. Female sea lions napped on the sand while a big bull roared at everything that moved. In the water, green turtles surfaced and then disappeared back into the water; silver fish leaped clear of the wave tops to escape their predators below, only to be caught by the waiting birds.

Spotting a tree that looked familiar, Goh ripped the fruit off the branch, peeled off the outer layer, and bit into it but found it so bitter he spat it out. As he did, he shook his hands, trying to get rid of the burning sensation. Within moments, an itchy rash spread across his hands and up to his arms, neck and face. He stumbled back toward the sea. When he couldn't stand the itching anymore, he tore at his skin. Each time he scratched, it only relit the fiery itch and spread the rash.

Rana found him sitting down in the shallows, head down, eyes closed, letting the wave fringes break over him as the rash spread across his face, chest, and arms. "I'll get you something to calm that down," she said, taking his arm when he didn't move. "In the meantime, you can wash off some of that burning in some fresh water. There's a little stream over here."

Fen wandered away from the shore, humming as he hefted the two land turtle cages onto his shoulders. When he found an open grassy spot, he set the cages down and called to the turtles, singing them out into their new world. Slowly they stretched out their necks and looked around before they took their first steps.

"You've spent many days in a cage at sea, but you're meant to be on land. It's a good place here. At least I hope it is. Good luck," he called as he left them.

Laido and Darna remained on their boat.

"Call Sula," Laido said. "Tell her she doesn't need to stay."

When Darna returned, Sula came with her.

"Thank you for your offer to stay on the boat -" Laido started.

Sula hunkered down next to him, taking his arm, searching his face. "You're ill. I didn't know. How many days?"

"Many," he said slowly.

"I don't remember," Darna added.

"Where is the pain?"

"My gut is full of stones," Laido replied. "I have no strength."

"I might be able to help," Sula said to Laido, "though the medicine might kill you. You and Darna will need to talk. I'll return later. We'll decide then."

As Sula left them, Darna wept, her sobs escaping even as she tried to hide them.

Laido took her hand. "I thought it would take the heart from the others if I said anything while we were at sea. Now I have much I want to say and little time to say it. Please listen.

"First, you are the best part of my life. I never said that to you before. I have no excuse except I was afraid that giving it life in words would threaten its existence. As the days went by, we talked of other things and the most important ones went unsaid.

"When I die, I will wait for you at the far side of the Bridge of Birds. I will stand there, waiting, until you cross over. I promise."

"But surely you -" Darna began.

He waved her objection aside. "Let me finish. You must help Nina and Tahn reach their dreams. They hesitate, just like I did. They stand in their own way. Tell them what I wasn't brave enough to say."

She gripped his hand.

"And Ryu," Laido said. "He's like a son to me, yet not. I gave him all the responsibility as navigator and only a bit of the knowledge. I was jealous because he's going to live, and I'm going to die. His success only highlights my failure."

"You haven't failed. Not in any way."

"It's strange," he said, moving her hand to his chest, "how much we don't see even though it's right in front of us."

Darna bent down, putting her head on his chest over their clasped hands.

When Sula returned, she brought medicine balled up in a leaf. "It will dim the pain, but it will not make you well."

Laido chewed the leaf ball slowly and forced himself to swallow.

"Thank you," Darna said as Sula rose.

"I'm sorry I cannot do more. I'll let you two talk. He will feel better off the boat, in the fresh air."

"She's right," Laido admitted. "I need to get off this boat. I wish I had a small boat, so I could simply float away." His eyes closed.

"Would you help me get him off the boat?" Darna asked.

"Of course."

They settled him in the shade of a scrub tree.

"It's beautiful here," he said, opening his eyes. "And strange. Mountains coming out of the sea."

Darna sat next to him. When Sula offered to leave, Darna shook her head. "It's good to have you here," she said unsteadily. "I feel as if nothing is real."

"Shall I send for your children?"

Darna wrapped her arms across her chest and tried to stop shivering. "I don't know where they are. I don't know where I am. What is this place? Why did we come here?"

"Because we chose to."

"Then we chose stupidly. Why would he abandon me in this place?"

"We all die. The place is irrelevant."

"Laido!" Darna yelled.

Laido opened his eyes though they seemed focused elsewhere. "Put my bones out to sea, please. Look to the Travelers Path at night." He paused, turning to Sula. "Thank you for your help. It makes the journey simpler."

"What has happened?" Darna cried.

"Once the pain stops, there is nothing to force the body to continue," Sula said as she rose. "I'll send for the others."

CHAPTER 26
A FUNERAL FOR A CHIEF

After Laido's death, the women prepared the body and made a funeral wrap for him; the men built a pyre of driftwood. While the fire burned, they left gifts for him to take to the afterlife: decorated gourd bowls, a knife, fine stones, a necklace of long feathers, strings of trade shells, a black spear, a container of salt, another of shark teeth, a carved turtle shell ornament, a white sash. Colbee, Jin, Tahn, and Goh made the little boat that Laido wanted. Along the waterline, they carved images of the original wind raft, the burning mountain on the Fat Men's island, the fight at Masali, the kite races and flying man, the wedding party, the flattening of time, the mountains in the sea, and every person on the boats so he would have many companions on his journey.

"He was our chief, though he never claimed the title," Colbee said when he presented the boat.

"He didn't need to," Hao added.

When the fire had left only bones, Darna and the other women dusted them with red clay powder, wrapped them up, added all of the jewelry and gifts, and set them on a bed of red flowers in the little boat. Nina, Tahn, Nulo, and Ryu – all Laido's children in one way or another – carried the boat out into the water. Behind them came Darna and everyone else, walking into the sea side by side. They walked until the seafloor dropped off underneath them.

"I'll meet you soon," Darna called, throwing red flowers into the sea as the little boat drifted away.

"We need you here," Sula said.

"Why? What is this strange land to me?"

"Today it's home to people you love. Don't abandon them."

Still in the shallows, Darna fell to her knees. Nina, Tahn, Ryu, and Nulo huddled close to her, their arms wrapping around her like a nest. Soon the others joined, forming a second circle and a third, all pressed in together.

"He's waiting to be sung into the Otherworld," Colbee said. "We need to make a fire, cook his favorite food, and sing him on his way."

When the fire was lit and the food cooked, Tahn began.

"I sing my father –

He was the chief, the navigator,

the boat-builder, the teacher,

the inventor,

and yet I didn't know those men;

I knew only my father.

We argued.

He looked at me with disappointed eyes.

We drifted apart.

Then I joined this group

heading into the empty sea,

and I saw my father worry.

I saw him fail.

He was only a man.

I wept for him then.

I saw a man, like any other man,

and yet

so much more.

A dreamer

hungry for a world as large as his dreams.

That is his gift to me, to us,

the treasure he leaves behind.
Take from him the dream he offered you.
Carry it on.

Sail on the wind with the endless flyers, Father,
until you reach
The Travelers Path.

Tahn added more wood to the fire as Ryu and Nulo stepped forward.

"We'd like to sing a song that my grandmother sang," Ryu said. "If you know the words, please help us sing it. It's a song for everyone we miss.

"I am more because of you," Ryu began.

"I am better, stronger, kinder
because of you," Nulo finished.

You add to all things,
even the sky.

When you leave,
the stars will remember you,
the sea will sing for you,
the rocks will carry your name.

In another time, I will see you again," they sang together as others joined them,

"somewhere behind the sun,
where tears turn into flowers."

"You need to eat something," Kiah said, handing the bowl to Darna. "Please."

Darna didn't notice the food. "What use am I here, Kiah? I can't navigate by the stars. I can't build boats. I wanted to explore at his side. I thought the monsters we'd face could be killed with spears."

"Don't belittle yourself. Exploration is our food, the air we breathe," Kiah said. "You are our sister, our mother, our friend. There are no substitutes for those."

"I'm stretched out, like light on the sea, only bits and pieces."

"Then let your friends help you."

"What can I offer in return?"

"Will you help me rebuild the garden boat?"

Darna shook as she took the hand Kiah offered. "I will. Yes. Of course I will."

* * *

After five days, the mourning period ended. In the old land, they would have marked it with a feast, but no one felt like feasting. Instead, they drifted away, some down the coast, others inland.

Ryu and Nina climbed the mountain more side by side than together; they kept climbing because the effort distracted them for a moment. Nina had never sung for her father; she'd hardly spoken since her father's death. Ryu also reeled under the loss. Laido had been the master navigator, the teacher. He could build a boat and take it anywhere, read the patterns in the waves. He saw the sea as a complicated relative, not a foreigner. While Ryu studied the stars, Laido knew them, not as names but as beings.

Ryu had never told Laido about the star changes or the disappearance of the No Shadow day and its strange return. These remained his secret and his disgrace. Late that night, when Nina slept, he climbed to a clear spot, studying the marker stars he thought he knew. *I'm a star keeper, a day counter. I should understand. The truth is I haven't been watching. I can't remember when I last marked the day shadow or tracked the visitor stars.*

For a while, he'd used the mast as the sun anchor on the boat, the way Laido taught him. At dawn, the sun rose along a point notched in the bow, then up onto the mast before it leaped into the sky. Its long shadow at dawn fell on a marker point on the stern, then shortened to almost nothing at the middle of the day. As the day grew older, the shadow grew to the opposite mark on the bow, before the sun sank into the sea over the stern marker.

Everything's different now. If I had a flat surface and a pole, I could check, but up here, what could I use? Any tall stick? A tree? If I stood in its early morning shadow, what would I know? With no reference point, I'd be watching the shadow of a tree, that's all. I need something else.

Nulo's stone. I could use it to set up a sun anchor, track the shadow, check it against the marker stars.

Pale light lit the eastern sky as he found his way back to camp, anxious to tell Nina about his plan.

"Nina?" he called into the silence of the empty camp. "Nina?"

* * *

She awoke to find Ryu gone. When she called his name, she heard no reply. Hearing a noise off to one side, she got up and headed that way with only the starshine to guide her. She worked her way down loose heaps of sharp rock and piles of light, tinkling stone, always feeling he was somewhere in front of her. As she stepped over a ledge, she found nothing under her foot on the far side. Pitching forward in the dark, she fell and rolled, her shoulder hitting tough scrub bushes and scraping along ropey stone formations, her elbow banging into sharp rock, her foot jamming between two stones before the fall wrenched it free again. She tried to stop herself, grabbing hold of prickly branches that tore away as she fell, but the fall carried her along faster, throwing her from one rock to another until she slammed into a rock barrier. For a while, she stayed still, wondering if she was alive or lost between worlds. Then the pain spread, everywhere. Her ankle throbbed; pain shot through her shoulder and neck. She felt sick.

At first light she hauled herself up against the side of the stone trough that had stopped her, a tube formed by the mountain long ago and now missing its top part. On the far side of the trough, the mountain dropped down to the sea with dizzying suddenness. Staggering back from the edge, she saw black stone columns lined up along the far side of the trough, each one twice as tall as a man, standing at the cliff edge like warriors guarding a land of spirits. Unbelievable sparkling stones lay heaped on the ground at the foot of the columns. When the sun's light hit the stones, they flashed with all-color fire.

"How beautiful!" she cried out.

Pain ripped through her shoulder again, doubling her over. With her good arm, she pulled herself up the side of the trough and slid down into it, looking for a way to follow it uphill. The sides swelled out in some sections, narrowed in others. Rainwater pooled in depressions along the bottom, littered with sticks and dead leaves. In the closest of these piles, she found several sparkling stones entangled in the debris. Extracting three, she cleaned them off and tucked them into her sash.

When she found a deep pool, she bent over, cupping her good hand in the water to drink. Beyond the pool, piles of obsidian shards as sharp as knives blocked her way up the center of the trough. Skirting them, she edged along until she reached a section where the wall had collapsed, giving her a clear view of the guardian columns and sparkling ground. Through the gap, flashing stones had spilled into the trough, forming piles at her feet. Their light pulsed in different colors around her, moving through her, filling her. She fell to her knees in the stones, reaching for them, pulling them toward her. *It's all light here! It's light inside me and outside me. It shines out my eyes, my mouth, my skin. Lights piled up on the mountainside, piled up inside me. Different colors, sun-pieces. Fierce lights. Terrifying. Incredible. Beautiful.*

She rocked back on her heels in the middle of the light, unaware of the sharp edges cutting into her skin as she scooped them up, pulling them closer to her, piling them up around her. *Brilliance so terrible and clear!* In a rush, she pulled yet more stones toward her, piling the lights ever higher until they covered her completely. *I want to be part of the light, to live here forever, in the gods' place.*

The light took her to another world. As everything else dropped away - the mountain, the rocks, the sky, even her pain, she flew into sheer light, blinding blue-white light. Yet something held her back so that she faltered as she flew, falling as the sky darkened. Something weighed on her, drawing her down to the dark world where the pain waited; something held onto her, calling her, over and over again. She knew his presence, his smell, the strength of his hands on her

"Nina! Come back! Don't leave me!"

She gasped as the pain reclaimed her. The fractured bones in her shoulder ground against each other with every movement. The pain tied her, like a needle through her skin, to this life and this person beside her. She didn't want it. The light called to her even as he held her. She flailed her good arm, answering the stones in words he couldn't understand.

With a shout, he lifted her up, shoving aside the piles of flashing stones that cut into his skin like knives. When he climbed to a spot clear of the stones, he set her down and called her name, but she didn't respond. She didn't even see him.

CHAPTER 27
ON THE CLIFF

Despite having the whole island to explore, Colbee and Kiah soon wound up back on the shore, working on the Sailfish and the garden boat. After a while, Darna, Goh, and then Fen joined them.

"Give me a job to do," Goh said. "Then I'll forget the itching."

"Let's go somewhere," Fen suggested. "We can look at the rest of the island. Maybe we could fly the kite."

"All those days at sea and you want to go back out." Colbee laughed. "I'm sorry. The Sailfish needs some repairs before it goes back to sea."

"What about the Wind Raft?" Jin said, joining them.

"It's not my -"

"I think Laido would like to see it on the water," Darna said.

Down the beach, Liwei propped himself up on his elbow, watching the group prepare the Wind Raft. "Where are you going?"

"We're bored," Jin answered.

"Or," Colbee put in, "we're exploring the island."

"What a good idea." Liwei grunted as he rose. "I'll join you."

Sula appeared as they readied the Wind Raft. "May I come with you?"

As the sun rose into the middle heavens, they paddled out into the open water then set the mat to help them head to the end of the island. On the far side, with the tide moving against them, they had to paddle again. Schools of yellow and blue fish flashed just beneath the surface. Sea turtles and rays glided through, scattering the fish until they passed.

"We should drop the fish trap," Colbee suggested.

"I'll get it," Darna offered.

"Wait!" Goh called. "Look! Up there!"

"Where?" Liwei called.

"Right there! About halfway up the mountain, just at the top of those cliffs."

"I see it. Something's flashing," Jin said.

Goh pointed. "Two people - up there."

"You're sure they're people?"

"Yes – or spirits."

"Spirits?"

"Well, they're shining. The whole cliff is shining."

"I can see that," Liwei said, "though I can't see any people. Can we get closer?"

As they all stared at the cliff, Goh said, "I think they're Ryu and Nina. Ryu is waving."

"Why are they standing at the edge?" Darna cried. "Are they all right?"

"They're stranded," Liwei said. "Look at the cliff. There's no way up or down."

"Then how can we help?"

"I have an idea," Colbee said slowly. "Jin, do you remember when we lifted Fen on the kite?"

"Clearly. What's your plan?"

"We could use the kite to land someone on the cliff edge. If it's really impossible to help them down the cliff, we could move them one by one by kite."

"Like the fishing kites Hao talked about!" Liwei said.

Colbee nodded. "Something like that."

"Right," Jin said. "What do we do first?"

"Darna, Kiah, Sula, can you put together two kites for us – a big one and a small one? Fen, climb up and untie the mat lines. And see what we can use to build a foot bar. It'll go right under the big kite."

"What can I do?" Liwei offered.

"Help build the kites. Once they're complete, you'll help anchor them."

Once they'd made the kites and attached the sling, they launched the assembly. The small kite rose quickly in the updraft, helping to lift the big kite. Jin stood on the stabilizer bar. He looked down only once as he was lifted into the sky. Gasping for air, clenching the bar, he made himself look at the cliff.

"How do I steer it?" he yelled into the wind.

Once it was flying, the kite stayed too high and too far from the cliff to be useful. Trying to turn the kite like a boat in the water, Jin pushed one side forward. Immediately, it lurched sideways, looping downward. After he let it go, the kite returned to its original position, still too high and too far. Next time, he turned the edge, making the kite loop downward, then pulled the edge back until he'd recovered part of the distance, pushed it again, straightened it, playing with how much he needed to drop down before the kite went dangerously out of control.

"The world of eagles!" he cried as the kite pulled him up.

With each pass, he drew closer to the mountain. From what he could see of the terrain, he had only one possible place to land: beyond the stone trough. Once he'd landed, he'd have to secure the line and check on Ryu and Nina. If they couldn't manage the climb down, he'd have to load one of them on the triangle, launch the kite, and get back to the boat before doing it all again. It had seemed more plausible when Colbee described the plan.

When he got as close as he could to the ground, he dropped down, hanging off the kite and pulling it with him. After a scrambled landing, he secured the line and climbed through the trough toward the figures at the cliff edge. Both had lost a lot of blood. Nina seemed unable to move.

"Nina?" he called. "I need you to help me."

She didn't reply.

"Nina! This can't work without you! Help me!"

She looked through him.

"Ryu!" Jin shouted. "The only way I can help you and Nina is if you help me! I need your help!"

"She's hurt," Ryu said. His arms and legs were covered with blood.

"Yes. I'm going to take you out one by one. If I take Nina, will you stay here until I get back?"

"I won't leave her."

"Either I take her or you take her," Jin replied. "We can't all go at once."

"We'll go together," Ryu said. "Or we'll stay."

"Fine. You'll need to -" Jin started. "Never mind, I'll work something out. We can use the foot bar as a seat. Can you balance while you're helping her?"

"We'll go together," Ryu repeated.

Jin rigged up a sling from his sash and wrapped it around Nina, then tied it to the bar. He helped Ryu onto the seat and yelled at him to keep hold of the brace. "Once the kite is launched, you'll fall out if you let go of the brace." When Ryu didn't reply, he made Nina's sash into another sling. In the process, the three sparking stones fell out, so Jin tucked them into his own sash. Then he tied both Ryu and Nina to the seat. "Hold on to her. I hope this works."

While the wind blew up the face of the cliff, the ledge blocked it so there wasn't enough lift for the kites. After trying several different spots, he held the small kite out over the edge until it caught the updraft, but it wasn't enough to lift the big kite even it didn't have two people aboard. He moved up the cliff and worked the kites into a better draft. When the small kite found it, it pulled up in a rush.

Jin settled Ryu and Nina and played out the line until the big kite took off. The second line he pushed over the cliff edge so it dangled below the main kite. From the cliff, he worked the kite, keeping it close enough to the cliff to catch the draft and far enough away to keep from crashing.

"It's up to you now, Colbee!" Jin cried as he played out more line. "Once you have the second line in hand, I'll send this one over."

From the field of flashing stones around him, he took a large piece carefully in hand, aimed it so the sun hit its smooth side, angled it down toward the boats, and swept it back and forth, up and down, hoping Colbee would see the signal.

Colbee and Liwei enlisted the help of all the others to haul the kites back down. Once the main kite was over the Sailfish, Sula grabbed the line and held the kite still while Colbee cut out Jin's knots and wrestled the two passengers off the seat. Nina and Ryu fell off the bar onto the deck.

"I'll look after them," Sula said.

"I'll help," Darna added.

"We have to get Jin," Fen called. "I'll go on the kite!"

Goh yelled, "He's coming down the cliff! Jin! He's climbing down the cliff!"

"We'll bring the boat in as close to shore as we can," Colbee said. "If he falls in the water, we can pick him up."

"If he falls on those rocks, he'll die before we can reach him," Liwei noted.

"We can still be close in case we can help. Grab your paddles. We're heading toward the shore."

As they got closer, they watched Jin move like a monkey across the cliff face, wedging his hand into a crack, swinging his legs up, searching for a tiny ledge barely large enough for his toes to balance on while he moved on to the next hold. At a spot where an enormous piece had broken off the cliff, he had to hang from his fingertips while swinging his legs forward until he could grab a new handhold, working his way from one spot to another across the gaping opening to the edge and then down before he could cross back to his original line.

Unable to help or to look away, the group on the boat traversed every part with him, leaning with him as he looked for a new grip or struggled to find his footing, gasping when he missed a hold and fell back, with only one hand wedged in a crack to keep him from falling.

"He's going to make it," Liwei announced.

"What a stupid thing to say," Goh snapped.

When Jin reached a long ledge, just wide enough for his feet, he stopped.

"What's wrong?" Fen cried. "Why did he stop?"

"I don't know," Colbee said. "Maybe he's tired."

"Can we help?"

"I don't think so."

"Climb down, Jin!" Fen yelled. "Keep going!"

"Keep going!" Goh echoed.

Liwei and Kiah started pounding on the side of the boat. "Keep going, Jin!"

From the ledge, Jin waved to them, dusted both hands with dirt, and began to climb down once more. He moved a little slower than he had before and missed several footholds. Bit by bit, he worked his way down the cliff face.

Near the bottom, jumbled pieces of fallen rock blocked his way. Moving quickly, he jumped from one flat surface to another. Some wobbled under his feet while others broke away, taking the surrounding stones with them as they fell. As he crossed an open area, a whole field of small stones moved suddenly under his feet, dragging him down as they cascaded down the cliff. Reaching out as the rockslide took him, he caught hold of a scrub thorn tree and dragged himself up onto solid rock. Near him, several other thorn trees clung to life on the cliff rock, twisting their roots into tiny crevasses. Moving from one to another, he picked his way down. Thorns as long as his fingers raked his skin and tunic until he bled, but the trees also gave him a path to follow.

He caught his breath as he stepped into the sea and the salt water found every scratch.

The group on the boat broke into cheers as they helped him onto the Wind Raft.

"Well done, Jin!" Liwei called. "I knew you'd be fine."

As she worked on Nina, Sula let out a whistle of alarm when she saw all of the cuts. "A strange place you've been to - no wonder you're having trouble returning." As her long fingers probed Nina's shoulder, Nina winced. "At least you're still in there somewhere," Sula commented.

With Darna's help, she mixed fresh water with honey in a half-shell. When Ryu didn't seem interested in drinking the mixture, she tilted his head back and poured it in his mouth. Spluttering, Ryu thrashed against her, knocking the water bowl from her hand.

"You're welcome," Sula said.

"Not very cooperative, is he?"

"He'll be all right. He bled a lot. I'm more concerned with her."

Darna took her daughter's cold hand. "So am I."

"She's going to need more days on shore. She'll stand a better chance of recovering there."

"We could gain many things from these islands while we're here," Darna said. "Unless I underestimate Liwei and his brother, they'll find a way back up the cliff."

"Why?"

"Treasure. Did you see Jin send the light signal?"

"Of course. It almost blinded us."

"It could work as a signal between people on different boats. It makes no sound, needs no fire, is visible over a great distance, and could mean anything. Liwei and Fuhua are always looking for something new. It means trade; trade means wealth."

"If they want wealth, they should start with the giant shells."

"I'm sure they will. Very little escapes them where wealth is concerned."

Sula shrugged. "It's useful sometimes."

"Your wealth allowed us to build the boats," Darna noted.

"Not all wealth is good. Some of those pearls were payments."

"Payments?"

"I sold dark magic," Sula said, rocking back on her heels.

"Why?"

"I was angry, so I became part of everyone's anger, everyone who had been assaulted, robbed, deceived, cheated. They asked me to avenge their wrongs so I did. I met Rana because she had been raped by two brothers. Their father, the village chief, knew what his sons had done, yet he did nothing about it. No one dared accuse his sons. When I did, I was punished. They claimed I was a witch, trying to curse them all. After they dropped the tree trunk on my face, they left me for dead. Rana took me in, cared for me. We knew worse punishment would follow, even if we did nothing more than continue to breathe, so we fled in the middle of the night, the two of us and three others. We split up along the way; I don't know what happened to the others. When Rana and I reached Seal Island, we set up a little business.

"With the puppets?"

"Yes. While Rana worked the audience, I'd fashion bits of clothing for the doll Rana would pull out of her sack. It was simple, just enough for the audience to catch: mostly tunic decoration or hair style, or a particular piece, like a necklace or a topknot decoration. Rana was so good, no one noticed me. I'd dress the puppet for her and tell her where to find the target. It was easy work, the audience loved it, and we made enough to trade for what we needed. But the pearls I saved. Some things you have to save for something special; otherwise, they become cheapened, and so do you." She glanced up at Darna. "I'm sorry if I've talked too much. You seem to be the kind of person who would listen without judging."

"I'm sorry for your pain," Darna said, "and honored that you would share your story with me."

Sula inclined her head in a small bow. "Now, we have a young woman to bring back, if we can find a way."

CHAPTER 28
NAVIGATING A NEW WORLD

When Colbee brought the Wind Raft back to shore, those they'd left behind waited to hear their story. Around the fire that night, Jin talked about flying high over the earth and maneuvering the kite down to the cliff. The others hung on his every word. Fuhua wanted to know about the shining stones. Tahn asked about the signal lights. Everyone wanted to know how Jin got down the cliff. As he was telling them, he remembered the stones he'd tucked in his sash. Explaining that Nina must have picked them up somewhere, he passed them around for people to see.

"Be careful. The edges are sharp."

Fuhua could hardly let go of them. "We have much to discover here before we leave," he said as he handed the stones to his brother, still keeping his eye on them. "Much to discover." Even Nulo found the stones fascinating, rolling them over in his hand, sliding his finger carefully along the angles.

"Well," Colbee broke in, "starting tomorrow, we have important work to do. We need a shelter near the beach, food, water, building supplies, and repair materials. It's also a good time for us to put the boats back in order. And please let someone know where you're going before you head off on your own."

* * *

"With Laido gone and Ryu ill, who will be navigator?" Kiah asked when she and Colbee took their turn staying with Nina.

"That's the question on everyone's mind," Colbee answered.

"You could be navigator."

"We need a lead navigator and a second. The lead navigator sets the course. If the boats get separated, the second navigator must be able to get the other boat where it needs to be."

"Why keep the navigation methods secret? Why not teach anyone interested? If we lose -"

"I agree. Others would like to learn."

"What about Hao?"

"He hasn't helped - with anything."

"Maybe he would if someone asked him."

"He told me he couldn't read the stars anymore."

"What? When?"

"Before we reached these islands."

"Why didn't he tell Laido?"

Colbee shrugged. "That's when he stopped helping."

Pointing to a group of sea lions basking on the shore, Kiah said, "Look at them. They don't worry about direction."

"They don't worry about much," Colbee agreed.

"Why do we need a navigator if we don't know where we're going or what we'll find when we get there?"

"The course was supposed to be east."

"Why?"

"Because that's where the last island was."

Kiah waited for a better answer.

In the silence, Darna joined them. "Am I interrupting?"

"Not at all," Kiah said.

"Ryu will be fine," Darna noted, kneeling down and taking her daughter's hand. "But Nina needs something more than honey water. I'll ask Sula if she has another idea. Thank you for watching over her. And," she added as she stood up, "I heard your discussion about the navigator."

"I meant no disrespect to Laido," Kiah said.

"It's not disrespectful to recognize our situation. The navigator needs to get people from one known point to another. Laido did that very well. Yet when we passed the last known point, all he knew was to keep going on that same course, into nowhere. I think trying to set a course with no destination killed him. Now Ryu is suffering, trying to figure out a new world based on the old one. Hao too. You're right, Kiah. We need to decide where to go from here after we've realized we're floating like a mass of plants swept off an island by a storm. Eventually it winds up somewhere, or it disappears into the sea."

"Darna -" Kiah stretched out her hand.

"No one else must die from shame of the unknown. The sooner we accept the sea as our home and teacher, the sooner we'll heal. All of us," she added, looking at the young woman lying on the mat. "I'll get Sula." Tears stung her face as she put her hand over Kiah's. "Thank you, friend. I forget sometimes that others will help save me from drowning."

CHAPTER 29
NINA'S JOURNEY

Nina heard sounds, not words. She was walking somewhere, but no matter how far she walked, she couldn't reach her destination. Though people along the way looked like people she knew, they said nothing when she spoke to them, as if they didn't see her. Ryu, involved in something else, didn't notice her. She passed by her mother and Kiah unrecognized. Nulo and Aeta spoke to each other, ignoring her. Someone started walking next to her, talking to her in clicks and squeaks, like dolphin sounds. Except for those sounds, the world fell silent. Since she couldn't say anything to her companion, she bowed. The man bowed in return, turned and walked away, leaving her alone the moment she recognized him. *Father! Wait for me. I can't breathe, Father. I can't do this anymore.*

On her mat, she curled up into a ball, retreating.

"No, I don't think so," a voice said. "Not now."

Pungent spice smells filled her nostrils, bringing with them a flood of memories: the taste and smell of her favorite foods so strong they made her mouth water, the feel of the wind in her face while the Wind Raft pulled through the sea, the image of Ryu reaching down to take the paddle from her hand with sea spray beading up on his skin; his smell when he was close to her; the feel of his skin under her hand as she put the red flower design on him. These memories, embedded in taste and smell and touch, called to her from far away; they were miniature souvenirs of a world she used to know, interesting and remote, as if she'd heard about them in a story.

"It's not enough," one voice said.

"Then we'll add some help."

Sula and Darna threw gourds of sea water down her body, one after another so it was a constant onslaught shocking her, soaking her, seeping into the cuts, stinging, burning, and washing her into the present. Nina screamed, thrashing her good arm. Everything hurt with a piercing, grinding pain.

Sula stepped back, waiting for Nina to stop trembling. "You've witnessed something that will change you forever, Nina. Even so, you're still you. This is not the last experience that will change you. Make it part of you and keep going."

"I was looking for something," Nina managed as tears came to her eyes.

"Yes." Sula clipped off the word. "We all are. It's part of the journey. We'll help you get cleaned up."

CHAPTER 30
TREASURES

The sparkling stones could not be forgotten. As people worked, their conversation returned to the stones: what magic they held, how many were on the cliff, how much they might be worth.

"I don't like all this talk about the stones," Aeta complained. "That place is very dangerous. Has everyone forgotten what happened to Nina?"

Nulo didn't reply. He too found the stones fascinating.

Aeta shook her head slowly. "Those stones belong to the spirits on the cliff."

Others didn't share her opinion. Some saw the gems as treasure waiting to be found. Others saw adventure, maybe a fortune. Recognizing the fever that took them, Colbee set aside two full days so anyone who wanted to could look around the rock fields. He imposed only two rules: no one could go alone, and no one could bring back more than one handful of stones.

Jin had seen an easier route coming in from the far side of the island, so Colbee offered to take the interested treasure hunters on the Sailfish. Fen went along, hoping the kite might be involved. Nulo and Hao opted for the overland route, walking up the mountain.

Though Colbee brought the Sailfish as close to shore as he could, the groups found a tangled confusion of mangroves blocking their way, broken only by piles of rocks that had fallen off the cliff and crushed the mangroves. When the searchers tried to scramble across the rock piles, the stones slipped away under their hands. Watching from the boat, Colbee thought Fuhua and Liwei would never find their way across the rocks and up the bank, but he underestimated the brothers' interest in the stones. They followed one of the streams up the mountainside. When the way became too steep, they hauled themselves up by branches and roots of the giant thorn trees that grew along the banks. As the blazing sun reached its highest point, they turned away from the river and headed inland.

Past the trees that bordered the river, they stepped into a bizarre world containing no trees, no bushes, nothing green, only heaps of rocks so sharp they were impossible to walk on, and beyond, ropey rock formations, tunnels, half-tunnels, and vents that dropped down past the limit of their sight into the depths of the earth.

Liwei stopped and stared. "Fuhua, look at this."

Far ahead, pulled toward a different treasure, Fuhua was already deep in the land of firerock, where strange formations lay exactly as they'd been put down at the moment they'd turned from fire to stone. Directly in front of him a vent tube large enough to walk through opened up. At his feet, the ground moved with shifting, dancing light bouncing off the sparkling stones. He started one way then turned another, torn between the places, hungry for all they held, not caring that the sharp rock cut through his mat slippers. Extraordinary stones lay waiting on these fire-blasted slopes. He picked up several large red stones and some beautiful crystals, yet farther ahead, more called to him.

When Liwei caught up with him, Fuhua was as deep inside one of the tunnels as he could get before it became too dark to see. In his hand, Liwei held the largest rock crystal either of them had ever seen, big enough to draw Fuhua away for a moment before he went back to running his hand along the vent wall.

"There," Fuhua said, pointing, "it runs right along there."

"What?"

"The amazing yellow rock." He removed a stone from his sash. "Like this one."

"That's Nina's stone."

"Well, I'm keeping it for her."

"That's a new way to describe stealing."

"She knows nothing of its worth. She could as easily have chosen a nice shell."

"But she didn't."

"So I'll give her another one, a prettier one."

"That one is hers."

Irritated, Fuhua tucked the stone into his sash and turned back to the wall. "Why don't you leave me alone? I have work to do here."

After Liwei walked away, Fuhua returned to the seductive golden vein. Where he stood, the tube was wide enough for four men to pass side by side, but walking required finding a way around the stone pieces that had fallen from the roof or tumbled in during floods. The rocks, piled up haphazardly, looked as if they'd just landed there, but rainwater and leeching minerals had cemented them together. Fuhua had to go back outside to find a rock to use as a hammer. With work, he broke a large rock loose and shoved it toward the wall, then steadied it with smaller ones and climbed onto his new platform.

The golden vein lay right in front of him, but it only gleamed, unconcerned, when he clawed at it.

"I need a chisel to get you," he announced to the rock.

He climbed back down and searched the length of the floor but found nothing suitable. At the mouth of the tube, he picked up a piece of black stone with a sharp point and found another piece for a hammerstone. Back in the tube, he climbed back up on his platform, set the chisel at an angle and tapped it with the hammerstone. A few small pieces of the yellow stone fell off and disappeared into the rubble on the floor. He tried again, slightly higher. The chisel bounced off the rock. When he hit it once more, it only slid against the surface.

"I want the yellow rock," he said to the wall, "and you are going to give it to me."

Setting the chisel back in the vein, he brought the hammerstone down hard, but the blow only buried the chisel, wedging it against the harder rock on both sides. Grunting, he tapped it upward to loosen it. When that didn't work, he tried from above. The chisel didn't move. Fuhua felt the yellow vein gleaming softly, calling to him, taunting him as it kept its treasure locked up tight.

Climbing down from his platform, he searched the floor of the tunnel for a bigger hammerstone. Loosening one bigger than he really wanted, he hefted it up on his shoulder with a grunt and climbed back up. Straining to hold the rock while he figured out where the chisel lay beneath it, he moved one hand to each side of the rock, lifted it with a gasp, and threw it against the chisel. As it fell, it broke the chisel, hit the wall under the seam and careened off, narrowly missing his feet before it landed and bounced across the tube floor. Frustrated, Fuhua jumped down, snatched up the big rock, and hurled it against the wall. The force ran along ancient fracture lines, finding each weak spot, transferring the movement, breaking fragile bonds with a splintering shriek. With each break, the message spread, amplified into rolling, booming sounds that swept through the tunnel. Over his head, splinter lines spread; pieces broke loose. The booming swept through again, running up his body, jolting him away from the precious golden vein. He took a step back as bits of ceiling broke off farther down. As he stumbled toward the entrance, a whole section broke away, catching him on the back of his shoulder and shattering into pieces at his feet. He pitched forward, reaching out to break his fall, but his left hand jammed between two rocks on the floor. When he pitched forward, the bone twisted until it snapped. Fuhua screamed.

Another piece of the roof splintered and fell. Underneath him, Fuhua could feel the whole tube shudder.

Hearing the crash in the cave, Liwei broke into a run, picking his way through the rock debris littering the floor. "Are you all right? Can you walk? We need to get out before more of the roof collapses."

"My arm," Fuhua moaned.

Liwei pulled on his brother's good arm, helping him to his feet. "It's probably broken. Right now, you need your legs more than your arm. Move! Once we're out of here, I'll wrap up the arm. And your hand," he added, looking back at his brother's smashed, bloody hand.

Once they passed the mouth of the tube, Fuhua tripped and fell again. Behind him, the rest of the ceiling collapsed in a roar as piles of rock slabs filled the interior. A cloud of rock dust shot out the tube mouth.

"Look what happened!" Liwei cried, coughing.

Fuhua didn't look.

"I'll tie up your arm so it won't move," Liwei offered. "If we can't find anyone to help us, we'll have to find our way down the mountain. Can you manage?"

"No. It was a struggle coming up, when I had two arms and two hands to help me."

"You may have to try."

* * *

The other treasure hunters waited on the boat until the shadows lengthened. When there was still no sign of Fuhua and Liwei, Jin offered to go look for them.

"I'll take one of the signal woods. If I find them, I'll signal you. Tahn, if they come back, signal me," he called as he headed into the mangrove tangles and insect swarms.

* * *

In the field of sharp rocks, Fuhua couldn't find a comfortable place to rest. His brother had tied his broken arm and mangled hand inside his tunic, but every movement awoke the pain.

"I apologize for being a little bit over-zealous," Fuhua said. "Still, the treasure yields to the hunter. I didn't get the prize today, but it's a setback, not an omen, right?"

"The real treasure right now would be someone to help us."

"Well, yes, that's true."

When they heard Jin tapping on the signal wood, both of them shouted to him, telling him where they were, explaining the situation long before he could understand the words.

Jin checked Fuhua's injury. "Getting you to the boat will be a challenge, even with Liwei to help," he said. "I'll send a message to Tahn to meet us at the edge of the woods with a staff and a torch. With the sun already in the late heavens, it could be night before we reach the boat."

Goh and Tahn arrived to help get Fuhua through the stands of thorn trees and over the slippery rocks. Each step had to be planned and executed. Fuhua fell several times, rolling over to protect his bad shoulder. Cutting short his complaints, he got his feet back under him with help from both sides and kept going.

In the cove, Colbee moved the boat close to the shore and extended the rope ladder.

By the time they heard the welcoming cries of their friends back at the campsite, night had fallen and early stars had appeared. Sula and Aeta put the last of the wormwood powder on Fuhua's mangled hand, placed broad leaves soaked in mineral clay on his arm, added an obsidian stone on top, and covered the whole thing in more clay-soaked leaves. When they were done, his arm looked like a tree trunk but the bones no longer ground against each other.

Before he went to sleep, he found Nina and handed her the stones he had taken.

"My deepest apology," he said, bowing. "I have no excuse except greed."

She rolled the stones over slowly in her hand, studying them. "I picked them up before I knew that place, before I understood its power. A long time ago." She held out the piece of gold. "This is for you. I understand it's what you wanted most. I'll give the others to Nulo."

Stunned, Fuhua accepted the gift.

* * *

Late that night, Darna sat by the fire with Sula, Jin, and Tahn. "I noticed today that Kiah has completely replanted the garden boat," she mused. "Perhaps it's time to go back to sea."

"Before someone else gets lost," Tahn added.

"Fine with me," Jin said. "The stones proved more trouble than treasure."

"The islands were a good stopping place," Darna said, "not a home. Laido wanted a land so vast and beautiful it was equal to dreams."

They made plans to leave, gathered materials, and stood together in the sea to leave offerings to the gods who had let them visit their home. Nulo buried a fine red stone; Rana and Goh each buried one of the stones they had found; Darna offered her shell necklace. Liwei gave back the large quartz piece he had taken though he wasn't at all convinced that the spirits had better claim to it than he had. As the water swept against them, the injured began to mend. The islands loosened their grip.

That night, Rana's wildest puppet told a story of a trickster who claimed he could wrap his arms around the moon. The local people called him a fool, but the trickster went on, saying he could also shake the moon so hard it would come apart, and after it was broken, he could put it back together again. When the villagers bet him a large pearl that he couldn't do any of these things, he swam out into the middle of the pond and held his arms around the reflection of the moon. Then he splashed around, flailing his arms, making the reflection shatter into many pieces. For his finish, he waited for the reflection to come back together again, bowed to the villagers, and asked who would be delivering his fine pearl. "Education," he said, "is always costly." Then he ran off, chuckling at his own wit, while the villagers chased after him.

Nina laughed for the first time since her transformation on the cliff.

CHAPTER 31
FEAR OF THE UNKNOWN

When he flew on the kite, Jin noticed lighter-colored water near the island extending toward what looked like another island in the distance.

"It might be wise," Fen said, "to have someone small and light check for the island from a better vantage point, such as the kite, once we are at sea again."

"It might be wise?" Colbee laughed. "Maybe. First we need to make a better harness and you need to talk to Jin about steering."

"I'll talk to him!"

Kiah and Darna wove a long sleeve that looked like a dragonfly body. Once Fen was fitted in it, he had only his head, neck, arms, and feet free.

"Be careful," Colbee warned. "The sleeve will help you be part of the kite, but it will make swimming almost impossible if you ditch."

"I won't ditch. Attach me to the kite and send me up."

Colbee hoisted the whole assembly into a good wind that pulled the kite aloft with Fen stretched out underneath.

"Can you see anything in front of us?" Colbee called.

Fen glanced down to check the boat's alignment and follow that course out to sea. The sea looked pale around the edge of the island then suddenly grew dark where the deep water swallowed the light. Up ahead, the colors seemed lighter again, though there wasn't an island. He glanced back to check the direction. Red trickles spilled

340

down the sides of the island they had passed on the way in. Off to one side, a pod of giant whales moved easily through the sea, oblivious to their observer. The long-winged albatrosses flew nearby, showing off their speed and agility in flight. *Taking Laido to the Travelers Path,* Fen thought.

"Well?" Colbee asked again.

"Yes," Fen called back. "I can see many things."

"Interesting but not very helpful."

"The shallow water seems to go straight on course in front of us," Fen called down, "though I can't see the next island."

"Submerged islands," Colbee guessed. "Anything else?"

"Yes. The island we passed when we first arrived is bleeding fire."

"Are you getting light-headed?"

"No, but I feel like a fish caught in a funnel."

"Well, keep looking and don't get too lost in dreams. I'll bring you down once we get the mats set."

Immediately, Fen lost himself in the joy of flying, working on banking turns just as Jin had said, swallowing great gulps of air as he headed into each maneuver.

"Hello! Are you still there?" Colbee called, as he started pulling in the line. "Last chance to look around."

Fen scanned the sea. The pale water still stretched in patches in front of the boat, with dark patches in between. The great whales had covered a surprising distance since he last looked; huge schools of flashing fish now swam where the whales used to be. Far out over them, his shadow danced on the water, mimicking his every turn. As Colbee brought the kite down, Fen waved to the sky and the seabirds. The opening for his feet didn't give him enough room to steady himself, so he hit the deck and fell forward like a felled tree trunk. Kiah tried to catch him and they tumbled onto the deck.

"Thank you," he said as he scrambled out of the sleeve.

"So," Colbee said, "what did you see?"

"Islands laid out like distant stepping stones."

"Where?"

"In front of us."

The news spread quickly.

"What's at the other end?"

"Maybe a whole new land."

"With other people?"

"Maybe."

"What will we do then?"

"I thought I wanted to find what lay beyond the edge, but now I don't," Kiah confided as she and Nina worked on the mats.

"Why not?"

"I'd rather stay at sea. It's better here. People don't fight as much. We have everything we need right here on the boats."

"What would you lose if we settled on land?"

"This world. The sea, the sun, my friends." Kiah rocked back on her heels, looking at her hands.

"I don't understand."

"Little lands are better. Big lands bring bigger trouble. Back in my homeland, warring tribes set fires to stop their enemies. When the dry winds took them, the fires grew into monsters, killing everything in their path, blackening the entire land. My parents and I escaped to the sea. For luck, my father brought the decorated skull of his ancestor, but it knew nothing of the sea. My father drowned in a storm; my mother perished on a little island with no trees. They left me to learn on my own."

"Yet you survived," Nina added.

"I did. And I found happiness on the Fat Men's Island. But it was a small world. I'm afraid we'll find a big world and the bad things will return. Maybe we should stay at sea. We're happy here."

"Why can't we be happy on land?"

"Look around. On the boats, we're all friends because we need to be. Once we land, who will be chief? The Fat Men? Jin? Ryu? Colbee? Nulo? Darna? What if we find a village that already has a chief?"

"I hadn't considered any of that."

"No, and we cannot set the future by worrying about it, yet it's coming at us, day by day, getting closer with each island we pass. This is it – the best time, before we find whatever it is we've been searching for."

"How do you know? Maybe we'll find the most beautiful world we've ever known."

Kiah patted the younger woman's hand. "Maybe we will."

The first islands they saw barely cleared the surface; the sea churned foamy over hidden rocks. Later they came across rocky outcrops where seabirds rested among tough grasses and an occasional stunted tree. Much later, they reached an island covered with thick forest from hilltops to shore. At no point did they see any sign of human settlement. Instead of villagers, colonies of sea lions and birds claimed the open areas. Even the natural harbors held no sign of people, not even the remains of a cook fire or an abandoned boat rotting on the shore.

While many grew quiet as they watched the islands pass, Hao talked even more, going on about spirits and winged children who flew out of the trees and circled the heavens. His nervous twitches returned. At Nulo's suggestion, Colbee asked him to design some tools for them, including a pair of flashing signal stones. For a while, it seemed to help. Hao spent most of his days grinding two of the stones he'd found on the islands.

Long before Goh called to them to say he'd sighted a large expanse of land on the horizon, they had seen the land that lay ahead of them. It haunted their dreams, alternately a place of horrors and a place of delights. No one mentioned the wild dreams that left them shaken; no one repeated the wild tales they had heard about the land at the edge of the world. If they were unusually quiet during the day, no one felt it right to notice.

Nulo's dreams filled with visions. They came in a flood, every night: a bird flying impossibly high into a dark sky, blue-green lightning forking across the clouds, Aeta with silent tears on her cheeks, a strange circular diagram carved in stone, a giant turtle that rose out of the black water and lunged at him. It was so close that he could see its hooded eye, its domed body moving surprisingly quickly, its feet pushing against the sandy bank. In a single snap, it swallowed him and took him down into the darkness which had no bottom, where the earth was waiting to be born.

He said nothing about the visions.

They sailed on in boats weighed down with unnamed fears. Every day the land grew bigger, spreading out along the horizon like a world unto itself. Since the current pulled them north, they went with it, searching for the right place. A few times, they went close to the shore and then pulled away again, afraid, using the weather or the tide as a reason to keep going, doing what they were used to doing, while they waited for something to convince them to change.

Late one day, Nina was watching a fish eagle soar over the water when she felt a prickling along the back of her neck. The sky darkened suddenly. The air crackled. The eagle swept up higher and higher, seeking something in the high clouds. When she called to Ryu, he joined her, already aware of the change, like a buzzing in the air. The boats drifted quite close to the shore.

"Look! The mountain!" Goh called. "It's exploding in lightning!"

On the land, the ground was growing dark while the sky filled with lightning. It pulsed in orange, blue, green, yellow, and blinding white, forking extravagantly around a black cone, flashing continuously, one branch spreading while another's ghost still lingered. With a crack, a huge white bolt lashed out from the cone and threw a ball of lightning, then another, some landing with a hiss out on the sea. On the other side of the cone, golden lightning flashed all the way to the ground and back, leaving a fog of light along its path. Green lightning coursed up and down the edges of the cone, which seemed to be rotating, like a cyclone coming out of the mountain and ending high above in a large, flat cloud that spread outwards.

Mesmerized, they watched, witnessing the power of the gods unleashed.

"We must leave," Nulo called to Ryu. "Now."

Ryu couldn't tear his gaze away.

Grabbing Ryu's arm, Nulo cried, "It is death to stay. Head away from the spreading cloud!"

Around the cone, lightning forked and flashed in all colors, sending out side flashes that spawned more lightning balls.

"We can't put up the mats," Ryu said, without taking his eyes off the lightning, "not with that storm coming in."

"It's not a storm," Nulo answered. "It goes with the lightning mountain. We need to get as far away as possible, quickly."

They hoisted the mats to catch the erratic winds and watched in the night as the earth and sky gods battled under a rose-colored sky. The next morning, the cloud spread out and ash began to fall, even out on the water, leaving a grey coating that shifted thickly with the waves. Sweeping it off the boats only put more of it in the air, so they tried wetting it down with seawater and then sweeping it up, but the ash fell faster than they could get rid of it. While some swept and cleaned, Ryu and Colbee pushed the boats harder, racing the spreading cloud. All the next night they kept going, pushing farther north, away from the dust. When it was light, they saw the cloud still chasing them, spreading out across the sky. Though they covered their mouths, the dust crept in anyway, and it hurt to breathe. It burned their eyes, scraped their skin raw.

"Cover up and keep the boats moving!" Colbee called. "We'll try to outrun the cloud."

Days passed in a blur. They worked, slept, and worked again, pushing the boats to go faster, sweeping up ash and dumping it into the sea.

When the ash finally stopped, they drifted, exhausted, for many days.

* * *

Hao saw the bird first. The red-beaked white bird with the long curved tail-feathers, bobbing gently with the waves, the same bird that had welcomed them to the black rock islands. Sure it was an omen, he pointed it out to Nina, who pointed it out to Ryu, and so the news of its appearance spread, until everyone on both boats saw it resting there on the water, considering them. The land behind the bird lay waiting for them as well. A broad sweep of golden beach bordered the blue-green water and a mountain of forest rose behind it. A silvery river fanned out as it entered the sea a little way down the beach. Long-legged birds strutted along the shore.

Ryu nodded.

"We're here!" Nina cried. "This is it. This is the place."

Jin, Goh, and Tahn set off to scout the area before the general landing. But they were hardly off the boats before most of the others jumped out after them and ran toward the beach, yelling and splashing. Nulo and Aeta followed the others, dropping gently into the water. Only Hao stayed, volunteering to guard the boats. Rana, Colbee, and Fen ran through the surf while the golden sand yielded softly under their feet. Off shore, coral heads showed off their colors as schools of fish darted in and out of the swaying blooms. An eagle ray swam by Nina, slowly moving its great wings up and down. Fuhua bumped through the surf and crashed belly-first into the water, sending up waves on both sides. Kiah darted through the sea like a seal, rolling over underwater and then diving once again. Sula walked into the surf as if she were strolling down a road, while Rana splashed her from behind.

When Jin returned to the beach, he raised his hands, pressing them together in front of his mouth while tears leaked from his closed eyes.

"It's for you, my family," he whispered. "This land of wonder is for you. How I wish you could have seen it."

Beside him, Goh and Tahn dropped their weapons and raced into the surf.

Colbee called to Hao, "Lower the anchor stones! You need to see the beach."

When they tired of the sea, they soaked in the river or slept under the arching broadleaf trees. When they got hungry, Kiah harvested what was salvageable of the garden vegetables and Tahn caught a big jackfish that fed the group handsomely. As the day started to fade, they sat together, listening to the snap of the fire and watching the colors of the old sun spread across the sky.

"It seems as if everything we've done has brought us right here," Nina said, "because this is where we're meant to be."

CHAPTER 32
THE NEW LAND

Ryu named it The Land of Four Bays. Each of the bays along the shore had a different character. One had a calm, protected harbor, another had high, crashing waves, and the third was quite deep while the farthest was so shallow the water stayed warm all night. Where the land surrounding the shallow bay was rocky and dry, filled with cactus trees and dry shrubs, the other bays nestled into lush forested slopes. In the sea beyond the bays, Ryu found marlin and sailfish almost as big as the boat, giant tuna, sharks, rays, eels, conchs, clams, lobsters, crabs, sponges. The manatee looked something like a dugong, but much bigger, longer than two grown men and fatter than six. Paddling slowly along, it grazed on the water plants growing on the bottom, unconcerned that Ryu swam with it. Where the river spilled into the sea, it lifted its strange rounded head to look at him. Apparently satisfied, it took a long drink from the fresher water by the river mouth and returned to its grazing.

A long-tailed otter slid on its belly down the hill and into a pond. When another joined it, they played with a flat stone they found. Howler monkeys found the camp before the sun rose, whooping and howling as they crashed through the treetops. Scarlet macaws screeched their arguments and flashed their color as they flew. Each day the explorers found more: big lizards and bigger butterflies, ants the size of a finger, stinging caterpillars, tiny monkeys no bigger than a hand, gigantic animals they'd never seen before that walked the forests and grazed on the grasslands, others that clung upside-down from the trees, a falcon that seemed to laugh as it hovered, huge spotted salamanders, tapirs and giant anteaters digging holes in the forest floor, blood-sucking bats, stinging ants, scorpions, cockroaches, brightly colored frogs, spiders, snakes as long as a person, and more flowering plants than they could remember. The forest itself was a wonder, so vast it was hard to comprehend, sweeping as far as they could see in every direction, split only by the rivers winding through it. Up in the foothills, the trees grew to be giants, their bases spreading wide, their trunks bigger around than all the people together could encircle with outstretched arms, their trunks soaring up through the understory and fanning out into the canopy high above. Every space that snagged a bit of sunlight grew something: ferns on the forest floor, climbing vines, orchids and mosses that dripped from the branches.

No matter how much they learned, they wanted to know more, about the lay of the land, the different bays, the rivers and lakes, sources of good stones and clays, weaving materials, game animals, dangerous areas, beasts, and insects, medicinal and edible plants. Every day, they explored more, pushing farther along the coast and into the interior.

As Tahn, Colbee, and Fen went up the coast on the Sailfish, they came across one cove with a peculiar rock formation jutting right out of the water. It looked exactly like a huge cat lying down, its long tail curving out behind it.

"It's only the way we're looking at it," Tahn said, though Colbee hadn't mentioned the resemblance.

"Then let's look at it from the other side."

The view from the other side was the same. From the front, it looked like a cat's head resting on its big paws. The long sweep of tail was unmistakable from any direction. The only part that seemed more rock than cat was the hindquarters, which dropped off more than they would have with a real cat. The rest looked so lifelike, they thought the great animal had simply curled up there for a nap and might later rise, stretch, and head off into the mountains.

When they got back to camp and described their find, Fuhua and Liwei added a different discovery. In the middle of one of the coves, they had come across a black rock mountain. Its matched sloping sides led up to an almost perfectly flat summit, making it the stunning centerpiece of the bay. Fuhua, who saw it first, named it Eagle Rock after the harpy eagles that nested there.

"It would make a great place for a Sky Circle," Ryu mused.

"Or a lookout post," Jin added.

* * *

Heading back to her hut late one day, Nina suddenly felt the hair on the back of her neck rise. She felt something was behind her. As she turned around slowly, she found a pair of yellow eyes studying her. She could just make out the shape that went with the eyes: the broad head with small ears set on the sides. The great cat lifted his head and opened his mouth slightly, as if taking in her scent and breathing her, while shafts of light played over his spotted coat. Except for the small movement of his long tail, he stood motionless, as did she, unable to move even if she had wanted to. His eyes held her. As she sank into his gaze, he took her into a different world, a world older than time, unmeasured by days, where ages swept through like summer storms; the land changed, the sea rose and fell, rivers changed their course, flooded, dried up and rose anew, yet through it all he stood, always, right there. He stayed because he *was* the land. It was his, all of this, the trees that crowded the hillside, the flight of the bats, the shining bays under the moon, the cries of the birds, the howling storm, the great animals who walked the forest floor - every part was his. It had been his since the moment the land was born. She slid into the golden center of his eye. He was the sun at night, the prowler through the Underworld, the carrier of the light yet to be born, undisputed destroyer with blood on his face, ruler forever, no matter who might lay claim to it for a little while.

She fell to her knees and bowed her head to the ground.

When she raised her head, the sky behind the jaguar flared red and purple. With a final look, he burned his image onto her spirit and then turned away, leaving her watching the spot where he used to be, still seeing the light ringing through the irregular circles on his coat as he disappeared into the forest. Trembling, she sank down, holding on to the dark earth until the light was lost and night dropped down around her.

The following day, she told Nulo. Though she showed him the place she'd seen the jaguar, they couldn't find any tracks.

"It's his land," Nulo said. "All of this. It will always be his land. It's his marker rock out in the bay."

"He could have killed me, easily."

"Certainly. Yet he didn't."

"Why did he -? Why didn't he -?"

"He wanted you to understand."

Though she didn't mention it to anyone else for a long time, she often felt the jaguar's presence out there somewhere, not far away. Even when she couldn't see them, she could sense his golden eyes glowing like the night sun in the Underworld, watching the visitors in his world. And she wondered if he was curious about these new creatures so excited to explore his land. Or jealous.

CHAPTER 33
IN THE COURSE OF DAYS

In the rush of activity establishing the new settlement, they found it easy to forget those who weren't part of it: Aeta and Hao.

Aeta hadn't told anyone she was pregnant. After a while, she assumed everyone knew, so there was no reason to mention it. And she had other reasons. The night of the lightning mountain, something had gone wrong. In their desperate efforts to escape the ash cloud, she hadn't had the time or energy to talk about it, even to Nulo. Later she didn't want to. Now, with every day in the new land, she felt more shut off from the excitement. Mostly, she said nothing at all, busying herself with the gardens or the weaving. When someone pressed her for a response, she said she felt a little sick. That covered many possibilities.

Hao, on the other hand, was the most talkative he had ever been, rambling on about arcane subjects. He sought out Nulo, and the two talked about stone cutting, water systems, engineering, time, values, and eventually, personal concerns.

"What is the meaning of our past?" Hao asked one day. "Does it shape us? In what way? If no one else knows your past, how could it affect others' perception of you, unless you wear it somehow so it's obvious to them?" Before Nulo could answer, Hao went on. "Could you create a different past? If you told yourself a different story enough times, would it, after a while, become your real history?"

"In your dreams, you would know the real story, the first story."

"No," Hao objected, "sometimes we don't know our own history, especially what happened when we were young. And dreams can be lies. We accept what people tell us. Or we make up our own lies and repeat them so often they become our history."

When Nulo didn't reply, Hao studied him. "What makes one person's life worth more than another's?"

Nulo looked out at the clouds piling up in the distance over the sea. "These are hard questions. I suppose a person must use the gifts the spirits gave him. We couldn't have gotten across the sea without your help, without your knowledge. That's a gift."

Hao acknowledged the compliment with a nod before he waved it away. "What if someone did something terrible early in his life? Is there any amount of time that could erase or even dim that mark on him?"

"Yes, I believe there is."

"Then you do not bear the burden."

Nulo waited for him to explain.

"My mother named me Son of Black Lightning because I was born during a lightning storm. She assumed I had been struck by invisible lightning. She hid me for a long time, but eventually, the townspeople found out and banished me.

"After traveling around the islands on a boat I made, I fell in with a group of other cast-offs. Though a few of them were wonderful people, most weren't. Many were so dangerous their own people had exiled them. Being the youngest and smallest in the group, I became an easy target. When I refused to do some things one man wanted me to, he beat me senseless. He thought it was funny, beating the hunchback. As soon as I recovered, I poisoned him. There's no other way to say it; that's what I did. He suffered a terrible death, calling out for someone to help him. He wasn't the only one. I was always angry, especially around stupid, handsome men who were surrounded by women. If the men laughed at me, I found a way to hurt them.

"The anger dug a hole inside me that was never filled. I tried throwing myself into projects. I designed tools and boats and buildings, mostly very good ones, but I built my anger into them and it came out eventually. The captain of a boat I built was murdered, his body thrown into the sea. Another time, I designed a bridge across a river. It was strong and worked well, but a woman in distress jumped off it to kill herself, so people decided the bridge was cursed.

"Nothing worked, no matter how hard I tried. As the anger got worse, I lapsed into fits, attacking anyone in front of me. One time, I killed a kind man who had never done anything against me or anyone I knew.

"I tried to run away, taking the most dangerous jobs with the explorers far out at sea. It didn't matter. The madness would always come back." He ran his finger absently over the edges of a rock. "The last time I was sent off to live on my own, I agreed it was for the best. That's when Darna wandered into the woods, so sick with fever, yet so kind. I was astounded to meet someone like her." His voice broke.

Nulo put his hand on Hao's shoulder. "I'm sorry."

"I thought for a while that I could change."

"Haven't you?"

"Everyone here treats me well, even when I don't deserve it. I lied about knowing what was on the other side of the sea. I've never been here and know of no one else who has. Colbee knows I've failed; Ryu does too. Day after day, I do nothing to help. It's not their fault; it's mine. The problem lies underneath where the damage can never be undone."

"Why are you telling me this?"

Hao held out a woven bag. "Would you give these to Darna and to Aeta?"

"Why don't you give them their gifts?"

"It might seem odd, my giving gifts to other men's wives. Anyway, I'd like it better if you did."

Nulo accepted the bag. "When should I do this?"

"The day after tomorrow," Hao said, turning away, as if to end the conversation. After a couple of steps, he turned back to Nulo. "How did you escape? The anger - how did you survive without being driven into rage?"

"Naia and my friends saved me."

Hao nodded slowly. "Yes, I suppose so. How I wish I could see myself through your eyes, Nulo. Unfortunately, I can see only through mine."

The following morning, Nina chose to stay in camp instead of going with Ryu on the Wind Raft. When Hao said he wanted to explore some of the bays, Ryu offered him Nina's spot on the boat. After she saw them off, Nina walked over to help Sula, Darna, and Aeta make nut flour. Nina noticed that Aeta's hands shook as she struggled to remove each shell. She was about to ask Aeta if she was all right when Aeta doubled over, crashing into their work surface, scattering the piles of nuts and hulls.

"I'm sorry," Aeta said dimly, as if she were somewhere far away. "I'm sorry."

"You're coming with me," Sula said, grasping Aeta's arm. "That's enough silence."

Aeta rose unsteadily from a pool of blood, her face a pale mask of pain as Sula helped her back to the hut.

"Nina," Darna called as she rushed to help, "I need you to find some herbs for me."

"I don't know them, Mother! You go. I'll stay and help. Please!"

"Listen to me," her mother ordered, then listed the herbs she needed. "Ask Kiah. She might have some in her garden, especially the breadfruit. Check with her first. And hurry."

Finding Kiah mending her garden beds, Nina tried to tell the story as quickly as possible. Before she'd finished, Kiah started picking leaves and placing them in different spots in her basket.

"Is she having contractions?" Kiah asked, still picking and sorting leaves.

"I don't know; I don't think so."

"We'll give her chanana," Kiah said. "Do you know it?"

"It's the one with the strong spicy smell, right?"

"Yes. The other plant has the yellow cup flowers and smells sweet. Pick those leaves too, if you can find them. Keep them separate and remember which is which. I have some honey, spearmint, and breadfruit leaves that I saved from the garden boat. We could use guava and plantain. Even thistle would help. I should have had the garden ready for us. I'll bring these and some water and gourds. Well, don't stand there. Go!"

On his way up the mountain beyond the settlement, Nulo stopped suddenly, turned around and ran back down the path toward camp.

At the entrance to the hut, Nina stood, staring at the blood soaking Aeta's wrap until a sharp look from Sula moved her into action. She handed the herbs to Kiah and knelt next to Aeta, taking her hand.

"The baby," Aeta said. "The baby is dead. Everyone's dead because of me."

At a loss for something helpful to say, Nina put her hand on Aeta's. "It's not your fault. It happens, sometimes, for reasons we don't understand."

Aeta looked away. "I know why."

Kiah and Sula made a tea sweetened with honey and offered it to Aeta. When she refused, Sula said, "This baby will be born today, whether it's alive or not. It's not your place to say no to that. Your giving up won't help any of us."

For a moment, the old fire returned to Aeta's eyes, but it was short-lived. She drank the tea and fell back on her mat, still bleeding. When Darna returned with gourds full of water, she almost knocked Nulo down as he stood just inside the doorway.

"Go to her," Darna whispered as she passed. "She needs you."

Kneeling next to her, he put his hand on her shoulder. As he watched the tears slide down her cheek, her pain cut through him.

When the herbs took effect, Aeta's contractions began, but she didn't have the energy to see it through. The women yelled at her to push when it was time, and she did; as soon as they stopped yelling, she stopped pushing. Dazed, she looked around yet recognized no one. Nulo felt the ground crumbling under his feet. It was happening exactly as he had seen it. Somehow, even with his gift of foresight, he'd failed to prevent it. The huge black turtle loomed close, ready to swallow him and everything he cared about and drag all of it down into the place below the Underworld where the world was waiting to be born.

* * *

"I want to check on something on Eagle Rock," Hao told Ryu. "I'll meet you back on the bay in a little while."

Watching the tiny blue fish and green turtles swimming around the coral heads, Ryu acknowledged the comment with a short wave.

On top of Eagle Rock, Hao felt suspended in a single moment like an insect stuck in amber. The eagles had gone, leaving only the flat rock, the middle ground between the water below and the sky above.

"My life is my contribution," he said, kneeling down, bowing his head down to the rock. "My death is my offering. It's a request, not a payment. A request for someone else, not me." Slowly, he rose

357

and walked to the edge of the rock, watching the waves moving in wrinkled lines so far below, the water amazingly blue. Storm clouds piled up on the horizon, so dark behind the sunlit rock.

Hao threw himself off the edge of the rock. Ryu had just returned to the boat when he heard the ricochet off the rock and saw the splash.

* * *

Late that night, the storm rolled in, bringing thunder and lightning before the rain. Rana fixed a meal but no one ate it. Aeta lay unresponsive, half-dead, while the women worked on potions and the storm rose around them. Nulo never left Aeta's side. His thoughts flowed with the storm winds. He felt the lightning before it struck the hut, drawing him up before it shot down with crackling, blinding light, running right through the hut from the roof to the ground. It counted them all, measured them. It sought out Aeta and found her, blasting life through her, leaving as quickly as it had come.

Outside, the storm rolled on; inside, a flame was rekindled.

* * *

Days later, Aeta, though still weak, could look around her once again and see friends. By the hut opening, Nulo was working a stone in the sunlight.

"Nulo," she said quietly, "what will we do now?"

Setting his work down, he moved over to her side. "We'll grieve our child's death. We'll wrap him up, sing his death song, and place him high in one of the tall trees. From there, his spirit will be free to fly up into the heavens with the other winged children. He and the others will turn into clouds where their sparks will join with the sparks of others. Then they will become lightning and return their energy to the earth and sky."

"And the bundle in the tree?"

"After his spirit is free, we'll bury his body and Hao's in a cave near Eagle Rock."

"And will you still be happy to be with me?" Her words were a whisper.

"Always. And when death takes us, I'll walk by your side along the Travelers Path into the Otherworld."

* * *

The gifts Hao had left for Aeta and Darna were polished grey stone mirrors. In each, a hollow stem ran from a fish bladder sac in the back through a hole in the bottom of the front. When the threaded wick it held was lit, the mirror intensified the flame's light. A woven strap strung through holes in the mirror stone allowed it to be attached to an upright.

"A way to light the darkness," Nulo said when Aeta showed it to him. "A beautiful gift."

CHAPTER 34
DARNA'S REQUEST

On the hill high above the shore, Darna sat alone, her arms wrapped around her knees, talking to Laido while she looked out over the sea.

"Well, we've weathered the storms and established the village. The land and water are generous here, Laido, the harbor waters calm, the sun warm, the fish and game animals beyond number, the fruit easy to pick. You would have liked it very much. On every side, we have plenty. You'll be a grandfather soon, and this is a beautiful world for a child to be born into, yet with all of this, something stops us from taking this land into our hearts. The young men wander far away, the young women too, searching up and down the coast or far inland as if it hurts their feet to walk the paths in our village. I stay behind, waiting for something, though the truth is I feel it too, the pull to be someplace else. Perhaps it's what happens when people stay on the open sea as along as we did. They become accustomed to the endless spaces spread out in all directions, a world ruled by the spirits of the sea and sky. After that, the land, even a very good land, seems foreign. Maybe the small boats kept us together on the endless sea but now we're free to drift apart. Or this land is keeping us from putting down roots, waiting to see if we're meant to be part of it. Or perhaps the ancestors are too far away to help us.

"So we're all in good health, but the group is failing. Everything feels as if it belongs only to today. I thought I'd see a struggle for power as soon as the village was established, but it hasn't happened.

No one seems to want to be the chief. No one speaks up, suggesting plans for the village. Liwei and Fuhua are trying to recruit some of the others to go back with them across the sea, to set up a trade route. Tahn seems restless enough to join them. Goh would stay to settle down with Rana, except like Colbee, Kiah, and everyone else, he's bewitched, seduced by the unknown lands beyond the horizon.

"Nulo grew so disturbed by his dreams of strange circular marks carved in stone that he set off to find them, on his own, wandering the hillsides where the great beasts with curling tusks graze. No one has seen him since the moon was empty. Aeta spends half the day staring at the point where she saw him last. Ryu takes the Wind Raft up or down the coast for days, searching farther each time. Sometimes others go with him, but many times he goes alone. We have no way of knowing if he's lost or hurt – or worse. Sula says she's gathering plants, but she disappears for days at a time without telling anyone where she's going. One of these days, she'll choose to forget the way back.

"Why can't we find contentment in this perfect land? We've lost our way now that we found our destination. We see our friends, those as close as family, and we can't wait to leave them behind.

"Maybe you and I were wrong. Maybe we gave these people a hunger that can never be filled, a desire for the impossible. How I wish you were here! You need to help us find our path. You were always the navigator. We're adrift here and we need you to set the course. Otherwise, people will leave, by land and by sea, and we'll all die because the few left behind will have no one to support them. Please. Guide your people, Laido. Not just for me or for the children, but for all of us. The battle is on us now, and it's a fight with ourselves."

Darna dropped her head to her knees. "Help us find our way," she whispered.

CHAPTER 35
MESSAGES

Day after day, Nulo worked his way farther into the interior. Out in the grassland, he skirted herds of beasts, some with long necks, some with long horns, some with long tails that flew behind them when they ran. Bitten, scratched, tired, and hungry, he pushed on, trying to find something he couldn't name, waiting for a sign, finding none. Each day's sun was clear and hot, the forests on the high hills thick and heavy, the night's dreams empty.

He found mosses growing on stones in strange patterns, colored lines on a cliff face, caves that held only bats and scattered animal bones. At night he listened to the howls of the night hunters, realizing how foolish he'd been to come out this far alone. *This world belongs to another, the one Nina saw. Maybe he's angry at the outsiders walking on his paths, drinking his water, killing his prey. Perhaps people were here before. Perhaps they tried to leave marks on the stone, but he drove them away or killed them while they slept. Or he used others – scorpions, blood-sucking bats, poisonous snakes. Who can say? We find his world beautiful – so beautiful that we keep wanting more, searching for it in every direction. Like them, I want something. I want the sign I was given in my dreams, perhaps by this spirit. If it exists, it means we were invited to be here. If not, it's only a wish that took shape in my dream. Hao said dreams can lie. But I don't think so. This dream is true. It has to be.*

One day when the sun was new, a fluid, whistling sound of light glinting on water called him awake and drew him on until he reached the stream that sang. For days he followed it as it twisted across the valley, under the brush. Along the way, other streams joined it, adding their quick, tumbling sounds, singing to him with overlapping melodies. As the river crossed a hard ledge, it spread out, thinning into a dozen smaller streams that crossed each other like braids joining, separating, and joining again before sliding over the edge with a shout, plunging down, and losing themselves in the mist. Far below, the streams crashed into a pool while the mist fell slowly, pulling on him as he half-slid down the wet rocks. Behind the waterfall, where the rock had been worn away, he picked his way across wet slabs, checking each spot as he moved. Oddly, after all his hurry, his feet seemed to stick to the rocks, slowing him. When he neared the far side, he stopped in mid-step. Sounds of the pounding streams retreated, leaving only airy whistles in their place, bits of sound hovering in the spray.

On the flat stone in front of him, he found what he had been looking for.

It had been carved.

A circle about an arm's length wide formed the edge of the carving. Inside it lay a smaller circle, and along its circumference thirteen very small circles, all carefully chipped into the rock face. Each small circle held a mark: a dot, a series of dots, a line, or a series of lines and dots. Lines connected the small circles, crossing each other in the middle of the large circle.

It was exactly the figure from the vision he'd had so long ago.

As the mist whistled behind him, he studied the carving. Someone had been to this rock pool, had stood right here on this spot, had found this to be exactly the right place to leave this mark. It had taken a long time to carve this design, to make the stone hold this idea. It had to be measured and marked, then pecked away carefully. And once it was created, the design's power proved so fierce that the image had reached the inner eye of someone the maker had never met.

Nulo leaned against the stone and drew his finger along the lines, tracing their paths over and over though he knew each mark by heart.

"Thank you, rock carver," he said, "for sending this message. Thank you, stone, for holding it." His hand shook as he went over the small circles. "Thank you for calling me here."

In the shadow on the far side of the falls, another watched him. When the sun's last rays slanted across the falls, the watcher took the light and stored it inside. As the beast turned his head, his huge eyes flashed red and gold.

* * *

The Misfits and Heroes saga continues in the
third book of the series, *A Meeting of Clans.*

Check out the Misfits and Heroes blog at
misfitsandheroes.wordpress.com

76412309R00205

Made in the USA
Columbia, SC
04 September 2017